HAWKER STREET

RICH HESKERTON

<u>WARNING</u>
Hawker Street is intended for adults over 15 years and contains strong language throughout, descriptions of comic violence, smoking and alcohol abuse. It is a work of fiction. All names, characters, businesses, places, events and incidents in this book are either the product of the author's imagination or used in a fictitious manner. Any resemblance to actual persons, living or dead, or actual events without satirical intent is purely coincidental.

Copyright © 2022 Rich Heskerton. All rights reserved.

For my Ma and Da,

Thank you for everything.

CONTENTS

1	Episode I	Pg 1
2	Episode II	Pg 28
3	Episode III	Pg 56
4	Episode IV	Pg 81
5	Episode V	Pg 119
6	Episode VI	Pg 143
7	Episode VII	Pg 174
8	Episode VIII	Pg 198
9	Episode IX	Pg 224
10	Episode X	Pg 247
11	Episode XI	Pg 269
12	Episode XII	Pg 290
13	Epilogue	Pg 317

HAWKER STREET

RICH HESKERTON

ACKNOWLEDGMENTS

Others are also somewhat responsible for this:

Dan Ebertz
Jon Oliver
Nadine Minagawa

Thank You.

EPISODE I

Tuesday
7:58am
North West London, Tossingdale Tube Station

The doors slid open. Half a dozen crooked necks straightened and the commuters stepped out onto the packed platform. Thousands of footsteps echoed around the ceramic tiles along with hushed mumbles of general dissatisfaction. The crowd steadily squeezed its way into the narrow tunnel to a cauldron of vaguely musical sounds bubbling and burbling.

Clara Baker wrestled with her jacket and briefcase, as she shuffled along the walkway with the rest of the commuters. As she neared a smiling busker, she passed the most discrete of glances into his guitar case and saw he wasn't doing well. Her eyes met his and she saw an earnest face. In an unconstitutional moment of altruism, she reached into her purse for the one coin she had, normally kept for the trolley at Asda. Still being dragged along by the current, she was smiling at the young busker when the coin slipped out of her fingers. She cursed and looked back at him to see an amused and appreciative face. The well-intentioned Clara shrugged, smiled and pressed onwards. She heard the amplified twangs of a guitar and a voice.
"This one's for-"
A blinding flash and a deafening crack, shook the tunnel.
Blackness.
Numb.

Clara became aware she was on the ground, as were dozens of other people. The air was thick with dust and the patient fury of tinnitus. The busker was just…gone.

Tuesday
7.59am
North London Hendon

A ray of sunlight shot through the crack in the curtain. The dust from a mountain of cigarette ends danced and sparkled in its warmth.

Detective Frank Ruggerman awoke in a start, face down and naked. He attempted to summon the cooperation of his aged, hungover muscles. As he clawed his way onto his back, his feet clinked the empty whiskey bottles and crackled the discarded cigarette pack cellophane. Frank pressed his lips around another cigarette and heaved himself upright. His left foot splashed the contents of his *Masters of the Universe* bedpan onto the floor. An automated voice cried *"I have the powerrrr!!"* After a moment, growling, Frank left the bed and shuffled towards the bathroom, shaking his left foot every third step.

In the kitchen, Irish cream splashed off the Cheerios in the takeaway curry tin and onto the sleeve of Frank's suit jacket. He turned on the radio, summoning two breakfast dj heroes, babbling and playing songs.
"That was Jurgen Tosshaus with "Funky Toss", which is a great vibes tune, don't you think Brad?"
"Yeah, I totes do Nick and that's what today's show is all about, great vibes."
Frank poured instant coffee directly from the jar, mostly into his mug and added water.
"Yeah Brad, cos' we all give out vibes don't we?"

"Yeah, and today we'll be talking about how our great vibes can affect other people, whether you're-" the radio clicked off.
Frank stood a moment and surveyed his kitchen the way a bomb disposal unit looks at a playground after an explosion. He had his packed lunch ready, but needed a mixer. He grabbed the nearest, a tin of golden syrup, and went to work.

Tuesday
9:45am
London Met Police HQ, Hawker Street

Despite the quad-annual spruce up of the headquarters of the Metropolitan Police, the station still had the overwhelming aura of the 1970's with its ubiquitous greys and browns.

The bustling corridors were filled with the usual complement of officers, perps, prostitutes and food service operatives. An officer appeared in the hall from an interview room, beckoning his suspects to follow. As they danced into the corridor, the light skipping of their handkerchiefs and bells only partially distracted from their nudity.
"God damn Morris dancers."

In a nearby gents toilet, sheltering from the pandemonium, was Assistant Detective Rosch Kunnypacken. Born of the last remnants of the Bermerian elite, Rosch had inherited his pale brown skin, slim build and stock portfolio from his mother and his formidable hygiene anxiety from his father. Despite his formidable hygiene anxiety, this particular toilet had provided much respite from the tempest of cruel derision and callous indifference that lay outside. At 28 he was the oldest Assistant Detective in the history of the Met and he was preparing himself to respond to the barrage of texts ordering

him to the office of Chief Commissioner Rudolph Leathers. Rosch took a deep breath and cautiously left his safe-place. Outside Leathers' door, Rosch paused, gathered himself and gave his best attempt at a 'confident knock'.
"Enterrrr!"

Rosch turned the ornate brass door handle and stepped inside. Leathers' office was a mahogany slow cooker for cigarette smoke and neuroses. Chief Leathers sat at his desk like an old Viking warlord dealing with new medication.

Another man, Reyka, an American in his fifties, stood with his back to the window smoking a cigarette. His foggy grey eyes calmly watched Rosch enter through twisting plumes of blue smoke. Perched at the end of Leathers' grand desk sat Renfield, the Chief Commissioner's minion. A man of such caustic vinegar and spite, he had had to wear spectacles from the age of three.

As Rosch sat down, he locked eyes with the large stuffed fox that adorned Leathers' desk.
"Assistant Detective Rosch Kunnypacken." said Leathers.
"Yes sir." replied Rosch.
"Do you know who I am?"
"Yes sir, Chief Commissioner of Police, Rudolph Leathers," Rosch paused and turned slightly, "it's written on the door of your-"
"Let's get to it." interrupted Leathers. "We're here to discuss your new and, to be quite frank, probably last detail. Due to your 'incident' last month we have decided to transfer you to a more suitable area of the force."
"You're taking me off homicide?" asked Rosch.
Renfield awkwardly placed his fist on the desk and screeched:
"We ask the questions here Kunnypacken!"

Rosch had worked homicide for six years. He knew for sure the fallout from his 'incident' would be weighty and sustained but the thought of being transferred floored him.

"After what you did young man, you are extremely lucky to have a job." reminded Leathers.

As Leathers spoke he slowly rotated an iron handle that was protruding from the rear of the stuffed fox, the mechanism pushing butter out of the fox's eyes, ears, nose and mouth. Rosch had heard it wise not to rise to Leathers' 'eccentricities', so there he sat, listening intently.
"Were it not for your Aunty Caroline, you'd already be in Siberia servicing lavatories." said Leathers.
Rosch could feel Reyka's calm but intent gaze as Leathers, slowly rotating the fox handle, continued to address him.
"And in light of your Aunty Caroline, it has been decided that you will transfer to the Western Tactical Unit, effective immediately."
"Western Tac-, the baffled department?!" said Rosch, incredulously.
"The Western Tactical Unit requires men, who-" said Leathers, powering through.
"My stats have surpassed anyone else in my year group." contested Rosch.
Leathers' anger exploded and he growled viciously while he turned the fox handle faster and faster, spraying butter wildly across the desk.
"Your insolence has griddled my gonads for the last time Kunnypacken!" gnashed Leathers. Reyka grunted to attract Leathers' attention and Leathers reluctantly calmed. Reyka lit another cigarette.
"You'll be working with Detective Frank Ruggerman." said Reyka, with a voice that was a blend of silk and sociopathic indifference.
"He's a violent drunkard." retorted Rosch.
Leathers leaned in.
"I see you need severe clarification, Kunnypacken, on just how much this particular trouser soiling of yours revealed how very arrogant and undisciplined you really are."
Rosch felt his indignation begin to deflate like a sad bouncy castle.

Reyka took one step away from the window.
"We need to lower your profile while the heat dies down."
Rosch's mouth filled with the bitter tonic. The meagre Renfield placed an envelope in his in-tray,
"There is another aspect to this detail." he smirked.

Rosch glanced at Renfield, then focussed on Leathers.
"For nearly two decades now," said Leathers soberly, "Detective Ruggerman has been running the W.T.U. Bizarre, figures-crippling cases that would otherwise collapse our regular departments are now his sole mandate. He tackles freak occurrences, inexplicable happenings and all manner of undetanglable danglings. It remains true, however, that all too frequently his bull-headedness, like yours, brings these turds drifting onto my hairpiece," Leathers grunted, "...and we need a closer eye on him."
"You want me to spy?" asked Rosch, hesitantly.

His mind flooded with what playing informant to the brass would do to his already laughable reputation around the station.
With his chalky soft tones Reyka explained, "We have chosen you, Kunnypacken, because were it not for your lineage, we would have healed the reputation of this office by feeding you to the dogs like a '70's radio host. You will join the Western Tactical and keep us updated on a daily basis."
Renfield rudely signalled to Rosch to stand and Leathers shuffled desk papers.
"So, there it is." concluded Leathers.
"Yes sir." said Rosch, simmering as he departed.

***

The lift dinged and the door slid open revealing an embittered Rosch Kunnypacken. He stepped out into the elderly-rhino-grey corridor that enjoyed the same ambience as an abandoned fire escape. Rosch became aware of the scraping of his soles as he walked and the sound changed to a more focussed stride. Beyond two left turns came a door with a sign that someone had crudely altered to read; 'Wasted Testicle Units'. Rosch sighed, adjusted his immaculately selected Hugo Boss tie, knocked on the door and entered, quickly hitting a stack of boxes bursting with documents. Growling, he pushed the boxes back into the office and stepped inside.

Upon entering the woefully small office, he looked up to see a barrage of clippings, posters and mugshots strewn across every single inch of wall space. Pictures of corpses with extra limbs or limbs in the wrong places and blueprints of futuristic aircraft. His eyes drifted over the walls like someone who visits a neighbour for the first time, only to discover that their hobby is upholstering furniture with human skin. He saw a poster of Santa Claus riding the Loch Ness monster with the caption reading: 'Reality is Overrated'. Rosch sat down in a chair opposite Frank when he noticed another picture that caused a sudden burst of anxiety to race through his chest. Painful memories and the echoing sound of an agonised yelp were brutally cut short by the sound of Detective Frank Ruggerman addressing him from his desk.

"Jesus H.Kenobi - the Star Wars kid! To what do I owe the pleasure?"

Rosch winced as a familiar flash of bile flooded his stomach. Frank took a long swig from a bottle that looked like mineral water.

"I've been assigned to-"

Frank gasped as the clear liquid burned its way down his neck. Rosch recoiled as the 184% proof vapour reached his eyes and nostrils.

"I've been assigned to assist you." said Rosch. "Needless to say I'd rather flat-press my testicles than be reassigned here - but I'd rather we didn't begin with antagonism."

Deep inside Frank, a tirade leapt to its feet.

"Listen, you F-" he began, only to be stopped dead by the phone ringing. Frank answered the call.

"Ruggerman..." he said, curtly, "...no that's my name."
Frank's eyes turned sharp as he listened intently. He noticed Rosch sitting awkwardly so he turned away as he listened. Frank slammed down the phone, grabbed his jacket from his chair and made for the door.
"What is it?" asked Rosch, still sitting.
"Oh yeah, you're still here." said Frank, disappointedly. After the briefest hesitation Frank extended the most begrudged grunt in Rosch's direction and Rosch quickly followed him through the door.

10:38am

Along the grey dual carriageway Frank's squad car, containing himself and Rosch, was speeding its way out of town. The journey was spent mostly in bitter silence aside from one truly savage exchange about the tidiness of the vehicle. After a few miles, the grand buildings of Central London had given way to the bookkeepers and kebab shops of the Northern burroughs. Rosch was checking the bars on his phone when he noticed the sign for the tube.

Tossingdale Tube Station, North West London

Closely followed by Rosch, Frank lit a cigarette as he marched into the shabby, art deco entrance of Tossingdale Station. In light of recent changes in procedure involving the cordoning off of crime scenes, it was now commonplace for regular officers to become fatally entangled in dense networks of excess police tape. As they neared the escalator, Frank and Rosch gingerly squeezed past a P.C who was trying to reassure a trapped colleague.
"Calm down!" the P.C. barked, "Stop crying, Jimmy!"
Crawling flat on their stomachs, they clawed their way out of the bottom of the escalator and through the police tape which, by this time, had congealed into a dense resin. They

followed the trail of destruction along the filthy cream tiled tunnel. Debris and body parts mottled posters of supermodels, job sites and those takeaways that send you the bits in a box and you cook it yourself. A forensic officer in a biohazard suit bagged a guitar, snapped at the neck and caked in blood.

Removing handfuls of police tape from themselves, Frank and Rosch approached a decimated pile of remains covering a 10 foot radius. Huddled over the pile, carefully dusting with his little brush, was Sodermine. Head forensic, Chicago born, mid-fifties, his rain mac and Trilby the same age. Frank inhaled his last and put out the cigarette,
"What have you got for me, Sodermine?"
"Morning, Frank," said Sodermine, "in the thick of rush hour a busker by the name of Lee Henderson spontaneously exploded. Born in Surrey, early twenties, slim build, eczema sufferer with a penchant for boiled cheese. No trace of explosives or accelerants, seventeen commuters injured by flying offal. The first suspicion was a terror attack but there's not a single piece of evidence here to indicate that."
"Jesus H. Corbett." said Frank.
Sodermine adjusted the brim of his Trilby,
"I'm gonna level with you Frank, this is a total noodle scratcher."
Rosch surveyed the extent of the blast.
"Oi." said Frank.
Rosch snapped to.
"...Head to the station office and grab any CCTV you can."
Rosch nodded and made his way back towards the entrance to find the station office.

The dust had begun to settle and fragments of broken tiles and scorched overcoats cracked and snapped underfoot. Turning left at the bottom of the escalators

Rosch found the station office. He fingered for his badge and opened the door.

"Police, Western Tactical."

Rosch stepped into the dark, cramped office. Five TFL workers huddled around a CCTV screen. On the monitor he saw an explosion. 'Kablaaarrrgh! Kapow!' The TFL workers cheered and threw up their arms.

Rosch cleared his throat.

They spun around in their chairs like startled lemurs. He showed his badge.

"I'm Assistant Detective Rosch Kunnypacken with the Western Tactical Unit and I need to see that footage."

"The baffled department." mumbled one of the staff derisively.

A portly gentleman in his late 40's stood and extended his hand.

"How do you do, Detective? Bob Davies; Chief of Staff, Tossingdale Station."

He eagerly shook Rosch's hand with the same vigour as his bubbly pan-south-western accent charmed his ears.

"You lot get off back to work now." he said, dutifully.

The staff dissipated like giggling children. Rosch glanced over each shoulder as they departed, before returning his focus to Davies.

"I'm afraid," said Davies, "none of my lot were present during the explosion. Carol's birthday, we were all having cake by the escalators."

"I need a copy of that footage." said Rosch.

"Can do detective, Geoff uploaded the whole thing onto Yourtube, it should be accessible if you've got the app on your phone."

"Hmf, thanks." said Rosch, turning to leave.

"Oh, Detective?"

Rosch begrudgingly faced Davies once again.

"You know of late, I can't help feeling there's something not quite right in this town. We've been seeing more and more of these ... inexplicable things, something tells me, this is just the beginning."

Rosch tucked that in another of that day's boxes and left.

***

Frank stood up, removing his oven mittens as Rosch returned.
"Did you get the footage?"
"We all did," replied Rosch, "not much use by the looks of it, though. None of the station staff saw anything and the commuters not covered in liquified busker or late for work say the same thing: he was playing a song and boom, he exploded."
Frank shifted a blood-soaked fragment of clothing with his shoe,
"No signs of a terror attack, no trace of explosives, what the hell could have done this to a man?"
Rosch pondered the same.
"I need you to compile and archive all the CCTV on or around the explosion."
"Wait." said Rosch. "I have a hunch about what could have caused this."
"Stick your hunch," said Frank, "I need that footage catalogued."
"I don't know who you think you're talking to!" Rosch returned abashed.
"I'll tell you who I'm talking to," sneered Frank, "I'm talking to the second gunman on the forest bastard moon of Endor!"
Rosch felt a stab of self-loathing rip through his insides.
"You're lucky to be on the toasty side of a carbonite freezer pal, and last time I checked, I ran the W.T.U."
"You're the only one in it!" cried Rosch.
"Until now." said Frank. "Now get that fucking footage catalogued."
Rosch stepped close to Frank.
"Piss off, Ruggerman."
Rosch turned on his heel and marched out. Over his shoulder he shouted,

"Catalogue your own bastard footage."
Frank turned his back which meant he did not see Rosch's next steps and subsequent wrestle with police tape.

11:34am
London Met. Police HQ

Back at HQ, Frank scanned his ID at the entrance that led into the library and crime resource archive. He held his breath as he pushed through the rotating turnstile as once he had sharply caught his testicles on the triptych.
The dusty stillness of the library said nothing of the accounts of violence, despair and horror contained within its pages. Frank sat down at a terminal and news articles began to spin across the screen. Sepia time capsules, each bearing witness to some terrible murder or horrific wheat thresher accident.

'FREAK EXPLOSION DURING JAZZ ODYSSEY KILLS HIPPY, CITY REJOICES'.
'SUPERMARKET ADVERT SHOOT DELAYED BY SPONTANEOUS HUMAN COMBUSTION'.
'X-FACTOR FINALIST LIQUIFIES SELF IN NAIL BITING ELIMINATION ROUND'.
'TAKE THAT KILLED BY EXPLOSION IN CELEBRITY GLADIATORS DEBACLE'.

Frank found his attention drawn to a small footnote 'Gary Barlow unscathed'. Frank pondered the data as a neat, petit man in a suit approached him.
"Your port sir." said the petit man.
"Thank you." said Frank.
Frank lifted the stout mug off the tray by its sturdy handle. He sniffed the exquisite ruby depth and thought to himself; 'Barlow. I have to find out what song the busker was playing.'

12:10pm
The Olsen Twins HQ, Harrow, London outskirts

Harassed by the elements, on a deserted piece of scrubland there is a battered and cranky Winnebago. Probably the last place you'd expect to find three of the best intelligence specialists in Europe.

The wind took Rosch's hand and slammed the car door shut. He wrapped his long black overcoat tightly around himself and traversed the slippery mud on the way up to the Winnebago. In the merciless gale, Rosch struggled to catch his breath. He reached the doorstep, cursing the ineffective tread of his Dior shoes for such conditions. Eager to escape the cold, his impatient knock rattled the rickety door.
"What's the password?"
Rosch sighed deeply.
"Three M.C's and one DJ." said Rosch.
With the cold slowly penetrating his ribs, Rosch doubled over and blew warm air into his hands. There was a murmur inside.
"Is that the album or the single version?"
"For god's sake let me in!" roared Rosch, tearing open the rickety door and forcing his way in.

The inside of the Olsen Twins HQ was an intensive laboratory of video recorders, radio scanners and every imaginable kind of surveillance gadgetry. Chris Olsen, the only Brit in the firm, helped Rosch inside. Ostracised from a militant group of Warhammer 40,000 enthusiasts Chris, who was also the largest of the Olsens, handled the door protocol for the Winnebago. He extended his hand towards Rosch.
"Phone." he said.
Rosch reached for his phone in his coat pocket.
"I'm not going through this again." said Rosch.

Nathan Olsen leaned back and stretched subtly in his demob leather chair.

"You know the drill Rosch, phone scan and cavity search."
Chris Olsen removed the back of Rosch's phone.
"We need to make sure you weren't followed here."
Leaning against the cardboard covered window and sipping from a mug reading 'Resistance is Fertile' was Hansen Olsen. At nineteen he was the youngest of the three, and one of two of the U.S born Olsens.
"Security is everything in our line of work Rosch." he said soothingly.

Three men, unrelated but all sharing the surname Olsen, these three ultra-specialists had found each other through frequenting comm-tech expos, wargame testing ranches and a website for Eerie Indiana fans. Rosch slipped off his long damp coat.
"You can check my phone but if any one of you goes near my arsehole."
"Relax Rosch", assured Nathan Olsen. "We have a bio-scanner, we can check you as you are."
Chris Olsen brought forth a black metallic device shaped like a stretched-out rabbit. It came to life with an electronic 'twoodly-deety-doo'. Chris waved the device up and down Rosch's body as Rosch raised his arms.
"You know it still amazes me," said Rosch, "that you guys think someone can put something inside my rectum whilst also somehow, magically circumventing my attention."
As it reached Rosch's crotch, the device sounded an electronic squeal.

Five minutes later...

The Olsens huddled around an X-ray picture of Rosch's colon. Rosch peered at the image.
"Balls." he said.
True enough, the picture showed a small hand grenade shaped device in Rosch's colon. Nathan Olsen inspected the picture.
"It's an MXC-5 tracker, fairly short range, looks totally fried though. Indian last night Rosch?"
"Curried goat." he replied.
The Olsens gasped in unison. Nathan Olsen took to his desk.
"What can we do for you?" he said.
"I need to know all you know about spontaneous human combustion, with large crowds of spectators. Fairs, Klan rallies, that sort of thing." said Rosch.
Hansen Olsen put down his mug.
"Have you ever heard of *group convergence telekinesis*?"
"I know the words." said Rosch confidently.
"Group convergence telekinesis or G.C.T" said Chris Olsen, "is a rarely occurring but tremendously powerful phenomenon. It occurs when a group of people share an intensified common mind set, within a very confined space."
"Yes," continued Nathan Olsen, "and if that group of people reach a sufficiently heightened emotional state, say a hostage crisis or a septic tank disaster, with enough pressure their brain waves can align, creating a super-consciousness."
"What we're saying Rosch," said Hansen Olsen, calmly, "is that in moments of catastrophic terror, this super-consciousness can manifest its will in a tangible form."
Rosch paused.
"You're saying the busker exploded because the commuters 'willed it'? That's insane."

"No sign of explosives or accelerant," said Hansen, "No trace of a perpetrator, and let's not forget, he had no prior history of spontaneous combustion whatsoever."

Rosch flailed as he processed the idea.

"Jesus. What could the busker have been playing to inspire that level of hatred?"

Nathan Olsen flexed his chair back and stroked his short brown beard.

"These days? Mars, Bieber, take your pick."

Hansen Olsen refilled his coffee mug.

"Do you know Frank Ruggerman over at Western Tactical?"

"Don't." implored Rosch.

"He's untouched in this kind of work," assured Chris Olsen, "we've worked with him for years."

"He's nothing but a low rent, alcoholic piss-monger who thinks he's Fox Sherlock bastard Columbo." said Rosch loathingly.

"There was that unexplained zoo exodus in '93," added Nathan Olsen, "Frank figured out the orangutans had become sentient and-"

"Yes and we will never hear the end of that one" said Rosch.

Chris Olsen pondered.

"He cracked the Jackson murder in '98 because he exposed that televangelist who had been using subliminal cuts of dogs in his infomercials."

"Yes, well,..." said Rosch.

Hansen Olsen looked at Rosch with his peculiar otherworldly steadiness.

"Face it Rosch, if you're going to crack this case, you need Frank Ruggerman."

HAWKER STREET

**1:37pm
London Met. Police Science Lab**

The Met. Science Lab was cared for and supervised by Jojo Binks. Hailing from Hackensack New Jersey, former Golden Gloves and waste management consultant. He moved to London many years ago and had made a successful home in the UK. Now in his late fifties, his powerful frame still put the seams of his lab coat to the test. The double doors into the lab swung open and in strode Frank Ruggerman,
"What have you got for me Binks?"
"Eyyyy!" sang Binks, "Bring it in."
Frank and Jojo embraced and shared a deep, nourishing hug, both subtly moaning with relief.
Binks turned to a sophisticated chemistry setup and poured two large scotches.
"A salut."
Jojo savoured his scotch and got to business.
"We set up the tests like you asked."
He led Frank over to a series of windows, each looking into a small room. Each room contained a lab assistant with headphones and a desk, at which sat a member of the public.
"As per request," continued Binks, "we started playing songs to randomly selected members of the public. We took measurements from their pulse rates, sugar levels and urine samples as indicatements of their emotional state. We tried different songs, changed the temperature... mostly we tried to recreate the charm and comfort of the London underground rail system."
"You find anything?" said Frank, removing a cigarette from the packet.
"Well," said Binks, "we discovered that boy bands inspire the highest emotional intensity, usually, rage. The Jonas Brothers, Boyzone, that kinda thing."
Frank lit his cigarette and patiently waited for the good bit.
"The responses were generally pretty intense. Watch this."

Binks tapped on one of the windows, inside, the lab assistants played the music to the subjects. Frank and Binks watched in silence.

"The rooms are all soundproofed, thank god." said Binks, crossing himself.

In quick succession the subjects displayed intense degrees of emotional distress. The first had ripped paper from the lab assistant's clipboard and was stuffing it into their ears. The second, desperately wrenched at the door handle trying to get out, finally collapsing in tearful sobs. Binks led Frank to the third window where a small, bald, bespectacled man sat calmly. Frank looked on and exhaled a dervish of blue grey smoke.

"Ask the lab tech to play some Gary Barlow." he said.

Binks tapped the window and gave the lab assistant the slightest of nods. The lab assistant put the needle on a record player. Within seconds the bald man jumped to his feet and slammed a fist into the lab assistant's face, sending him careening off the chair, papers flying.

"Bloody hell!" said Frank coughing and spluttering.

"Oh, ho ho!" laughed Binks in shock, "You know Frank, with this kind of emotional intensity we could have a real catrasmaphy on our hands."

Frank tried to fathom the consequences.

"Great god's gonads." he said.

Frank's phone buzzed.

"Ruggerman." he answered.

Rosch's BMW sped past Baker Street.

"It's me." he said.

"Where the fuck have you been!?" barked Frank.

"Look, I know," said Rosch, "you can chew me out later. I think I've got something."

"Yes, the I.Q of a beanbag." hissed Frank.

"No, something interesting, some kind of group hysteria thing."

Rosch steered his way through the traffic.

"Alright, meet me back at the station" said Frank.

"I'll be there in fifteen to twenty." said Rosch.
Frank hung up.
"Cretin." he said.
He turned to Jojo Binks.
"Thanks for the help, Binks."
"Ey, forget about it, anytime, you know that."
Binks slapped a hand on Frank's neck.
"Come on, bring it in."
The two embraced. In the hug, two joys converged from the very middle of themselves. The sound of deep humming moans followed by slaps on backs.
"But seriously. Thanks, for everything." said Frank.
"One hand washes the other Frank, remember that." said Binks smiling.
"Sure thing."

2:51pm
London Met. Police HQ East Car Park

Frank stood with his car door open, about to enter, when Rosch pulled into the car park. Frank's phone received a text that read:

EXPECT A VISIT FROM A ROSCH KUNNYPACKEN (AKA THE PHANTOM MENACE) LOVE MARY, KATE & ASHLEY

He thought for a moment and then turned his attention to Rosch exiting his car in the next bay.
"This better be good." said Frank, "I don't appreciate being left alone to trawl through hours of Yourtube dribble."
"I have a theory." said Rosch, "have you ever heard of group convergence telekinesis?"
"I know the words" replied Frank, earnestly.
"It's basically when a group of people, in a confined space, all hate something intensely. Their collective psychic

energy can somehow manifest itself physically." said Rosch. "I think it's what killed the busker."

Frank pondered the theory.

"That fits." said Frank. "Together with the lab findings on rage inspiring boy bands, we could be on the brink of cracking this thing."

Rosch smiled cautiously as he felt a burgeoning mutual respect.

"So, what now?" he said.

"We'll get back in the lab first thing and squeeze out something more solid." said Frank.

Rosch smiled a subtle smile and went to re-enter his car.

"Oh, one last thing..." said Frank, "Don't ever consult the Olsen Twins without me again."

Rosch paused and then closed his car door.

"Excuse me?" he said.

"You heard." said Frank, "I've got open investigations."

"You piss-head bastard Ruggerman! You are not the only police with ongoing cases you know! I've built a network of sources from Mudchute to Cockfisters! Before this cowpat of a detail, I was working homicide, for six bastard years! Now you want to have me as some kind of deputised Jimmy Krankie? Forget it."

Frank stepped towards Rosch.

"You are in no position to be going all 'maverick goose' after being suspended for killing an Ewok."

Rosch recoiled and leaned against his car as a flash of guilt seared through his gut. His mind lurched back to that evening five weeks ago…

Rosch had been sitting at his desk in a small office adjacent to the rest of homicide. He was pouring over crime scene photos and forensic analyses. He had five bodies to deal with, all horrific violations found in West Central. The brutal nature of the attacks made for high grade tabloid fodder, the headlines seared onto his mind.

'BIZARRE ANIMAL ATTACKS TERRORIZE LONDON!'
'WINTER WONDERLAND CLOSES AFTER RAMPANT ANIMAL ENCOUNTER!'
'IS ANYONE SAFE?'
'HUNGRY, HUNGRY HIPPO' BAGS FIFTH!'

That night, Rosch had followed a lead to an illegal fox gambling club in Soho. The front entrance was manned by three serious looking men, so Rosch made his way to the rear through a series of dark, wet, alleys that separated the building from Chinatown. Suddenly, from behind a bin there dashed a strange creature, hissing and growling. In a flash it was gone, into the next alley. Rosch drew his weapon and slid with his back against the wall, nearing the corner. He heard strange animal mutterings. He cocked his pistol, flinching as a bin crashed over, spilling its contents. Rosch dashed round the corner and came face to face with something inhuman. Rosch fired and fell backwards against the wall, gasping for breath. His weapon still trained on the creature, he tried to compose himself, steady his breathing. He carefully approached the body. The alley was dark but Rosch could just make out that the creature was face down and motionless. He pressed the muzzle of his pistol against the rain soaked and furry back of the figure on the ground, no response. Rosch's thoughts suddenly turned to puzzlement then flooded with abject horror. He turned the body over to reveal the startled face of an Ewok. Rosch's spine turned to meltwater as he realised his mistake. The gravity of it bloomed inside him like a rose and his veins filled with the promise of an incoming guilt tsunami. Eyes streaming with tears, Rosch cradled the Ewok in his arms and cried the saddest, longest "Why?" that would be heard in Soho that evening.

Rosch was still sobbing as Frank was berating him.
"Bottom line is-" barked Frank.

Rosch opened his tearful eyes and sniffed in a giant glob of mucus. Frank momentarily recoiled and continued;
"Bottom line is, I don't need some trumped up brat, nephew Wookie whacker-"
"Ewok!" sobbed Rosch.
"...Ewok whacker, making me a ton of noisy pig shit to clean up! Understand?!"
Rosch stood broken and helpless.
"Now go home!"
Frank entered his car, cursing to himself. Slowly, and tearfully, Rosch did the same.

3:52pm
London. I Love Dogs Way

His face stained with tears and mucus, Rosch drove along the avenue. The swollen clouds heaved and swayed the tall trees like seaweed in the current. Thoughts like stinging nettles flooded and scratched Rosch's mind one after another in a continuous deluge. 'How dare that drunkard tell me how to use *my* sources? That complete and total bastard! God, what am I doing? I'm fucked. I've lost fucking everything and everyone, finds it fucking hilarious. I'm a fucking joke... But no one could work with that wanker. That's why he's tucked away in the arse end by himself in the fucking basement. Yes! Bollocks! Fuck him! Fuck him in his stupid, Star Wars put down shitting face!'. Rosch shook and hammered the steering wheel, gritting his teeth and writhing in his seat.
"Fucking bastard bastards!"

Five minutes later...

Rosch felt numb now. Dry tears and mucus were splayed across his collar. He sniffed and turned on the radio. An Australian dj hero said some words.

"Great stuff. If you're just joining us we are celebrating the tragic death of pop legend Gary Barlow with a special memorial programme."
His colleague took over.
"And we continue now with this gem from 2000 and blah blah blah nobody gives a shit."
A song started. Rosch heard familiar piano chords.
"Oh I fucking hate this song-" Rosch froze.
Snippets of thoughts from the day began assembling in his brain.
'This is a total noodle scratcher', 'Kablaarrgh!', Celebrate the tragic death of Gary Barlow', 'Group Convirgin Telegmony', 'Deputized Jimmy Krankie!' 'Latest trouser soiling!' 'Ochli - doody!', 'trouser soiling!', 'Gary Barlow', 'Wookie whacker!' 'Ewok!', an agonised yelp… and then silence.

Rosch thought of the countless performances of Gary Barlow numbers that the buskers of London would be singing during rush hour tomorrow. So many commuters, so many stations, so much hate. It could mean hundreds of explosions linked together by the tunnels, all taking place during rush hour. Rosch slammed on the brakes and did a U-turn, racing off at full speed.

4:24pm
North London, Frank Ruggerman's House

The car door slammed shut and Rosch raced up Frank's garden path. He hammered on the door.
"Ruggerman, you bastard!" he cried.
Out of the corner of his eye, he spotted Frank curled up on a small bench with his trousers around his ankles, hugging an empty bottle of amaretto.
"Ruggerman! Get up!" he shouted.
Frank snarled as he surfaced.
"The fuck do you want, Lando?"

"Barlow's dead!" said Rosch, "It's all over the radio!"
Frank snapped too, sitting upright in a flash.
"Jesus H. Mary and Mungo! The tribute songs! By 10am tomorrow, half of London will be rubble."
"What do we do?" asked Rosch.
Frank pondered this a moment, before gruffly whispering, "Huffnagel."
Frank reached under the bench pulling up a bottle of scotch. Rosch paused only a moment before saying;
"I'm driving."

5:10pm
Whitechapel. City Hall

The car screeched to a halt next to the marble steps leading to the mayor's office. Frank leapt from the car as Rosch carefully exited the passenger's side, nursing his nose with his head back.
"Come on!" Frank yelled, racing up the steps.
Frank and Rosch burst through the heavy ornate doors of City Hall. Many had left for the day but the halls of office were still busy. With Frank leading and Rosch opening another pack of tissues, they marched down the hall towards the mayor's office. Sat at her desk was Alice Cooper, the mayor's P.A.
"We need to see the Mayor, now!" demanded Frank.
"Okay then." she said, stoically.
Mayor of London, Harry Huffnagel was a known eccentric. Along the corridor Rosch noticed the collection of portraits depicting the Mayor's prize winning horse Ginger, Michaela Strachan and veteran comedian, Rodney Dangerfield. Rosch cleared the last of the blood from his nose and readied himself. Frank barged through the heavy door into Huffnagel's office.
"Mr. Mayor, we have to talk. "

Rosch scanned the room and there he was, Mayor Harry Huffnagel, standing with a watering can, pouring onto a large plant pot, containing a giant stuffed elephant toy.
"Ello, Princess." he said.

It didn't get talked about much anymore but Harry Huffnagel bore an uncanny resemblance to a 1960's era Michael Caine, in both appearance and manner.
"Mr Mayor," Frank began.
The mayor stopped pouring.
"This best be quick, I'm a guest judge on 'Salsa Time with Arsene Wenger' in 'alf an hour."
"We're investigating the exploding busker case," Frank continued, "We know for definite it wasn't a terror attack."
"No?" barked Huffnagel, "Then what the bleedin' hell was it?"
"We don't have time to explain," said Frank, "but with the death of Gary Barlow, the resulting rage caused by the countless tribute acts on the London underground tomorrow will unleash unimaginable destruction and tear apart the city."
Huffnagel reflected deeply and put down his watering can.
"What?" he asked.
"We found a link" said Rosch, "between condensed public hatred and spontaneous human combustion. What happened with that busker will be multiplied to a city-wide explosion."
"If we don't stop those tribute songs," said Frank, "it'll mean the total destruction of London."
The mayor adjusted his thick rimmed, black spectacles.
"Right, you mean to tell me, you want me to announce to the city that no one can perform tribute songs for one of the most highly regarded members of the most popular boy band in British history cos Keith Floyd and Luke...Skywanker know how to use wankypedia? Not a chance."
"If we're wrong, we're wrong." said Frank. "We go back to our grind of tedium and indignity and the whole of

London does the same. But if we're right" he paused, "Harry…"
Huffnagel's face briefly contorted into a peculiar facial gesture at Ruggerman's over familiarity.
"You...will have saved the lives of millions of registered reality show voters."
The mayor smiled cynically. He looked at Rosch who slowly nodded in agreement whilst nursing a broken nose. The mayor lit a cigar.
"Alright." he said.
Rosch turned and smiled at a truly nonreciprocal Frank Ruggerman. The Mayor pulled and exhaled the exquisite blue plumes,
"So, what do you need from me?"

**7:37pm
London**

All across London, the Mayor appeared on screens announcing his mandate for the city.
In the Ham & Organ public house in Islington, the regulars stared, transfixed as Mayor Harry Huffnagel 'laid it out'.
"*Ello, you lot. It is with heavy breathing, that we witness the passing of Gary Barlow.*"
On a commuter train to High Wycombe, faces stared at tablets and laptops.
"*I appreciate...*" the Mayor continued, "*the London music community's desire to pay homage, to the fallen soldier, of Great British tosspop.*"
In the Dog & Hotpot, in a ladies toilet cubicle, Jenny Taylor watched the broadcast via her Twittlechat feed. With a crunching clear of the throat, she wiped.
"*But I implore you all to be strong. To stand defiant, to mourn only with quiet dignity.*"
On a huge screen in a packed Wembley Stadium, the Mayor's face towered over the crowd.

"Cos if anyone tries to perform one bloody tribute song, it'll be your arse!"
The crowds erupted with joy.

9:55pm
London Met. Police HQ East Car Park

Frank and Rosch approached their respective cars. Frank had rolled the dice on using the disabled space and saw no ticket.
"Well, we did it" ventured Rosch.
"Yeah, see you tomorrow." said Frank, opening his car door.
"Ruggerman," said Rosch gingerly, "I thought it might be appropriate to celebrate with a drink?"
Frank paused thoughtfully. It was the unstoppable hope versus the immovable indifference.
"Fuck off." he said, thoughtfully.
"Oh come on you crusty old bastard" pleaded Rosch.
Frank Ruggerman acquiesced with a grunt.
"You're buying." he added.
The two cars pulled out narrowly avoiding a collision, the deafening cacophony of angry car horns and muffled abuse rang into the night.

EPISODE II

Friday
12:56am
Little Toffle Woods, near Kilburn

Daniels had been running so long he thought his heart was about to explode. Stripped to his underwear and with his hands bound, he ran through the dense woods of Little Toffle in north west London. The rainwater splashed up his body from the long grass and scrub. The wet leaves lashed his face, blinding his eyes. He could hear someone behind him. Daniels stumbled over someone lying on the ground but kept running.
"Hey what's the big idea?" the homeless man shouted after him.
"Sorry!" gasped Daniels as he raced on frantically.
The stitch in his side felt like it had begun to haemorrhage. He paused breathlessly, scanning for an escape.
Way behind him he heard:
"Hey what's the big idea?"
Daniels spun around to see his pursuer but there was no-one there, only swaying trees. He called out.
"Hello?!"
No reply, only silence save for the wind gently rustling the treetops. Daniels turned to continue onwards when he felt a sudden, tight grip around his throat that stopped his scream dead.

6:30am
Little Toffle Woods, Near Kilburn

Footsteps, conversations and barking dogs ravaged the serenity that you would normally find when this deep in the woods. The crime scene was in full swing. Officers and forensics scurried between the trees like an ant colony. There was a pop-up lab, interview tents, extensive craft service tables and police tape as far as the eye could see. Sheriff Sheila Reed of the Kilburn Sheriff's dept. approached Officer Sam Honken as he shooed off a trio of crime scene photographers.

"Go on now." he said.
Sheriff Reed removed her beaver skin gloves.
"Howdy Sheriff." said Honken.
"Mr. Honken." said Sheriff Reed.
Honken shuffled uneasily.
"It's Daniels." he said.
"I can see that." said the Sheriff, ruefully.
"They're never gonna stop ya know, … until, … ya know?"
"I know. I know." said the Sheriff.
At that moment, Officer Downe entered the scene.
"Sheriff." she said brightly.
Officer Downe ducked under a line of police tape and put on her marigolds. Sheriff Reed was becoming increasingly impressed by her plucky new recruit.
"Officer Downe." said the Sheriff, smiling subtly.
"Where's that then?" asked Downe. "Okay," she continued, "it's the same as the others, early hours of the morning, stripped, bound, tied to a tree stump with the mobile phone inserted part way into the colon."
"How long has he been like this?" asked the Sheriff.
"Just a few hours." replied Downe, lifting the police issue tarpaulin. "He's not even hypodermic yet."

There, underneath the cover, naked, except for his underwear, tied to a tree trunk, with hands bound and a mobile phone inserted into his rectum, the still very much alive Daniels shivered in the bitter cold of the early morning.
"To see such degradation." sighed the Sheriff.
Daniels was exhausted, slowly succumbing to exposure. His faint whimpers for assistance became muffled as Officer Downe replaced the sheet over his head.
"Some people are just callous.", she said wistfully.

7:56am
London Met HQ. Chief Commissioner Leathers' Office

Leathers hammered the button on his intercom with the finger he had just sprained, hammering the button on his intercom.
"Arse biscuits!" he winced, "Just tell them to eat around it!"
"Yes sir." replied the intercom.
Leathers was examining his throbbing finger when Renfield, the wretched lackey, sprung from a long line of wretched lackeys, stuck his head through the door.
"Rosch Kunnypacken, sir."
"Show him in forthwith." commanded Leathers.
Leathers opened Rosch's report and within seconds of reading had reached catastrophic levels of confusion.
Rosch entered.
"Sir." he said.
"Kunnypacken, be seated." said a befuddled Leathers.
Rosch watched uncomfortably as Leathers reviewed his report in the same way a labrador inspects a dildo it had mistaken for one of its litter. Leathers deemed the exercise a write-off and cut to the chase.
"How is your relationship with Detective Ruggerman?"
"uhm."

Rosch thought back to a few nights prior when he and
Frank were in the Met. local pub, the Dog & Hotpot.

"So, why did you join the force?" Rosch had asked.
Frank had groaned, stood, sank the last of his pint and left.

Back in Leathers' office, Rosch pondered.
"I'd say there's a burgeoning respect." he said.
As Rosch spoke, he was all too aware of the calm but
malignant gaze of Reyka, who stood with his back against
the window, his omnipresent cigarette fuming away.
"Not good enough Kunnypacken." said Leathers "We have
an exploding busker, no concrete reason why, no signed
afterdavids and no arrests of any description."
"No sir."
"This is a disgrace!" Leathers roared. "I've seen accidental
enemas with better findings."
"I understand sir, it's just..."
"Nevermind what it's just, Kunnypacken! It is impossible
to ignore what it just, wasn't was, isn't it, wasn't it?"
"Sir." replied Rosch gingerly, fearing complete mental
collapse.
"Be still" said Leathers, "Begin your account...I want you
to tell me every last detail."

Leathers and Reyka listened intently as Rosch relayed
his account of the Henderson busker case. Rosch had
annotated the report with professional judgements on the
performance of his new super, including;
"He apparently, 'forgets' to fill out incident reports"
and...
"He's totally smashed, and I mean constantly."
Once Rosch had delivered his account, Leathers sat back in
his chair and pressed his fingertips together.
"So, it was spontaneous human combustion?" inquired
Leathers.
"Yes, sir."
"Proof?"
"Not as such, sir."

"This is precisely what we need trampling out. Ruggerman's wild theories and speculations are causing severe chafing in City Hall. Governor Denton can barely use his space hopper. His gusset's like an estuary at low tide." said Leathers.

Reyka lit another cigarette.

"Rosch, we want you" said Reyka, "to keep Ruggerman on a more PR friendly keel."

"Yes," interjected Leathers, "and stop him turning every case into an episode of bloody Scooby Doo. I trust we can count on you, Rosch. Keep Ruggerman on the straightened arrow and we may be able to salvage your career just yet. Well, there it is. Now, you have a case in Little Toffle so get a move on and try not to kill anyone."

8:34am
Wood Green, the home of Councilwoman Caroline Ahem

The mist danced around the expansive and immaculate country house. The grounds lay deathly still, save for the occasional blood curdling cries of the Howler Monkeys. The wings of the house were connected by corridors, lined with large windows that sucked in every photon of light they could.

Along one of these corridors trundled Caroline Ahem in her motorised wheelchair. A fiercely glamorous woman who wielded her titanic fashion budget with formidable precision.

As a child, her mother, a member of the Bermerian aristocracy, had taken her to a charity benefit hosted by a handful of obscure British royals. During the evening, the 7-year-old Ahem had been left alone whilst her mother was negotiating the sale of 14,000 Kalashnikovs to the Earl of Tewkesbury. Her tiny frame had wandered out into the rear garden and through the servants entrance, only to be swarmed upon by the Corgis. Eventually, a waiter by the name of Hassan spotted the poor child under the mound of churning fur and teeth. In a mortal struggle, he struck each of the Corgis with a bottle of '73 Chateau De Mon Oncle and returned the child Ahem to her mother. Hassan was thanked, docked the cost of burying the Corgis and given a fifteen minute break to treat his injuries. The attack left Ahem unable to walk and bound to a wheelchair and Hassan out of work, bound for the Job Centre.

Now aged 63 (or 52 depending on publication) Ahem was amongst the most powerful figures in London. At her side, jogging to keep up, was her assistant Grace. Ahem pulled her chair to a stop at a window overlooking a fountain.
"Get me Leathers." she ordered.

In his office, Leathers, having just shooed out Rosch, moved onto his next task for the day. It was whilst he was feeding stills of fornicating animals into a shredder, that Ahem's call came through. Leathers clasped the phone between his collar and shoulder.
"Speak."
"Leathers, Ahem."
"Councilwoman! How does you?" said Leathers, briefly perusing each image before shredding.
"What's the status of our boy?" inquired Ahem.
"Well, your nephew is lucky to still have his sheriff's badge, but he's in place."
"He's playing ball?"
"He has to be," warned Leathers, "his reputation is a crusty glob on the rim after this Ewok fiasco, he hardly has a choice."
Ahem removed her dry Manhattan from a passing tray and savoured the aroma.
"Good." she said. "You just grind the monkey and he'll dance all night long."
She took a sip of the stirred down bourbon and briefly considered when had been the last time she had taken pleasure in anything.

"Rosch is a good boy" she explained, "sensitive and eager to please. Keep him close with a dangling carrot and he'll spill every nugget on Ruggerman."
Leathers fixated on a picture of mating giraffes: "Received."
"Oh, and Leathers, if you ever want to escape the drudgery of being chief commissioner, you get our boy on top and Ruggerman gone with the wind, are we clear?"
"Understood, Councilwoman."
The call ended. Ahem continued down the corridor.
"Tosspot." she hissed under her breath.

10:12am
Little Toffle Woods, near Kilburn

Several officers leapt out of the way as Frank Ruggerman's car pulled to a stop between an ambulance and an organic ice cream wagon. Frank and Rosch exited the car and approached the centre of the scene. Sheriff Reed was on hand.
"You must be Reed." said Frank.
"I agree." she said, shaking his hand warmly. "Listen, I've got a real mess here and I hear you're my best bet at getting it cleaned up before mom gets home."
Reed lifted the tarpaulin exposing Daniels, who, desperately fatigued by now, sobbed wretchedly, shrinking away from the bright flashing cameras of the forensics. His feeble pleas for assistance still sadly went unnoticed.
"I take it no witnesses stepped forward?" asked Frank.
"None that speak English." said Sheriff Reed, indicating a nearby Romanian family desperately miming their testimonies. "Also, no traces of his pursuers found yet, either."
"Pursuers?" asked Rosch. "What makes you think there's more than one?"
"Just a hunch, I guess," said Reed, "I've got to admit I am in way over my head here. Normally, my job's giving talks

at schools or scraping poo off the windscreen of the riot van.
"Don't worry..." assured Frank, distractedly watching Daniels' attempts at relieving a cramp in his leg without aggravating the mobile phone in his bottom.
"...This seems fairly straightforward by my standards." Frank approached Daniels and the forensics scattered like cockroaches in the light. He paused thoughtfully for a moment before replacing the sheet over Daniels' head.
"In these parts, do you have much trouble with aliens?" he asked.
"Aliens? No." replied the Sheriff.
"Witchcraft?"
"No."
"Mind altering parasites?"
"Nope."
"Feral beastmen of the woods?"
"No."
"Demonic possession?"
"No."
"Restaurant reviewers?"
Reed hesitated. Rosch sensed a tangible change in mood like that which follows the discovery of ringworm at an orgy.
"Look, I'm sorry I can't be more helpful," said Sheriff Reed, slowly stepping away. "I'm sure you'll find everything you need in the popup labs."
The last of her sentence was lost as she turned and sprinted off into the woods.

A cold gust of wind blew through the clearing, lifting the rear of the sheet covering Daniels' whimpering form. Frank stood and surveyed the scene.
"Such callous disregard." said Frank. "First off, we need the full prints, swabs and cavity analysis."
"Nooooo." sobbed Daniels.
"Results should be back within the hour" said Rosch, checking his watch. "or it's free, or something."

Frank stood and scanned the extensive crime scene with its myriad tents and trailers.
"Yeah," he said, turning to a nearby officer. "I've got to say you're well organised here. What was the time of dea... uhm, moment... of... penetration?"
"About 8 or 9 hours ago." the officer replied. "But he was only discovered at about 5am."
"So you got all this set up in just a few hours?"
"Nah," said the officer. "most of this lot was already here. Old Jeff (...) had his lawnmower nicked yesterday mornin'."
Only then did Frank and Rosch notice the old bearded man standing atop the ridge.
"Thieving bastards!" he wailed.

After retrieving the initial forensics report and a truly thorough cavity analysis on Daniels, Frank and Rosch returned to the car.
"Restaurant reviewers?" said Rosch dryly. "Well I'm glad we can write off your usual alien-crossdressing-sasquatch-routine."
"If I was you," growled Frank "I'd take the opportunity to clean the Wookie shit out your ears and learn something."
Once again, Rosch felt the familiar twitch of bile in his stomach.
"Fair enough, but if you would be kind enough to let me in on whatever it is you think is happening here? Because something tells me you've seen this before."
With the subtlest of grunts, Frank grudgingly accepted and led Rosch back to the car

1:17pm
London Met HQ. Western Tactical Unit Office

Frank entered the office making a beeline for a drawer heaving with documents. Rosch wearily dumped his jacket and slumped into the dusty couch.

"Whenever you are ready, Ruggerman." said Rosch.

"Shut the fuck up and listen." said Frank, briskly as he switched on the projector.

"I've got cases with similar tropes dating back to the advent of mobile phones. Frances MacGillikudie, sixty-five, found in the woods just outside Kilburn, tied to a tree stump, bound and gagged in just her underwear. It was only thanks to a team from Gardeners World Live that we found her."

At the press of a button the projector heaved its aged bones onto the next slide.

"Robert Clancy, thirty-three, found once again in the woods, this time in Scrunt near the 'Stop n' Gobble'. Notice the phone inserted into the rectum again, unlucky for him this took place during the 'Saved by the Bell' era of mobile phones."

Rosch pursed his lips and blew a short sharp breath.

"These are just a few of a hundred cases like this pre 2000. That's when things really get interesting. Since then, we're averaging twenty to thirty a year between here and St. Pivot's."

"Twenty to thirty a year?" said Rosch. "How's that possible? Surely twenty to thirty people being found every year, bound and gagged with a phone inserted into their anus' would at least be on Tik Tok?"

"And not one arrest." said Frank as he garnished an augmented pina colada.

"So, what? A cover-up?" asked Rosch.

"Has to be." said Frank sipping from the straw of his weapons grade rum cocktail.

"It's the same old business. Look for those who stand to profit, those who stand to lose. Silence... has a tremendous clarity to it."
Rosch pondered the case against a mental backdrop of his recent life choices.
"The last four recorded cases have all been in that same woods, outside Little Toffle." said Frank.
"So, what now?" asked Rosch, quietly bracing himself.
"Not sure," said Frank, with contempt bordering on disgust, "but it'll probably involve going to Little Toffle."
Frank picked up his jacket and made for the door.
"Jesus Christ." he spat, disdainfully.

2:59pm
Little Toffle Main Street, near Kilburn

A flurry of net curtains twitched as Frank's car arrived on the Main Street of Little Toffle. The street was lined with old timey stores and restaurants. Each had their own wooden deck with either tables or goods on display. An old man rocked menacingly in his chair as he smoked his oversized pipe.

Rosch exited the car and immediately became aware of the locals' tense gazes. A trio of moody looking bearded folk stared from the porch of 'Clandestine Clams and Hammers' As Frank and Rosch neared the store, the trio turned their backs.

Frank took out his phone as they progressed down Main street. Next door was Mr. Dbrovnik's 'Mirrors U Like'. Again, its patio held a complement of disapproving onlookers. They, too, slowly turned their backs in an effort to shun the outsiders. However, this group were confronted by a screen of large mirrors that reflected all, causing them to revolve, awkwardly.

"Maybe we should split up, collect statements, interviews?" said Rosch.

Rosch's suggestion fell on deaf ears as Frank scrolled through something on his phone, stopping only occasionally to survey the street.
Rosch was losing his patience.
"Ruggerman, we-"
"Lando, when I need your kind of input I'll use the toilet. Until then you're surplus so jog on and get us a couple of miniatures."
"Fine." said Rosch. "Do what you want, I'm getting to work."
Frank sat on a bench and stretched out.
"May the force be with you!" he sang.
"Fuck off." snapped Rosch.
Frank leaned back and felt the sun on his face. He sipped from his hip flask and returned to his phone.

5:10pm

Rosch sluggishly stepped off the last step in front of 'Barry's Bagels'. He closed his eyes and filled his lungs with the piney air. So far, the few locals who had not slammed the door in his face hadn't given him anything. From the rest there wasn't anything even close to a complete sentence.

Some progress had been made in 'the Toy Shack'. Rosch had managed to obtain an interview with the 19-year-old clerk, Jamie. Conventional conversation had proved impossible, however. Rosch had managed to engage the boy by using the accoutrement from a game that was to hand. As Rosch would describe facial features or hair styles, the boy would shake his head or nod. Rosch would then flick down the flaps until only one suspect would remain. After some fleeting success the interview collapsed into bedlam as the clerk attempted to flee the scene in a Wendy house.

Out on a street bench, Frank was sipping his fifth, large pina colada as a despondent Rosch approached.

"Productive day, dear?" asked Frank, wryly.
"Not a bastard thing." grumbled Rosch.
Frank slurped the last of his drink, stood and burped. A little distance down the street Rosch spotted a strange old lady placing a note on the bonnet of Frank's car. She was trying to casually hurry away, glancing over her shoulder. Rosch subtly directed Frank's attention to her. Frank approached the car and removed the note. On it was a strange drawing like a crude hieroglyph. He looked up at the woman who suddenly panicked and fled.
"Police! On the ground!" shouted Frank as he drew his pistol and sped off to follow her. Frank and Rosch raced down the street in pursuit. She ran around a corner into an alley where she stumbled over a large collection of bagpipes. As she scrambled to her feet, Frank leapt and drove his shoulder into her abdomen, sending them both crashing to the floor.
Frank came to lie on top of her. Sitting up he cocked his pistol and roared: "Calm down!"
his pistol waving maniacally in the air.
The old lady struggled frantically.
"Please! They can't see me talking to you!"
"Who?!" said Frank.
"You!"
"No, you idiot! Who can't see you talking to us?!"
"I can't say! They'll kill me!" she cried, struggling and kicking.
"Who are you and why did you put this on my windscreen?!" he demanded.
"My name's Greggs, but just check out Mr. Sanderson, he owns the Firenze Pizza Shoppe! I've said too much already. Now please let me go!"

In a wild effort Mrs. Greggs lashed out with her leg and caught Rosch in the testicles, buckling him to the floor. Frank finally released her and she clambered off. He stood up slowly as he got his breath back and studied the crude hieroglyph more carefully. It looked like the depiction of a figure with three legs and a sombrero.

"Get up Lando. We've got a thread to pull."
Rosch barely heard the words over the sound of his rupturing kidneys, as he lay dry heaving.

5:20pm

After some digging online, Frank had found the Firenze Pizza Shoppe. Rosch's testicles had suffered tremendous trauma, making him breathe like he was in labour.
"Pipe down, Lando." said Frank. "This is the place."
Frank brought the car to a stop outside the rustic looking pizzeria.
"Of course." said Rosch, nursing himself. "Why would you conduct interviews? Surely a real detective waits until a demented old woman gives him a napkin depicting a Mexican bandit with a deformed penis."
"How would you like to add concussion to your shattered scrotum?" Frank retorted. "According to his Wikipage," he continued more calmly, "Rene Sanderson doesn't just own the pizza shop, he's chair of the local businessman's guild. If there is anything shaky going on with this lot, he's in charge. Now wait here."
Frank got out of the car and removed something from the boot. The slam of the lid closing caused a lightning strike in Rosch's abdomen. Parked outside of the pizza shoppe was a vintage Mercedes Benz 330SL. Frank sauntered over to it and slid a long thin object down the inside of the driver's door. With a few wiggles the door opened obligingly.

 Inside the Firenze Pizza Shoppe, Rene Sanderson was preparing for the evening. A tall, broad man, even at the age of fifty-eight his physique spoke of a rugby player. He had capitalised on his father's success in the area and had become a prominent community leader. He was laying out cutlery when he heard the familiar roar of a powerful engine. He approached the window and gently drew back

the curtain. In his purring pride and joy, he saw Frank, revving the engine and smoking a cigarette. Sanderson coolly stepped out onto the porch, approached the car and entered the passenger side.
"Detective Ruggerman I presume?" he said, smoothly. Frank took one last roaring rev and switched off the engine.
"You know this is truly a lovely motor." said Frank, "I always imagined myself having one by now, on the long drive of a manor house in, uhm…Coventry."
"Too busy chasing the Loch Ness monster I suppose." Frank swivelled in his chair towards Sanderson.
"I'd check that lip of yours, sunshine. I'm here with the long arm of the law and I'm going to stick it right up your browsing history."
"I'm fairly certain I don't know what you're talking about, detective."
"Citizens being publicly humiliated in ritualistic displays and abandoned in the woods,"
Frank pulled out niche porn magazines from the glove box.
"...and judging by your taste in literature, I'm guessing the mobile was your idea."
"Well, I'm currently at a loss, detective, but I can assure you I will attempt to aid your investigation as best I possibly can. Here, my card." said Sanderson. "Now, if you don't mind, I have the dinner service to prepare for."
As Frank opened the car door, he noticed a small matching hieroglyph tattoo on Sanderson's hand.
"Where did you get the fancy tattoo?"
"A momento from my rambunctious youth. I've not the heart to see it removed." said Sanderson.
"Well, tattoos are all the rage where you're going." said Frank exiting the vehicle.
Sanderson sat calmly and watched in the rear view mirror as Frank returned to his car.
"Anything?" said Rosch.
"Oh, it's him," said Frank, "or at least his show. He's as cool as they come. Right, let's check in the BnB."

7:23pm
The Randy Salmon Guesthouse, Little Toffle

Torrential rain hammered the latticed windows of the creaking guesthouse. Having been given their respective keys, Frank and Rosch took to their rooms. Frank, with a lit cigarette in his mouth, dumped his things on the bed, rubbed his hands and made his way to the bar.

Rosch carefully unpacked his clothes for the next day and set up his laptop to begin the day's report. He rubbed his eyes and took a moment to evaluate his surroundings and subsequently, life's purpose. His laptop came to life and he began to write.

'Yet again I believe our progress to be unnecessarily hindered. Ruggerman and his obsession with conspiracy and the bizarre. He is perpetually at the mercy of his wild imagination and his tenacity for such can sadly lead him to overlook the obvious. He has a chronic distrust of people and the world around him.'

Meanwhile, down in the saloon, the landlord pointed from bottle to bottle on the backbar shelves. Leaning over the counter, smoke billowing from his face, Frank pointed at his desired choices with increasingly agitated grunts. The landlord endeavoured to assist, running up and down the bar pointing at bottles. Eventually Frank went behind the bar, removed three bottles, gestured that this would do him fine and returned to his room. Rosch continued his report.

'There is no doubting his eye for the criminally intent, but his caustic manner and chronic use of words like arse and tosspot make him difficult to engage with professionally.'

He stopped a moment and slowly deleted the last entry.

'He is....a....total fucking arse head...fuck fuck fuck fucking! Fuck candle arse bastard!'

Rosch swept the laptop and most of the guesthouse stationery onto the floor and buried his face in his hands.

3:00am

Rosch awoke with a start, just like he did every night at this time. His mind temporarily reminisced of attempted sleep therapies and medication. The vague and perfidious memories dissipated as Rosch became aware of the sound of lashing rain on brittle glass. Also, the rain mixed with the sound of an unconscious Frank across the hall, who was by the sound of it, clearcutting a forest. Even the dense oak doors of the guesthouse couldn't subdue Frank's slumberial nasal onslaught. Rosch got out of bed and peered out into the dense monsoon. Outside in the hall, he heard something fall over. He opened the door and looked out onto the landing. At the end of the corridor, he saw a cloaked figure disappear down the stairs.
"Police! On the ground!"
Rosch grabbed his weapon from its holster and raced out across the landing, stopping at the top of the stairs. He paused, his gun trained down into the candlelit stairwell. Carefully, he made his way down, scanning for the intruder. Rosch slowly crossed the hallway and entered the saloon. The room was dark save for the dim mustard colored lights of the backbar and Rosch carefully scanned for any sign of movement. At the sound of footsteps, Rosch ducked behind a large bookshelf only to see Frank enter the bar where he removed a bottle of brandy before returning to his room.

"Ruggerman!" Rosch hissed.
Rosch got up to follow Frank when he came face to face with the cloaked figure who struck Rosch with something heavy. Rosch and his weapon were thrown to the floor. A heavy kick to the chest smashed through his preoccupation with the current fragility of his testicles. Winded, Rosch parried the follow-up kick and his assailant tumbled on top of him. A forearm was thrust onto Rosch's neck and pressed down hard. Rosch swung punches into his assailant's abdomen with all his might but his attacker was

a lot heavier than he was. Rosch clawed for any kind of possible weapon as he felt the forearm on his throat begin to restrict the oxygen to his brain. He kicked his legs, knocking over a decorated table that celebrated the landlord's enthusiasm for humorously shaped vegetables. He fumbled amongst the tumbling carrots and aubergines until he found a mighty squash. He grasped it tightly and smashed it against his opponent's temple, sending him reeling into a coat stand. Rosch gasped for breath as he pulled himself up. Down the hall, the noise snapped Frank out of his sleepwalk. He took a second to realise where he was, which in itself was not that out of the ordinary.
"Ruggerman! Fucking help!"
Frank turned quickly before he noticed the magnum bottle of brandy in his hand. He held it to his mouth and took a big swig.
Rosch swung a knee fiercely into the middle of his attacker's gut, slamming him against another table. Rosch threw heavy blow after heavy blow with what was a truly formidable squash. The figure twisted in Rosch's grip and slammed its forehead onto the bridge of Rosch's nose. Rosch's vision multiplied into seven and his knees collapsed. He awoke a short while later as Frank pulled him to his feet. Again, Rosch was flooded with panic.
"I'll fucking do you!"
"Easy Lando." said Frank, "He's gone. I followed him into the garden while you were sparko but he got away."
Rosch groaned as he felt his ribs grind against one another.
"Actually, on that note," said Frank, "we best get you fixed up."

5:26am
The friendly local doctor stood and waved on the steps of the Little Toffle Surgery practice.
"Thank you!" hollered Frank, holding aloft his free lollipop.
Rosch winced as he touched the stitches on his nose.

"Look," said Frank, savouring his cherry-cola lollipop, "we all take a shoeing in the line of duty every now and then-"
"Oh, piss off, Ruggerman!" shouted Rosch, immediately regretting it, "if you hadn't been paralytic and insistent on doing everything your own way, I might not have a bastard concussion!"
"Alright, alright!" said Frank. "You're right. Now listen, I've figured out what's got this town so riled. Each victim was an active BingeGripe reviewer. Look."
Frank showed Rosch his phone. It displayed the homepage of BingeGripe, the most widely used restaurant review app in the Little Toffle area.
"Here's the profiles of several of the previous victims. See here. Dirk Jacobi, forty four, three weeks before he was found in the woods he posted this scathing review of *'Mama Feelgood's Karaoke Lounge'*. *'Uncomfortable seats, warm prosecco, poor song selection, way too much Phil Collins, I'm never coming here again.'* Within a fortnight Mama Feelgood's Karaoke Lounge had gone into liquidation. This is what they're all so afraid of, and why no one will give us anything cos they're all in on it."
"So, what now?" said Rosch.
"That's easy." said Frank. "We wrangle the weakest link and do some fishing."

9:34am
Little Toffle Main Street

The morning light was as crisp as the air. Frank and Rosch walked once again down the main shopping street of Little Toffle.
"And we're looking for what, exactly?" said Rosch.
"Just keep your eyes open." said Frank, scanning left and right as he progressed down the street.
"Here." he said.
Frank approached a doorway overgrown with marauding foliage. He removed handfuls of vines and revealed a sign.

'OLD LADY GREGGS' TUPPENCE TEA AND TAPAS'.

"You go in the rear, watch your step." said Frank.
Frank quietly lifted the door latch and entered. Inside was a charming and lovingly maintained tea room. As he stepped across the tiled floor, he picked up a menu, which detailed the extensive selection of teas all available for tuppence.
English Monkfish Tea
Boofnondle
Devon Crankshaft
Forty Minstrels
Japanese Mourning
Wobbly Scallops
Rolf's Harum
Victorian Anecdotal
Hank's Passage
Plymouth Peregrin

Passing some discarded crates and pallets, Rosch approached the rear door. He drew his pistol, placed one hand over his testicles and crept inside.
At that moment a terrified Old Lady Greggs appeared from a doorway. She dropped her tray of plates, screamed and kicked Rosch sharply in the testicles. As he descended, Rosch again burst into tears, only this time in silence.
Alerted by the crash, Frank burst in with his weapon drawn.
"Freeze Greggs!"
She threw a charity bucket at him. As he recoiled, she hammered a mighty punch across his jaw before wrapping her arms around his waist and slamming him into a cupboard. Frank struggled with the tenacious, pitbull-like frame of Greggs. He managed to free his hand holding his pistol, reached up and struck a series of heavy blows on her back. With each blow Greggs' grip on him weakened. After what must have been a good five minutes, Frank struck the last blow and he and Greggs slid down the wall into a breathless heap.

A short while later....

In the middle of the Tuppence Tearoom, Old Lady Greggs woozily awoke, tied to a chair.
"We haven't opened yet." she croaked. "You're going to have to wait like everyone else."
"We know what's going on here." said Frank. "We know you want it to end."
"It's never going to end! They're too powerful!" said Greggs, returning to this universe.
"You have to trust us." said Frank. Just then, Rosch vomited, as he lay sprawled on the cold floor.
"You have to trust me," repeated Frank. "I know a way to bring these bastards into the light of day."
Greggs spat out a tooth and surveyed their faces. Rosch just about managed to sit himself up. Spotting the vomit on himself he desperately fumbled for his antibac spray.
"This is your chance to do the right thing." said Frank.
After a moment, Greggs nodded.
"Alright," she said. "What have you got planned?"
"I just need to put the cuffs on you," said Frank, "but first, have a swig on this."
Greggs cautiously accepted Frank's hip flask and took a long swig.

   The sun was shining as Frank led Greggs out to the car, followed by Rosch, shuffling gingerly. Net curtains twitched once again as Frank lowered Greggs' head into the back seat.
"We're taking her to the local lockup" said Frank, turning the key in the ignition.
"What if we can't trust them there?" said Rosch. "Who says the locals aren't involved?"
"I'm banking on it." said Frank.
The car slowly pulled away across the dusty gravel, under the grave scrutiny of the locals.

11:14am
Little Toffle Sheriff's Station

After arriving in the car park, Rosch assisted Greggs from the back seat the way a petting zoo accepts a new Velociraptor. Whatever it was in Frank's hip flask, it had done the trick for Greggs. Her wobbling form sang and slurred as they escorted her into the station.
At the front desk sat Dawkerman, the clerk.
"Mrs Greggs? What is the meaning of this?"
Greggs held tightly onto Rosch's hand. Her buckling knees swayed her hips to and fro giving her a strikingly Orangutan-like posture. Frank removed his badge.
"Detective Frank Ruggerman London Met. Drunk and disorderly, decided to trade in tea for a bucket of amaretto and Windolene."
Dawkerman sniffed as he assessed Greggs in the throes of an intense blood alcohol adventure.
"I really, really, love karaoke." sang Greggs evangelically.
"Lewis Hamilton, he's good."
"Best let her sleep it off." said Dawkerman.
He buzzed and Frank led Greggs through the turnstile into the holding area of the station. Upon hearing a rendition of Shaggy's "Mr. Boombastic", Dawkerman peered at the hall mirror and waited for the door to close behind them. He reached for the phone.
"It's Dawkerman. They're here, they've got Greggs…" he said. "…Okay bye."
Frank and Rosch returned to the front desk.
"She's in number 4." said Frank. "We'll be back tomorrow morning for an interview once she's sober. Let's go."

6:34pm

The last of the day's light was being strangled into vivid pinks and oranges as the sun fell towards the horizon. After moving the car, Frank and Rosch were staking out the station from a cluster of trees and bushes across the road. Rosch checked his watch as the faint sound of Greggs in her cell, doing an impressive Oliver Reed, drifted over to them.
"Wild Thing!..." hollered Greggs.
"It's going to get cold soon." said Rosch.
"You just stay put, Ja Ja." said Frank.

10:18pm

"Alright, fuck it, let's...oh hold on." whispered Frank.
A blacked out van slowly drove into the station's car park. From it emerged four tall figures in black cloaks and masks. They cautiously surveyed the scene and went inside.
"Just hold on." whispered Frank.

Inside her cell, Greggs lay on a hard plastic cushion. She was mumbling lyrics from De La Soul's "3 is the Magic Number" when she heard a knock on her door.
"What do you want?" she barked. "You want to taste *my* tuppence you c***?"
There came another knock, this time louder.
"All right," she mumbled resignedly, dragging herself to her feet. "I'll warn you now… I've pissed myself."
Greggs peered through the small hatch and came face to face with the dark, contorted face of a hooded demon.
From outside, Frank and Rosch heard Greggs' most peculiar scream. It sounded like a scream of someone in mortal terror mixed with the revelation that it is happy hour for ten more minutes.
"Just wait, here they come." said Frank.

The front door of the station burst open. The four figures dragged a vigorously protesting Greggs outside and towards the van.
"Hold it right there, Sanderson." said Frank, drawing his pistol.
One of the figures grabbed Greggs, held her close and placed a pistol against her temple. The other figures also drew weapons, one of which was a shotgun. Rosch took up position behind a car and covered the other three figures.
"There's nowhere to go, Sanderson." said Frank.
The figure grasped Greggs even tighter, their passionate speech sadly rendered incomprehensible mumblings under the mask. Frank stood wide eyed with weapon trained.
"Take the mask off." he said, more out of impatience than anything.
The figure obliged.
"Yes, I do suppose we are beyond such formalities." said Sanderson.
"Let the pisshead go, it's all over." said Frank.
"Yes, for you detective, and your gimp."
Rosch resisted the urge to consider Sanderson's reason for that comment.
"Don't be a fool!" said Frank. "Some bad online reviews from a handful of happy-meal nazis can't be worth this!"
"You don't get it, Ruggerman. Those same 'happy-meal nazis' almost collapsed this town. Everywhere simple high streets are being destroyed by giant shopping malls, family-owned businesses fighting for their lives. And then came the reviewers. Such devastating power in the hands of bored, unfulfilled control freaks. Just being spiteful. It is as if complaining is the bulk of the fun. It's like they can't get off unless they're being a c*** to somebody. They were putting good people out of business. Places that had thrived for generations being shut down because of a lack of quinoa smoothies or a pube in a sundae."
"That doesn't give you the right to make an example of these people. Look," said Frank imploringly. "even if you just stop the 'phone in the arse' thing."

"They just grow and grow and become more and more influential." Sanderson continued with increasing mania. "Nothing can stop them. Businesses are filled with young workers terrified of offending people and getting a bastard bad review. Do you know more under-25's suffer nervous breakdowns now than ever before?"

Rosch emerged from behind the car, his weapon still trained on the figures.

"Sanderson." he said.

"What are you doing, Lando?" Frank warned.

"Yes, what are you doing?" reiterated Sanderson.

"Nice and easy now," said Rosch. "I may have found something that might help. It's an app called 'Them Apples'. It's an app for reviewing Bingegripe reviews. You spot a review on your page that you think is malicious or unfounded, review it on 'Them Apples' and voila, their rating as a reviewer drops, meaning they have less sway. Over time, users will have to learn to play nice in order to have their reviews listened to. Which is what it's all about really, isn't it? Being listened to?"

"This community is fighting for its life, detectives." said Sanderson, beseechingly.

"I know. We get it." replied Frank. "It's your livelihoods, your families. But if one more civilian gets 'Motorolla'd' in the arse, I'll know it was you, and I'll be back down here with two dozen lads and tear gas to return the favour."

Sanderson let go of Greggs and she collapsed like a bean bag. With weapons still drawn and nerves still jangling, the figures slowly backed away towards the van.

"We'll be keeping an eye, Sanderson." called Frank.

After the locals had left, Rosch and Frank assisted Mrs. Greggs to her feet.

"Let's just hope the Tuppence Tea Room does coffee." said Rosch.

**Monday
8:32am
London Met HQ**

Frank and Rosch pushed through the double doors into the morgue. It wasn't the ideal route but it was by far the quickest way from the east car park to the main building.
"Yes," continued Rosch. "but we still have no arrests, no statements, nothing."
As they crossed the morgue, Frank and Rosch passed several bodies on examination tables. One with a mobile peeking out of its anus moved feebly.
"The important thing is," said Frank, as he strode onwards, oblivious to the pleas of the still painfully unassisted Daniels. "I think Little Toffle has seen its last ritualised rectal violation. As more often happens in a case like this, we just have to stay vigilant, attentive, and make sure no more good people suffer such horrendous indignity."
Daniels sighed and sobbed as the double doors closed behind them.

**3:21am
Streatham Aircraft Hangar**

Along the grey corridor echoed the sound of Caroline Ahem's motorised wheelchair and heavy military issue footsteps. She arrived at a doorway manned by two soldiers. With a salute they stood aside and allowed her in. The interior of the hangar itself was dark and huge. In the centre was a table, surrounded by another complement of soldiers. Ahem approached and came to a stop at the desk.
"Ambassador." she said.
Sat at the table was the petite form of Ambassador Crunk, chief liaison for the UK. A member of a species known as Reticulant, his short grey legs kicked under the table and his giant bulbous head swayed gently under its weight. Fortunately for Ahem, Reticulants have a supernatural

talent for languages and Crunk spoke English like a recently laid-off scaffolder.

"Put a sock in it, Gsa Gsa." snapped Crunk.

Ahem could see her cool reflection in the vast black eyes of the Ambassador.

"Your world's ability to conceal our presence has reached an all time laughable." he said. "We warned you about smart phones."

"As indeed you did-" began Ahem.

"Now, we have to go public." said Crunk, "To execute a '*Friends From Beyond The Stars Welcome To Earth*' media campaign because your people, cowards that they are, can't handle change without celebrity endorsement."

"Colonialism is not an *alien* concept to my people, Ambassador. In this age, PR is a necessity for enacting any kind of... progressive action."

"Well, we're stuck with it now." grumbled Crunk. "Are we on schedule?"

"Absolutely," assured Ahem. "Key personalities are being brought on board. Your people's "arrival" will be welcomed the world over with a glistening fanfare spectacle. The start of a bright new future of cooperation between worlds."

"Fucking hell." Crunk smiled. "I see why they chose you."

Ahem was an exceptional diplomat and so did not respond to the Ambassador's bladder release under the table. She calmly held her poise during the sustained splashing sound on the concrete floor. The difference between the gravity on Earth and the Reticulant homeworld meant that bladder control was an issue, just not for the Reticulants.

"What's the score with piss head?" inquired Crunk, disdainfully.

"My nephew has been assigned to his department and is reporting his activities on a daily basis." replied Ahem. "Ruggerman can't even fart without my knowledge."

"That better be so." warned Crunk. "People like him still have the chance to knacker this whole thing if you don't get them silenced."

"Trust me Crunk," said Ahem with a gentle grin. "Frank Ruggerman is as good as neutered."

EPISODE III

Wednesday
9:51pm
Texacana Recording Studios, Mumford Hacks, London

The dark, shaggy carpet lining the walls, floors and ceilings sapped all vibrations and gave the place the sense of vacuous horror, normally only encountered in deep space or Luton airport at 4am. Jessie had long regarded the silent studio as the place where sound came to die. She'd had yet another day of moving goal posts, faulty equipment and self-entitled slide guitarists on a come down. Jessie could not remember the last time she felt the excitement of bringing an artist's sonic dream to life. These days it was all about cutting corners and making do with increasingly less.

Her colleague Keith entered the booth she stood in, dumping armfuls of reel-to-reel tapes on the shelves.
"How are you holding up?" he asked.
"Like a rhino's water-bed." Jessie retorted.
"What did Davidson say about the overtime?" Keith pressed on.
"He okayed it," Jessie replied, "then, in his infinite wisdom, he shaved three days off the deadline."
"You're kidding?" said Keith sceptically, sipping a bottle of water.
"I should tie that stupid ponytail of his to a *Seaworld* orca that's been off its meds and having a really crap day."
"This is ridiculous." exclaimed Keith, water tumbling from his jaws. "It's not your fault their label slashed the budget for the recording."

"Yeah? And it's not my fault he's such a-"
Abruptly, the door to the booth was wrenched open.
"Country music isn't going anywhere," said studio boss Rupert Davidson on his phone as he poked in his head, "you mark my words, it's in the clubs, it's in the cars. Next year every advert on telly will be awash with wailing steel guitar and good old-fashioned fiddling... Alright ciao."

Davidson ran the studio and enjoyed the same workplace esteem as a rabid gastral parasite.
"We on schedule, yeah?" he queried.
"I don't know how you expect me to record this album within four days, it's-"
"Jessie Jessie Jessie!" cooed Davidson condescendingly, "We all have to make sacrifices in these crucial stages. It's important now that we all focus on the bigger picture. Anyhoops, if this doesn't work you can always go back to sound engineering open mic nights at Jimmy Gristle's. Now, you two head home, you're back in first thing to redub that cowbell."
Jessie and Keith donned their jackets and left the booth after Davidson, pulling faces and flashing rude gestures behind his back.
"See you tomorrow." they both chimed as they left.

Davidson cursed his poor phone signal as he made his way through the corridors to his office. He paused and peered at the shadowy fire escape at the other end of the corridor.
"Oi! You need to clear out, I'm locking up." he shouted.
Silence.
"Hello?" No response.
"I must be going mad." he muttered to himself.
Just then a swift chill cut through his body. He wrapped his coat tightly around himself and strode toward his office. Once inside, he touched the radiator, which he found to be ice cold.
"Ah, fuck this." he said, grabbing his bag and overcoat.

Davidson switched off the desk lamp which sparked violently, causing the whole floor to descend into a dark gloom. Only the pale blue neon light from the pharmacy next door crept in through the window.

In the twilight, his breath became a vivid apparition as the temperature plummeted. He removed his phone and shone the torch at his *'The Wright Stuff'* thermometer on the wall. As he watched the mercury continue to descend, he didn't notice the latch to his office door closing tightly.

    Davidson bundled the last of his things together and tried to open the door.

"Oh, you must be fuckin' joking." he scoffed.

Suddenly, his heart was shot through with an icy spear-tip as he became aware of a presence behind him. He spun around only to face an empty office. Taking a deep, reassuring breath he tried again to open the door.

There was, however, no escaping the cold hand gripping his shoulder. Frozen panic raced through every inch of his body, paralysing him.

"Please?" he whimpered.

Whatever it was, it smashed his helpless body against every wall and sharp corner in his office until all traces of life were long gone.

Saturday
8:15am
Rome, Vatican III: La Vendetta

The light of dawn spoke only of adoration as it caressed the rooftops of the Italian capital. Father Pantoliano smiled as he crossed the floor of his chambers. His rooms on the fifth floor had arguably the best view in Catholicism. After watering his plants, washing his breakfast bowl and a few rounds of darts he sat and began to write a letter.

Dearest Father McKoy,

I must call upon you once more, regarding those evil forces that threaten to impede upon the realm of man. Even in this modern age, we remain the first and last line of defence against the gluttonous beasts of hell. I'm sure you will be aware by now of the Texacana Davidson affair via its tepid response on Twittlechat. I ask you to investigate any spiritual aspects which may prove irksome for Il Papa and our brotherhood. I trust you will handle this latest incident of 'paranormal phenomena' with your usual discretion and fortitude. The detective assigned to the case is one Frank Ruggerman, a man of mixed reputation and, undoubtedly, a man of great enthusiasm and colourful language. I fear him somewhat lost to the love of our lord, embittered from wandering in the cold. But I sense that within him lies a torch, albeit dim, fading and cantankerous.
Take father Younger to assist you and hit me up with updates when you can.
Sincerely yours, Father Darren Pantoliano.

"Angelo?" said Father Pantoliano.
The tanned boy looked up earnestly from his jigsaw puzzle.
"Pop this letter in an email and ping it off pronto there's a good chap.

8:17am
London Met. HQ

Rosch slowly slid out of the door to Chief Commissioner Leathers' office. Leathers' rant had gone omni-directional, so Rosch took his chance to escape. Through the door the tail end could be heard all down the corridor.

"Here's your bloody figures!" roared Leathers as he stuffed successive handfuls of paper into his assistant Renfield's mouth.
"We don't need arrests! No! We just get old ladies pissed and fight them in tea rooms!"
Behind the closing door the tirade became muffled but lost none of its wrath, like attempting to hide a dog fight under a duvet. Rosch stood a second rubbing his eyes when a text message arrived on his phone.

'TEXACANA RECORDING STUDIO, MUMFORD HACKS NOW. GRAB A BOTTLE.'

9:51am
Texacana Recording Studios, Mumford Hacks, London

Frank Ruggerman entered the lobby of the Texacana before stopping at a line of police tape. He glared at a nearby forensic as he waited. The forensic turned in his crinkling head to toe bio-suit, gestured apologetically and tapped a button on a remote control. With a loud metallic groan, the police tape slowly rose to the ceiling allowing Frank to pass underneath.

Upstairs, Frank passed along the corridor to Davidson's office where he found Rosch and Sodermine already at the scene.
Frank looked at Rosch and clicked his fingers.
"Good morning." said Rosch, stoically.
"Bottle" demanded Frank.
"A bit early, don't you think, Ruggerman?"
"One fucking job", growled Frank as he knelt down next to the body and lifted the sheet. Rosch gagged at the released aroma.
"Steady now, Ja Ja." said Frank. "Hello Sodermine. He's ripe, this one. How long?"

"Morning, Frank." said Sodermine. "Yeah, it looks like this guy's been here at least 3 days."
"Was anyone else here?" Frank asked.
"As far as I can see, it's been business as usual." Sodermine replied.
"And no one wanted to speak to him? He must have been a real man of the people. What's the score?"
"Rupert Davidson, fifty-two," recounted Sodermine, "C.E.O of the Texacana and label boss for Rootin' Tootin' Records. The main man behind the South East London country revival."
"Any idea what happened to him?" asked Frank.
"It looks like he was mangled like a Play-Doh rag doll. Whoever did it turned his bones into hummus."
"The first on the scene had to break in," Rosch interjected, "the door and windows were all locked from the inside."

Frank pondered this briefly before standing up and opening a large cupboard. Inside, another suited forensic was dusting for prints. Without a word the forensic slowly reached out and closed the cupboard door again.
"The CCTV shows he was the last one in the building," said Rosch. "He re-entered his office at 21:58, and never came out."
"So," said Frank, "unless we can find this invisible polar bear, we can assume he didn't do this himself."
"I searched everything" said Rosch, "there's nothing but some contracts, expense accounts and an accordion signed by someone called Rupert Everett…hopefully forensics will-"
"I think I know what we're dealing with." interrupted Frank.
"Oh no." sighed Rosch under his breath.
"Sodermine," called Frank, "get onto Binks and tell him to send us the E.V.P monitor, tape recorders and two cameras, both with infrared."
"Can do." Sodermine replied.
"We'll set up in-"

Frank was interrupted by the heavy *clunk* of the intercom that connected each room in the studio.

"Ahh, Detective Ruggerman," said the voice, "can ya please come to the reception? There's someone here to see you."

Clunk

Frank and Rosch made their way downstairs into the foyer where they were met by two priests. The elder was Father McKoy. Arizona born but now a Londoner, his short grey afro had kinks and scruffy patches after decades of touring the globe.

"McKoy." said Frank, amicably.

"Hello Frank." McKoy greeted him, "It's been a long time. How have you been keeping?"

"Same old, mate, same old." replied Frank.

The slim and boyish-faced Father Younger nodded and beamed a smile as he wrestled with the weighty tomes in his book bag.

"Shall we?" asked Frank, as he led the priests upstairs.

***

Back at the body, Frank, Rosch, Younger and McKoy all huddled around Davidson's lifeless corpse.

"Male, dead." said Frank beginning his brief. "No footage, no witnesses, no prints, no forced entry and with everything locked from the inside. I'd say we've got a level 5 transmorphic free repeater, mean fucking temper on it, too."

"Textbook." replied McKoy.

Rosch looked across their faces.

"I'm sorry, to be the one man idiot convention, but what are priests doing here?" asked Rosch, quizzically.

Frank and McKoy exchanged concerned glances.

"Come over here a sec." said Frank calmly as he led Rosch out of the office and into the hallway.

Frank looked up and down the corridor before opening a door.

"In here." he said.

Rosch entered the doorway. His exasperation with Frank's 'unorthodox' approach shifted gears as the small room immediately fell into black and the door locked behind him.

"Wait a minute." cried Rosch, feeling for the walls in the dark. "It's a fucking cupboard!?"

Kneeling back down next to the body Frank continued. "I've got the kit en route, should be here within the hour-"

A loud, splintering crash heralded Rosch's escape from the amps cupboard. Rosch stormed back into the office.

"You total arsehole!" he screamed, "Locking me in a cupboard!? Are you doing Harry Potter now as you're out of Star Wars material?! I should-"

"Alright, alright," soothed father McKoy. "Let's calm this down. Now, what's your name son?"

Rosch tried to calm himself.

"I'm detective-"

"Assistant." Frank interjected.

Rosch felt the bile in his stomach begin to affect his vision. "I'm assistant detective Rosch Kunnypacken."

"Good, I'm father McKoy and this is father Younger. We're here on behalf of the Church, 31st street Prezboluskian chapter."

"Yeah," said Frank, feeling charitable, "every now and then there's a ramp up in cross dimensional turbulence. Restless spirits causing hooha with the odd case requiring 'divine intervention'."

"Our job is usually to invalidate hoaxes but, every once in a while..." continued McKoy.

Rosch closed his eyes and exhaled deeply.

"So..." he inquired, treading carefully, "this is...ghosts, is it?"

"Yes." said Frank, both priests and the forensic still in the cupboard, in almost perfect unison.

"Oh good, another day at the baffled department." chirped Rosch.

Father Younger noticed the new hint of derangement in Rosch's eyes.
"Detective," said Younger, kindly. "I understand your scepticism. I'm somewhat still adjusting myself, but I implore you these things are very real, and very, very dangerous."

9:33pm

Across the rooms of the studio, thermographic sensors and video cameras were being readied to pour information into the main booth. Frank was finishing off the final connections whilst savouring a rye heavy Manhattan. Father McKoy walked up and down the corridors, clutching his holy scriptures. At certain points he would stop and feel the walls, making a mental note of where the vibrations were strongest. McKoy looked back down the empty corridor. He recognised all the signs of a presence but there was one thing in particular that currently disturbed him: the unshakable feeling of being watched. As McKoy continued on his thoughts were briefly driven onto the more worrisome parts of his last medical check. There was something here and whatever it was, it was very nasty indeed.

Father Younger entered the office at the end of the hall to find Rosch sitting against a speaker, staring at a poster of Willie Nelson.
"Rosch," said the priest, "I see much sadness in you."
"Yes," he replied drily, "but I imagine if you were being treated like a human urinal cake you would have a fair amount, too."
"He seems very capable." said Younger, "But I can see he likes a drink."
"Between the cases, the drink and that, quote unquote, 'brain' of his...Trying to adhere to protocol, having it all signed and sealed is all but impossible. It's like trying to herd wasps using morse code."

The priest sat next to Rosch and carefully placed his bag of heavy tomes next to him.

"I think I'm having a breakdown." whispered Rosch.

"Rosch, you must believe me when I say I understand. I wasn't always a priest, you know." said Younger. "I wanted to be a Yourtuber, make vlogs, set trends. But one day, when I was eight years old, my sister grew terribly sick. My mother wouldn't let me see her. Later that night, Father McKoy came. I remember he was so kind. He just had this way about him, like if your grandad joined the X-Men. As he entered her room, I snuck a glance through the door as it closed. I saw her face, it seemed so angry, and there was so, so much vomit. Thanks to the benevolence of our lord, that night Father McKoy saved my sister from the demon. She works in Mothercare now. Ever since I've dedicated my life to fighting evil, armed with the righteous sword of god's love."

"Well, no offence, Younger." said Rosch.

"Please, call me Father."

"I'm not very comfortable with that, I'm afraid."

"Fear not my son. God's love is shared amongst us all, trust in me, Rosch...

I am your father."

With that came the *Clunk* of the intercom and the sound of a deeply hecklesome laugh from Frank in the other room.

Frank released the intercom button and sat back in his chair. The tail end of his laugh sounded like wringing out the very last drops from a filthy dish cloth. In the neighbouring chair sat McKoy.

"Why torment the child so?" said McKoy.

Frank waved his hand lazily and made a guttural sound. The sound of a *ping* from the console signalled that all data streams were now synced.

"Right," said Frank, "it looks like we are all linked in, cameras set, audio feed live."

He leaned forward and pressed the intercom again.

"Okay. You two get comfy but stay alert. We're in for a long night. Younger, I want sweeping walk-arounds every thirty minutes. We'll monitor the cameras and the audio feed."

Clunk

Frank turned to McKoy and looked earnestly into his kind, battle worn face.

"It's game time." said Frank, opening another case of whiskey.

11:42pm

Rosch's face was vacantly bathing in the pale blue light from the pharmacy when Father Younger approached him again.

"Rosch, let me show you something." he said. "This is an original account, recorded in the 4th century, Luxembourg."

Rosch had to admire the ancient book. Its time ravaged binding opened dutifully, revealing ornate scripture of the most exquisite intricacy.

"If you see here, a farmer named Jean-Jacques Frivello became convinced that a demon had possessed his favourite pig. According to this he had accidentally left the gate open when, 'whoosh', it got him." said Younger.

With tears of despondency beginning to well, Rosch said "That's very interesting."

"Oh Rosch, what's the matter?" said Younger, gently.

"I can't do it! I'm done, I'm out, I'm going home."

"But Rosch..."

"I'm sorry, I don't mean to make you think that I believe you're all deranged, but I do, so that's how it's going to look." said Rosch, searching for his bag.

"Detective Ruggerman is going to need your help."

"He needs E.C.T and sectioning." said Rosch.

"Oh no, Rosch. Father McKoy has been solving these issues for decades and he is convinced that a tremendous threat

haunts this place. He believes there is danger of a powerful demon entering this realm. Look here… this book details the battle between good and evil, spanning four generations, circa 300 CE to 340 CE. It holds a few rare cases in which hauntings escalated into full blown demonic encounters."
"Encounters?" said Rosch.
"Oh yes." said Younger. "Hauntings are often mostly harmless. Paranormal phenomena, such as lights blinking on and off or the toilet seat raising by itself and dropping just as you let go. But what we call 'encounters' are very serious. You see, everything we know and otherwise, works in terms of vibrations. Light, chemistry, love, hate, all of it: vibrations. When people die with excessive intense emotion in their soul, the demons can smell it as they cross out of our realm. They hunt it down and feed like swarming piranha. Hate is their favourite. As they devour the soul, it becomes trapped in a feedback loop, rage, hate and pain all growing and growing with no escape."
"Sounds like Twitter." said Rosch.
"The cursed," continued Younger, "cannot leave hell by themselves, but as they feed, their strength grows. Then all they need is a weak point, between their realm and ours. If strong enough the demon can break free and come in you, into you, come in to you, come inside you."
"Lovely." said Rosch, dryly.

2:21am

In the main booth, Frank sat alone monitoring a mess of devices, sipping an elaborate, tropical-looking cocktail. Suddenly, a long, distorted screech tore through the speakers with snippets of fiddle and banjo. Frank pressed the intercom. *Clunk*
"McKoy, I just got a big spike on the M-graph, you got anything?"
He watched as McKoy, Younger and Rosch converged in the corridor on the night-vision monitor.

"Big temperature drop." said McKoy, his breath drifting as vapour through the light marking the fire escape.
"Any souls trapped here, let yourselves be known."
Silence.
In the corridor, doors began to rattle louder and louder.
Clunk went the intercom. "McKoy, Younger, Lando, get your arses back here now." said Frank. *Clunk*
"Let's go." said McKoy.
As he turned, a large glass picture frame shattered and fell from the wall with a deafening crash. McKoy, Younger and Rosch ran, covering their faces from flying shards of glass and plastic. They crashed into the main booth and slammed the door shut behind them.
Frank sipped his cocktail and turned his attention back to the monitor.
"The readings went off the scale..." he said, twisting knobs on the mixer. "Let me try and clean up that E.V.P track."
Frank applied several filters and replayed the recording. From muddy, grinding sounds emerged voices, southern U.S voices, male and female and the sound of wistful, plodding, country music. The recording distorted again with the sound of seething hisses. Then nothing. The four men in the booth looked at each other's faces.
"What on god's earth?" whispered Younger.
Frank typed enthusiastically on the computer.
"What the hell was that?" asked Rosch.
"A band." said Frank.
"A band?" repeated Rosch, incredulously.
"A band."
Frank turned the monitor around revealing a picture of five people in overalls, standing around a gate smoking pipes.
"Hank Jarvis and the Goat Piss Gang, to be precise."
McKoy stepped closer.
"How do you know it's them?" said McKoy.
"Five voices," said Frank, "same instruments and they were the only group to record a love ballad through a megaphone. It says here they were signed to Davidson's

label, they were touring the disastrous second album when they all died in a bizarre coach collision."

"Bizarre?" said McKoy.

"Collided mid-air with a zeppelin." said Frank. He tapped a key to reveal an image.

"Sweet potato pakora." exclaimed McKoy.

"So why did the second album tank?" asked Younger.

Upon hearing these words, Rosch once again felt that familiar feeling like he was born on the wrong planet. It was comparable to the feeling of being refused entry to a nightclub for only having one head.

"A mix of constant infighting and excessive washboard solos." replied Frank, "Davidson wouldn't record the third album but wouldn't release them from their contract either."

"So that's what's keeping them between the realms." said McKoy.

"To record a follow up." said Frank.

"And there it is." sighed Rosch, failing to mask his anxiety.

Frank took a long swig of an alco-pop.

"I don't believe this." said Rosch.

"Believe it, slippery nips." said Frank. "McKoy, can you open a gate and keep it defended while we record?"

"It'll be tough." said McKoy thoughtfully. "It's hard enough just to keep it from collapsing. Even if they're fully rehearsed, it'll take hours to finish."

"Ruggerman please, look at yourself." said Rosch. "We're here to investigate a murder and your plan is to help a cross dimensional country band from Streatham. Leathers is-."

"Fucking Leathers." Frank exasperated. "You still don't get it, do you? Little Darth Fauntleroy trying to walk the line, tick the boxes. Be another little puppet stuffed up to the elbow on the dirty hand of the top brass. I know, why don't you find something more useful to do like getting us a bottle out the vending machine?"

Frank threw a handful of coins in Rosch's general direction. Rosch kicked over a stack of guitars and left the room.

"Finally." said Frank. "You know what I don't get? It's how a country band goes from squabbling with their manager to mauling him so badly they turn his bones into goulash."

"They must have fallen in with bad company on the other side." said McKoy. "Frank, play the last E.V.P again."

Frank cued up the recording and let it play.

"Cut 190hz to minus eight and apply the filter again." said McKoy.

Frank played the recording. There was a swirling cacophony of otherworldly growls and voices, blended with the unmistakable sound of a banjo tuning.

"There." exclaimed McKoy.

"What is it?" asked Younger.

"Hank Jarvis and the G.P.G has five members. Jarvis, Keith Bishop on bass, Margie Williams on drums, Bubba Hampton on slide guitar and Screamin' Sue Pollard on banjo. On the recording I heard a 6th voice. Bring it back 3 steps and filter out the fringe waves."

After a few clicks, Frank replayed the recording.

"Stop the recording." said Younger. "I know that voice."

McKoy looked up into the face of his young charge.

"I've heard it before. It's Banghalla." said Younger.

"Who is?" queried Frank, opening another bottle.

"A demon." said McKoy.

Younger closed his eyes as the tears welled. McKoy placed a reassuring hand on the back of his neck.

"So, this demon," said McKoy. "found the Goat Piss Gang and is now using their purgatorial anguish as a bridge to our world."

"How long?" asked Frank.

"A matter of hours maybe," McKoy replied, "the fact that we haven't seen him yet means time could still be on our side."

"Then we've none to lose," said Frank resolvedly.

Suddenly, through the glass of the booth, they saw a rift of swirling blue light rip open, bathing everything in an

ethereal glow. Five blurry figures cautiously stepped through the portal.
"That's them." said Frank, powering up the main mixer.
"McKoy," he continued, "no matter what it takes, keep that gate open."
Frank pressed the intercom.
Clunk
"Erm, alright listen, can you hear me?"
Whispy, glowing tendrils from the portal slowly danced around the periphery.
"Well sure we can, good buddy!" sang Jarvis.
The rest of the Goat Piss Gang joined in the conversation then.
"What the hell is going on?" "Where in the Sam hell are we?" "Is this the Texacana?"
"Listen up," ordered Frank, "we know why you're here. We're going to help you record your album."
"Well oowee! I'd say that's mighty kind of you, folks!" said Bubba Hampton cheerily.
"Now wait, hold on a dang minute, where's that son bitch Davidson?" said Hank Jarvis.
"Dead." said Frank, resetting the EQ's to flat. "Time is running out guys, you picked up something real nasty with you on your travels so we need to get to work sharpish and get this done before it breaks through."
Frank pressed the intercom and spun around in his chair.
"Now, everyone in position, McKoy?" he said, releasing the button.
The old priest turned back towards him.
"Are you up to this?" asked Frank.
"I'd say there's still some grit left in this old horse Frank."
Then, in a flash, McKoy whipped out his bible, put a hand on Frank's shoulder and looked him squarely in the eye.
"Let's get busy."

3:34am

Father Younger groaned as he hoisted the dolly carrying five crates of whiskey and malibu to the booth. McKoy traversed the studio, continually reading psalms, brandishing his crucifix. Frank had rolled up his sleeves and the air in the booth was thick with cigarette smoke. *Clunk* went the intercom.
"Alright, that was good." said Frank, labelling the sound files.
"Woop Woop! That was a mighty fine ding-dong!" cheered Screamin' Sue.
"Hampton," barked Frank, "remember, nice and easy with the harmonies, you're not the Ronettes."
"Uh, copy that, good buddy." he replied.
Frank looked to the songlist on the clipboard.
"Right, next up "My heart deserves a ramblin'" in A. And one, two, three, hit it."

Meanwhile...

In a quiet room at the end of the corridor, Rosch was contemplating if Alaskan oil rig workers got good benefits. He then reached a conclusion.
"I'm out." he said, grabbing his jacket.
Rosch made his way into the corridor and, approaching Davidson's office, he paused. Listening intently he slowly poked his head inside the quiet office.
"Oh, sod this." he groaned.
As he turned to leave, he suddenly came face to face with a Father Younger he did not recognize. Rosch felt his breath freeze in his lungs. Younger leered at him. His once boyish face now a sea of cuts and sores. Bloody saliva pooled on his chin before slowly descending to the floor, but Rosch could only see his eyes. Edged with blood, Younger's irises had turned the colour of bubonic magma. Behind them

Rosch could see a wildfire of hate and pure, unequivocal evil.
The door slammed into the wall as Rosch's body was flung into the office. He crashed heels over head onto the desk and tumbled onto the chair, flipping it instantly. Rosch gasped for breath and, clutching his ribs, clawed his way back on his feet. Younger crept closer to him, eyes glowing in the dark like those of wolves on night-vision. Younger hissed and the room was suddenly ravaged by a powerful wind, shattering picture frames and sending a flurry of documents into the air. Rosch drew his pistol but Younger smirked as the gun disintegrated into dust. Rosch slipped under his arm lunging for the nearest object to hand which was the *Rupert Everett* signed accordion. He lifted it to protect his chest as the demonic Younger leapt towards him. The two wrestled. Rosch felt rancid saliva splash his cheek. The accordion groaned and wheezed, sandwiched between them as Rosch fought for his life.
Clunk "Listen, Lando you're going to have to knock off that accordion or it'll show up on the recording. The walls to the session studio are only sound proofed from the rear." *Clunk*
Rosch gritted his teeth and tried to shove his weight back against his attacker.

Meanwhile, back in the booth...

McKoy coughed discreetly, as he reentered the dense smoky fog of the booth.
"Okay, that was nice." said Frank, holding three lit cigarettes in his mouth. "Let's nail that middle sixteen and we're ready for Sue's 'abridged' washboard solo."
McKoy dropped an umbrella with a cherry into a pina colada and raised it to his lips. He stopped and froze as he noticed Rosch on the CCTV, performing either a truly passionate accordion solo or, as was more likely, being

engaged in mortal combat with a malevolent supernatural force.

The beginning of an uptempo banjo number fell to silence as McKoy dashed out into the corridor. He ran down the hall and smashed through what was left of the door into Davidson's office.

He saw his devoted companion, now a slave to a most vile being, with claws clasped tightly around Rosch's neck.

"Demon!" McKoy roared.

The possessed Younger flung Rosch into the corner and turned to face McKoy.

"That's *our* word priest." hissed the foul creature.

McKoy raised his crucifix and began to read.

"Oh, such light and unconditional love! Let your benevolent grace be our guide!"

Younger staggered back, clutching his swollen abdomen in agony. Just as the demon screamed and reached for McKoy, the old priest ramped up the passion in his reading with a salvo of fire from deep in his belly.

"And he! Whose power knows no earthly constriction! Seize in thy grasp the vile intruder!"

The demon's body contorted in a violent spasm, locked in the shape of a bizarre hieroglyph.

"Abomination be thy name, destruction is thy destiny! Take thy place!"

Younger's helpless body flew back into a chair. McKoy shouted to Rosch over the cacophony of the tornado.

"Now Rosch! Tie him up with those mic cables!"

Rosch picked up the bag of cables and cautiously approached the struggling beast.

"Do it now, Rosch!"

With that, Rosch jumped in and began tightly wrapping the cables around Younger.

Rosch, ribs broken, cried in anguish as he pulled the knots tight.

"As it was above the precipice! So it was below!", McKoy bellowed.

Younger turned his head towards Rosch, his mouth tore wide open and he doused Rosch in gallons of putrid green bile. Rosch was paralysed by his repulsion. He considered reaching for the anti-bac spray in his pocket. However, he quickly realised that it was very much bolting the gate after the horse was already covered in rancid vomit. As he struggled to tie the last cable, Rosch was locked, once again, in mortal combat only this time with his gag reflex.

"Great job son!" McKoy shouted. "Now, take this bible and read!"

Rosch took the second bible from McKoy's hand and took position on the other side of the room. As the heaves wracked his body, he began to read.

"Though he...was, n-not...a popular...shepherd..."

"Louder Rosch!"

Rosch tried to clear his throat and read again as loud as he could in the face of the nauseating stench of putrid stomach acid.

"Though he was nohhhrrt, 'urgh' a pop..ular shepherd!"

"That's it Rosch!"

Clunk went the intercom. "McKoy, I need you back here, the gate's weakening." said Frank. *Clunk*

McKoy braved the spinning maelstrom of debris and handed Rosch a crucifix.

"Here! Take this! I'll be back as soon as I can. For the love of god just keep reading!" implored McKoy as he left to join Frank in the booth.

It is safe to say that Rosch did not want to be left alone with the demon again. He also thought, momentarily, about previous jobs he'd had. Side stepping another dose of hell's stomach contents, Rosch took as firm a stance as he could, and began to read again.

"Long...and d-dark, is the...sh-shepherd..."

Through the double doors and once again into the silent corridor, McKoy raced to the booth.

On the way, he rushed past a cleaning lady who was locked in her own battle, trying to retrieve a granola bar from the vending machine. She was tutting and cursing lazily, repeatedly hitting the buttons.

"Jesus Christ.", she complained.

McKoy reached the booth and entered, closing the door firmly behind himself. He reached under his arm into his coat, pulled out another crucifix from its holster and began to read.

The portal containing the five apparitions regained its integrity and the room glowed with its former, deeper blue. Frank pressed the intercom into the session room.

"Alright, we're getting there. Let's crack on with... "More Moonshine, your Majesty?"

A distorted, vicious hiss tore through the speaker.

"Oh, for fuck's sake, what now!?" ranted Frank. "That better not be on the recording."

McKoy looked at the monitor and saw that the demon had broken free and Rosch was in serious peril.

As McKoy rushed out to help Rosch, Frank chuntered exasperatedly, "Tell him to stop doing ANYTHING, if he can't contribute at least, he can stop messing around with the-" The last few words fell silent as the door closed. The only sound audible now was McKoy's frantic breathing. Unwavering, he raced onwards, once again past the cleaning lady negotiating the troublesome vending machine.

"Oh, Jesus, no. Christ." she said, now pressing any buttons visible.

McKoy slammed through the double doors and through the remaining splinters of the door to the office. He recoiled, shielding his face from the hurricane surrounding Younger. Rosch cowered behind an overturned cupboard. Younger tore away the table and debris as he stalked closer and closer to Rosch.

"Rosch!" McKoy shouted.

Rosch had sadly lost his previous battle and was now covered in his own vomit as well as that of the demon. To his credit, Rosch persevered with the reading, stopping

only to wipe the pages clear of vomit when the text became obscured.
After releasing one last shower of stomach contents in Rosch's general direction, Younger turned menacingly towards McKoy.
"You are getting too old for this shit, McKoy." hissed the demon.
"Rosch! Take the left side!" McKoy bellowed.
He and Rosch took up flanking positions on the creature and began to read, employing all the brimstone they could muster. McKoy threw back his head and the room shook with the might of his voice.
"And you, foul heathen! When the lambs fell into the great quagmire, the light of the good lord spoketh unto his chosen livestock!"
Rosch's knees wavered back and forth as the recently qualifiable 'dry heaves' continued to course through his body.
"...be-because, the longer...the sh-shepherd..." he read.
"For no forfeiture could undo the desecration of his laundry basket! Thus, he cast out his unwanted house guests!"

There was a deafening rip as another dimensional rift tore open behind Younger. This time, the portal was not of an ethereal blue, but coloured red by the scathing flames of attrition. As old as the universe itself the fire swirled downwards, spiralling into the abyss. Its hunger for the souls of the avaricious and the vile swelled with a sadistic glee at the prospect of reclaiming one of it's lost. Younger's tortured frame locked, contorted once again and was thrust back into the chair.
"It's working!", shouted McKoy.
He continued reading as he made his way towards the intercom button.
Clunk
 "Frank! How much longer?"

"We're nearly there," said Frank, "just "the ballad of Tracy Chapman" and we are finished. Okay. 1,2,3,4!"
A few notes of another uptempo banjo number began.
Clunk
"Foul demon! Born not of this world!" raged McKoy.
Clunk "*The gate is weakening!*" yelled Frank over the intercom. *Clunk*
"God damn it." grunted McKoy.
The maelstrom surged around the room and the chair holding Younger levitated into the air.
"God damn it!"
McKoy took a deep breath and channelled every fibre of his being.
"For he who can reapeth of the bountiful linen, can hold the almighty in the guest room! Rosch! You can do it! Just believe! And as was foretold, beholdeth! There came the form of the Des O'Connor!-"

Meanwhile, back in the booth, Frank bounced playfully in his chair as he listened to the Goat Piss Gang, playing his 'air banjo' and spilling whiskey as he poured it into a thermos.
In Davidson's office, the windows blew out, spraying shards of glass everywhere.
"That's it Rosch!" yelled McKoy.
"...My...h-humble, shhh...shepherd..."
In that instant, the apparition became torn from Younger's writhing body. The ghostly form screamed and clung to its host with merciless claws. It writhed and stretched as the maelstrom tugged on the demon's soul.
"We got him Rosch! You're doing great son! Just keep going! Believe!"
"...And w-wouldst th-thou dine...at the *H-Happy Eater*..." persevered Rosch.
Younger collapsed to the floor as the demon lost its grip and was now being dragged into the portal. It screamed in rage sounding like an angle grinder on steel. In a flash it extended one last lunge of its arm and buried its claws

deep into Rosch's shoulder, causing him to cry out in agony. McKoy stopped reading. He saw the demon's glee as it dug its razor sharp talons into Rosch.
"Get off my plane of reality you evil son of a bitch!" screamed McKoy.
He ran towards the demon, leapt over the desk and lunged at the writhing hellspawn. Rosch fell to the floor as the claws were ripped from his flesh and McKoy grabbed onto the demon, sending them both tumbling into the fiery depths.
The next moment the portal zapped shut leaving only an unconscious Younger, a breathless Rosch and sheets of A4, drifting slowly down from the ceiling.
Clunk
"What's happening? McKoy!" shouted Frank. "McKoy?!"
Rosch dragged himself to the intercom.
Clunk
"Ruggerman..."
"Lando?! What's happening? Where's McKoy?!"
"...He's gone...he took the demon with him." said Rosch, in disbelief at his own words.
"...*Right*..." said Frank quietly.
Silence.
Clunk...
...Clunk
"*Get back to the booth...*" said Frank, "*I think we're done here.*" *Clunk*

Back in the booth, Frank's face bathed in the blue glow of the portal, a picture of quiet satisfaction. Rosch and a broken Father Younger entered the booth. Frank did the briefest double take at their condition but said nothing.
"Nice work guys," beamed Hank Jarvis. "We finally did it. Say thank you to Frank and the boys."
"Thank you, Frank." cheered the Goat Piss Gang.
Frank pulled on his cigarette and signalled a casual salute.
"Good job guys."

As the G.P.G packed up their instruments, the portal slowly changed colour to the serenest pink. They waved their final thank yous and returned to the other side. Then they were gone.

5:05am

Out through the Texacana's front reception doors, into the cold dawn air, emerged the three. Without breaking step, Frank turned onto the pavement and left.
"Write that one up, Jabba." Frank called, over his shoulder, inhaling deeply from his cigarette.
Rosch and Younger stood, exhausted and shell shocked, as Frank strolled to the nearest tube.
The bin truck rumbled into view at the far end of the street. The municipal workers, dragging bins, back and forth.
Rosch looked at Younger, who bore all the signs of severe PTSD combined with the aftereffects of a Berlin Stag night.
"Did we just-" began Rosch.
"Another time, mate." croaked Younger, slowly turning and walking away.

Rosch looked on as the broken young priest walked his fragile way down the road, back to normality. Rosch pawed the ancient bible he still held in his hand, flicking through the pages not stuck together with stomach lining. What had he just been through? What would Leathers say?
"For fucks sake." he sighed dropping the book in a nearby bin before making his way to his car.

EPISODE IV

**Saturday
11:42pm
29 Adam West, Little Edinburgh, Kensington,
London**

London has many pockets of congealed affluence but few postcodes hold as much media money as Little Edinburgh. This one neighbourhood is populated by the most esteemed and influential purveyors of the arts and many of their personal trainers.
Sandra Buckfaster pulled her car onto the driveway of her carbon neutral, mock Georgian home. Slamming the car door shut and kicking the head off a gnome she stomped her way into the house.

Once inside, she threw off her jacket and marched upstairs to her study. It was here where she would post her passionate and often show-run destroying reviews of West-end musicals. Most notably, her scathing review of David Lynch and Andy Bell's *Erasure Head,* involved both a figurative and literal 'hatchet job'. She sat at her computer and began to type. As she did, she read aloud her thoughts in her formidable Edinburgh accent.
"Thank you very much Sir Mandeep Lloyd Throbber for a truly dreadful evening of so-called musical theatre. This production of Catnips is absolutely fuckin' gash! It's nay more an accurate portrayal a'the day to day life a'cats as it is about the time a reanimated Elvis Presley fought Jackie Chan at Wembley stadium."

Sandra paused to open a can of *Taggart's Uber-Brew lager,* took a hearty swig, gasped and continued.
"And despite popular opinion, you actually can get bored of watching a fully grown man in a catsuit lick his own testicles."
Her rant was interrupted by the sound of breaking glass downstairs. Sandra was a woman who was often frustrated by her inability to act out her titanic rage on those she deemed deserving, so a break-in was a well-timed cup of tea.
"Right." she said, as she stood, sank the last of her can, slapped her smartphone on her desk and rubbed her hands together. As she barreled down the stairs, she ranted.
"All right you slags you thought you'd try your hand at a wee bit of burglary eh? Well believe me you fucking hoodrat you've picked the wrong fuckin' hoose."
Her vitriol was deflated instantly as a wet slashing sound robbed her last few words of all gusto. At the bottom of the stairs she stood, her warm sticky entrails slowly leaking into her hands, dribbling through her fingers. Behind her she heard a deep purring sound. With her face now as frail and white as a snowflake she slowly turned to face her attacker.
"...Testicles?" she whispered.
Without the means to scream Sandra could only watch as her body was torn asunder.

Sunday
8:22am
Wood Green, The Home of Councilwoman Caroline Ahem

As the mist drifted over the grounds, Councilwoman Caroline Ahem sat in her study. Her assistant Grace was showcasing the latest promotional material for '*Earth's Got Visitors*', the forthcoming celebrity gala heralding the arrival of an extraterrestrial presence. Ahem was all too aware that in order to hoodwink the entire country, only the perfect celebrity line up would do. It was at such a time of immense pressure that she felt she needed rumblings from the Western Tactical Unit like a sheepdog needs a pilot's licence.

"Get me Leathers." she growled .

As the call came through, Chief Commissioner of Police Rudolph Leathers was at his desk. Today, he had chosen to adorn himself with full kayaking gear, complete with helmet, life jacket and a full-length paddle, with which he was miming long, slow strokes. He pressed the button to receive the call.

"Strooooke?" he queried.

"Leathers? Ahem. Can you tell me why the most comprehensive account of my nephew's last case is in the album reviews of the Big Issue?"

"Councilwoman, hello!" chimed Leathers. "The Big Issue's connection with the music scene in general has given it a-"

"Leathers!" she snapped, "this is a rhetorical conversation. Now, we are two weeks away from the official arrival of the Reticulants and with it the biggest media event the world has ever seen. We've got celebrities to coerce, news to fabricate, costumes to sew and vol au vents to fill. Now how is Ruggerman still blitzkrieg-ing the bowl of your department?"

"It's... rhetorical." said Leathers.

"Good boy." said Ahem. "Ruggerman's cage rattling is getting louder and moving beyond the demented ramblings of an inebriate. Six months ago his Twittlechat followers consisted of the last two dozen *Eerie Indiana* fans. This week, his post got liked by Richard Osman - Osman Leathers!"

"Hmmm," replied Leathers, thoughtfully, "...rhetorical"

"Right again, now-"

"However, Councilwoman, if I may." interjected Leathers, gingerly. "I hold you in the highest respect as a community leader and ruthless tyrant and I am fully on board with 'Go Team Ahem', but with Ruggerman's profile as it is, don't

we risk turning his crusade into a chunky, stubborn movement?"
"Hmm." pondered Ahem, "...perhaps we don't have to stop him, just slow him down. You have got to turn your rabid dog into a housebroken chihuahua. Give the maverick enough red tape to hang himself with. Put Toltattler on it. He's been dying to assess Ruggerman for years and is so anally retentive he makes you look like Jerry Garcia." Leathers internally rebuked her description but was well versed in top-level corruption.
"That's?.."
"Rhetorical, good." said Ahem. "Now Leathers?... do not, disappoint me."

8:50am
London Met. HQ, Front Entrance

Amid the usual morning bedlam, Frank Ruggerman stumbled, bleary eyed from the back of an ambulance. The on-hand paramedic looked confused as Frank gave him twenty pounds and patted his face. Frank adjusted his suit jacket and entered the fray.

Watching Frank from across the street, hidden from view, was the scrutineer extraordinaire. The scourge of the maverick, the bane of the inefficient, a man who loved protocol more than he could a human child, Standards Officer, Eugene Toltattler. Through his windscreen, Toltattler peered over his copy of *'How To Win At All Costs with Richard Madeley'* and watched Frank enter the building. He quickly made a note of his exact time of arrival. He didn't have to, it was just good practice. Toltattler slurped the last of his supersize cola, exited the car and followed Frank inside.

The reception area of the London Met was especially busy on Sundays. Officers dragged a struggling mime artist towards an interview room, his invisible glass window sadly failing to protect him against their brute force. The local Girls Brigade chapter were elevating their charity drive biscuit sale to another level by selling items from the armoury after accidentally acquiring the key. One concerned officer intervened but was quickly placated by the unbeatable value of the firearms on sale.

Both on crutches, a mother and child were waiting patiently as Toltattler strode through the double doors. The desire to check the validity of their disabled parking permit flashed in his mind but he had to focus, he was after bigger game today.

Toltattler was a tall man of considerable heft but he crossed the floor of the Met reception with the stealth of a pine marten. He believed indeed that the weasel was his spirit animal, which partly explained the dozens of taxidermically preserved *Mustelids* in his home. He admired their tenacity and their explosive ability to pounce on unsuspecting prey. A little way ahead of him, Frank was proceeding further into the building. As Frank paused to talk to the receptionist who was midway through tasering a new trainee, Toltattler dashed into cover behind a trio of Beefeaters playing snap. At that moment, upstairs, Asst. Detective Rosch Kunnypacken was pouring his heart out.

"...And ever since I've been getting rogered from every possible angle. My career is in the toilet, Leathers is scrutinising everything I do from somewhere inside my colon. Aunty Caroline is calling everyday asking why I'm not chief yet and reminding me just how disappointed my parents would be if they were alive. The entire department thinks I'm a joke and my only, only chance to get things back on track is to rein in the abominable piss-head. It feels like I'm swimming in cement. I'm just not sure how much longer I can take it."

"...Sir, please say your order, slowly and clearly into the microphone." said Jakub, the cafeteria attendant, looking at Rosch with a balanced blend of confusion and contempt.

The Met cafeteria was housed in bulletproof glass after pudding cups were decreased by forty-five ml in 2006.
"Um, sparkling mineral water please." said Rosch.
Jakub placed a glass of blue milk onto the revolving tray and smiled. Rosch was considering the pros and cons of self-immolation when Frank arrived behind him in the queue.
"We've got one." said Frank.
"Hello." said Rosch.
"No time." said Frank, brusquely. "Sandra Buckfaster found dead in her home in Little Edinburgh. Looks like an animal attack."
Rosch winced with dread.
"Are you listening to me?" snapped Frank. "Forty two years old, musical theatre critic, writes her own blog. High profile, holds a lot of sway in those circles."
As Frank continued, Jakub free-poured the five great white spirits into Frank's thermos.
"...so we'll need to restock our supply of tranquillisers." said Frank.

He and Rosch exited through the reinforced doors of the cafeteria. As they made their way back to the ground floor, they passed a wooden cut-out photo opportunity of a policeman referencing his baton as his penis. Behind this, lurked Toltattler. He slipped out behind them and carefully tailed his unsuspecting marks. Toltattler followed them down the corridor that led to the armoury. As they turned the corner Frank spun around, grabbed Toltattler, drew his pistol and thrust him against the wall.

"Toltattler you've been up my arse all morning now what's the fucking crack?" barked Frank, pressing his gun barrel firmly against Toltattler's nostril. Toltattler believed wholeheartedly that it was the bureaucrats who really tended the gates of the justice system and it was not the first time that an agitated colleague had thrust a gun in his face.

"Leathers wants me to supervise your little circus here with all happenings to be fed back and checked under the standards and practices." said Toltattler.

"Ah!" said Frank, "the perfect job for a tedious, bureaucratic cretin like you."

Toltattler snorted into Frank's gun barrel making the sound of blowing atop an empty bottle.

"Save it, Ruggerman. We need to go out today. If I'm to observe you and the...

'*farce awakens*' conduct, we must-"

"All right, all right. Fucks sake." snapped Frank. "You're taking your own car."

Toltattler inhaled slowly and exhaled again through his nose producing two long and sustained notes.

"Fair enough." said Toltattler. "29 Adam West in Little Edinburgh, takes twenty-six point four minutes. The budget requires that to ensure maximum fuel efficiency-"

The rest of his sentence was lost as Frank walked away.

"Fuck me." cursed Frank. "Now I've got a bag on each hip."

Frank stopped at a vending machine, inserted coins and awaited a heavy thud. He bent down and removed a large glass of Shiraz.

"I take it you're not a fan of Toltattler." said Rosch.

"I'm not even gonna dignify that with a punch in the face." said Frank, taking a gulp of wine.

"Who knows," said Rosch, "maybe having a third set of hands around might help us."

"Whoa." said a voice.

Frank and Rosch stopped and waited patiently for a shepherd to pass as he guided his llamas into the corner office.

"God you are vacant aren't you." said Frank.

"Look, I'm just saying that-" began Rosch.

"Toltattler is not police." said Frank. "He's a company man, a bean counting, walking dildo with the intuition of a turnip."

"Maybe so, but just maybe, accommodating him might be a good way to appease Leathers and get him off your back. Get some breathing space." said Rosch.
Frank looked at Rosch like a parent who has noticed a trick or treater has returned for a third helping. He flattened the last of his red and placed it on the tray of a passing waiter.

9:43am
Buckfaster Residence, Little Edinburgh

A host of police vehicles were already on the scene when Frank and Rosch arrived. As they came to park, Frank swerved to avoid the organic turkey dog cart and sent the car halfway up the embankment at the front of the house. The car rolled back slightly and came to a precarious stop. Rosch opened the passenger door sending dozens of empty bottles crashing onto the pavement. They proceeded up the driveway past an officer attempting to shoo away chimpanzees that had disguised themselves as press. The exterior of the house was now just a dense shell of police tape. Thankfully, subsequent officers had been able to cut through, revealing the entrance.

Inside the house, an army of forensics were filling out paperwork. Toltattler calmly paced the living room with his hands behind his back and wearing a smile of immense smugness. Tending the body as usual, was Sodermine. Frank and Rosch approached him and he stood, lifting his Trilby and mopping his brow with a handkerchief.
"Frank, Lando." he said warmly.
"Sodermine." said Frank. "What's the special?"
"Nothing healthy Frank." said Sodermine. "Sandra Buckfaster, forty two, Junior division swingball coach and theatre critic. Died about 1am this morning. Looks like an animal attack, something big. Barely a mark on her apart from the massive haemorrhaging and catastrophic tissue loss. Looks like this was her last gig."

Sodermine handed Frank a ticket stub for Catnips.
"Detectives!" barked Toltattler, marching towards them, carrying armfuls of clipboards.
"Sick him Ja Ja." said Frank as he turned quickly and slipped up the stairs.
Rosch stood quickly, just in time to be handed the clipboards.
"I need you both to fill these out." said Toltattler.
"We literally just arrived." said Rosch.
"I clocked the precise time of your arrival." said Toltattler. "This is your crime scene appraisal, your daily expenses estimate and this is your review of Detective Ruggerman's driving on the way over."
Upstairs, Frank quietly surveyed Buckfaster's study. She had framed some of her shining moments as a critic. On the wall were cuttings that read

'CHRISTOPHER BIGGINS CLINGS TO LIFE AFTER ROCKY HORROR REVAMP
GETS BUCKFASTERED' and 'FORMER BROADWAY DIRECTOR PROMOTED TO DRIVE-THRU WINDOW'.

Next to these was an A2 gloss photo of her stamping on a photographer at the 2006 Tony awards. He carefully touched a key on her computer, removing the dancing Rottweiler screensaver. He leaned in and began to read Buckfaster's last ever review.
"...Bloody hell." he said.
He finished reading the incomplete review and returned to surveying the room. He paused a moment and knelt down by a dark patch on the carpet next to a plant pot. A preliminary sniff identified the stain as something pungent.
"Yep. That is piss." said Frank, dabbing his eyes with his handkerchief.
Frank borrowed a flick knife from Buckfaster's desk and carefully cut out the square of carpet around the stain. He positioned a plastic zip bag open on the floor and wrung

out a good pint and a half of the reeking chardonnay coloured liquid. He zipped the bag shut and fingered the ticket stub in his pocket. Downstairs, Rosch handed two large binders back to Toltattler.

"What's the next step in procedure?" said Toltattler.

"Start local." said Rosch. "Most likely, Kensington Wild Cat Safari and Possumarium. Check with the night watchman, do a count of the mid to larger animals."

"No, do a full count." said Toltattler sternly. "There's no such thing as a harmless beaver."

"Beaver?" gulped Rosch.

"Sure." he replied. "It might look warm and furry, but it can bite through a tree trunk."

Frank jumped the last two steps of the stairs and approached.

"You're wasting your time." he said.

Frank threw the plastic bag of urine to Rosch who caught it without thinking.

"Oh god." said Rosch, recoiling as he wrestled to grip the large bag of liquid.

"We've got one attack," said Frank, "no witnesses. The Kensington Wild Cat Safari is within two hundred yards of Oligarch's Row, with a housing estate on three sides. You'd have thought someone would notice a Bengal Tiger firtling through the recycling."

"Suggestions?" said Toltattler.

"Until forensics comes back with the report," said Frank, "all we've got is the bag of scrumpy. We'll get it down to Binks for analysis. Toltattler you stay here and-"

"Nice try." said Toltattler. "Anyway, I've had your car taken in for diagnostics checks so you'll be riding with me. You can fill these out on the way."

10:33am
London Met Police HQ

Frank, Rosch and Toltattler strode through the entrance of the Met and across the floor of the reception. To his left, Rosch noticed the Girls Brigade stall was showing a lollipop lady a selection of knuckle dusters when Toltattler stopped.
"Detectives," he said, "this investigation is to be temporarily suspended while I partake in a brief adjournment."
"Tick tock Toltattler, this is time we ain't got." warned Frank.
"I'm afraid I must insist. I was eating protein bars whilst on surveillance this morning. I may also be dehydrated, as I am yet to have a bowel movement. Whilst I evacuate, I suggest you retire to the cafeteria and wait. Any further progress without the assessing officer to observe will result in disciplinaries."
The toilet door swung closed behind Toltattler and Rosch turned to Frank, who simply snorted and immediately pressed on with the case.

***

The London Met Police science lab was quiet on a Sunday but senior lab tech Jojo Binks was hard at work. The double doors swung open and in walked Frank and Rosch.
"Eyyyyy, what it is, Frank?" cheered Binks.
"Jojo." said Frank, approaching him with arms wide.
The two embraced and shared mutual nourishment.
"I hear they lumped you with that fuckin' hump Toltattler." said Binks.
Frank gave a short, guttural gesture of contempt. After checking that he was not in fact, invisible, Rosch took the initiative and extended his hand.
"Binks, Rosch Kunnypacken." he said.

"Hey kid." said Binks, as he placed a reassuring hand on Rosch's shoulder. "Relax huh? Don't try so hard, a little less you talk, a little more you think."
Binks gently slapped Rosch's face.
"Atta boy. You're all right." he said.
Binks sat at his countertop with the bag of urine. He smeared a sample onto a slide and carefully placed it under the microscope.
"I need to know who or what made it." said Frank.
"Well, you came to the right place." said Binks. "If it breathes, walks on two or more legs then we got its piss on file."
"Wait a minute." he said, adjusting the focus.
"Now what do we have here?"
Binks sighed.
"To be frank Frank we got nothing close to this. The last time I saw something like this?.. Christmas 2009 when we drank those Hairy Ballbangers."
Frank reflected deeply, whilst Rosch did not know where to look.
"All right, cool" said Frank, "Thanks Binks."
"Anytime." said Binks.
Frank turned to leave.
"Wait. Where are you going?" asked Rosch.
"We my dear," said Frank, "are going to the theatre."

12:40pm
The Royal Rodolfo Theatre, Soho

The Royal Rodolfo had stood tall amongst its peers on Shaftesbury Avenue since the days of *Arthur Atkins*. It was an institution loved and revered that had showcased often the most critically acclaimed and thematically progressive productions on the strip. The grand art-deco marquis bore the title of the latest production of Catnips and today, the hallowed venue was filled with patrons, cast members and the production team for a promotional press conference. The patrons had acquired their complimentary prosecco and taken their seats in the main theatre.

On stage and in costume were the leading cast members. Their Olympian bodies were perched comfortably on stools as the penultimate co-star of Catnips walked out on stage to warm applause. Known to theatre goers as Taum-Taum Tugger, he sauntered confidently towards the mic stand.
"Thank you, thank you." he said "Through the combined efforts of the crew, especially the actors..."
He gave a wink, inducing a sycophantic laugh from the audience.
"...all of the fabulous supporting dancers from Fortnums College, our glorious producer Sir Mandeep Lloyd Throbber..."
Then came an appropriately enthusiastic applause complete with an exclamation of 'We love you Mandy!"
"But," continued Tugger, "this year's production is our greatest yet. The longest running hit on the strip now gets to lead the way in promoting social awareness… for Cats. And it's all thanks to a legendary actor, my mentor, my friend, Jamelius Whiskers. Make him feel welcome folks, give him a hand, c'mon out here Jamelius."

Onto the stage walked Jamelius Whiskers. A man in his late sixties, he wore profound mutton chops and his vast belly was subdued tightly underneath an ornate, bejewelled waist coat. He carried himself with the poise and authority of an 18th century naval admiral. He had a remarkably commanding and stealthy quality that was only gently masked by his smile and feigned modesty. He took his place before his audience.
"Taum-Taum Tugger ladies and gentlemen." he said, calming the crowd with a gesture resembling a reverse nazi salute.
"One cannot resist the magic of theatre, when such an inspiring story is brought to life by so many talented, passionate actors. Shola Tarrington - Boothe, one of our

longest serving cast, gave birth on the afternoon to a litter of three beautiful girls, all destined for a career on stage I hope..."
Cue. Wait for laugh.
"only to be back on stage within the hour, ready for opening night. Give it up ladies and gents."

As Whiskers continued on with the programme, Frank and Rosch arrived in one of the empty balconies overlooking the stage. Frank looked down on the press conference and then began loading AA batteries into a laser pointer.

"Do you mind sharing what it is you hope to achieve by being here?" said Rosch.
"Watch and learn Fauntleroy, watch and learn."

Frank clicked the laser pointer closed.
"So, what?" said Rosch, "You believe a musical theatre actor is responsible for relocating a woman's entrails from inside to al fresco because of a shaky review?"
"I've got cases." said Frank, taking position near the edge of the balcony.
"Cases?" asked Rosch.
"Cases. Back to 1981. Coincidentally, the same time as the first premier of '*Catnips*'." said Frank.
"1981?" said Rosch, automatically.
"Brutal animal attacks, same m.o, all during full moons."
Below them, Jamelius Whiskers continued to avail the crowd.
"...ensuring this production will never, ever die. Thank you all so much for coming, I hope you will now sojourn with us across the street to The Closet Thespian for a measure of gin."
The audience applauded and began to reacquaint themselves with their bags and coats.
"But-" began Rosch.
"Look Lando, you've got to move beyond the textbook bollocks. The truth often can't be seen with logic alone,

you've got to feel it. The first thing you learn is that you know nothing. Second, the lady of fate twists and turns and the older I get, the weirder she is. All we have is the ticket stub of the critic's last gig and a rare piss sample, and that's all we need."

Frank leaned over the balcony and shone the laser pointer in the direction of the cast members who were calmly making their way off stage and into the crowd. The first to spot the red dot was dance troupe leader Kitty Widdler, who instinctively leapt off the stage in pursuit and onto the back of Dame Waphner-Hogget. The Dame screamed and flailed as the backing dancer frantically tried to subdue the red dot. Then in quick succession, the other cast members lost control and joined in. In a heartbeat, the area in front of the stage was a churning furnace of panic and enthusiasm. The fur of a dozen cat costumes and the fur of a dozen mink wraps were indistinguishable in the carnage. Frank chuckled as he clicked off the laser pointer and grabbed his jacket.
"Shall we?" he said.
As Frank and Rosch left for the exit, from the shadows, they were observed by a mysterious, unknown woman.

Outside, Frank and Rosch crossed the street away from the *Royal Rodolfo* towards the '*Thesp*'. Two serious looking bouncers stood guard to the VIP event in front of a long, bristling queue of hopefuls. Without breaking step, Frank approached the serious looking bouncers and removed his badge. "Fuck off." he warned.
Frank returned his badge into the inside pocket of his overcoat and he and Rosch continued inside.

The '*Thesp*' was packed to the rafters with the elite guard of the theatrical arts. In the deep red ambient lights, they milled and cavorted as a DJ played gentle house music. Frank carefully scanned the venue as he slowly made his way through the compacted bodies between the bar and the seating areas. Towards the very rear of the venue, Frank spotted the booth he was after.

At the table sat Jamelius Whiskers, Taum-Taum Tugger, Shola Tarrington-Boothe and a handful of young dancers. Frank approached, took a seat and helped himself to a nearby, elaborate looking, tropical cocktail.

"Can I help you inspector?" said Whiskers.

"Detective." garbled Frank with a mouthful of ice, fruit and liquor.

"Apologies. Can I help you detective?"

Whilst Rosch stood by and experienced yet another bout of epi-cringe, Frank spat the remaining ice cubes and fruit pulp onto the table.

"Some mighty mixed reviews this year, Whiskers." said Frank, "An overemphasis on testicle licking being at the forefront."

"That is just the typical ignorant hate speech-" began Shola before being coolly calmed by Whiskers. Frank had still not made eye contact with anyone around the table and was busy stirring and mixing his commandeered drink.

"You know how bad reviews are?" said Frank. "It's like a wildfire. People are very impressionable, especially on the internet. I wouldn't be surprised if your lot took bad reviews, very, very seriously."

"How seriously?" asked Whiskers, with effortless menace.

Frank sipped his straw steadily until the sound became a rattle of ice cubes.

"Deadly."

"Well, that's where you're wrong, detective." beamed Whiskers. "We find it more nourishing to perform from one's inner self, rather than to fawn to the critics."

Whisker's eyes became locked with Frank's as Frank tossed a strawberry into his mouth and chewed on its rum soaked goodness.

"Do you guys like *Bonio's*?" inquired Frank.

The *Catnips* stars exchanged nervous and confused glances with each other, all except for Whiskers and Tugger who maintained their poise.

"You like beef cuts, in marrowbone jelly?" said Frank.
"Jamelius." said Shola.
"You like a nice game of fetch?" said Frank.
"Ruggerman." said Rosch.
"Jamelius please!" said Shola, losing her cool.
"Because if I toss your pockets and I find any catnip, I've got six Dobermans in a cage who'll be calling you guys Garfield all night long." said Frank.
"Detective Ruggerman..." said a commanding voice from behind Frank's chair.
The voice belonged to Sir Mandeep Lloyd Throbber. The critics and patrons alike had come to regard him as musical theatre's answer to Vlad the impaler. He had an unshakable reputation for producing hit musicals and brazen self-promotion. He wore his bespoke *Saville Row* suit like a daggers sheath.
"I will advise you," he said, "that unless you have anything imperative to discuss with my actors, to kindly leave them in peace, before my lawyers get back from the bar."
While Rosch stood speechless, Frank slowly stood, popped a cherry into his mouth and dusted off his hands.
"Be seeing you Whiskers."

As the detectives departed, the atmosphere around the table slowly became relaxed once again, all except for Jamelius Whiskers, who did not take his eyes off Frank. Frank and Rosch left the venue and turned into the alley beside the building. Frank was enjoying another cocktail he had taken for the road when Rosch spoke.
"Aaaand that achieved what exactly?"
"Just putting the wobble on 'em." said Frank, smiling.
"Detectives." said a hushed voice from the shadows.
Rosch turned and saw a woman in her mid-forties. She cautiously but quickly approached the detectives. Her long brown curls bounced playfully on her overalls.
"Walk with me, for my pleasure." she said, in a Parisian accent thicker than an elephant seal's love handles.

They followed her further into the alley. When the woman was confident of their privacy, she began.

"Detectives. My name is Suzy Harper, I work at the theatre. We don't have much time but I know who you are and why you are 'ere."

"Even him?" quizzed Frank, pointing at Rosch.

"Especially him. It is nice to finally meet you, Rosch. Bravo for dispatching that Ewok, they are, how you say? Not as 'armless as people think."

Rosch turned away slightly and wiped away a tear as the feeling of human kindness hit him like an unexpectedly deployed airbag.

"Do you want to get to it?" said Frank, with growing impatience.

"I cannot talk here," she said, "I just wanted to tell you that you are on the right track. My father and I have been keeping an eye on these mangey bastards since the '80s. He was the caretaker at the *Royal Rodolfo*. He passed away last year and ever since they've been getting bolder in their tactics. Coercion, intimidation...and now murder."

"I am sorry for your loss." said Rosch. "Who have? And... what?"

"The key to nailing them will reveal itself on '*Late Night with Butterman*', watch Jamelius Whiskers. Now allez before you blow the whole thing."

"Can I give you my number?" said Rosch.

"Just watch *Butterman* tonight." she said. "I will contact you tomorrow with the next step. You must go now, they are, how you say? Bastards."

    Harper hurriedly continued down the alley, while Rosch and Frank retreated back towards the street. After they had left, in the dark recess of a fire escape, two feline eyes opened wide and burned with malicious intent.

3:05pm
London Met HQ. Western Tactical Unit Office

Frank and Rosch entered the office and immediately recoiled. Binks had left them a truly comprehensive collection of rare urine samples, carefully labelled, placed on every available surface and now unfortunately, at room temperature. They braved the tangy ambience and proceeded inside the office. Rosch slumped onto the couch and Frank turned on the TV.
"Found it." called Frank.
Rosch dragged himself onto his back and watched as the dusty television set filled the office with the sound of live jazz and rapturous applause. '*Late Night with Butterman*' was the longest running pre-late-late night chat show on the IBS network. The audience calmed and the logo faded away revealing the host, Butterman, sitting at his desk. Joining him were the core members of the cast of '*Catnips*', each in their lavish feline costume. Butterman smiled like a man facing a firing squad, shuffled his notes and began.

"And we are back with the cast of the hit West End musical Catnips and we are joined by Shola Tarrington-Boothe, Taum-Taum Tugger and Jamelius Whiskers. How are ya guys? It's great to see ya. Now, I hear, this current production will appeal to the woke generation."
"Yes indeed." said Tugger.
"And why is that?" said Butterman.
"We felt a responsibility… to speak for those going unheard." said Shola.
"Yes," continued Tugger, removing a speck from the fur collar of his spandex catsuit, "we felt the production had reached such success that we could use the exposure to bring some important issues to the forefront."
"For the lives of cats" volunteered Butterman.
"Precisely." smiled Tugger.

"It seemed almost vulgar to us," said Jamelius Whiskers, "how some, perfectly natural practices for cats, were being reviled by many as... 'unnatural'."
"You refer to the licking of one's own testicles." said Butterman.
"That is correct Damien." said Whiskers. "We feel that we owe it to this generation to join the rallying cry against prejudice and bigotry."
The audience, amongst one of the hippest and reportedly well-read of NYC, cheered and applauded riotously.
"Now, Jamelius," said Butterman, "we spoke backstage and, I was hoping, just hoping, you'd maybe…give us a demonstration?"
The crowd erupted.
Whiskers delivered an accomplished, pseudo-awkward shuffle in his seat as the crowd whooped and hollered. His ego spurned the audience with gallon after gallon of his exquisite modesty. Tugger stood up and pumped up the crowd further.
"Damien, I'd be happy to." said Whiskers.
The audience reached fever pitch.
"Jamelius Whiskers Everybody!" said Butterman. "Give him some encouragement!"

Frank and Rosch stood transfixed as the onscreen Whiskers contorted himself and began to lick his own testicles. The house band burst into another lively jazz piece, which only partly drowned out the enthusiastic licking sounds coming through Whiskers' collar mic.
"Shola, Taum-Taum, you show us too." said Butterman, revelling and laughing. "Amazing. How about that, folks? We'll be back with more from Jamelius and the guys after this."

Frank muted the TV and pondered deeply.
"He really, really likes to lick his testicles." said Rosch.
"Anything about that strike you as unusual?" asked Frank.

"You're kidding?" said Rosch, fearing death by incredulity.

"Whiskers outweighs me three to one and I can barely reach my hands to my pockets. He's pushing seventy... but just look at him go."

"So what does this mean?" replied Rosch.

"Firstly, a drink, cos I'm gasping." said Frank, opening a bottle of whiskey.

He looked around for a glass. Unable to locate one, he reached for an empty specimen jar left by Binks. Frank took a brief sniff of the jar and poured in the best part of a pint from the bottle. With the subtlest, begrudging grunt, he placed the bottle in Rosch's general direction.

"I'm-" said Rosch, declining.

"Whatever." said Frank, curtly.

Frank swivelled in his chair to face his computer, his craggy face illuminated by the glowing screen.

"From here on," he said, "it's all about the sample. We can use the catnip angle to warrant a drug test from the cast, full blood, stool and urine samples from everyone. Leathers will never okay it but that won't matter provided we don't run into-"

"Toltattler." said Rosch, cheerily.

"Shit." whispered Frank, placing his whiskey in amongst the other specimen samples.

Toltattler stood in the doorway with arms folded.

"Detectives, you were given strict instructions about pursuing this investigation without the assessing officer."

"We left a message." said Frank. "Wait. Were you on the lav this whole time?"

"There were...complications. Something has disturbed my duodenum. I bought your mail."

Toltattler threw a handful of letters, mostly onto Frank's desk before immediately returning his hand to clasp his abdomen. He was being ravaged by the same colonic irritability that had plagued his ancestors, all the way back to his great grandfather, Woolacombe Toltattler. It was his cross to bear, along with the crusade against wanton inefficiency. Toltattler stood stoic and battled to keep his composure amidst terrible wobblings in his gut. On the floor, amongst the scattered envelopes, Rosch noticed a handwritten note.

"Toltattler. You're here just in the nick of time." said Frank. "We need to know what these urine samples can tell us about who or what attacked Buckfaster. This is the cutting edge, where science *is* police work."

Rosch carefully opened the note, it read;

'It is blown! Come now!'
S.H.

Rosch's mind filled with thoughts of their mysterious new ally, that and whether the French have innuendo. Frank raised the specimen jar containing his whiskey and began to gently swirl the rich, golden liquid. In his fragile state, Toltattler stood firm and battled his tingling gag reflex.

"I hereby notify you," said Toltattler, closing his eyes as the aromas of the room began to overwhelm him, "that after a complaint by members of the national theatre board, you both must undertake a six-week sensitivity training course where... I hope these samples have been refrigerated properly?"

"Of course," assured Frank, "but we have to let them get to room temperature before we can identify all the nuance."

Frank then took a long, deep sniff of the contents of his jar. Toltattler's knees quivered beneath him.

"Surely,...the chemical analysis-" he said, slapping a steadying hand on the door frame.

"Ah for a particular analysis, sure, but for a case like this, you need a nose to truly know what you're working with."

Frank appraised his jar with great reverence and took a hearty swig.

"Ruggerman, don't think I don't see your vain attempt to- Oh god!"

Toltattler's resolve collapsed and he made a desperate dash for the nearest toilet.

With Toltattler gone, Rosch leapt to his feet and showed the note to Frank.
"It's Harper." said Frank.
"I think she is in danger." said Rosch.
"Cool your chaps *Darth-Tanien*, we're going. I've just got to make sure Toltattler stays… occupied."
"What do you have in mind?" said Rosch.
"Just keep a lookout." said Frank, grabbing his jacket and heading for the door.

Out in the corridor, the Hon. Judge Connors, adorned in full wig and gown, fought like a lion underneath the five officers struggling to subdue him.
"Old Connors on the navy strength gin again eh?" said Frank to one of the officers.
The officers wrestled the judge's arm and pressed it up behind his back. Connors roared in pain. He was pinned to the floor, but he flailed wildly on the ground like an upended Catherine wheel. Another officer brought Frank up to speed between baton strikes.
"Someone thought *whack* it would be a good idea to introduce *whack* martini breaks into the *whack* court proceedings."

Frank cooed apprehensively and directed Rosch to hug the wall and slip past the fray. Frank slowed his walk as they neared Toltattler's office and came to a stop at the corridor junction. He peered around the corner and saw no one.
"Remember, you're on lookout." Frank, whispered gruffly.
"Ruggerman wait." said Rosch quietly, as Frank slipped towards the door of Toltattler's office. A quick swipe of a *Londis* loyalty card, a wiggle, a click, and Frank was inside.
"Ruggerman!" whispered Rosch, nowhere near loud enough to be heard through the door. He scanned for any onlookers and followed Frank inside.

Toltattler's office was immaculate. Frugally decorated with a peace lily, a range of grip exercisers fixed to the wall in ascending order of size and a poster that read 'THINK... WARNING SHOTS WASTE AMMO'.

Frank was huddled over a basket of 12-inch records next to a record player.
"Ruggerman, please now, what are we doing?" implored Rosch.
"You are a terrible, terrible lookout." hissed Frank.
"Ruggerman for Christ's sake-"
"Argh! Okay! For fucks sake. Listen. We have to stall Toltattler, yes?" said Frank.
"Okay." agreed Rosch, his brain a galaxy of caveats.
"Well then know thine enemy." said Frank.
He removed a copy of *the Beatles' white album* from the basket. He carefully scrutinised the cover and then gently removed the pristine vinyl.
"I think there's someone outside." whispered Rosch.
"Nearly there..." hushed Frank.
Frank's eyes scanned the densely packed grooves of the record. He stopped, and removed a safety pin from his pocket. Then, very carefully, he took the pin and made a tiny notch in one of the grooves. He put the record, notch side up on the platter, placed the tone arm at the beginning, and hit play.
"Quick, let's go." said Frank.
Frank and Rosch slipped out of the office into the thankfully empty corridor.
"That should hold him." said Frank. "Right, let's grab the essentials and head to the theatre."

A heartbeat after they left, Toltattler emerged from the other end of the corridor, now more stable, but still in some colonic peril. As he neared his office, he heard familiar music. He stepped, ninja-like towards his door and slowly wrapped his hand around the door knob. He slammed the door open and lunged inside with his pistol drawn. With

the corners checked and no sign of an intruder, he stood and returned his weapon to its holster. The lively music from his record player continued. Toltattler began to enjoy it and considered again why anyone would ever prefer the Rolling Stones. On the beat, Toltattler leapt in the air, struck a pose and sang
"DON'T KNOW HOW LUCKY YOU ARE BOOYYYY!"

4:03pm

Frank and Rosch crashed through the door into the W.T.U. office.
"We're going to have to be quick." said Frank as he rushed over to his munitions cupboard. He began emptying the cupboard of boxes of ammunition.
"Hold these." he said, piling the boxes in Rosch's arms.
"*Choc-ammo?*" asked Rosch, barely.
"It's a 9ml round, high velocity, filled with chocolate."
"Chocolate."
"Correct." said Frank, closing the cupboard. "It's toxic and causes fatal diarrhoea in cats."
"Yes, but we-" began Rosch.
"-Are dealing with cats." said Frank, filling magazines with the *choc-ammo*.
"Yes but-"
"Have you heard of werewolves?" asked Frank.
"Of course, but-"
"Well, here we are." said Frank, chambering the first round.
"Werewolves?"
"No! Cats! Jesus Lando this is obtuse even for you."
"Actually, I would venture that at least one of us... is completely insane." said Rosch.
Frank hurriedly stuffed the remaining boxes of *choc-ammo* and weapons into a war torn sports bag.
"Think about everything you've seen." said Frank, bristling. "Can you lick your own testicles?"

"No." said Rosch, with tangible disappointment in his voice. "But that can't mean-"
"These are no Saturday morning cartoon fairy cakes Lando, these are the real deal."
"For the love of god Ruggerman, you are going over the edge...or maybe, more like in freefall for the better part of a decade, but if Leathers gets wind of this-"
Frank grabbed Rosch firmly by the shoulders and shook him violently.
"Don't fight it Lando!" he barked.
"No!" sobbed Rosch, "It can't be!"
"The testicles Ja Ja! The testicles!... Trust your eyes if not your instincts! We have to stop these furry arseholes!... Think about Harper."
Rosch inhaled deeply and slowly as he tried to keep at least one foot in this reality.
"Okay." he said, wiping his eyes and grabbing a bag of weapons.

Frank and Rosch slid quietly down the corridor towards Toltattler's office. They could hear looping music becoming louder and louder.
*'Back in the U.S, Back in the U.S,(*pop*) Back in the U.S, Back in the U.S...'*
As they peered into the doorway, Toltattler stood with his back to them. He was wearing his tie around his head, singing along and swinging his arm round and round as he played his air guitar, trapped in a perpetual loop.
"Back in the U.S, Back in the U.S (pop) Back in the U.S, Back in the U.S..."
"Got him." whispered Frank.
Confident that would hold Toltattler for at least an hour, the two slipped away quietly and headed for the theatre.

4:47pm
The Royal Rodolfo Theatre, Soho

Thanks to the TV hit; *Celebrity Crumpet Showdown*, the streets of Soho were empty. The wind blew past closed shop fronts and a thousand neon tube lit promises of satisfaction.

Since its construction, the *Royal Rodolfo* was the envy of the strip. Its bright marquis had celebrated the very cream of British actors, Helen Mirren amongst the creamiest.

As night fell, powerful, orange flood lights made the facade of the old theatre look like a stern, ancient face by a fireside. It began to rain and Frank and Rosch wrapped their jackets tightly against the cold as they proceeded down the cobbled alley leading to the theatre.

Once in the alley next to the venue, they located a side door and slipped inside. With weapons drawn, Frank and Rosch began searching for Harper. The long corridors of the theatre were lined with yard after yard of blood red carpet, the cream walls glowing with warm, ambient light. Silently, the detectives covered both sides and proceeded down a long hallway.

"Where the fuck is everybody?" whispered Frank.
"Ruggerman." hissed Rosch, frantically signalling down a side corridor that led away from the main hallway, at the end of which, tied to a chair, was a gagged and bloodied Suzy Harper.
Rosch immediately raced towards her with his weapon drawn.
"Easy now, Lando!" warned Frank, looking left and right for danger as he followed.
Rosch removed her gag.
"I'm sorry Rosch! Frank! This is a trap for you! You must leave now and do not take me with you, I deserve to rot in a puddle of my own cowardice!"

"Are you wounded?" said Rosch, as he cut through her bonds. "There is a lot of blood here."
"It is a coward's blood!" cried Harper. "It looks worse than it is because they hit me in the face repeatedly."
"Let's move it Lando." said Frank, "I don't like that we've not been greeted yet."
"Agreed." said Rosch as he cut the final bond and helped the battered Harper to her feet.
"Can you walk?" said Rosch.
"Yes, I can walk," said Harper painfully, "Like a coward!"
Frank cracked open a nearby door and peered through.
"It's clear this way." he said.
"No!" grimaced Harper, "We must first get to my father's office, we will need things there. Come this way."
Harper led the detectives through a double door that opened onto the foyer upon which sat the concessions stands. She paused a moment and peered over a counter top.
"We are clear," she said, "we must head towards that door and cross the hallway, past the main entrance. My father's office is there."
Crouching low, the trio scurried over to the doorway.
"Okay," said Harper, bracing to open the door, "so it is through 'ere, straight forwards and next to the left-hand staircase."
Frank and Rosch readied themselves to sprint.
"Allez!" she pushed through the door and raced forward before her pace faltered to a dawdle.

In the main foyer, two long staircases mirrored each other, curving around, framing the huge room. Gathered on these staircases, were hundreds of supple bodies in catsuits, their eyes flashing bright yellow in the low light. The door behind the trio closed and locked shut as the horde of feline horrors slowly advanced. From atop one of the staircases came the commanding voice of Jamelius Whiskers.
"Detectives."

Rosch reluctantly let his gaze drift upwards to see tier upon tier of alcoves and balconies, all writhing with cat bodies. He did a rough count of targets and a mental tally of the ammunition he had.

"The game's over Whiskers," said Frank, "give it up."

"Oh detective." laughed Whiskers, as he slowly descended the lavish stairway. "It gives me such joy to watch non thesps try and be passionate about their work. It's the greatest gift we give to the world, to inspire those with ordinary mundane jobs to pretend they have meaning."

Harper sat bravely on the panic that was slowly creeping into her heart as the way to her father's office became obstructed by feline beasts with deadly claws. From across the floor, Taum-Taum Tugger approached, his pupils now long, black slits, he smiled, stretching strings of saliva between razor sharp fangs, elongating with every step he took.

Frank cocked his pistol. "Not another fucking step Tuggernuts."

Tugger halted momentarily and hissed like a cornered rattlesnake.

"Why detective?" said Whiskers, "surely you must understand that your weapons are useless against the likes of us? Our species has evolved distinctly from your own. Whilst your mothers frightened you with folk stories in the bath, we have thrived for centuries in the shadows."

Harper spat out a bloody tooth.

"Then why wait until '81 to begin the musical?" she said.

"Hard to say," said Whiskers, "market forces, the success of these things is 90 percent timing."

"And now you are murderers!" she added.

"Oh, we were always murderers, darling, it's just the first time we got caught."

The horde inched closer and closer.

"Now if the three of you would kindly join us in the basement," he beamed, "it is time to wrap up this little adventure."

"Oh absolutely." said Frank.

Frank fired and Tugger's expression fell from Bengal Tiger to frightened kitten. Tugger screamed wretchedly, collapsed onto the floor and evacuated his bowels in a loud, violent and liquid movement. Whiskers' eyes flashed with the fury of a wildfire.
"*Choc-ammo!*" he roared.
In a heartbeat, the horde descended, screaming with fangs bare.
"That's our cue!" said Frank.
"This way!" shouted Harper.

The trio raced towards their attackers. Round after round of high velocity bullets tore through sinewy flesh, the air rang with the deafening combination of gunfire, feline screams and catastrophic bowel movements. Countless bodies fell as the trio cut through the savage mob towards the door. The horde closed in. A backing dancer from *Fortnum's College* lunged at Rosch's face. Rosch caught the creature sharply on its nose with his pistol and fired a round under its chin. Minus the top half of its head, the creature dropped to its knees and slumped to the ground, emptying the contents of its intestines like a sluice gate. One, two and three more fell revealing the doorway that led to Harper's father's office.
"Come on!" yelled Harper, crashing through the door.
Once through, the trio immediately slammed the door closed behind them and frantically began barricading it with all the furniture with any weight to it. The door slipped open a crack and a hundred furry hands with razor sharp claws scratched and tore furiously. Frank leapt atop the barricade and hammered the door shut with the butt of his weapon.
"Fucking bastards!" he roared.
Rosch loaded in his last clip.
"How are you looking?" he shouted.
Frank counted his remaining shells as the door bulged and splintered under the weight of the horde.

"Last clip and a few spare." he answered. "We need to shift it. This won't hold and they'll be trying to flank us."
"Detectives! In 'ere!" directed Harper.
She led them into her father's office, she raced over to a large dusty cupboard and threw open the doors. Inside, was a fine selection of high calibre automatic weapons and hundreds of boxes of *choc-ammo*.
"Oh get in you filthy slag." said Frank, smiling.
"Quickly!" she ordered, "My father knew that one day, they would cross the line, and when that day came...we would kill them all."
She threw Frank and Rosch a rifle each and they grabbed all the choc-ammo they could carry. "Allez!"
The trio raced back out into the corridor just as the barricade gave way. The horde tore through the shattered remnants of the doors and crashed in a writhing mass onto the floor.
"Remember, courtes, controlees!" shouted Harper, before opening fire.
In a plague of bullets, the furious creatures disintegrated. Exploding muscles were torn from ligaments and colonic contents were strewn up the walls, but still they rampaged.
"Ruggerman!" shouted Harper, "Head to that back right doorway and check it's clear!"
Maintaining short bursts of fire, Frank retreated towards the rear right side of the hallway. As he neared the door, it burst off its hinges, flattening him to the ground and pinning him underneath. On top of the door was a huge, rotund creature called Ginger Tom. His evil smile contorted his pendulous jowls and he swung a weighty paw down with all his might. Four claws of obsidian pierced through the dense wood stopping an inch from Frank's face. With all his strength, Frank heaved the door upwards and forced the muzzle of his rifle through a crack. He squeezed the trigger and the white-hot bullets tore through the belly of Ginger Tom. The humongous creature screamed and defecated. As his torso was transformed into mincemeat, Frank was showered in cat blood and excrement. He ceased fire and swung what was

left of the door and carcass off him. Breathless, Frank got to his feet and carefully advanced into the next corridor.

"It looks clear," he shouted positively, "we just-" The end of Frank's sentence was drowned out by the sound of gunfire and cat screams.

"Rosch! Quickly!" shouted Harper, as she directed him to follow Frank. Maintaining a suppressing line of fire, she and Rosch retreated and joined Frank.

Harper led the detectives through a door labelled 'CREW ONLY'. The lavish drapes and thick carpeting of the theatre gave way to a dank, musty corridor. The sound of frantic, racing footsteps echoed around the concrete back of house.

"We must get to the fire escape!" commanded Harper. "It is not locked during the week but it is connected to the kitchen, which has three ways in."

"Entry on three sides." said Frank, forebodingly. "Let's hope they haven't twigged where we're headed.

"Last clip." said Rosch, reloading as he ran.

Behind them, two doors crashed off their hinges, flooding the corridor with an avalanche of fangs and spandex covered bodies. They slammed through the kitchen doors to find a maze of steel work units, the surfaces reflected the pale blue light of the bug zapper.

"That way!" shouted Harper as she pointed for the fire escape, situated at the rear left corner of the kitchen.

Frank and Rosch were busy shoving the large steel fridges and workstations against the doors when the barricade lurched towards them with the weight of an entire mutant dance troupe. Harper ran towards them and hopped up onto the barricade and fired through a small round window. Rosch glanced over his shoulder and noticed several cats had crept in through one of the side doors.

"Argh shit! The side door!" yelled Rosch, as he turned his fire towards the breach. He and Frank drew down fire on the cats inside the perimeter, tearing their nubile bodies asunder in a wail of screeching yelps and part digested tuna chunks.

At that moment, the doorway that led out to the cafe slammed open and in rushed the swarm.

"The fire-escape! Now!" roared Harper.

"Harper, move!" screamed Rosch.

Harper was cut off. The air in the kitchen was thick with gun smoke, faces flickered yellow in the light from countless muzzle flashes. Empty casings rattled and bounced off the aluminium work surfaces as cats vaulted over counter tops towards Frank and Rosch, their bodies exploding on impact with the high velocity choc-ammo. First Frank's, then Rosch's rifle fell silent as the last few rounds were spent. On the other side of the kitchen, with her rifle spent and only her pistol left, Harper stared down the cats approaching her.

"Go!" shouted Harper.

With cats approaching on all sides, Frank grabbed Rosch.

"No! We can't leave her!" yelled Rosch as he kicked and pulled.

"There's too many, Lando! Think! If we end up as the fucking main course there's no one to stop them! Now fucking come on!"

"Harper! Fucking bastard, Ruggerman!" protested Rosch.

Frank dragged Rosch through the rear fire escape and down the stairwell into the open air. They raced off the final stairway, onto the cobbled street and away from the Rodolfo. Back inside, Harper threatened to use her pistol on the next cat who got too close. Shola Tarrington-Boothe approached stealthily through the encroaching mob and smiled, exposing her razor sharp fangs.

"There's no way out now Harper." she said, calmly. "You and your father's quest to stop us, dies now, in this very moment. I'm afraid you really should have used your last bullet on yourself because... this will not be quick."

Harper trained her weapon on Shola and squeezed the trigger.

Click

Harper rethought and threw her gun as hard as she could, striking Shola on her left breast.

Shola clasped herself, as a pain unlike any other, savaged her nervous system like a gopher in the jaws of a polar bear. Fighting for breath, she dropped to her knees and sobbed.

"Enough." said Jamelius Whiskers, calmly.

The subordinate cats parted and Whiskers, with hands behind his back, strolled authoritatively towards Harper.

"Subdue her." he said.

The closest two cats pounced and pinned Harper up against the cold ceramic tiles on the wall.

"Oh Miss Harper," said Whiskers, "removing such a long troublesome thorn gives me both joy and regret."

Harper struggled against her captors' grasp.

"Ta mere etait un gros cochon cretinuex." hissed Harper as she spat squarely into the face of one of the cats holding her.

The cat did very, very well to keep a firm grasp on his victim's arm considering he was so deeply, deeply horrified to the very middle of himself. Whiskers laughed from deep in his belly.

"I do so adore French cuisine." said Whiskers.

He stepped closer, his pupils extended into long black gashes as he opened his vast, salivating jaws. Harper ripped open her vest revealing dozens of custom *Ferrero Roche* grenades.

"...Here's your pudding fuck face."

Outside, Frank and Rosch had reached the car and were about to radio for backup when the Royal Rodolfo was rocked by a cataclysmic explosion. A chorus of a hundred agonised feline death rattles sang out into the Soho night, followed by a tsunami of involuntary bowel movements. The detectives stood a moment in the cold, night air.

"Adios, Whiskers." said Frank.

"Maybe she..." began Rosch.

"Not a chance." said Frank.

Frank removed a whisky bottle from the wheel arch of his car and took a hearty swig. Rosch stood silent. As Frank

noticed Rosch, something possibly resembling empathy flickered inside him. To Frank, it felt like the feeling caused by the first cigarette of a bad hangover, unpleasant and deeply unnecessary.
"By morning she'll be having a victory *sancerre* with her dad." said Frank as he entered the car.
Without a word, Rosch entered the passenger door and the car pulled away.

6:21pm
London Met. HQ

Councilwoman Caroline Ahem trundled through the corridor of the Met leading to Tolttatler's office, as she did so, she muttered to herself;
"Who do I have to blow to get a fucking update around here?"
As she approached Toltatter's door, she heard a loop of music, repeating ad infinitum. She drew her wheelchair to a stop and peered inside the office where Toltattler lay, face down and twitching sporadically.
'Back in the US, Back in the US, Back in the US (pop) *Back in the US...'*
"God damn it Toltattler." she said.
Ahem pulled away down the corridor and pressed her 24/7 com link to her assistant Grace.
"Grace? Listen, Ruggerman has managed to shake off the tail I put on him…
I don't know, he's dead or, paralyzed or something, point being, I need a car to bring the laptop over here before I go to see the Ambassador at the hangar. Righty ho chop chop."

11:54pm
Secret Hangar, Streatham Airfield

Inside the miles of electrified, chain link fence, protected by guard dogs and landmines, a tucked away hangar had become Ambassador Crunk's preferred location for his meetings with the human representatives. The entrance was currently manned by squads of Reticulant and human soldiers. The humans were greatly superior in stature to their short Reticulant counterparts, but the Reticulants found a great source of confidence in the astonishingly horrific effects their weapons had on humans.

Escorted by armed guard, Caroline Ahem was led inside the hangar and over to a table, at which sat Ambassador Crunk, a lonely desk lamp providing the only light in the vast, dark hangar. Once at the table, Ahem opened the laptop and turned it towards the Ambassador, with a few clicks, a video clip began. Ambassador Crunk peered intently at the screen with his large black eyes.
"This was taken last week at the Peter Cooke Music Hall in Wolverhampton." said Ahem.
On the screen, Detective Frank Ruggerman was giving yet another speech regarding his thoughts on the 'Visitors'.
"So, you see ladies and gents," said Frank, "not only do the Reticulants exist, they have been monitoring and manipulating human affairs since their arrival in the 1930's."
Frank clicked the remote of a dusty old projector revealing a photo of a man in a lab coat.
"See here, in 1939 they helped inspire Dr. Paul Herrman Muller with the idea of using DDT as an insecticide. Promoted as a way for the world to finally overcome the blight of nature's 'pests'. In reality, it was the unleashing of untold devastation across the whole ecosystem and of course, human kind itself. Later, in the 1970's..."

The projector carousel rotated one notch revealing a photo of a teenage boy with thick black hair and a waistband that stopped just shy of his nipples.
"They awoke a then teenage Simon Cowell to the fact he had no admirable qualities or talents of any description, and that he should focus his sights...on the entertainment industry."
Click
The next photo showed Susan Boyle smiling in the stocks covered in crushed tomatoes and an adult Simon Cowell leaning on the stocks, holding fistfuls of cash.
"In 1981…" *Click* "the McRib…"

Over the lid of the laptop Ahem could see the emotionally vacant face of Ambassador Crunk twitch imperceptibly with what she assumed was rage.
"…and believe me," continued Frank, "we're only skimming the surface. Several governments of this planet are collaborating with an extra-terrestrial menace. It is an attempt to conceal the greatest conspiracy in the length of human existence."

Ahem stopped the video and closed the laptop. The Ambassador pondered a moment.
"Fucking piss-head." spat Crunk.
"Your people had better be ready to move in the next seven days." said Ahem. "It is 'show time' and we are days from executing the biggest spin campaign in history and all the palms are as greasy as they're going to get. Now we-"
"Don't you forget Councilwoman," said Crunk, gesturing contemptuously towards the laptop. "that it's your inability to quash the likes of... Admiral Driptray, that means we have to reveal our presence on your planet in the first place."
"And this marks the beginning of a whole new era of opportunity for all of us." said Ahem gently, "All I'm saying is that we are at critical mass. If this doesn't go ahead now then everyone we silenced or coerced to play

ball will have to pipe up and spill the baloney and that my friend, will Weinstein everything."

"Calm down, Gsa Gsa." said Crunk, "Three ships containing the High Conqueror and the Ambassadorial leaders will drop out of hyperspace and enter your atmosphere in two days. The times, locations and selfie ops will all be sent via the twittlechat group."

"That reminds me, the High Conqueror," said Ahem. "Our team thinks that title is too aggressive for today's market so we're going with this."

Ahem showed Crunk an A3 artist's mock-up of 'the High Buddy Liaison' promotion. The poster displayed a Photoshop job of the aged Reticulant ruler on a university campus with sporty young types smiling.

"The High Buddy Liaison" said Ahem brightly.

Crunk tapped his long grey fingertips together and gently tilted his head.

"He's gonna love that." he said.

EPISODE V

Monday
12:37am
Hackney Canal

Away from the bright lights of Hackney Central, on a remote stretch of canal, a solitary boat was moored in the darkness. Inside, Duane Pegg, a tired, elderly man from Newcastle Upon Tyne awoke in a panic. His blurry eyes wrestled to adjust as he frantically looked all about him. Breathless, all he saw was the familiar interior of his trusty boat and home of the last twelve years. Suddenly, a blinding white light shone outside, penetrating through the grimy windows.
"Oh no, not again!" begged Pegg, "Please! Why won't you leave me alone like?!"
An invisible force thrust Pegg flat onto his bed and held him fast. He cried, helpless, gripped by paralysis. He strained his eyeballs to his left, through the patches of dirt on his windows he saw a line of Reticulant aliens form. His eyes drifted over them, their grey, wrinkly skin catching the odd glimpse of moonlight, their huge black eyes peering in and several streams of urine splashed on the windows. The old, swollen timber of the canal boat groaned and the invisible force slowly lifted the paralysed Pegg from his bedclothes. Pegg screamed and tears flooded his face.
"...Your Honour? Are you okay?"
The Right honourable Judge Duane Pegg awoke, still wracked with panic and terror, he calmed himself and tried

to steady his breathing. Prosecutor Janet Middleton looked sympathetically into Pegg's earnest and harried face.
"Are you okay, your honour?" she repeated coolly.
"Uhm, yes. Sorry pet," said Pegg, "I'm going to have to...take a brief recess and that. Go on, y'all piss off and have a smoke or summat. Thirty minutes."
"Your Honour, we-"
"Ah, come now lass, it'll be alright, I just need a breather. Alright, I'm calling a brief recess, to be resumed in thirty minutes."

Pegg gathered up his gown and descended from the bench chair, slipping into his private office that was tucked neatly behind the courtroom. Once inside and the door was closed behind him, he tore off his wig, sat heavily in a chair and wiped the tears from his face.
"Fucking alien bastards." he sobbed.

A few minutes later, Pegg was washing his face in the en suite. He turned on the television in time to see an historic address from the Prime Minister, Joffrey Wiff-Waff Donovan. Donovan looked like a pink toad in the midst of anaphylaxis and today was clearly revelling in himself more than usual.
"It is an unimaginable honour, as your Prime Minister, to, in my lifetime, witness that moment, in history, when we discovered that we were not alone in this universe. Yes, today I announce, with unbridled, British pride, that Visitors from another world, join us, with a host of celebrities, tomorrow night as guest judges on the hit talent show Britain's Got Performers."
Pegg looked on in unfathomable despair while the PM continued.
"I've appointed Councilwoman Caroline Ahem to be chief liaison with the Reticulant Ambassador."
Pegg watched a short video clip of Ahem accepting her 'new' role. Ahem drove her electric wheelchair towards a podium, sending several members of the council tumbling into the orchestra pit.

"I believe, with her flawless track record, tireless humanitarian work and no less than seventeen acquittals for fraud, she is the perfect representative, to help facilitate our country's path, into a brighter, limitless future. A future of cooperation and opportunity-"
The television clicked off.
"Fucking alien bastards!" roared Pegg.
He slammed his fist on the counter and shook off his gown revealing his holstered, standard issue revolver. Pegg tore into his wardrobe and put on a bright green bomber jacket and a bright blue curly wig. Before he left, he caught a glimpse of himself in the mirror.
"It's time to take a stand." he said.

Tuesday
11:33am
London Met. HQ

Standing in the office of the Western Tactical Unit, Frank was watching the same historic address as Judge Pegg.
"...a future of cooperation and opportunity," Donovan turned the page of his speech,
"...and intergalactic fornication."
Frank clicked off the TV.
"Fucking alien bastards." he said.
Just then Rosch entered the office with his arms full of requisition forms.
"Are you busy?" Rosch asked, hopefully, "It's the budget report."
Rosch dumped the mountain of forms on a desk and collapsed into a chair.
"Toltattler wants the serial numbers of all the bullets we fired at the Rodolfo."
The last few words of his sentence became muffled as his face slumped into his hands. Frank removed his raincoat from the back of his chair.
"I've got to be somewhere, back at two." he said.

Before he left, Frank grabbed a half bottle of Scotch and put it next to Rosch.

As his car crept onto the North Circular, Frank pondered how little effect an imminent alien invasion was having on the amount of traffic in this part of North London. Further along the road, he saw signs that the great sham was already in full swing. He saw a large billboard displaying a group of students playing hacky sack with an alien called 'the High Buddy Liaison'. The slogan read 'LSE welcomes the Visitors.' Frank smirked as he contemplated the forthcoming game. Why would the Reticulants show their hand now? Or even at all? They must be on the back foot somehow, which means there is a weakness, somewhere. As he pulled off the dual carriageway and out of the impacted hell of the North Circular, Frank put those thoughts aside as he had something vital to take care of first.

12:44pm
The Roswell Tiki Bar, Burnt Oak

The large chrome sign of the Roswell Tiki Bar sparkled in the sunshine as Frank pulled into the car park. Frank rubbed his hands with excitement as he hurried up the steps of the second-floor and third-rate cocktail establishment. Sitting back away from the street, the large reflective windows of the bar commanded a great view of the glistening skyscrapers of the Burnt Oak business district. Decked out in red and chrome, the Roswell Tiki Bar was reminiscent of a 1950's diner that had been redesigned by a psychedelic Gyles Brandreth.

Frank opened the door and stepped inside, as he approached the bar, he passed a handful of patrons including a gentleman, sat with his back to him, wearing a bright green bomber jacket and a big blue curly wig. Frank smiled and drummed gently on the bar top next to a sign reading

'Tuesday Lunch Deal 2 - 4 - 1 Caipirinhas.' as a bartender approached.
"Four caipirinhas please." said Frank.
"Is that two and two?" asked the bartender.
"Four and Four." said Frank, beginning to grow slightly impatient.
"Nice." said the bartender, smiling, "What are you celebrating?"
Frank became puzzled.
"...Two for one caipirinhas." he said.
"Oh." replied the bartender.

In the far corner of the bar, a large television rolled out 24 hr news coverage and Olympic dogging. At this moment, the screen showed flashing cameras as Caroline Ahem gave a series of press conferences regarding the Visitors. Far away and totally disinterested, Frank sat at a table with a tray of eight caipirinhas. This had been one of his favourite drinks ever since he attended a barbecue with a group of Brazilian barbacks. The ever-deadly tango between lime and sugar provided a fat bottom end and the perfect seasoning with which to celebrate cachaca. The sugar cane distillate that carried caramel and nutty notes and filled the soul with pure Samba. Frank was gazing adoringly at the eight frosty beauties in front of him when the man in the bright green bomber jacket and curly wig, tore off his wig and leapt to his feet.
"Alright, this is now a hostage situation! Everyone remain calm!"
Frank rolled his eyes in gravest disappointment and slurped his first caipirinha.

1:15pm
Councilwoman Caroline Ahem's Country Home

Light poured in through the tall windows that lined the long corridor that led to Ahem's study. The slight figure of her assistant Grace ran towards the study, the sunlight beating a steady rhythm as she passed each window. In her chaise lounge, Ahem was watching a nature documentary about an insect hive.

"It is not known why these ants allow the invaders to enter the hive. Scientists hypothesise it could be due to pheromones secreted by the invaders, the effects of a spore disorienting them or simply, they are c****s."

Grace stood gasping for breath in the doorway.
"You might want to see channel two, ma'am." she said.
"Sure, why not, sounds fantastic." drawled Ahem, lazily.
Grace turned toward the big screen and put on her best, deepest, Spanish voice.
"Channel dos."

The television switched to channel two, revealing a breaking story on C.U.N News. The reporter was Miss Shagney Kluft. Kluft was born in South Korea, raised in Los Angeles and had relocated to London many years ago. In her 20's, she had adroitly negotiated the politics and the misogyny of the L.A news circuit and become a veteran, but as she entered her 30's, things were changing and one too many fistfights with one too many editors had her bound for the UK.

"...just moments ago," she said, "a currently serving new old Bailey judge, Duane Pegg, fled mid-trial this afternoon and has seized control of here, the Roswell Tiki Bar. Taking at least five people hostage, it is believed that the incident is in response to the arrival of the intergalactic visitors."

1:18pm
The Roswell Tiki Bar

Revolver in hand, Judge Duane Pegg paced along the windows of the Tiki Bar, surveying the gathering of press and police outside.
"More. Needs to be more." he said to himself.

With a caipirinha in each hand, Frank slowly approached Pegg.

"Take it easy there, friend." said Frank.

Pegg instantly turned his gun on Frank.

"That's it." said Frank. "Just keep it on me. If we talk, we have a much better chance of getting out of here alive."

"Oh, I'll talk," said Pegg with a tremble in his voice, "and they're going to listen. I'll make them stop. I just want it to stop, like."

"Who?" said Frank, inching closer. "What, stop?"

"Ah man, they've been coming for years. They're pretending like they've only just turned up. Out of the bastard blue."

Frank stopped and looked at the man, desperate and fatigued.

"How many times have they taken you?" said Frank, quietly.

Pegg turned his tearful eyes on Frank.

"Lost count." he said. "But it's been roughly twice a week since I was fifteen."

"You see the white light, you feel paralysed," said Frank.

A flash of trauma tore its way through Pegg's mind and he cried in anguish.

"It became routine. I wanted to speak," he said, "but anyone who would listen would just think I was nuts."

Pegg turned back towards the window.

"But this?! This is too far." he said, indignantly. "They're just taking the piss now like!"

"And you just want to be heard right?" said Frank calmly. "Why don't we see if we can make that happen."

1:24pm
Sandalhoof's Golf and Country Club

Over a hill of gently undulating, pristine greenery, strode Chief Commissioner of Police Rudolph Leathers, accompanied by his vinegary lackey Renfield. Sandalhoof's

was, by a country mile, the most revered country club in the country. It was an institution so exclusive that at least a quarter of the caddies employed were technically oil barons. Renfield carried in his arms the full complement required for a full eighteen holes, which for Leathers was a trumpet, a trombone, an oboe and a variety of smaller woodwind instruments. Leathers came to a stop. He took a moment to feel the wind on his face and appraised the hole.
"Oboe." he said.
Renfield handed him the oboe and Leathers lay down a few feet away from the bright white ball. After a moment, Leathers blew an almighty toot, however, the ball remained motionless. Leathers rose to his feet and solemnly traded the oboe for the trombone. Just then, a phone attached to Renfield's backpack rang loudly. Leathers checked the screen and answered.
"Councilwoman. Lovely day." he beamed.
"Leathers? This is a situation." she bellowed. "It's game time with the visitors and we are zero tolerance on negative press. I want Rosch to be assigned as main negotiator for the Roswell Tiki thing and get it done now."
The phone went dead. Leathers replaced the receiver and relayed the order to Renfield.
"She says get Kunnypacken to negotiate the Tiki Tiki."
Renfield nodded and began texting. Leathers lay down once again with the trombone and blew a long raunchy parp.

**1:55pm
The Roswell Tiki Bar Car Park**

To a chorus of Chewbacca impressions and lightsaber noises, Rosch approached the police cordon wearing a flak jacket denoting him as the 'main negotiator'.
"Use the force, Lando!" yelled an officer preceding a dozen high fives from her colleagues.
As he stepped through the barrier, Rosch was all too aware of this situation's potential to go full 'Hindenburg'. He

pondered what handling a hostage situation correctly could do for his career. But mostly he feared the less than perfect track record of the four snipers on neighbouring rooftops and the three dozen police, all with automatic weapons trained on the cocktail bar, especially since he considered them all, total arseholes. Rosch stood in front of the bar and raised his megaphone.
"This is assistant detective Rosch Kunnypacken. I'd like to talk to you, and maybe see if we can solve this thing without anyone getting hurt. What do you think?"
Inside, Frank was adding a lime wedge garnish to another caipirinha when he recognized the voice.
"Lando."
Pegg parted the blinds with his revolver and peered outside before turning to Frank.
"You. Come here."
Frank calmly acquiesced and approached. Pegg carefully placed the gun against Frank's head and led him outside onto the balcony. Down below, Rosch raised his megaphone once again.
"Ruggerman? What the hell are you doing here!?"
"Two for one caipirinhas." said Frank. "I left the gun in the car." he said, shrugging.
"Jesus Christ." said Rosch, mournfully.
"Wait a second. You're police and that?" said Pegg, cocking his revolver.
"Yes, I am," said Frank, "but you can hand on heart trust me that I hate these alien bastards just as much as you. I know this whole 'Visitors from the Stars' thing is bullshit."
Pegg thought carefully.
Frank continued, "I know dozens of people who have experienced what you have. The abductions, the levitation…the experiments."
Pegg dragged Frank back inside and began to sob. Once inside, the pair noticed a pungent aroma.
"Oh, Jesus what's that?" said Pegg.
It was then that Mark Ostrich, a telemarketer, who was amongst the five hostages, spoke.

"Yeah, apologies old spice but I appear to have wet myself in terror."

Frank turned to Pegg.

"It's going to get a lot tangier in here before too long." said Frank, sipping his caipirinha.

Pegg's mind was racing as he tried to review his options.

"Look, you've got me" said Frank, "and I've got a vested interest in getting your message out there. Why not let this lot go?"

Pegg trained his gun on Frank.

"No, you look mate. You seem a canny chap but don't forget I'm in charge here. Don't push us."

Frank raised his hands slowly, "I am with the program." he said.

"I want everyone in the middle of the room here. Come on get gan." ordered Pegg, directing the hostages with his revolver. He signalled to Frank, "You, take the bunting down from the bar and use it to tie 'em up."

Outside, Rosch tried once again to appeal to his suspect.

"Judge Pegg, it's me again. I just want you to remember I can't help you if you don't speak to me."

Pegg took a moment and looked across the faces of the hostages.

"All right! I'm ganna let some of these go, as a gesture of good will like! Don't take the piss though! I'm livid enough to make furniture out the lot of 'em."

"Understood, your honour." said Rosch, "We are ready when you are."

Pegg turned to Frank.

"Untie the pisser and the old girl. The rest of you are staying here."

Once free, the kind, elderly lady, known locally as 'Snakebite Ethel', gingerly assisted Mark Ostrich, most recently dubbed, 'the pisser', through the door and down the stairs. At the bottom of the staircase, they were greeted by officers in body armour and outbreaks of tepid applause.

As the two recently liberated hostages were stuffed into a police wagon, Rosch addressed Pegg.
"Judge Pegg. I think what you just did, tells me a lot about what kind of man you are. And I think that it's someone, who can be trusted, who doesn't want to see innocent people suffer."
"Ah I'm growing quite weary of this public school twatter." said Pegg.
Frank carefully approached Pegg.
"I know him," he said, "he's my partner. He's a complete tit but he's genuine. Look, can I speak with him?"
"Ah I dunno." said Pegg, forebodingly.
"Just two seconds." said Frank, "I'll bring him up to speed and calm that lot outside down enough to make sure they don't try anything stupid like come in guns blazing. What do you think?"
"All right." said Pegg, "But I'm coming with you. All nice and easy movements now."
With their bodies so close it could be called spooning, Pegg and Frank shuffled out onto the balcony cueing the bristling of automatic weapon mechanisms. With a gun to his head, Frank began.
"Alright listen. Firstly, there are four hostages left, including me, everyone's unharmed. Second. This man's actions are due to our government's part in a global conspiracy regarding the presence of extra-terrestrial creatures. They are claiming to have just arrived on our planet when in fact they've been coming here since the 1930's."

Meanwhile, in her study, Caroline Ahem was painting a portrait of herself on safari when her assistant Grace once again appeared breathless in her doorway.
"Ma'am, Detective Ruggerman is one of the hostages."
Grace flinched at the sound of a snapping paintbrush.
Then, Ahem spoke, with a voice resembling an avalanche with gritted teeth.
"Get...me Leathers."

2:32pm
Sandalhoof's Golf and Country Club

Amidst the flurries of toots and parps occurring at his feet, Renfield almost didn't hear the phone ringing. He answered, shielding his eyes from the bright sun.
"Hello?"
"Leathers! The bed is being shat as we speak, you are to get Rosch inside that situation immediately, with no more bellowing every word in front of the world's fucking cameras!"
An ear-piercing crack and the phone went dead.
"Okay then." said Renfield stoically. Seeing that his superior was still in the thick of his 'golf game', Renfield took matters into his own hands and began typing on his phone.
Back at the Roswell Tiki Bar, Rosch received a text.

'YOU MUST GET INSIDE IMMEDIATELY AND SHUT RUGGERMAN UP!'

Meanwhile, Frank continued his address. "This man, Judge Duane Pegg, is one of hundreds of people abducted by the Reticulants on a regular basis."
Rosch looked up at the balcony and realised that a catastrophic farce today was better than a disastrous shitstorm tomorrow, or something to that effect. Rosch attempted to corral his thoughts. "Uhm?" he said hopefully.

Frank continued. "Experimented on, abused, humiliated. Sleepless nights, living in fear. Tormented, like someone on a bad Tinder date, because...you never knew when they'd come."
"Ruggerman, do you think maybe we could…"
"Those brave enough to confide in their loved ones, were dismissed as crack heads."

Rosch accidentally triggered a blast of siren from his megaphone, before apologising via a din of feedback.
"Sorry, I'm sorry," said Rosch. "Uhm I-"
"Oh, for fucks sake Lando what!?" roared Frank.
"Listen, I can only imagine what that kind of trauma does to a person. But I want to know. I want to come inside." said Rosch, removing his vest and weapon. "Look. I'm unarmed, no tricks. I'll enter nice and easy."
While Pegg recoiled slightly at his choice of words, Frank placed a comforting hand on Pegg's shoulder.
"Like I said. He's a tit, but he's on the level. His aunty's a top councilwoman as well, he'll be a good bargaining chip, if it comes to it."
Pegg's eyes danced distantly with Frank's while he pondered.
"All right!" he barked, "Just you! Any other funny business and I start gardening!"

Rosch attempted to centre himself as he began walking towards the fray. The surrounding officers looked on with wowed expressions before they collectively opened the stakes, 'Star Wars Kid dead within 5 mins', steadying at 3 - 1.

Up the stairs and slowly into the doorway, with his hands raised, Rosch's mind was surprisingly clear, abject terror can do this sometimes. Pegg frisked Rosch and directed him to a chair away from the other hostages.
"Is everyone okay?" asked Rosch.
The three hostages, who included the bartender, a builder called Samson and a librarian named Olivia, all gave gestures indicating in the vein of 'not too bad' and 'can't complain really.'
"What are the SWAT team's orders?" asked Frank.
"They've just been ordered to hold. Until…" Rosch paused, "I… tell them to do… possibly something else."
"You?" Frank scoffed.
"Yes." retorted Rosch, with paper-thin confidence.

"Good old Aunty Caroline." smirked Frank.
Just then, the hostage Olivia, managed to sneak her phone from her pocket unnoticed. She carefully began typing a post on Twittlechat that read:

'I'M HERE AT THE ROSWELL TIKI BAR!! WE ARE OKAY. THERE ARE TWO POLICE IN HERE. ONE IS DEFS ALCOHOLIC.'

The screen flashed a tick and she returned her phone to her pocket.
Pegg paced anxiously by the window.
"Argh, I don't understand it," he said, "there should be more press here."
"It's precisely like you say," said Frank, pouring cachaca into four glasses, "they're protecting the charade."
"Bastards." said Pegg.
"I think it better," ventured Rosch, nervously, "maybe more productive if we focus on the situation at hand?"
Frank immediately sensed the tone of the room turn drastic and Pegg marched over to Rosch and put the barrel of his revolver against Rosch's temple.
"Do you think I'm here for a fucking leaving do? This *IS* the bastard situation at hand!"
Pegg's hand trembled as Rosch and the hostages became trapped in an extended flinch, beads of sweat descending on brows froze solid.
"What's the earliest time they came that you remember?" said Frank, gently.
After an excruciating pause.
"Well, you see, that's a bit complicated like." said Pegg, sitting on a chair. "Cos' I've only got full recollection of the ones that come later, the early ones I must've blacked 'em out, you know with the trauma and that."
Olivia covertly began another post.

"THE MAN IS A TOTAL NUTTER!.'

Frank lit a cigarette and offered one to Pegg.
"Who have you told about the experiments?" he said, sharing his lighter.
"Ah you're joking man." said Pegg, exhaling and scratching his nose with his revolver, "A magistrates court judge talking about being abducted by outer space men. One of the first times I remember like, I was strapped to a bed. They were injecting us with summat. They put me foot in porridge. I could just about see… they was all around us. Holding handfuls of what looked like money. They did such awful, awful things to us."
Pegg closed his eyes as he relived the sensation of being strapped to a table in a dark room. He recoiled as the memory of that alien finger, dripping with saliva, slowly poked into his ear.
"Aww don't man." he said, repulsed.

   As the judge recounted his ordeal, these hostages, who were all total strangers, looked into his vulnerable face and Olivia began to delete the post she was writing.
"I remember, for a while," said Pegg, "it felt like they was investigating us. Testing us, you know for weaknesses and that. But later on, it was like they had run out of ideas and... they were trying anything. Once they made us wear these cling film pants, and forced us to parade around the room, and then these others, were pelting us with little balls of sage and onion stuffing."
The hostages each closed their eyes as they tried to imagine the poor man's suffering.
Olivia began a new post.

'I CAN'T HELP BUT FEEL FOR THIS POOR MAN!
THEY PELTED HIM WITH STUFFING! :(
#SORRY4PEGG

The screen flashed a bright tick.

3:16pm
Caroline Ahem's Country Home

Grace appeared, once again in the doorway bearing her mobile phone and a look of sheer dread.
"Uhm, Ma'am, one of the hostages is posting on *Twittlechat* from inside."
"Good." said Ahem, smiling thoughtfully. "A human being's final thoughts, broadcasted live on the internet. Afraid, lost, wretched, a speck in the face of a universe where there is only futility. God, I love social media."
"Actually, they are quite sympathetic." said Grace.
"What?" said Ahem, her tone suddenly crocodilian.
"It seems the hostages feel...sympathetic."
"What's the response?" said Ahem.
"The post has been liked and shared by...a presenter."
"...Who?"
"...Presenter, naturist and sex goddess Michaela Strachan."
Ahem roared and sent her easel flying across the room.
"Patch me through direct to Rosch's comm link!" Ahem snarled, "And get me Oprah!"

Roswell Tiki Bar

Meanwhile, the remaining patrons and staff sat calmly, as the old man continued his account.
"I mean," said Pegg, "I fail to see the scientific merit of seeing what happens when you finger someone with a Toblerone."
Suddenly, a fizz of static shrieked in Rosch's earpiece.
"Rosch darling, Aunty Caroline. Don't speak, I know you can hear me. Look, I know you've done your best but I feel you need a little nudge along so listen close. Leathers has given the SWAT team the all-clear to engage in the next five minutes."
Rosch coughed to disguise his fervent protesting.
"Lando, please." said Frank, disappointingly.

"Five minutes honey and the boys are coming in. You need to get back outside and calm the whole thing down. Speak to the troops, update the press. The silence makes em' all... antsy."

Over by the hostages, Pegg continued.

"-and to think, they've got the nerve to pretend, to the whole world, that these bastards have just now showed up and they're our new BF-fuckin'-F's."

Rosch looked across the faces of the hostages as they listened to Pegg, and saw only sympathy, as he did so, his aunty piped up again on his earpiece.

"Don't be fooled, Rosch darling. Pegg is a deeply troubled, sad man, suffering with terrible paranoid delusions."

In her study, Ahem picked up and pretended to read a pack of peanut *M&M's*.

"I have here a copy of his prescription medication." she said. "Hydrocallaroxipine, *Lemsip*, fornacaphanol and max-strength Randy Quaaludes, honey this is a deeply troubled man."

Rosch felt his instincts slowly sliding back to where they felt more comfortable, gently pushed back down to Earth by his aunty's reasoning.

"He needs to be taken to a secure facility, where he can be cared for. First of all, Rosch, you have to put a pin in Ruggerman or he'll keep encouraging this poor man's torment."

Try as he might, Rosch could still not shake the looks of sympathy in the faces of the hostages.

"Now is there anything Ruggerman has told you that might indicate a personal hatred he has for our visitors?"

This question however did bring Rosch crashing into this dimension. His mind drifted back to a few nights prior, when he and Frank were sitting in a booth of a local pub, The Dog and Hotpot.

In the middle of the table were a dozen empty pints and a bottle of whisky with the optic and part of the wooden frame still attached. Rosch finished a pint and spoke.

"I take it you never married. Is there a reason for that other than that you're an arsehole?"

"I came close once, wanker." said Frank earnestly, "Beatrice her name was. Had this lovely, chocolate hair...really kind. We were together for years, we were happy, for the most part, I think. Still, the job got in the way like it always does. It wasn't long before the feelings of something not quite right became too loud to ignore and the whole thing fell apart."

"So, what happened?" said Rosch, failing to attract the attention of a waiter.

"The fights had become more frequent." said Frank. "Then it reached a stage where, when I could be home, she'd always be busy with friends or working. It was like she would find any excuse not to be with me. I kept finding weird things in the house, little signs here and there. A few nights later they came for her... I never saw her again."

"She left you?" said Rosch.

"Yep." said Frank, sipping a pint of Scotch.

"All that shit you give me for killing an Ewok and your Mrs ran off with an alien? You've got some stones 'ergh'!" At that point, Frank had reached under the table and seized Rosch vengefully by the testicles.

"Yes, I do Ja Ja." said Frank, coldly. "Now you listen and you listen good cos if I hear one crack about Mac & my wife, anal probing or *E.T's* Magic finger then I will crush the life out of you, are we clear?"

"Crystal." whispered Rosch, dribbling saliva onto the table.

   Rosch was lamenting his still dangerously brittle testicles when his aunty spoke.

"Rosch darling, the clock is ticking. Two minutes until the swat team get on the goodfoot, now do me proud... Ah! Oprah darling! Listen up-"

Rosch's earpiece fell silent at last, and he internally mopped up the last few pockets of resistance regarding his

career prospects and returned his attention to the scene. Frank was now also sharing accounts of alien shenanigans.
"-and inflate your arse as big as it'll go." he said.
"Aye, that's right." agreed Pegg, "And what's more, is they'll blindfold you, and ride you round the track."
Encouraged by the fact that he thought his logic circuits were about to melt, Rosch decided to step in.
"I think maybe I should…update… everyone." he said, "You know, give them an.update. Chill them out. I can speak to the press. Give them your side… of things."
"Ah, for fucks sake, man you're useless." said Pegg, "I've been wanting to get rid of you since you sat down. You're like a fart in a sauna."
In response, Frank mimed a gesture to Pegg by placing one hand flat on top of the other.
"Tit, level." he said.
"Ah what's the use." said Pegg, "There's never any changing owt is there? Go on get gan. And you three too. Let's get you back to your families."
Frank untied the hostages and they had begun to leave when Olivia approached Pegg.
"I hope you don't mind," she said kindly, "but I Twittlechatted a post earlier, saying that I felt for you, for your pain and stuff. It's getting some nice momentum. Look, it's been liked by Michaela Strachan, and she's amazing."
"Ah, bless you, pet. All of you, have been great. Very understanding. We'll see what happens though eh? Go on, now get gan."
With that, Rosch and the hostages headed toward the exit and Pegg turned to Frank.
"Excuse me mate." he said.
Frank slurped his caipirinha, pretending not to notice the man's immense vulnerability.
"Will you… stay with us?" asked Pegg.
"Absolutely." said Frank.
Just then, Rosch was the last to exit the door.
"Oi Lando." said Frank, "You're doing the right thing."

Rosch then left, saying nothing.
"Right." said Frank, rubbing his hands and heading behind the bar.
Pegg turned on the TV to see what the coverage was saying. Just outside, reporter Shagney Kluft was live.
"In a miraculous turn of events," she said, "it appears three of the hostages have been released thanks to detective-" Kluft paused and touched her earpiece, "Sorry, *assistant* detective Rosch Kunnypacken of the Western Tactical Unit."

   As the hostages were met with silver foil blankets, gingerly escorted away and then forced into Police vans, Kluft approached Rosch for an interview.
Inside, Pegg watched intently whilst Frank was enjoying the smell of fresh limes.
"Assistant detective Kunnypacken, what can you tell us about the current status of the situation?"
"It's still potentially volatile, detective Ruggerman is now alone with Pegg, but the hostages are now clear so…"
"And what of Pegg's state of mind?"
Rosch hesitated, just shy of the precipice and then tumbled over it.
"Pegg is a deeply troubled individual-" he began.
Inside, Frank stopped dead, listening to his partner's account.
"He has a long history of paranoid delusion; he is on a long list of medications-"
"And what of your partner? Detective Ruggerman?"
Rosch had jumped in and now could only swim.
"He's a long serving, highly experienced police officer…but he too suffered a mental breakdown caused by a traumatic end to a long relationship. It affected him very deeply, and it may contribute to irrational feelings of animosity towards our…visitors."
"So, there you have it." said Kluft. "With the world welcoming our first contact with visitors from another

planet, it seems some of us are finding it a tough pill to swallow. This is, Shagney Kluft-."
Pegg muted the television and stood in a state of existential collapse.
"For fucks sake!" roared Frank as he launched a bottle of cachaca across the room. His rage then turned inwards as he experienced the worst kind of disappointment, the kind that you should have seen coming and the possibility that that was the last of the cachaca.
"I guess the bed's truly shat now." said Pegg, "Better just lock us up like."
"Fucking Lando." spat Frank.
"Ah mate there's no use getting further twisted up about it all. I've said my piece and most folks don't even get the chance to do that."
"Your Honour. I know it all looks dark now, you're exhausted and we got sold out by a... poundshop Niles Crane. We're going to have to take you in, but I promise you hand on heart I'm not giving in until we blast this whole charade wide open. And I need your help to do it."

Frank remained steady as a tear rolled down the cheek of the old man, following the contours of the man's face as he birthed a smile.

Rosch arrived at his car, unaware that someone had written 'Uber-Wanker-Noobie!' in police tape on the passenger side. He opened the door and sat heavily, wincing immediately as his still tender testicles screamed in protest. Just then, his aunty came through once again on his earpiece.
"Rosch?! Rosch darling, congratulations," cheered Ahem, "you wobbled out the gates but came home in style. I'm proud of you darling."
Rosch removed his earpiece and started the car.
In her study, Ahem received another update from her assistant.
"#SORRY4PEGG just got picked up by Chris Packham and Ray Mears." she said.

A cold glaze came over Ahem's ordinarily leisurely face, this was going to get out of control, without her doing something...decisive. She reached for her phone and searched her text messages for a name: REYKA
She then casually wrote a text, pressed send and sipped a Manhattan.

The Lucky Orphan Restaurant, Chinatown

The reviews said that the duck in plum was to die for but at that moment, the action at the Lucky Orphan was happening in the rear. Away from the diners, a dusty and sweaty room was packed with people shouting, waving handfuls of cash in primal excitement. In the middle was a circle with sawdust stained by the blood of decades of animal brutality. An elderly man in black shouted and pushed the crowd back, creating a bigger space and revealing two opposing wooden boxes. The old man cried an ancient command and the room fell silent. The spectators waited, their eyes ablaze with anticipation. The old man cried again and the doors to both boxes fell open. From each box emerged a rockhopper penguin, honking buoyantly and gently rocking from side to side. The crowd erupted into a savage frenzy, money exchanged hands and fights broke out as the penguins honked and pottered jubilantly around the floor. Standing at the back of the room, smoking a cigarette, was Reyka. He reached into his pocket and removed his phone, finding a text from Caroline Ahem.

#SORRY4PEGG IS BEING PICKED UP BY TROUBLEMAKERS. END IT NOW.

Amidst the frenzied crowd, Reyka stepped on the end of his cigarette and made a phone call.

Roswell Tiki Bar

"Prison's not too bad for judges, to be honest." said Frank, placing the last of the bottles from the back bar into a sports bag.
"You know mate…" said Pegg.
"Frank." said the detective, warmly.
"Nah, it's Duane. Anyways mate, I wanted to thank you, for staying with us like. I didn't mean to hurt anyone. I was just so desperate, I let my anger get the better of us."
"You're right to be angry after what they did to you." said Frank.
"Aye. But I never wanted hurting anyone on my conscience, on top of my other woes. But now, thanks to you mate, I feel ready to face whatever comes next."
Thwip
A thirty-eight-calibre bullet passed through the glass window and through Pegg's jugular. He collapsed instantly, clutching his neck and gasping for breath. Outside, Shagney Kluft was frantically delivering her update.
"Shots have been fired, I can only assume that Detective Ruggerman, the last remaining officer inside was in danger or has lost control of the situation-"
"Pegg!" roared Frank as he rushed to the old man's side, quickly applying pressure with a bar towel.
"Ah mate, they've binned us." wheezed Pegg.
"Hold on your Honour." said Frank, covering Pegg with the remaining towels.
Pegg coughed, spraying dark red blood onto his face and chest.
"Ah mate, give over, I'm knackered. I'd rather it end here than face another Toblerone up my arse."
"Don't you fucking dare," barked Frank. "I need you to crack this whole thing. Pegg, listen to me."
The blood was flooding into the bar towel at roughly the same speed the life was leaving his body.
"My phone." croaked Pegg.

Frank, now soaked in blood, removed the old man's phone from his pocket.

"Hashtag mate." wheezed Pegg. "It's all about...mm-mm-Michaela."

"Pegg? Come on now, mate." said Frank.

Frank held the old man and called for the ambulance team. Then he felt the last whisper of Pegg's life leave the venue.

In her study, Ahem received a text.

'IT'S DONE.'

EPISODE VI

Thursday
8:36pm
Southend, Boardwalk

Even with the night air still moist from the earlier rain, the beach front at Southend was lively. Shirtless 'lads on tour' weaved smoothly between couples strolling the promenade and families eating candy floss. Raindrops fell from brightly painted awnings and pooled on the wooden decking. In the black pools of water, lay shimmering portraits of the bright neon lights. Screams of excitement commingled with sirens and the cacophony of the attractions. In the window of a shop called Alf's Darts and Nougat, a television displayed C.U.N News reporter Shagney Kluft, delivering her latest.

"The call for an investigation into the death of judge Duane Pegg, two weeks ago at the Roswell Tiki Bar, has been quashed today. Earlier, we spoke to the personal trainer of the sniper in question, officer Jeffrey Dushone, who gave us this dictated statement."
"*It's simple. The hostage was in danger, pishew! I took him out. Who cares anyway he was a nutter.*"
"Honey please!" said a little man, shuffling with excitement a few steps away from the shop window. "We can watch the news at home! I want to play the games!"

Upon hearing these words, Gloria, a towering and glamorous woman, diverted her attention away from the shop window and towards her love. She saw in his face the same innocence and vulnerability that had inspired the romance of her life. She took his hand and they strolled along the promenade, revelling in the whizzing, sparkling rides and attractions. The slight, petite man nearly burst with excitement upon seeing his favourite game, *'Slap the Mackerel'*. He looked up into the amazon's broad face and she smiled with a love from the bottom of the Mariana Trench. Gloria handed the attendant two pounds from her buffalo skin pouch. The attendant smiled shyly and cowed his head as, with the hair, Gloria stood at an impressive 7' 2". Emphasised by make up, her eyes shone like emeralds and her shoulders suggested a being of phenomenal physical strength. The attendant wisely kept his observations about the apparent mismatch of the couple to himself. Gloria beamed as her darling honked with delight, slapping his hands all over the five-ounce mackerel. She adored him. In previous lives, she had harvested thousands of souls across the battlefields of time, but when her eyes first met his, she became consumed with a burning desire to cherish, protect and ravish him, forever.

A while later, Gloria led her love up the hill, away from the bright lights of the boardwalk and into the vast pine woods that shrouded Southend from the inland. Beneath a large fir, she turned to drink in the view of the buzzing seaside town. Smiling, the little man unzipped his fly. Gloria's smile vanished suddenly, her demeanour changed to that of a tiger in the long grass.
"What is it honey?" enquired the little man.
Gloria stepped in front of him and stared into the dense forest with absolute poise. Suddenly, from the thicket to her left, a strong, hairy limb reached out of the darkness and grabbed hold of her arm. In a deep, commanding voice, she spoke;
"Run Antonio!"

With that, the little man shrieked and ran back down the hill. From the dark thicket leapt a large, feral creature, tall and covered in thick, black, matted hair. Gloria fell under the weight of the beast but swiftly used the momentum to roll him off. With a roar she rained repeated elbows onto the face of the beast. The beast however was also immensely strong, he thrust a powerful, hairy forearm into her middle and sent her reeling. In a flash she was back on her feet, the beast lunged for her and they were locked in a desperate wrestle.

At the bottom of the hill, Antonio had reached the road and was running for his life when a terrible and muscular scream stopped him dead in his tracks. The little man looked back. Then with his eyes flooded with tears, he turned and ran back towards town. Back up on the hill, the feral creature anxiously examined the face of the now still Gloria. Her lifeless eyes, wide open in frozen oblivion. The beast reared his head and howled in deepest anguish.

2:31am
London, Stockwell

Stockwell was a particularly ill-fated borough of London. The green park areas had been decimated by rabbits and international money had converted both the foodbank and the hospice into luxury flats. It was here, down a dark, dank alley, that security expert Nathan Olsen was hunting an exceptional target. Two streets over, Hansen Olsen was also searching, carrying a large rifle, fitted with darts containing a powerful tranquilliser. Carefully, Hansen stepped over an abandoned canoe and shone his torch down the side street next to *'the Hot Calippo'*, a former strip club. Hansen pressed his walkie talkie.
"Chris. Anything?" he said.
Sitting back on the main road was the Olsens' Winnebago. Inside, Chris Olsen was observing a bank of monitors and enjoying a varied selection of salted treats.
"Nothing on the infra-red," he said, "or the dog-cam. Bessie's not having the best night I don't think."
Chris watched the feed from the terrier mounted camera and after observing what he believed was his limit on other dog's anuses, he turned off the monitor.

"Nathan, anything on the motion tracker?" said Chris.

"Not a dot." said Nathan. "God damn, it's like looking for a needle in a haystack, only if the needle is...incredibly pissed."

Nathan and Hansen exchanged foreboding nods as their paths converged between two buildings of the old steel works. Suddenly, a blip pinged into existence on the motion tracker.

"Wait, I think we got something." said Chris, wiping his hands on his '*Dungeons & Drag-Artists*' tee shirt.

Nathan and Hansen heard a crash and the sound of scrambling up above.

"The walkway, up above you!" yelled Chris over the walkie talkie.

At that moment, the Olsens saw their target, a panicked and rampaging Frank Ruggerman, scampering across the rooftops and fire-escapes.

"Oh, god, he's naked." said Nathan, ruefully.

"What did you expect?" said Hansen, stoically. "Come on, let's move"

Inside the Winnebago.

"Don't lose him!" said Chris. "He's making a break for it!"

"Frank!" yelled Nathan.

Frank's naked form leapt from the fire-escape, landed in a large wheelie-bin and then vaulted over the wall and into the park. Nathan raced around the corner and through the entrance. The swings, slides and other monuments of the play area stood frozen in the moonlight. Nathan slowly passed the light of his torch across the structures. Hansen joined from the opposite side, his rifle raised.

"You should get a clear shot as you come round the silly-slide." said Chris.

"Copy that." said Hansen, under his breath, as he stalked his friend.

At that moment.

"I got him." called Nathan.

Hansen, doubled back on himself and joined Nathan as he stood, watching the naked Frank, rock backwards and forwards on a spring-mounted butterfly. Hansen lowered his rifle as he observed his friend in a state of deep, nihilistic oblivion. The two stood a moment and observed a man, distraught, smashed and involved in an unprecedented level of self-destruction.

"I think you better still..." reminded Nathan.

"Oh right, yeah." said Hansen, casually raising his rifle and firing a dart into Frank's back. With a groan and a gurgle, Frank quickly lost consciousness and slumped onto the floor.

7:45am
London Met HQ

Two weeks had passed since the arrival of the Visitors and the Roswell Tiki incident. Rosch made his way across the floor of the Met reception, headed for Leathers' office. All around him he saw features of the new normal. A charming, young man was about to lead a group of Reticulant tourists on a tour of the Met. Rosch saw the young man's attractive and earnest face, smiling as he oriented the eight to ten strong group of petite, grey, wrinkly aliens. The Reticulants, adorned in Hawaiian shirts, straw hats and bizarre looking devices which Rosch assumed were cameras, milled about with varying degrees of enthusiasm at the prospect of the tour.

On the other side of the entrance, Rosch saw some of the new Reticulant recruits being drafted into the police force. The traditional Met Constabulary uniform had been tailored to fit the four-foot bodies and large cranial circumference of the Reticulant form. Having successfully completed the three-day induction, these recruits from another planet smiled and blinked their large black eyes as they were handed badges and firearms. The human training officer mimed something to the effect of 'Okay you're all set, have fun.' and the group of uniformed aliens cheered, bundled together and ran off into the street. Rosch's mind may not have been able to fully understand what was going on around him, but what he did know, aside from sporadic acts of wanton vandalism, Frank had all but disappeared from the force and that life for Rosch these days was generally smoother, provided he didn't think too much.

Upstairs, Rosch reached Leather's office, knocked and entered. Inside, he found Chief Leathers dressed as an orchestra conductor and Reyka and Renfield gazing at Rosch with their usual malintent.
"Sir, Frank Ruggerman has-" began Rosch.
Immediately, Leathers' face took on a look of pure fury and he hammered his baton on a brass frame which was holding some sheet music. Then, Renfield, Leathers' vinegary minion shrieked.
"Kunnypacken how dare you march in here and start barking your problems at his Majesty!"
As Renfield brayed, Reyka lit another cigarette, standing in his usual spot by the window.
"Rosch," he said calmly, "we want to thank you for your exceptional service you've-"
With everyone talking over each other, Leathers fired a round from his revolver into his waste paper bin. With the room now silent, apart from everyone's tinnitus, Leathers gestured for Rosch to sit and begin.
"Sir, Frank Ruggerman has destroyed the office and my car, he is totally out of control-"
With a stroke of his baton, Leathers stopped Rosch, and directed Renfield to begin.
"Kunnypacken how dare you march in here and start barking-"
Leathers' baton whipped through the air, silencing Renfield. Leathers closed his eyes and tenderly directed Reyka to start.
"Rosch, we want to thank you for your exceptional service in this latest matter. Homo-reticulant relations are at a-"
"All due respect sir..." interrupted Rosch.

Leathers glared at Rosch for disregarding the conductor.
"...but I'm afraid I'm hoping you'll allow me to transfer."
"Transfer?!" barked Leathers.
Leathers stabbed his baton into his desk via Renfield's hand.
"Where to?" enquired Leathers, with effortless menace.
"Somewhere...else." said Rosch.
"Rosch this is a crucial time." soothed Reyka. "Your role in the Pegg fiasco has helped solidify our relations with the visitors and while detective Ruggerman is in such a...volatile state, we think it best you remain close to him."
"With respect sir," said Rosch, "he needs to be brought up on charges and dismissed."
"Young man," added Reyka, "what if I were to tell you we are making you, acting head of the Western Tactical?"
Rosch, quickly stepped over the fact that he was currently the only officer in the detail and dared to dream. His mind timidly appraised the implications of what was being said.
"My own department?" he said.
For the first time, Rosch felt somehow that clouds were parting, albeit in an insane set of circumstances.
"Well, at the moment it's just you and Chevy Chase but yes it'll be your own department." admitted Leathers.
With as close to a smile as Reyka's face could muster, Reyka spoke.
"Keep up the good work Rosch, it's working."
Rosch looked into the face of Reyka. Reyka was approaching his sixtieth year and rumour had it that in his previous gig with the C.I.A. he had proved invaluable in the United States' most insidious and despicable affairs. What was undeniable, was that Reyka carried himself with the manner of a man very comfortable with coups, assassinations and the ability to make life and death decisions about the lives of others with astonishing ease. Rosch's mind was flirting with the apparent darkness of the man, with whom he was now getting very comfortable in bed, when Leathers spoke.
"Well then good job man in charge there it is off you go good day."

The door to Leathers' office closed behind Rosch and he set off for the day's roll call.

London Met HQ, Roll Call

With the faintest whispers of hope beginning to colour Rosch's usual emotional state, he made his way down to the ground floor of the Met, along an empty corridor, through a doorway and into the flat-out bedlam, that was Roll Call.

Upon opening the door, Rosch was confronted with a large room, lined by glass partitions and an officer, who had somehow caught fire, leaping out of a window. Phones were ringing constantly, sheets of paper floated down from the ceiling and officers, both human and Reticulant, yelled and squabbled, impatiently waiting for their assignments. At the centre of it all was the aged, wiry form of former NYPD Captain Marge Kowalchik. Sporting a huge shock of wispy, grey hair and thick rimmed spectacles, Marge held court and distributed the details.
"Alright!" she barked. "We got a warrant for a Mrs Tatagglia, 84 year old housewife wanted for multiple D.U.I's and 2nd degree vandalism, she's a live one so you'll need the rhino mace, Parker, Tolstein, it's yours."
She slung a file across the room, hitting the wall and sending paper flying everywhere. Amid the chaos, Marge spotted Rosch and reached for a file from underneath the counter.
"Hey Chewie! I got yours right here buddy." she yelled, hurling a folder loosely in his direction.
"It's in Southend."
"Southend?" shouted Rosch, struggling to make himself heard over the hysteria. "But our jurisdiction? Don't they have police?"
"What is it Lando? I'm god damn busy here!" shouted Marge, immediately losing interest and returning to the task in hand "Alright, Walker aaaaand...Kazzalkeeorb."

A human female officer and a Reticulant officer looked up from a game of *Trivial Pursuit*.
"Mrs. Wachowski, 424, 26 and Threadneedle says the guy next door keeps moving her door mat. Will somebody answer the god-damn phone!?"
Rosch gathered up the last of the documents from the floor and went on his way back to the office.

The office looked like a tornado had passed through on a combine-harvester. Empty bottles were strewn everywhere and in huge letters, scrawled on the wall, a message read:
'TOFF CRAP LANDO JUDAS PISS!!!'

Rosch grabbed his jacket just as his phone received a text from the Olsen twins.

'WE FOUND HIM, YOU BETTER COME AND PICK HIM UP.'

9:18am
The Olsen Twins Winnebago

Upon a desolate piece of waste ground, sat the Olsen twins' Winnebago. Inside, at the rear, were makeshift bunk beds, upon which lay a distraught and barely conscious Frank Ruggerman. Dribbling, mumbling and nursing a bottle of whiskey, Frank writhed, his cheeks stained with tears. With Chris and Nathan standing over their fragile charge, Hansen appeared, replacing his phone into his pocket.
"Rosch says he'll be 20 minutes." said Hansen.
"What should we do?" asked Chris.
"Well," said Hansen, "he's had a Hogarthian amount of booze since yesterday. He's lost the use of his legs above the knee but judging by the state of his pants I'd say his kidneys are still functional."
Chris tried to reach for the bottle clasped in Frank's arms eliciting a fierce snarl.

"I think as long as we don't try and take the BOTTLE off him," warned Hansen, "he should stay calm until Rosch gets here."
Nathan gently placed a blanket on Frank.

As Rosch arrived in his replacement squad car, twenty or so metres from the Winnebago, he could see flames flickering up the side of the war-torn vehicle. Frank, who was now mobile, was fending off their attempts to subdue him with blankets by using a fire extinguisher. Rosch then observed the situation diffuse as Nathan managed to taser Frank into submission. Rosch exited the car and approached the trio of breathless security experts.
"We advise he keeps drinking." said Chris, nursing a broken nose.
"Jesus Christ." said Rosch, ruefully.
"Look after him Rosch," said Hansen, "he needs you now more than ever."
The Olsens assisted the paralytic and twitching Frank into the passenger seat of Rosch's car and tucked his legs in. Leaving the Olsens bruised but waving amiably, Rosch headed for Southend.

10:45am
Southend

The signpost signalling 'You are now entering Southend' stood at the edge of the dense pine forest that surrounded the little seaside town. They had come this far without incident and Rosch cracked the window and took a moment to smell the peculiar blend of mustiness and fresh growth. With a bottle still, clasped firmly in his arms, Frank began to stir.
"How are you feeling?" enquired Rosch, cocking his pistol.
Frank coughed, hefty, guttural expulsions, instantly gave up on figuring out where he was and removed the cap from his bottle.

"Anything from you and I put one in your leg." said Rosch, firmly.

With his eyes, slowly adjusting to his surroundings, Frank stretched and twisted, trying to get the kinks out.

"You." said Frank, dryly. "...I underestimated you."

"Oh, for Christ's sake, Ruggerman." Rosch implored.

"All this time," said Frank, peering out of the window, swigging his whiskey, "you were the ultimate company man, eyes on the prize. And here I was thinking you were just a... fucking twat."

"All right enough, Ruggerman."

"Pegg's dead. Sniper got him straight through the gullet, pishew."

"It was Leathers who put the snipers on code red." insisted Rosch. "They said the sniper thought you were in danger and-"

"Oh, piss off." scoffed Frank. "We were walking out. I was going to bring him in and see him looked after but you towed the party-line, gave the press what Leathers had shat out that morning and made him, and me look like dribbling tap jobs. Nobody cares if some headcase gets shot, what's one less loony for the public to worry about?"

"Look I'm sorry he's dead I really am, but he wasn't who you thought he was. He was dangerously unstable."

"Mehh."

"Did you see the list of meds he was on?" protested Rosch. "Antidepressants, mood stabilisers, antipsychotics... and that's just the Downey Jr. stuff."

"Well, you did your job," said Frank, "you served that horse shit to the press giving Leathers' private black and white gun-club the all clear to silence him and he's dead now and it's your fault."

"Wait, hold on," said Rosch, "it looks like we're here."

The car came to a stop next to a line of police tape and the Southend Sheriff's department were on hand. Four, portly officers in cowboy hats and khaki uniforms, peered contemptuously at the vehicle as Rosch exited and Frank staggered towards them.

"Okay what have you got for me Sodermine?" said Frank, collapsing in a ditch.

Rosch approached and spoke with the nearest officer.

"Officer... Piper?" he said.

"Yep?" said Piper.

"I'm Asst. Detective Rosch Kunnypacken with the Western Tactical Unit, London Met, I was hoping you can bring me up to speed."

After cautiously glancing at his colleagues, Piper relayed the situation.

"Young, out of town couple made their way through the woods after enjoying the funfair. Then something attacked them."

"Something?" said Rosch.

"Someone!" corrected Piper, quickly.

It was then that the hulking form of the man in charge appeared, a mountain of pure gristle, seasoned with tobacco and whiskey.

"This is clearly a case of tourists wandering off the beaten track and running into trouble with a vagrant...Howdy Mr. Kunnypacken, I'm Sheriff Lorenzo Baldenbach, welcome to Southend."

From beneath the far-reaching brim of his hat, he wore the smile of a Cheshire cat that had just been cleared of all charges in the case of the lost sausage rolls.

"Thank you." replied Rosch. "I have the initial report that was sent to my department. I'd like any updates from the latest forensics and I'd like to interview the witness."

"The witness is recuperating with his mother in a five star resort up in Blackpool." said the Sheriff. "They've requested to be left in peace so we're going to respect that."

"Well, I'm afraid," said Rosch, "my investigation requires interviewing the witness."

"Mr Kunnypacken, even a small-town sheriff like myself knows what you get up to there in the Western Tactical Unit. Now, I believe the nature of whose investigation this is, is still in dispute and without any evidence to make this case 'paranormal', it will remain a local case for local cops. I'm sorry but... there's nothing for you here."

Rosch looked to Officer Piper, who bowed his head, sheepishly.

"Yep," continued the plump sheriff, "as far as I can see it's another by the numbers case of tourists preyed on by a scumbag. Now, if you don't mind, we'd like to continue our investigation."

"I don't mean to sound impertinent, Sheriff," said Rosch, "but I was assured cooperation."

"Like I said, Mr. Kunnypacken, the matter of your jurisdiction here is still one of some discrepancy but saying that, I can allow you some limited access to the spartan resources of this office. Call my number anytime."

"Thank you, Sheriff." said Rosch, reluctantly.

With that, Rosch wrestled Frank to his feet and the two of them descended the hill towards the beachfront.

Progress was painfully slow, with Rosch carrying Frank, his arm draped around Rosch's neck. The beachfront was lined with fifty-three concrete bollards over which, the intoxicated Frank, insisted on stepping over each and every single one. Rosch tried to discourage this, insisting that 'time was wasting' and that 'they needed to press on.' but deviating from the bollards invariably cued a fistfight.

Along the promenade, Rosch carried Frank past the stalls and attractions, attempting to piece together what had happened the night before.

"It's a big bollocky mess is what it is!" roared Frank, in between a mixture of dry and not so dry heaves. In the file Rosch had been given, was a headshot photo of Gloria, the recently deceased Amazon. He went from stall to stall, wrestling to keep Frank upright and enquired if anyone recalled seeing the couple. Frequently, Frank would break away into the crowds, meaning Rosch would spend the next ten to thirty minutes searching for him.

Three hours later, a ladybird carousel was rotating slowly and the organ music droned on endlessly. Rosch, exhausted and with blood coursing down his face, finally cuffed Frank's wrist to the handrail of a cartoon ladybird. As Rosch clambered his way off the ride, he handed a baton to the attendant and gestured 'any funny business, just crack him'. He then found a gents toilet, washed the blood from his face and patched himself up the best he could.

As he stepped out once again into the sunshine, Rosch winced at the pain in his swollen lip. He peered around him into the fog of the bright lights and hysterical noises when up on the pathway, he spotted Officer Piper.

"Officer Piper!" he called, wincing at the sharp pain in his head.

Piper looked about him anxiously. He spotted Rosch, considered fleeing but lacked the energy. Rosch ambled up the pathway and took position next to Piper, leaning on the old iron railing overlooking the sea.

"Detective." said Piper, the gravel in his voice gently coloured by an unmistakable melancholy.

Officer Piper was another American residing in the UK. He was originally from Houston but had become an Anglophile after watching an episode of *Columbo* where he goes to London. When he came of age, Piper joined his local Sheriff's office and later transferred to the bright lights of Southend.

"Hello again, Officer." said Rosch. "You seem like a man who knows this town inside and out. How long have you walked this beat?"

"Too long." said the officer. "I took it as a temporary post back in the late-80's."

"Something tells me you don't buy the whole mugging gone wrong story." said Rosch.

"Something tells you right sir. There's something strange up there in them woods, comes down every now and then. Wild, hairiest thing you ever saw."

"You've seen it?" said Rosch.

"Just glimpses."

"The sheriff is reluctant to investigate, I take it?"
The old police man paused a moment before he spoke.
"These seaside economies are...very fragile. A scare like this could mean the end of this town. I'm three weeks away from retiring, Baldenbach could ruin me if he saw fit. Don't judge me too harshly, detective. I'm not a bad guy, just complicit in covering up multiple homicides."
"Where did you see it?" asked Rosch.
"The last time was in the jungle, Southend's homeless community."
"And where do I find that?"
"Far side of the Casino car park, behind the boardwalk. They're a mix of down and outs who've accumulated over the years. Mostly old *Love Island* contestants. Not a bad bunch really, but I wouldn't go down there without my assault-rifle."
Rosch thanked Piper, bid him good day and set a course for the jungle.

4:57pm
The Jungle, Southend's Homeless Community

Around a torn, wire fence, Rosch stepped onto the gravel footpath that ran behind the casino. Lining the rear of the building, was a never-ending string of large cardboard boxes, converted into modest lodgings. True to rumour, the occupants were mostly former contestants of the hit reality show, *Love Island*. Exquisitely muscled torsos and breath-taking cleavages milled about, wrapped in mangey blankets, orange skin smeared in grime. They got by on barbecuing locally sourced roadkill and selling items scavenged from wheelie bins as well as the occasional organ. As he proceeded along the stretch, Rosch covered his mouth with his handkerchief and clasped the anti-bac spray in his pocket. Just then, Rosch spotted a grizzled, bearded man acting very agitatedly, hoarding a collection of tattered magazines from the 1980's.

"The porter shrimp." said the grizzled man. "Noooooo! Can't. Unnnngh! Panda pops."

Rosch flinched violently as a voice spoke disturbingly close to his ear.

"He's perfectly harmless, you know. He's just very protective of his… magazines." he whispered.

Rosch had been addressed by a rake-thin, bald man in hotpants who locally went by the name of Kettlechip.

"So, what brings such a handsome Tarzan into the jungle?" said Kettlechip, swigging from a hip flask.

Rosch removed his badge.

"There was a murder yesterday evening-"

"And there was something rather, animalistic about the attacker right?" said Kettlechip, playfully.

"What can you tell me?"

"Apologies detective, I've had nothing but carbs today and my memory is…"

Rosch sighed and removed his wallet. As he opened it, Kettlechip gasped a long, awkward gasp.

"Is that?" he said, quivering with excitement, "Bea Arthur?"

In a flash, Kettlechip snatched the *Top Trumps 'Mama's of Comedy'* trading card from Rosch's wallet. It was an exceptional card. The picture displayed Bea Arthur at the height of the *Golden Girls* days, the categories including Wit, Delivery, Timing and Sultriness, all indicating a 9 if not 10.

"It's signed." added Rosch, coolly.

Kettlechip dropped to his knees, inhaled deeply and emitted a long silent scream. Within a heartbeat, Kettlechip was back on his feet with his face pressed firmly against Rosch's chest.

"Now you have to listen to me very, very carefully." he said, in an ecstatic whisper. "I want that card…I can show you what you're looking for. It comes by here, most nights."

"Show me."

As requested, Kettlechip, sauntering gleefully, led Rosch deeper into the jungle. Rosch reached for his handkerchief once again as they passed ex-models, ravenously devouring suspicious looking barbecue and performing backstreet bikini waxes. Then, like a mouse, Kettlechip dashed into one of the large, modified cardboard boxes. He began to rummage, throwing out items and paraphernalia. At last, he returned, unfolding a shabby piece of paper and handed it to Rosch. Rosch carefully looked at the paper sheet. Upon the paper had been drawn a crude, single line sketch of something resembling a sasquatch.

"Are you trying to get arrested?" asked Rosch.

"That's it! I saw it!" exclaimed Kettlechip. "As far from me as we are now! I swear on my life as a neurologist! I swear it!.. He's out here most nights...Be careful though detective, he spooks real easy."

8:37pm
Southend Boardwalk

As Rosch returned to the boardwalk, many of the rides were closing up. Tired and frustrated, he returned to the ladybird carousel to see the lights turned off and an open set of handcuffs dangling from a handrail.

"Shit." snapped Rosch, bitterly, almost cueing the phone ringing in his pocket. He answered to the harrowingly upbeat voice of Chief Leathers.

"Kunnypacken?" he said. "Just checking in! How does it do?"

"Well sir, Ruggerman's racked up at least five incidents of gross misconduct since we arrived. We are being sued for desecration of the *Tollaguska Beer* brand and I'm fairly sure I'm concussed."

"Ah. Still being a handful is he?"

"Sir, he needs to be dismissed. I can't control a deranged lunatic."

"Well Rosch, if it turns out that you can, we may have to discuss making you...full detective."

"Full detective?" said Rosch.

"That's correct. So, keep up the good work my boy! Keep it up up up!"

The phone went silent. Rosch couldn't help but let the nightmare of his current circumstances be temporarily soothed by the thought of an end to all the heckling and the *Star Wars* put downs. These thoughts were soon overtaken by his awareness of how much talking aggravated his split lip. Rosch looked at his watch and quickly began preparing for his stakeout in the jungle.

1:00am
The Jungle, Southend

In amongst the residents, Rosch was wrapped in a blanket, his face illuminated by a nearby oil drum fire. He had commandeered Kettlechip's box for the night, dressed in casual clothes purchased at a charity shop and now lay in wait. Rosch gazed at the crude sketch of a mythological creature he held in his hand. He wasn't thinking about how cold it got after dark, how these people lived in these conditions or what Kettlechip was up to in the hotel room he had rented for him. He wasn't even thinking about how much sasquatches reminded him of Ewoks, or where Frank was. Only two words recurred in his mind,
'Full Detective.'

Most of the Junglists were bedded down for the night, a handful still pottered about in the firelight. Rosch stood and made his way to the edge of the stretch of boxes, finally choosing a space behind a wheelie bin in which to relieve himself.

"Ah not on the veranda!" mourned a voice behind him.

'Full Detective' he thought. All he had to do was somehow stay this bizarre course he was on. Just then, Rosch heard a strange rustling, a little further down the alley. He finished off, removed his pistol and slowly approached the source of the noise. Rosch's throat turned to an arid desert as he heard sounds that could only be made by a very large animal. He took two further steps when the sounds fell silent. He cocked his pistol and drew down around the corner of a wheelie-bin, but only saw a mattress covered in tattered newspaper. Suddenly, Rosch was struck by a large box filled with mannikin parts and he tumbled to the floor, sending his weapon skidding across the ground. Rosch saw a flash of something large and very hairy as it disappeared into a side street that joined the alley. Rosch quickly gave chase, cursing the loss of his weapon. He reached the side street and saw a hairy bottom disappear at the top of a fire ladder that led to the roof of the casino.

It's fast whatever it is, thought Rosch. He quickly dashed back to find his weapon, wiped a grimy hand across his forehead and sprinted back to try and head it off on the other side of the casino. He raced back around the corner and slipped over onto his back as he met the blinding white headlights of a local squad car. Rosch grimaced in pain, nursing his head and shielding his eyes from the high beams.

"Now hold it right there!" bellowed the large, square voice of local officer Tibadeauxs. She commanded him to raise his hands, which he did, slowly.

"Easy now, officers. I'm Detective Rosch Kunnypacken of the London Met. If I can just reach my badge…"

"Keep those hands where we can see 'em mister." she said, cocking her pistol.

Tibadeauxs' partner, officer Franklin exited the driver's side and drew her taser.

"Officers, please-" begged Rosch.

"He's comin' right at us!" yelled Franklin, deploying the taser barbs into Rosch's abdomen. Rosch's body twisted and writhed and the current coursed through his body like a stampeding gorilla, officer Tibadeauxs smiled and spat out a glob of tobacco spit.

"Hmm. Southend fried city folk."

1:41am
Southend Sheriff's Department. Drunk Tank

At weekends, the drunk tank at this hour was standing room only but tonight, officers Franklin and Tibadeauxs shoved a bruised and still occasionally twitching Rosch into the large communal cell in the centre of the building. Rosch tumbled onto a bench and the greasy, iron bars slammed shut.

"Goodnight cityboy!" chirped Tibadeauxs as she and Franklin departed, laughing spitefully.

Rosch coughed chestily and rolled his battered body onto his back. Aftershocks from the taser were slowly becoming less frequent, which was good news, as only when they had stopped would Rosch be able to shake his excruciating headache. Rosch clutched the picture of the creature in his hand and slowly closed his eyes.

The sound of a police baton cracking against iron bars almost split Rosch's brain in two. Rosch strained his eyes to focus on the large mass looming over him, it was Sheriff Baldenbach.

"Boy, I've had several reports today from locals about an out of town sort causing ruckus on my boardwalk. Apparently the *Tollaguska Beer* mascot was beaten severely and his assailant tried to...it says here, drink him."

"Sheriff you have s-something dangerous in this zzzztown and if you don't-"

"Young man" insisted the Sheriff, with a tone like the grave, "I've had just about enough out of you and your wild speculations disrupting my quiet seaside town. I'll be requesting your removal first thing in the morning but allow me to extend our hospitality until then."

The Sheriff casually turned on his heel.

"Oh and boy?...don't let old man Jenkins find out you're a cop."

Rosch turned and saw a jittery old man with a scraggly beard. The old man was asleep but clearly dreaming about being a squirrel trapped in a house fire. Laboriously, Rosch pulled himself closer to the bars of the grimy cell.

"You can only c-cover the truth for so l-long Baldenbach! As long as thzzzzere's breath in my b-body!"

Later, as Rosch drifted in and out of sleep, his head trauma from earlier coaxed vivid dreams and harrowing visions into his mind.

"But you had to tow the company man line."

"Alien bastards! They've been coming here ages like!"

'Pishew!'

"Wookie Whacker!"

"Make you full, detective."

Rosch awoke with a start, the faces of Pegg, Frank, Ahem and George Lucas still lingering in his mind. At that moment, the iron door scraped open once again, and Frank stumbled inside. Rosch stared as his partner collapsed onto an already fully occupied bench. Frank was clearly now being piloted entirely by whiskey, but his basic motor functions and certain baseline neural mechanisms were well trained. Frank found himself a corner to slump into and got comfy, whereupon he saw Rosch and burst into derisive laughter.

"Oi, Lando. How's the party-line treating you?"

Rosch remained silent.

"Why didn't you call Aunty Goebles to let you out?

"I don't know." confessed Rosch. "To be honest I haven't had a clue about what has been going on for about six or seven weeks now."

"Well, you've got yourself a special one here, but at the end of the day it's a textbook case with only one possible perp whoooooo…"

The last word of Frank's sentence evolved into the ejection of his stomach contents, decorating the floor of the drunk tank. With that, Frank slumped backwards and passed out.

"Wait, wait! A textbook case of what? Ruggerman?! For fucks sake."

Rosch repeatedly slapped Frank's face, bravely stopping himself before it became too indulgent but there was no response. Rosch came to the conclusion regarding his next move about as reluctantly as a thirty-year-old man approaches being circumcised. His phone had been buried in the folds of his homeless garments and had not been confiscated by Tibadeauxs. With the coast clear, Rosch dialled and waited.

"........Aunty Caroline, hi."

3:34am

The gruelling sound of the iron cage door opening shook the cell once again and Rosch carried the unconscious Frank past a deeply unimpressed Franklin and Tibadeauxs. As they shuffled out of the cell, the Sheriff, glaring at Rosch said nothing, just slowly chewed his gum.

"Thank you kindly." said Rosch politely as he hoisted Frank back onto his feet.

After a step, Rosch returned his attention to the Sheriff.

"I need to borrow an office." he said.

The door to the dingy office slammed into the wall releasing chunks of paint and Rosch quickly dumped Frank into a chair. With Frank near surfacing, Rosch frantically ransacked the drawers of a desk to find gaffer tape. He found a roll in a drawer marked 'invoices' that was filled with old memory sticks and cotton buds. Rosch was securing Frank's extremities to the chair when Frank, groggily came round. In the corner of the office was a coffee machine that looked like it was requisitioned from Pearl Harbour. Rosch poured a cup and began feeding it to Frank who instantly began swigging heartily. Suddenly, Frank stopped and a terrifying panic took hold. Realising that this was the first non-alcoholic substance to pass his lips in over a fortnight, Frank began to writhe desperately against his fastenings.

"Jesus Christ Lando! What are you doing to me?!"

"Ruggerman, I don't want to do this but-"

"No! You don't understand!" grimaced Frank. "Sobriety, ungh! for me at this stage is more akin to a... pensioner... taking ayahuasca."

Frank contorted in his chair, gritting his teeth, totally unprepared for the incoming sobriety.

"Ruggerman!?" said Rosch, shaking his shoulders.

"For fucks sake Lando, get me a Bailey's or something!"

"Bailey's?"

"Yes! Miniature. Left, ungh! ankle holster!"

Rosch quickly reached down and yet again to his total disbelief found said Bailey's miniature. He twisted off the cap and poured it down Frank's neck. Gasping, wracked with pain, Frank slowly began to calm.

"Are you okay?" said Rosch, quietly contemplating the strength of the gaffer tape.

"Seventeen per cent, we don't have long." said Frank.

"Right. Get on the computer."

Careful not to take his eyes off Frank, Rosch sat at a desk and wiggled the mouse to clear the screensaver, which was a rendering of Jesus sat on a *Harley Davidson*.

"Search for hairy sex gods of the 1980's." said Frank.

Rosch immediately stopped and began to question his own sobriety.

"Uhm." said Rosch.

"Just do it." grunted Frank. "Hairy... sex gods, of the...1980's."

Rosch buried his face in his hands.

"Ruggerman! Any minute now, Baldenbach and his goons will be out looking for that thing. They're going to find it and when they do-"

"Cos it's Tom Selleck." interrupted Frank, coughing and wrestling with his dangerously low ABV.

After an inordinate silence.

"Tom Selleck?" said Rosch.

"It's Selleck, it's Selleck," said Frank, still twisting in his chair, caffeine still marching around his blood stream like the Gestapo hunting for hidden alcohol. "it was always going to be Selleck, come on it's obvious! Selleck!"

Rosch typed the enquiry into the search bar and the top hit was a collection of pictures including the likes of Burt Reynolds, Robin Williams and Tom Selleck. Rosch was momentarily captivated by the on-screen machismo as Frank spoke.

"Mankind's genetic structure is in a perpetual state of flux." he said. "For these men, freak hormonal imbalances met abnormal genetic nuance to create a perfect storm. A biological maelstrom of hairy sex."

"But I've seen it," replied Rosch, "this thing is more like *Addam's Family* stuff."

"And that's precisely the problem." said Frank. "Selleck has evolved from a conventional macho man to some kind of unstoppable, randy savage. However, after decades of success, his ageing body will be struggling to handle the breakneck metabolism required to sustain that kind of charisma."

"But why Selleck?" said Rosch. "Why here? Doesn't he live in America? And even if this absurd drivel miraculously had some science behind it, it could be anybody. At least any of the hairy sex gods of the 80's, Robin Williams, Burt Reynolds."

"No! Use your head!" bellowed Frank. "Look at the victim! A woman that glamorous is out of the league of Burt Reynolds and he knows it... He peaked at Sally Field whereas Tom Selleck was rogering Courtney Cox as late as the mid 2000's! No. Despite his hairiness turning him basically feral, Selleck thinks he's still got the goods. It is him and he is here."

"How do we find him?" asked Rosch.

"There's an old flame of his that sings at the Bukkake Lounge. I think it's what brought him here."

Rosch sat back in his chair and briefly considered his next move.

"I think we best get you a drink."

4:12am
Southend, The Bukkake Lounge

With Frank swaying and sipping a bottle of absinthe, the detectives stood outside the entrance of the Bukkake Lounge Karaoke and Cocktail Bar. Even at this hour, the Bukkake Lounge was swinging. From inside they could hear what sounded like a riotous crowd watching a striptease performed by a raw chicken.

"Uhm...Maybe we can get her to meet us outside?" said Rosch.

"Nice." said Frank, congenially.

Rosch sprayed his anti-bac spray and pressed the button of the intercom. For a moment, Frank and Rosch waited outside the looming, jet black facade of the most notoriously fun venue in Southend.

"Yes?!" said a female voice.

"Good, err, morning," said Rosch. "We're from the Western Tactical Unit of the London Metropolitan Police, we're looking for a...Patricia Groats?"

After a moment's silence, the voice, which had somehow transformed, to a now deeper and more gruff register returned.

"There's no one by that name here."

Rosch looked back at Frank who was struggling to hold focus on any one object. Frank raised the arm holding the bottle in gentle encouragement. Rosch paused and then spoke again.

"It is regarding a...Tom Selleck."

The intercom clicked off and they waited. After a minute, heavy iron latches slid across their rusty housings behind the solid black door, and tentatively, a woman emerged. She was middle aged with short black curly hair and olive skin.

"Miss Groats, we are detectives Ruggerman and Kunnypacken with the London Met."

Rosch showed his badge and Frank gestured agreeably with his bottle before swigging.

"We need your help to locate Tom Selleck." said Rosch. "We understand you know him."
Groats stood, wavering.
"That was a long time ago. I'd love to assist you gentlemen, but it's peak season and...I can't leave the show before the final act. We're recreating the last supper and-"
Frank then snatched the sasquatch rendering from Rosch and showed it to Groats.
"Listen," he said, curtly, "if we don't take him in, you can guarantee Sheriff Ballbag and the rest of the 'Dicks of Hazzard' will be out in their pickup trucks looking to wrangle him and tie him to the bonnet."
Groats slowly took the picture from Frank's hand and she gazed at it, memories of a long-lost love threatening to breach the perimeter of her heart. She clutched the picture to her breast and acquiesced.

Back at the Sheriff's office, Baldenbach, his officers and the team of sniffer dogs, hollered and hooted, firing shotguns into the air as they climbed aboard three pickup trucks. Then, shouting and cheering, they sped off into the night in search of the troublesome beast man. When he was sure they were out of sight, Rosch quickly dashed from his hiding place beside the station, carrying nets and a tranquiliser rifle. He stashed them in the boot of the car and raced into the drivers' side to find a worried Groats and an unconscious Frank. Rosch glanced at Groats' troubled face in the rear-view mirror.
"Don't worry," he said kindly, "I'll make sure we find him before they do."

4:35am
Southend Beachfront

At this time, the promenade was silent, the rides and attractions were all closed but the string lights that lined the boardwalk were still shining their warm glow. Groats, cautiously, walked the promenade and sat on an old iron bench. As a message came through, she touched her earpiece that Rosch had given her.

"That's it Patricia, you're doing great." he said.

Rosch and Frank had taken position under a large bush with a clear view of Groats.

"Remember you'll be in my eyeline the whole time." said Rosch.

For fifteen minutes, Groats sat anxiously on the bench under the watchful eye of Rosch and the now, fast asleep, Frank. Rosch checked his watch and noted that in one hour the sun would be up.

"Come on." whispered Rosch, eagerly.

Groats sat on the bench, shivering slightly, looking up and down the boardwalk when she suddenly froze at the sound of strange, heavy breaths behind her. She felt sniffs of her hair and the placement of hairy hands on her shoulders. The beast's vaporous breath descended around her and she relished the familiar touch. In a flash, she stood and held him, locked in a deep embrace, their two loves converging and filling every cell in their bodies with radiant light. Suddenly, bright white high beams illuminated the pair and screeching tires came to a halt.

"We got him Sheriff!" yelled one of Baldenbach's troops.

Panicked, Groats and the beast fled into the undergrowth, making their way towards the woods. Rosch removed his pistol and raced forward in chase. Frank, disturbed by the commotion, gathered himself best he could and dutifully made after the enamoured pair albeit via a very different route. The pick-up truck backed up and with spinning tires displacing sand and shots firing into the air hurtled after them. Rosch dashed into the undergrowth and sprinted after the pair. He raced onwards into the woods, lashed by wet leaves and branches. He reached a clearing and shone his torch left and right. Nearby, he could hear the barking dogs, engines and gunshots of the local Sheriff's men as they tore about, searching for the beast man. Frank staggered his way into the trees. He pushed through the undergrowth and slipped down an embankment, landing in a pile of dead wood.

Deeper in the woods, with the sound of the Sheriff's men appearing to be moving further away, Groats and the beast stopped and tried to get their breath back. Groats looked at the beast as he held her. She carefully parted the dense, matted hair obscuring his face and saw those deep, oceanic eyes. It had been so long since she felt that connection with someone. She had made a reasonable life for herself, she lived alone, looked after herself and work at the Bukkake Lounge was regular. But still, there was no happiness she knew like being in love. The beast held her close and he declared his love as undying. Tom Selleck had long lost the power of conventional speech but via a sequence of grunts and hand gestures, Groats understood.
"Hey! I got 'em!" shouted a voice, followed by several bullets whipping close by. The two darted away into the ever darker thickets. Upon hearing the shots, Rosch stopped and frantically looked this way and that, his torch blinking on and off. Cursing, Rosch tried to get some life back into it by rubbing the batteries.

At the bottom of an embankment, surrounded by dead wood, Frank growled as he strained to stand up, his bones screaming at him in many languages. His absinthe bottle, now empty, thudded on to the ground. Swaying, Frank shone his torch and tried to get his bearings. He continued further into the woods which had become so thick, there was next to no assistance from the moon. Further on he pressed until he came to a clearing. Frank shone his torch onto what looked like some kind of survival shelter, a crude structure that could possibly provide some sanctuary. Frank crawled on all fours into the shelter, the dry leaves underneath him cracking under his knees and hands.

Once inside and with immense difficulty, Frank sat himself up and searched for his cigarettes. There he sat, the woods had begun to fill with the morning chorus, a sound

Frank personally despised, but his mind was quiet as he smoked. The thought of being smashed and alone in a woodland shelter at 4am would probably upset most people, but humans are remarkably diverse creatures. Under his left hand Frank felt something strange. With brief investigation, he found what appeared to be a power cable. He lifted it and discovered that it was attached to something inside the shelter. Curious, he crawled forward, a cigarette hanging from his lip. Covered in twigs and leaves, he found a large metallic box. He opened the front hatch and a bright light illuminated his face. Inside the strange metal box was the best part of a dozen, refrigerated vodka bottles.
"Oh, get in, you hapless bastard." beamed Frank, tears welling in his eyes.

Back up on the road, local officer Piper was in his squad car, returning home from the office. He had been watching the drunk tank patrons while the rest of the office was rampaging around the woods. Piper slammed on his brakes and the car stopped just short of Groats and the beast. Piper grabbed his radio but said nothing. He simply stared in horror at the wild man. His eyes naturally descended to the beast's crotch but anything worth seeing was obscured by dense body hair. Then, Piper saw the look of earnest vulnerability on the face of Groats.
"This is Piper…" he said.
Just then, Groats stepped in front of the beast, her face demonstrating only her resolute desire to protect him. Piper paused a moment before speaking into his radio.
"...Target located to the rear of the casino" he said, "...target is on the move."
Just then, a little way away, the Sheriff replaced the handset to his radio and shouted to his officers.
"He's near the casino! C'mon boys!"
In the distance, a chorus of barking dogs and truck engines erupted as they sped off, back towards town. Groats and the beast stayed motionless as Piper half exited his car.
"Go on now." he said.

With that, the pair raced off into the woods. Piper sat back down in his car and remembered his own wife who had sadly passed away four years before. Knowing that the couple had a chance to escape and be happy, or whatever can constitute happiness in this life, caused Piper to smile. He sat, thoughtfully in his car when a realisation dawned.

"Oh, wait he killed somebody." said Piper to himself.

He looked back to his radio handset, contemplating calling it in before deciding it was too late. He turned on his favourite country music station and sat peacefully with a cigarette.

Suddenly, Rosch, now filthy from scampering in the woods, also appeared on the road in front of Piper's car. Rosch saw Piper and approached. Piper rolled down his window and spoke.

"I doubt we have a chance in hell of finding them before the sun comes up."

"Anything from Baldenbach?" said Rosch, wiping twigs and bracken from himself.

"Well, if you ask me," said Piper, "the Sheriff and his men are going to be out in these woods an awful long time, an awful long time indeed."

Rosch went to speak again but Piper pulled away leaving him alone on the road.

"Nice." said Rosch, as he began to make his long walk back to town.

**Monday
11:12am
Harvey Nicholls' Cafe Forecourt, London**

Rosch sat, with his latte untouched, in the luxuriously appointed, open air cafe forecourt of the top end London store. Across from him, for what seemed an eternity, his aunty, Councilwoman Caroline Ahem, stirred her Manhattan.

"Tom Selleck" she said, curiously.

"Absolutely." he said firmly.
"Preposterous. Doesn't he live in America?"
"Aunty, I know what I saw."
"Look Rosch, don't you see how these things work? Ruggerman is days away from the nut house, you did us so proud with your Pegg testimony, now you are full detective and acting head of the W.T.U. Don't throw it all away for the sake of a psychotic inebriate."
Rosch stood.
"I better be getting back. Thanks for the coffee."

8:39pm
Southend

The air was thick with the sound of crickets as Sheriff Lorenzo Baldenbach reappeared on the porch of his mother's home, carrying two mint juleps. His mother, a haggard and bitter woman, sat under a blanket, she grunted as her son handed her the mint and whiskey cocktail.
"Now what's that face for?" she said, grumpily.
"Well ma." said the Sheriff. "I sure let them city folks make a chump outta me. And I still gotta find a perp for this murder. Sheeit. It's enough to break a dawgs ass."
"Ah hell why dont'cha just blame it on one of these here aliens?!"
"I can't just blame it on no foreigners no more ma." said the Sheriff,
"...things have moved on in Southend."
Then, sipping their refreshing drinks, mother and son spent that night on the porch in silence.

EPISODE VII

Tuesday
1:26pm
London, Leytonstone

The reflections of endless white picket fences and green lawns slid along the jet-black flanks of Rosch's car. The sun shone brightly in the flawless sky and despite the city getting weirder by the day, here in the depths of suburbia everything seemed painfully normal. Mile after mile of homogenous houses, each more identical than the last. Flowers spilled out from raffia pots and the songs of a thousand pressure washers came from all corners of the neighbourhood. Hulking 4x4's sat like engorged toads on driveways, their offspring spilling out onto the streets, lining every inch of the kerb with cars. Sadly, the astonishing sense of normality here couldn't quell the turbulent voices in Rosch's mind. For the longest time now, each step he took seemed only to take him further away from what he thought his life was.

Out of his window, Rosch saw a trio of children on a lawn sitting solemnly around a spinning top. They looked in a state of near hypnosis. They sat quietly devoid of the excruciating bedlam for which children are most notably recognized. They raised their arms in the air and the spinning top began to flicker. Bright red lights flashed and raced all over the device and the top slowly lifted off the grass to the height of about a metre where it stopped and hovered. Then, red lasers shot out and traced grids of geometric lines across the faces of the three children.

Further down the street, Rosch saw a father and son playing catch. They too seemed strangely dispassionate. The son threw a ball to his father. Much to Rosch's surprise, the father simply stood motionless, his arms remaining outstretched as the ball thundered its way into the man's crotch. Rosch's neck was craned backwards as he tried to process what he had just seen. In his rear-view mirror, he saw the father remain standing, unphased, still with arms outstretched.

With all his might, Rosch tried to focus on the fact that he was now acting head of his own department. He clung to the notion that this was what he wanted. He tried to ignore the unshakeable feeling that the city and in fact the world, were changing fast and too often in ways that were devastating to his mental health.

2:56pm
Burnt Oak

Rosch had been so deep in his thoughts whilst driving that he hadn't noticed that he had arrived at the Roswell Tiki Bar, just like he hadn't noticed the three roundabouts, the car wash and the cake sale he destroyed as he drove through Highgate. Something had drawn him here, but whatever that was, Rosch was in no place to deal with it. He pulled to a stop and watched the fracas that was occurring outside of the bar.

Waving placards and wearing t-shirts bearing #justice4pegg, ten civilians were making their voices heard, C.U.N News reporter Shagney Kluft was reporting.
"What started with a twittlechat post, sent right here at the Roswell Tiki Bar, has grown into a movement of almost a dozen people. The burgeoning group is campaigning to reopen the investigation into the death of magistrate Judge Duane Pegg. The hashtag rocketed into our feeds after being given a like by naturist and television sex furnace Michaela Strachan. The question now is 'will the Met reopen the

investigation?' or is it just a matter of, to quote Prime Minister Donovan, 'T'dah to some sad, loony oik, wasn't it? Isn't it?' Let's speak if we can to one of the protestors-"
Rosch decided to return to the office, as he did so, he drove past the platoon of armoured riot vans, preparing to descend upon the protestors.

Reticulant HQ, Ambassadorial Chamber

In a secret location, the Reticulants had set up a large fortress from which Ambassador Crunk, the chief liaison with the British government, was to oversee his affairs. The ability to camouflage an artificial structure the size of a town was just one of the technological nuggets the visitors had in their arsenal. Inside the base was a fully functioning community complete with markets, domiciles, three churros outlets and an ice rink.

Up on the fifth floor, at the end of a long, curved corridor, lined with ambient blue lights, was Ambassador Crunk's office. On a magnificent TV screen, Crunk and his two seniormost officers were watching Kluft's report from the Tiki Bar. For a moment, the trio of bulbous headed, grey despots sat in silence.

"Shagney Kluft?" said Lieutenant Rabz, quizzically.

"This is getting out of control." grumbled Crunk, "Michaela Strachan is a party size Toblerone jammed right up my-"

'Ping' went a notification on Deacon Smash's phone.

"Ambassador." said Smash, "#Justice4Pegg has just been liked by John Snow."

"Channel 4 News or Game of Thrones?" asked Crunk.

Deacon Smash looked at his phone and then looked again.

"Ooh, both." he said cheerily.

There then came the sound of Reticulant urine splashing under the table as Crunk spoke.

"Okay, it's game time. Rabz, get me Williams over at Cloning and Infiltration. You, put me through to Ahem."

The big screen flickered to life and a head shot of Caroline Ahem appeared with a dancing phone icon.

"Ambassador, how are you?" smiled Ahem, from the comfort of her chaise lounge.

"Shut it." snapped Crunk. "Where's Ruggerman?"

"Strictly compromised." she said. "In two days, he'll be committed to a rehab centre where he'll be so medicated, he's likely to drown in his own dribbling idiocy."

"Not good enough." said Crunk. "Ruggerman needs breaking now. We will handle him. You get on top of that Strachan bastard and squash this 'just-juice-4-pegg shit'."

"Ambassador, Michaela Strachan is-"

"Hanging up." said Crunk.

Ahem's big screen turned black.

"... a national treasure." said Ahem, quietly.

Ambassador Crunk took a moment to consider the two officers currently sat at his table. Lieutenant Rabz was a decorated officer in the military who had been promoted to top brass after successfully invading Dalmanek 7, filming it and creating the hit reality show; *Whose War Crime Is It Anyway?* Deacon Smash on the other hand was a lifelong friend of the Ambassador. They had schooled together and managed to remain in fairly close proximity as they ascended the ranks of the Beta 3 Invasion Services. Smash had made his career in what you might call the clergy. The closest thing the Reticulants had to religion was a loosely organised movement born from a group of militant TV critics who had assembled to prevent a reboot of *Dallas*. Since its inception, the quasi-religious sect known as 'the Brigade', had been a driving force in the spread of the Reticulants across the universe.

Just then, Crunk's screen fizzed again as the face of Williams, the chief engineer in the cloning and infiltration department, appeared on screen.

"Ambassador." said Williams, brightly.

"Williams, listen up. I'm sending you a dossier of a Frank Ruggerman, I need a clone unit deployed for a psychological breakdown job."

"Nice." said Williams.
"Yeah," said Crunk, "he used to be married or something. Apparently, she ran off with one of us a few years back."
"You're joking?" said Williams.
"Nah. It's disgusting really, but times are moving on. Anyway, get that skin job up to spec and deployed pronto."
"Can do." said Williams.
"Remember Williams, I want this human broken...Okay, bye."

**Wednesday
11:13am
The Dog and Hotpot Pub**

The black timber woodwork of the Dog and Hotpot would dissipate into dust if you scratched it with a key. Since the smoking ban, the aromas of generations of sweat and stale lager were now free to drift around the venue and permeate their way into the clothes and minds of the patrons. The roster of post-brunch / pre-lunch drinkers was thin on the ground today. A handful of silent contemplators, each lost in the void as their thoughts were being romanced and then numbed by gallons of grain derived medicine. They included a dental assistant, a milkman who, having finished his rounds, was out of ideas for the day and lastly, Detective Frank Ruggerman.

Frank sat alone in a booth, gazing into the bottom of a glass of whiskey. His posture resembled that of a monk who had spent his life copying religious scripture and the pool of saliva on the table spoke of a man in crisis. His lifelong ally, the nectar of the maverick and the distilled tonic of the overactive mind was turning on him. Whereas for the longest time, Frank's thoughts were free to wander uninhibited across the boundaries of plausibility and logic and now, there was only a meaningless fog. Frank's mind was deaf to the screams of his body that were signalling with all their might that his vital functions were collapsing. It was too late now. He was just so very, very tired. Best to just let it drift away. All of that struggle and sacrifice should now be left to ebb away like sand on a shore, the waves removing layer after layer with each retreat. Frank's fog was so dense and disorientating that he was totally unaware that someone was standing next to his table. Suddenly, the mire of Frank's mindscape was penetrated by a familiar touch as a delicate hand caressed his face. On some unconscious level, feelings of tenderness and longing swelled and the paralytic Frank leaned into the soft hand and tears began to roll down his face.

"Hello Frank," said a soft voice, "I've missed you."

11:30am
London Met HQ. Western Tactical Unit Office

Rosch had the door to the office open as he typed out the new codes of conduct for the Western Tactical Unit. Outside in the corridor, he heard shouts and squabbles and the unmistakable sound of a riding mower. The chug-chug-chug of the mower became louder and louder and flashes of amber hazard lights appeared on the wall. A moment later, the mower came into view and sat on top was Senior Officer Marge Kowalchik. Cursing and grunting, Marge brought the 250cc gardening vehicle to a stop and reached for a folder of documents. She threw the folder through the door of the office sending paper flying into the air and knocking over a pot plant.

"Chewie!" roared Marge, "New assignment from Leathers. Congratulations, you're on diplomatics."

Rosch crossed the floor of the office and picked up the scattered documents which most notably included black and white photographs of alien dignitaries.

11:31pm
The Dog and Hotpot Pub

Frank was unable to focus on the person that now stood before him, but inside he recognized her. Long buried feelings of nourishment and security told him in no uncertain terms who this was.
"Beatrice." he whispered.
His hands trembled as they tried to reach for hers and his eyes welled again. Just then, Frank's malaise changed in tone as he tried to gather himself and regain some degree of poise. Unable to prevent himself from dribbling, Frank centred his thoughts on the clarity of her visage in his memory. He cherished the contrast of her pale skin with the deep, dark brown of her long, wavy hair and the piercing blue eyes that shone from beneath her dense fringe.
"I'm sorry to just… surprise you like this." said Beatrice, awkwardly. "I couldn't...muster the courage to contact you. I tried… The lads down the station said you'd be here."
Beatrice took Frank's hands and held them tightly.
"Can we go home love?" asked Frank, his eyes closed tightly and holding her hands to his forehead.
"I was hoping you were going to say that." she said.

12:24pm
London Met. Diplomatics Briefing Room

With the arrival of the 'Visitors', the Met had created a special ops detail assigned with providing close protection for alien dignitaries and council. The officers assigned to Diplomatics came from all over the Met but they were each highly ambitious, politically adroit and all at least momentarily, enjoyed the favour of the top brass. Rosch sat patiently in the briefing room with a dozen or so other officers, one of whom was sitting at the back and watching Rosch with grievous scrutiny.

Finally, in waddled Sgt. Major Katherine Breville. Hailing from Wolverhampton, Breville had first made a name for herself in the prison service. Later, after moving to London, she had brought order and financial frugality to some of the toughest garden centres in the country. Now, she was a senior in the London Met and had recently been assigned with overseeing the protection of prominent Reticulants. She took to her podium, grunted and shuffled her papers.

"Afternoon." she said. "Devlin, Stills, Nash, you'll be accompanying Grand Troubadour Kizzphat to the Grand National try-outs at Chepstow. Man, they love them horses."

"Uhm Sarge?" said Devlin, gingerly.

"I know," said Breville, curtly, "just try and encourage him to use the toilet before he goes in. Davenport, Bunty, you've got the big dog, Ambassador Crunk himself. First off there's a meeting with the PM, then a few personal errands and, as fortune would have it, you will also be joined by *'full'* detective Kunnypacken, on loan to us from the Wasted, err Western Tactical."

Rosch clung to his professionalism as the sniggers popped around the briefing room.

"I'm sure his presence fills us all, with a new hope." said Breville, stifling a smile.

The briefing room broke out into hysterical laughter but was quickly hushed by Breville.

"Enough." she barked. "Now go on, get out of it."

The officers, many still chuckling and making Wookie noises, gathered their things and departed. Rosch was still unknowingly being carefully observed from the back of the room. Rosch stood and politely shook hands with his new colleagues, officers Bunty and Davenport. Bunty was an ex-doorman from Luton and Davenport was on a long-term exchange program from Melbourne, Australia. As the trio reached the lift, Davenport's petite and cheery form, turned to Rosch and addressed him with her usual bounce.

"Oh, my God!" she beamed. "Don't you just love diplomatics?"

"I don't know, it's my first time." said Rosch, repeatedly pressing the lift buttons.

"They took me off domestic disturbances when this lot touched down. I'm telling you it's the biggest piece of piss since *Kinder Surprise* toys came prebuilt. Plus, I can barely get from A to B without all the perks tumbling out my arsehole!"

Finally, the lift pinged, the door slid open and they entered. Once the lift was on the move, Davenport spoke again.

"Detective Kunnypacken," she said with a hint of flirtatiousness,

"...May I call you Lando?"

3:02pm
Frank Rugerman's Home, North London

The conventionally Dresden-esque interior of Frank's home was being given a thorough spruce up as Frank lay unconscious on his bed. After carrying him home in a wheelbarrow kindly loaned by the landlord, Beatrice had stripped and bathed him, and laid him gently to rest. She then began to process a load of laundry which had constituents dating back to dial-up internet. Whilst this was running, she had changed several blown fuses, prepared a stew and cleared the guttering. Putting the step ladder away, she closed the door to the cupboard and stared vacantly at a framed photograph. The photo depicted Frank and Jojo Binks on a fishing trip. As her face, void of any feeling reflected in the photo, she remained stoically unaware that this was the only photograph of Frank smiling in existence.

As Frank slowly began to surface, his brain felt like a cement mixer full of rusty chainsaws. At that moment, Beatrice entered with a bowl of stew, she smiled and placed the bowl on the bedside table. Sitting on the bed, she heaved Frank into an upright position, adjusting him occasionally

when he would slump over. Beatrice began to feed him the stew. Frank, with eyes still rolling in his head, tried to focus.
"I don't know where I am." he said, trembling.
"It's okay, Frank. You're home safe."
"Did I…have too many?" Frank asked.
"That's one way of putting it, love, yes." she said.
Frank laboriously raised his head and looked into Beatrice's face.
"Why now?" he whispered.
"Oh, Frank. I've been wanting to see you for years. I've been beside myself."
"It's like…I can't believe it's you." he said.
"Of course, it's me, silly piss-head." she said, smiling. "Just rest up now we've got to get your strength back. Ooh, let me get you a water."
Beatrice stood.
"Wait." said Frank.
Beatrice listened.
"I'm sorry…for all the times, with the job and that."
Beatrice smiled and made her way out onto the landing.
"I know." she said, quietly.

3:10pm
Secret Hangar, Streatham Airfield
Meeting with the PM

A series of black diplomatic cars arrived in tandem on the large concrete plateau. From them exited several officers in suits, including Rosch. Holding the car door open, Rosch spoke into his cuff.
"Bringing the Ambassador in now, do you copy?"
"Copy that." said a voice in his ear.
Shuffling his little grey legs as he descended from the rear of the car, Ambassador Crunk led his entourage to the entrance of the hangar.
Rosch took position at the front of the party as they progressed inside and down a long grey corridor, lit by

overhead lamps. They arrived at a set of heavy double doors, manned by soldiers. Rosch showed his I.D to the guards, as he did so, he caught a glimpse inside of a fidgety, dumpy man scampering around a large round table. The doors were opened and they made their way inside. Officers Davenport and Bunty took positions around the perimeter of the room and stood patiently as Ambassador Crunk, along with his colleagues Lieutenant Rabz and Deacon Smash, joined the PM at the table. The PM, Joffrey Wiff-Waff Donovan, wiped the sweat from his hands and turned on his £26,000 a semester charm.

"Ambassador, welcome." he chimed.

"Let's make this quick." said Crunk, "We're offering you the fastest and most fatally addictive operating system ever conceived, which will allow you to manipulate the public like a pissed marionette."

"Yes, we-" began the PM.

"Have failed to deliver on the first clause of our agreement." finished Crunk.

"Yes, and it's precisely this which I have-"

"We said, an additional five seasons of *Malcolm in the Middle,* original cast, no substitutes." said Crunk.

"Yes, I understand, it's just-"

"We have the power to reanimate deceased cast members if needed." said Lieutenant Rabz.

The other Reticulants nodded in agreement.

"Oh absolutely. It's just that I uh-" said the PM, diverting his nervous gaze from one huge wrinkly grey face to another.

"I can see you're having a stroke," said Crunk, "so let me simplify it. We want content, you can give it to us. We'll sort you out with a few helpful innovations. But ultimately, don't forget that we have weapons capable of atrocities far beyond even your despicable, inbred imagination. Orbiting space lasers that can discolour the tap water of a single household. We have death rays that don't mark the skin, they just swap your organs about."

"Swap your kidneys with your eyeballs." added Deacon Smash.

"Yeah, or put your brain in your urethra." grinned Lieutenant Rabz.

"Point being," said Crunk, "you are sitting at the kids table. The grown-ups table is handling business and the truth is that we have got this planet firmly by the terrestrials."

"Yes." nodded the PM.

"Get it done," said Crunk, standing, "we're out of here."

As the Ambassador led his party from the room, the PM leaned towards Rosch and the other officers.

"I must insist," he whispered, "it is paramount that you don't discuss anything you see here. 'Shhhh' Very bad. 'Shhh'."

5:29pm
Frank Ruggerman's Flat, North London

His surroundings were slowly becoming more familiar as Frank's senses began to stabilise. Gritting his teeth, he slowly twisted himself onto his side, instantly triggering a savage bout of acid reflux. Groaning, Frank slowly slid off the bed and onto his feet. He clung to the bedpost whilst he tried to find his balance. Step after wobbling step, he hugged the wall and ventured his way onto the landing. The effort caused saliva to drip from Frank's mouth and collect on his once upon a time white vest. His shoulder slid against the old, cream and burgundy patterned wallpaper that only clung to the wall out of fear of what was in the carpet. The bathroom door was open and even with his mind still full of distortions, he heard someone using the toilet and pondered just how long he had lived alone. He clawed his way to the bathroom door and looked inside. Beatrice flushed the toilet and was washing her hands when she saw him.

"Darling, what are you doing up?" she smiled.

Frank was still desperately trying to reconnect a galaxy of broken synapses in his mind, even simple connections the sober take for granted.

"Have you always pissed standing up?" asked Frank, clinging to the doorframe with all his might.
"I suppose as you're up, we can have lunch." said Beatrice. "Here, I've made your favourite."
Beatrice handed him a six-pack of Latvian lager.
"Oh sweet." he wheezed, his voice shaking.
Suddenly, he sobbed and wrapped his arms around her.
"I'm so sorry." he cried. "I've missed you so much."
"Come we go." said Beatrice, "Let's get you smashed."

5:36pm
Parsonbury Manor Country Estate
Meeting with the Hunts Club

The next appointment for the Ambassador led the motorcade far into the countryside. Winding lanes, lined by thick bushes that bristled with life. Butterflies and bees dashed from flower to flower as the passengers of each car savoured the charming aromas of industrialised agriculture. Eventually, the lead car turned onto a lane marked by a large wooden gate. After a few hundred yards, the expansive facade of Parsonbury Manor came into view. As they approached the home of some of England's most privileged, the rumble of the dirt road was soon replaced by the crackle of gravel.

Once at a stop, Rosch left the vehicle, surveyed the scene and opened the door for the Ambassador. Almost immediately, they were approached by a tall, moustachioed man of pure tweed. He walked with an immeasurable swagger, smiling as he removed his tanned leather driving-gloves. This was Lord Samson Fortitude. Recently returned from what he referred to as 'the colonies', his sun-blanched complexion competed with the bright red of his hair and moustache.
"Welcome Ambassador," he said. "Delighted we are to see you again."

Ambassador Crunk grunted and walked into the grand entrance of the house. Rosch and the other officers closely followed the Ambassador inside. From the entrance, the building spread far to the left and right with a huge staircase immediately in front. Atop the staircase was an astonishing stained-glass window.

A truly priceless piece, the window depicted the late Prince Philip wielding a broadsword and bragging triumphantly over a dead pheasant. Rosch was quietly admiring the grandiose decor when they were approached by an elderly butler, carrying a tray with a toilet brush and a folded newspaper.

"Ah! Pringle!" ejaculated Fortitude. "I trust we are all ready for the demonstrations?"

"Yes m'lord." said the butler with a voice as chalky as the white cliffs. "But... we've only got the two-"

"Yes-yes-yes, be still Pringle. Everyone, if you'll kindly follow me to the rear garden."

Rosch signalled Bunty to remain at the front entrance and for Davenport to go on ahead into the garden. Whilst the party made their way to the rear of the building, farm labourers were removing large, heavy cases from the last two vehicles in the Ambassador's motorcade. In the rear garden, a number of the rustic elite had gathered for the day's expo, labourers and waiting staff stood by patiently.

With the arrival of the Ambassador, the gathered gentry slowly congregated around the edge of a large enclosure containing two alpacas and a thin man in a lab coat named Steven Hapenny. Rosch looked on, trying to remain focussed whilst processing what was truly a surreal scene. His surprise continued as Bunty and Davenport had left their positions and reappeared with ice cream cones. She handed Rosch his cone before he had a chance to deploy his antibac spray.

"Perk time!" sang Davenport. "Honestly, sometimes I can't believe we get paid for this."

Crunk looked on and checked his timepiece as the labourers loaded the heavy cases onto a series of tables, a few yards away from the enclosure. Fortitude signalled to Hapenny who led an alpaca into the middle of the range. One of the labourers opened the first case revealing an impressive, rifle-looking weapon. Approximately four feet long, chrome plated, with a large purple crystal embedded into the barrel. Assisted by another two labourers, the weapon was hoisted onto the man's shoulder and he turned it towards the first alpaca.

"It'll just take a moment to align with your D.N.A." said Lieutenant Rabz.

The labourer exhaled deeply and braced himself.

Just then, Rosch was approached by another member of the landed gentry, Lord Speck.

"You know-" he began.

Before he had chance to continue, the labourer pulled the trigger to the Reticulant weapon. Speck spun around and dropped his half-eaten turkey leg onto the floor. From the barrel of the weapon came a bright, surging purple energy beam. The weapon sounded a low, gritty, rhythmic pulse and the Alpaca's screams gradually descended in pitch until they became a throbbing, gelatinous squelch.

"Gordon Bennet! Ha Ha!" cried Speck, licking his fingers. "Good heavens, what ever will they think of next?"

As was customary in these parts, Speck read Rosch's I.D badge and considered if the young man was of decent stock. After a moment's recollection;

"You know," he said, "I remember the name Kunnypacken. Bermerian couple, snuffed it if I recollect. Rodney! Come over here there's someone I'd like you to meet."

With that, Rosch was approached by another bouncing tweed legend carrying a paper plate of food.

"Rodney, I'd like you to meet detective Kunnypacken, he's escorting the 'grunt' visitors."

Speck took a turkey leg from Lord Rodney's plate.

"Kunnypacken, Kunnypacken." pondered Lord Rodney. "Ah of course! Yes! The wife, frosty little harpy. Her sister is old 'tin pants' Ahem."

Whilst the pair considered Rosch's pedigree, another alpaca was disintegrated by a different but equally terrifying weapon, invoking another warm round of applause from the gathered.

"Ah! Foxy Caroline!" said Speck.

"Yes, she's still drudging it out in politics I believe." added Lord Rodney. *Scoff* " Bloody mugs game if you ask me."

As Speck and Rodney enjoyed the sunshine and shared memories of the Kunnypackens, Rosch's gaze was locked on the enclosure. Never wanting to seem impolite, Rosch accommodated their attention. However, over their shoulders he watched intently as Steven Happeny, the man in the lab coat, who was tending to the alpacas, walked towards Lord Fortitude. He held his hands outstretched and as far as Rosch could discern, he was explaining that he had no more alpacas. With that, Fortitude raised his hand and two farm labourers escorted Hapenny into the middle of the enclosure.

"Oh nice. Verrrrry nice." said Hapenny.

Whilst Rosch looked on, horrified, Speck and Rodney were still lost in their own conversation.

"Yes, but sadly," said Rodney, "we need those buggers to keep the bloody economy afloat. Otherwise, we'd have comrade bloody Corbett charging the earth and I'd have to move the whole bloody lot overseas again... Isn't Ahem, liaison for...this lot?"

A third weapon blast destroyed Hapenny, leaving no trace except for a scorched print of his cardio-vascular system on the ground and another gentle round of applause from the nobility.

Rosch was speechless when he suddenly became aware that Speck and Rodney were awaiting a response from him.

"Uhm. Yes. I'm, sorry. I think so" said Rosch.

"Oh yes she is!" said Rodney. "Poor bloody bugger, having to deal with these hideous, ghastly creatures. But…" removing a martini from a passing tray, "…god help me I do love their toys."

"Cheers!" added Speck.

As the Ambassador's motorcade left Parsonbury Manor, the horizon was reclaiming the sun, the radiant pinks and purples smearing across the black vehicles like oil slicks.

7:05pm
Frank Ruggerman's House, North London

By now, Frank had greatly improved his 'swivel off the bed' manoeuvre, however, the incontinence was still very much an issue. Still wobbling and with a head like a diseased landfill, Frank made his way out onto the landing of his now spotless house. In the dark, he felt his way to the top of the stairs and peered down at the lights flickering from within the living room. As cautiously as his compromised brain would allow, he clung to the bannister and walked down the stairs. The lights and sounds from the TV grew more and more vivid as he neared the bottom. He clung to the bottom stair post and discerned that the TV channel was changing every three seconds. He slowly made the final step towards the open door to the living room and peeked around the corner. Frank's already harried face fell to despondency as he saw Beatrice vacantly blinking every three seconds causing the channel to change. Frank retreated behind the corner and braced as the disappointment and heartbreak flooded inside. However, the feeling of hopelessness and grievous humiliation barely had time to settle as Frank realised the danger he was in. The only questions now were 'what are its weak points?' and 'did he have sufficient weaponry in the house to kill it?'.

From the living room, Frank could hear the theme from *Malcolm in the Middle*. On the sofa, sat bolt upright,

Beatrice began to gently bounce up and down, humming along with the music.

'You're not the boss of me nooowwwwww! You're not the boss of me nooowwwwww!'

As the familiar lines echoed around the house, Frank crept back up the stairs as silently as he could. Over the years, being stealthy had become less and less a part of Frank's approach, so added to his age and the wildfire of lactic acid in his muscles, avoiding the creaky steps required the concentration of a Formula 1 driver.

"If your mother finds out that I did that in the toilet she'll go nuts!!!"

Frank reached his room, touched the photo of him and Jojo Binks as he always did and slowly opened a drawer at the foot of his wardrobe.

"What is the matter with you?! I will count to five and I want that dog to drive that car back where he found it, are you listening to me?!"

Downstairs, as she gently bounced, Beatrice raised a china tea cup to her mouth, took a bite out of it and chewed on the fine, crunchy porcelain. Frank removed a pistol from the drawer and as quietly as he could and took out the magazine. Empty.

9:13pm
Desmond Deckard Estate, East London

A sea of windows across the three-storey housing estate were filled with curious faces, looking down on the series of black vehicles parked in the courtyard. Leaning on the bonnet, Rosch and Davenport shared a Hawaiian pizza.

"Honestly, taste this life mate, go on taste it." chuckled Davenport with inner disbelief.
Rosch tried to empathise with Davenport's unshakeable sense of self-satisfaction with her life choices but when he tried, he repeatedly felt the straws slip through his fingers. Just then, Officer Bunty emerged from a doorway carrying a shotgun, followed closely by the Ambassador and his entourage. Davenport quickly closed the pizza box, licked her fingers and wiped her hands on her stab vest.
"We're done." said Crunk. "Drop us back at the Met."

London Met HQ

As they passed along the corridor towards the office that had been requisitioned for the Reticulants, Rosch paused to look at a poster. It depicted a young female officer, walking her beat in the sunshine, stopping to talk with an elderly resident. The top line read:

'HELP YOUR COMMUNITY'
At the very bottom of the poster the line continued:
'DON'T BE A C**T'

Rosch was gravely unprepared for the effect these simple words would have on him. Ambassador Crunk led his staff into a large dark office, lit only by the pale green glow of video screens.
"Christ, what a day." groaned Crunk, collapsing into a chair.
"I know," said Deacon Smash, "I can't stand those tweed mafia slags."
"They've got loads of animals there, though." said Lieutenant Rabz.
"True that." said Smash. "I feel bad I forgot which end you put the carrot in."
As his staff settled in, Crunk was deep in thought.
"I'm forgetting something." he said, to no one in particular.

"Ah that happens to the best of us." said Lieutenant Rabz. "You want to watch out for those kicks from the horseys. It'll make a carrot up the arse feel like a moistened towelette."

"Did you forget your catheter?" said Smash, helpfully.

"Shut up, I'm trying to think. And yes, I did... What was it?" said Crunk, tapping his long spindly fingers on his huge grey head.

"I can get more carrots." said Lieutenant Rabz, fearlessly taking the initiative.

"I've got it!" said Crunk.

"Carrots!" cheered Lieutenant Rabz.

"No. Shut up, pervert. I'm talking about that piss head Ruggerman."

Rosch had been lost in his thoughts but that name grabbed his attention.

"Get me Williams in Cloning and Infiltration." barked Crunk.

A fizz and a buzz and a voice appeared on the communicator.

"Hello, Ambassador." said Williams, "I assume you're after an update on the infiltration unit?"

"What's the score?" said Crunk.

"Hook, line and sinker. He's convinced it's his wife come back to him. Silly twat."

Rosch closed his eyes as his abdomen cramped with a grave, incoming realisation.

"That's probably enough emotional torture Williams. I can stream the replay, yeah?"

"Oh yes." said Williams.

"Good. Oh, and Williams?"

"Yes sir."

"We've had enough fun, put it on 'Norman Bates' mode and finish him."

"Copy that gold-leader." said Williams, smiling.

In his lab, Williams sipped his coffee and pressed a red button with a Reticulant symbol that translates both as 'terminate' and 'pleased to meet you'. On his computer

screen appeared a countdown indicating t-minus twenty minutes.
"Yes! The ticking-crock!" Williams chuckled to himself.

Back in the Ambassador's office, Davenport had returned from the cafeteria with a mega-gulp cola. She went to offer some to Rosch but he was gone, she saw only a slowly closing door and heard only the echoes of hard, fast footsteps as Rosch sprinted for the exit. He burst out through the doors and raced across the tarmac to his car.

Frank Ruggerman's House, North London

Frank cursed internally as he realised the only ammunition he had for his pistol was most likely downstairs in the kitchen. He breathed a deep breath and readied himself when he saw his badge on his dressing table. He stood a moment and decided that he wasn't going to die in his vest and pants. Slowly and silently, he donned his scruffy suit, not paying mind to the sudden awareness of the weight he had lost in the last month. He adjusted his tie, reached for his badge and clipped it onto his belt.
The TV still bellowed the sounds of quality tea-time programming and Beatrice continued to gently bounce on the sofa.

'Dewey! Malcolm! Reese! Get in here! How many times have I told you about pyramid schemes?!'

Frank hugged the wall once again as he crept back down the stairs. Avoiding the creaky steps again caused perspiration to descend his brow. He could feel his heart about to beat its way out of his throat.

'Lois! Honey! It'll grow back as soon as he hits puberty!'

Frank stopped as he reached the bottom of the stairs and waited. Beatrice's show had gone to adverts which clearly displeased her as she stopped bouncing. Frank waited, motionless, daring not to breathe. With the return of the theme music, Beatrice began bouncing once again and Frank slipped around the corner and into the kitchen.

In the dark he felt his way around the top cupboard. Inside, he found a box of Weetabix containing a clip with one bullet left. He cautiously and quietly clicked open the pistol, removed the clip and inserted the bullet. At that moment, Rosch's car screeched off the North Circular and tore it's way into North London. Rosch swerved between the other cars at blistering speed, fumbling with his phone with one hand.
"Fucking come on! You bastard! Pick up!"
Upstairs on Frank's muted phone, the screen lit blue and flashed the name 'Darth Waitrose'.
"Shit! Shitting shit it!" cursed Rosch.
Without taking his eyes off the kitchen doorway, Frank slowly opened the lower cupboard. He knocked into a wooden chair making the shortest scrape on the tiled floor. He froze and Beatrice stopped bouncing. Frank then opened a biscuit tin that was full of live 9mm bullets.
"Get in." he whispered.
"Get in what darling?" said Beatrice, coldly from the kitchen doorway.
Frank almost leapt out of his skin and momentarily considered how a heart attack might actually be the best possible outcome here.
"What are you doing dressed?" asked Beatrice.
"Nothing love." replied Frank, trying to regulate his breathing from *Defcon 1* to '*casual man about town*' "I just found some biscuits I was looking for."
"Do you want a pint of brandy to go with them?"
"Uhm, yeah, that'd be lovely."
Beatrice smiled.
"I'll just go to the cupboard." she said.

As she looked for the brandy, she had her back towards him.
"Darling?" he said.
"Yes love?" she said, slowly turning to face him.
Frank stepped towards what was a truly uncanny replica of a woman he once loved. With a combination of love, sick humour and an appreciation of exceptional craftsmanship he looked into her face.
"You hate *Malcolm in the Middle*."
Beatrice appeared to be looking through him. Her expression held the look of gentle curiosity that you can only see on the face of an A.I, as if it's calculating whether to rip out your larynx or make you a sandwich.
"Ha Ha. Nonsense love. It's genius." she said, jovially.
Beatrice turned away to leave the kitchen.
"Between the writing and the performances." she said. "Bryan Cranston's Hal is the most iconic Dad since Homer."
As Beatrice stepped along the dark hallway towards the living room, Frank was loading the remaining bullets into his clip.
"...I couldn't even watch him in *Breaking Bad*."
As she spoke the word '*Bad*', her eyes lit red and her voice dropped one octave and lost all trace of humanity.
Rosch's tires screamed as he swung onto Frank's road and brought the car to a skidding halt. He raced from the car, up the path and drew his pistol. The door had been smashed almost to pieces with just a saloon-like flap hanging from one of the hinges.
"Ruggerman!" he screamed.

    The house looked like a riot had taken place. As he crept further into the destruction, he glanced into the living room where the TV sparked glowing embers through the huge hole in the screen. As he walked further down the hall, towards the kitchen, he saw blood. A thick trail smeared across the floor and walls with a huge concentration on the kitchen table along with a junior hacksaw. The trail led him towards the back door. Taking a deep breath, Rosch slowly gripped the handle and cocked his pistol. He inched the door open and stepped out into the garden. The garden sloped steeply away from the house and red-brick steps marked the path downwards. Once at the bottom of the steps, Rosch stood speechless as he saw Frank in a woolly hat and scarf, cigarette in mouth and soaked in blood. Frank was rotating between swigging from a vodka bottle and feeding what looked like body parts into a woodchipper. Unable to speak, Rosch simply watched as Frank stuffed in the last two pieces, finished the vodka and collapsed in a deck chair. Eventually, Rosch walked towards Frank and placed a hand on his shoulder. Frank erupted with rage.

"Get off me!" he screamed, immediately losing his balance and collapsing into Rosch's arms. Frank sobbed hopelessly into Rosch's coat.

"Alright," said Rosch, "let's just get you back in the warm, shall we?"

The ground was deathly slippery with blood. Rosch did his best to carry Frank up the steps and back inside. Just then, Frank murmured something.

"What was that, Ruggerman?" asked Rosch.

Frank murmured again, only with more passion.

"Well, I'm afraid it's going to have to wait." said an encumbered Rosch, returning to the task in hand.

'Thwip!' A dart hit Rosch in the neck and he lost consciousness. Just then Frank summoned the very last of his lucidity and spoke.

"I said look out for the ninja." then he blacked out.

EPISODE VIII

**Friday
9:36am
Caroline Ahem's Country Home, Wood Green**

The engine of the golf buggy carrying Caroline Ahem and her assistant Grace roared as they powered up an undulating bank of the rear grounds.

"That's it, that's it, stop! Stop!..Nice and easy." said Ahem, as she trained her shotgun on the nearest and most oblivious peacock. Her concentration was shattered by the loud ringing of the telephone that Grace had installed in the buggy.

"Oh, for fucks sake." snapped Ahem as she shouldered her shotgun, triggered the firing pin and decimated the roof of the golf cart. Seething and with peacocks fled, Ahem centred herself and answered the call.

"Ambassador! How is my nephew getting along?"

"Not impressed, Gsa Gsa." growled Crunk, from his secret base, "Your boy's gone AWOL."

"AWOL?" said Ahem. "That can't be."

"Two days ago he ran out of my office like a demented gazelle. He hasn't shown up for work since so I've put the feelers out looking for him."

"Ambassador, surely there must be some kind of explanation?"

"His phone's off, he's not at home. He's missing...and the souse has gone too..."

Ahem's throat ran dry.

"...and I guarantee you if he's *not* with me, then he *is* with Ruggerman, and that means problems."

"Ambassador, if I can-" began Ahem.
"Save it for the tea rooms, Gsa Gsa. Your boy's a liability."
The line went dead. Ahem simmered steadily, she knew from experience that she would have to let the rage subside before her supernatural capacity for ruthless contingencies would kick in. Also well versed in these situations, Grace waited a minute before venturing;
"You look disappointed...Shall we go over to the monkey house?"
Ahem breathed deeply, looked into the face of her assistant and enjoyed her favourite feeling in all the world, the feeling of money well spent.

10:30pm

After driving continuously for two days, a car, driven by an unknown figure, was now deep in the woodlands that lie west of London. It was one of the last great wildernesses of Britain. Mile after mile of untameable forest, dense woodlands and unforgiving topography, sparsely populated by only the hardiest of English folk. The driver sat silently as the vehicle, containing an unconscious Frank and Rosch, left London far, far behind.

Before reaching their destination, the driver had to pull in at 'Acrid Hank's Gas and Goulash', a rest stop so remote it was seen by human eyes less often than Halley's comet. The unknown figure, slim and dressed top to toe in black, filled the tank and proceeded inside the rest stop to pay. Unbeknownst to the figure, sitting on the other side of the forecourt, pretending to read a newspaper, was Jazz Gabnit. During a previous colonisation, Ambassador Crunk had assembled a team of notorious Reticulant outlaws, misfits and estate agents to form a network of spies he called 'the feelers'. Amongst this team were some of the most wayward Reticulants ever born but Crunk had forged them into a highly effective squad that was just as good at finding things as it was at making them disappear. He had recruited Gabnit during a television awards ceremony, held on Levinson 6 of the Paramount nebular. On Reticula, *'How I Met Your Mother'* had become a pandemic smash hit. During the announcement of its award for 'Best Breakthrough', an inebriated Jazz Gabnit had rushed the stage screaming, 'There's no fucking jokes in it! What the fuck is wrong with you people?!' The Ambassador, who was on one of the premier tables at the event, looked up from his sushi and saw the petit, wrinkly, grey and naked form of Gabnit wrestle with a dozen security staff. He realised that he had not seen such a promising talent in years so he did what he always did, he had her family terminated and arranged an interview.

For now, Jazz Gabnit watched the screen door close behind the slim figure as they entered the rest stop. She carefully placed her paper down next to her, donned her XXXXL trucker cap and casually sauntered over to the car. Pressed up against the rear passenger windows, she saw the unconscious faces of Frank and Rosch. Just before the screen door opened once again, Gabnit leisurely returned to her bench, casually chewing on a long piece of grass. As the car pulled away, Gabnit touched the face of her watch and spoke;
"Yeah, it's Gabnit. I've got a message for the chief. Tell him 'get ready to love me.'

4:47am

The last five hours of the journey had been on dirt track as the car containing Frank and Rosch ventured deeper and deeper into the woods of Cranston. The first embers of the dawn were approaching the horizon but for now the woods were still as dark as could be. The headlights of the car were the only light visible for miles around. If it were seen from above, the car looked like a lost electron wandering a giant black circuit board. The car slowed as the dirt track began to ascend up a hill. Several deer leaped into the path of the car and stared, unblinking before racing off ahead. Finally, a cabin came into view.

The car pulled to a stop on a gentle bank that led to the front steps of the cabin. Constructed from giant timbers, it sat on top of a hill, in a large clearing that gently sloped away to the west. One by one, the driver carefully dragged the unconscious detectives up the front steps, across the porch and inside.

8:11am
Acrid Hank's Gas & Goulash

Jazz Gabnit was using the outhouse when a call came from Ambassador Crunk.
"Hello guv." said Gabnit, smiling.
"Where are they?" snapped Crunk.
"Some cabin in the woods outside Cranston. The brief said not to take action, but you give me the signal and I can have 'em ready and on the grill before lunchtime."
"No, can't do it." said Crunk. "Even with that piss head this close to the incontinence aisle, I can't risk martyring him. With these kids it's all 'hashtags' this, and 'Graham Linehan' that. If social media gets wind of it like we're involved, they'll turn Shane MacGowan into Che Guevara."
"...Che MacGowan." smirked Gabnit.
"...Don't try and be clever Gabnit."
"Sorry guv."
"No, this requires something of a light touch. Get onto Williams in Cloning and Infiltration and ask him for one of his new hypno-thingys."
"Hypno-thingy." said Gabnit, confidently.
"Yeah, it's the latest thing we're selling to human little ones. It spins round and has all flashing lights. It's fucking stupid really but they seem to like that kind of stuff."
"On it, Guv."

9:22am
The Cabin, Cranston Woods

The ground floor of the cabin was open plan. In the rear, the kitchen consisted of carved, tan-coloured cupboards and thick, heavy timber work surfaces. In the front, a series of ancient, dusty armchairs and a sofa sat encircling a huge hearth. The former occupier had been something of a hoarder and the place was littered with strange bric a brac like mannikin parts, old wheelchairs, bagpipes, stuffed animals and hunting gear. With the amber glow from the hearth dancing on Rosch's sleeping face as he lay in the Napoleonic armchair, the figure in black lay a thick tartan blanket on him.

The sound of a cocktail shaker in fairly close proximity sawed through Rosch's tender and abruptly awoken head. As his vision began to clear, Rosch quickly recognized the fact that he had no idea where he was. The tranquilliser had left him with a cruel and brutal hangover. His first step towards a thought triggered a wave of catastrophic nausea so horrible he was gutted it didn't kill him. Rosch was trying to minimise his actions to just breathing when he noticed the slumbering form of Frank Ruggerman in the armchair across from him. As Rosch looked at Frank's 'rarely this peaceful' face, inside him, guilt and indignancy gently wrestled for dominance.

Emerging from behind the chair, the figure in black sat next to Frank, holding a tray with a bowl of stew, a spoon, a tea towel and a Mai Tai. Still essentially paralyzed by the lingering traces of the tranquilliser, Rosch looked carefully at the stranger who was now feeding Frank the stew.
"And you are?" asked Rosch, the action of speaking shaving ten years from his life.
The figure in black turned coolly, looked at Rosch and then returned to feeding Frank. From what he could discern,

Rosch perceived the figure as a Japanese woman in her late 20's. Her jet-black cat suit stopped at the neck and her hair was wrapped in a tight bun. Rosch was considering how beautiful she was when the sound of her voice doused him like a bucket of ice-cold slops.

"Detective Kunnypacken." she said, with a voice like the dry, reluctant speech of someone woken up after a ten-thousand-year nap. For reference, think of a female, Japanese, Werner Hertzog.

"That is *my* name." said Rosch, with a hint of mania.

The toxic sensations in Rosch's body, combined with everything else that had happened to him in the last eight weeks had rendered Rosch in a volatile state of existential panic.

"And I'm…" said the woman, "not going through this twice so you'll have to wait until Frank is lucid."

Rosch groaned and his head slumped backwards.

"I'm awake, I'm awake." murmured Frank, groggily searching for his cigarettes.

"Good. Then I can begin." she said.

After another five, silent, exposition-less minutes while she set up a video projector, Rosch exploded.

"Argh! For fuck's sake!" he cried. "I can't take this shit anymore, will someone please shoot me in the fucking head."

"Calm down Ja Ja!" yelled Frank, wincing at the feeling of a chemical dagger in his cranium.

"Detectives." said the woman.

Frank and Rosch were both exhausted from their brief spat.

"I am Gimudzuke Rerata of the London Metropolitan Police Service. As you are both English and therefore ignorant, you may call me Gim."

"Uhm, my parents were Bermerian" said Rosch, hopefully.

"Whatever." said Gim.

"What do you want?" said Frank, lighting another cigarette.

Gim carried herself with permanent intent and indefatigable poise. She looked across the faces of her new companions.

"I am here to help you stop an invasion."

Outside Cranston Village

A gentle breeze blew and a flurry of yellow petals descended onto a stream before being carried beneath the sheltering boughs of the willow trees. The golden sun poked through the canopy and its rays bounced playfully on the gentle ripples of the fresh, mountain water. Across a wooden bridge, three young children scampered.

"Last one across gets chlamydia!" cried Elizabeth, her brothers following close behind.

As they reached the other side, their mother, in grimy, tattered clothes, groaning under the weight of bags and picnic baskets appeared.

"Nobody's getting chlamydia!" she cried. "Elizabeth, where do you learn these words?"

Breathless, she leaned against a tree for support.

"William! Harry!" she cried. "Don't go too far!"

Elizabeth left her brothers to wrestle and she ventured further into the undergrowth. She could hear their heated debate continue behind her.

"You're the one with chlamydia!"

"No! You're the big fat chlamydia face!"

"Boys! For Christ's sake!" screamed their mother, removing a hip flask from her battered cardigan.

Underneath a scarlet rhododendron, Elizabeth spotted something metallic and shiny. She inched closer to it and picked it up. It was the shape of a spinning top and decorated with abstract, ruby red symbols. She inspected it carefully and it shimmered with a flash of red light that coursed from the top to the bottom and back. In a flash, red lasers shot out from the device and mapped Elizabeth's face before writing rapid, intricate information onto her irises. Her brothers were still grappling and giving mutual wedgies as Elizabeth approached them. Her face was cold and vacant. As she neared, the boys stopped and looked at the strange device she held in her hands. A minute later, heaving their bags across the wooden bridge, their mother joined them on the bank of the stream. Her children all stared at her silently. Elizabeth aimed the device at her mother.

"What have you got there darling?" she said.

All the humanity ebbed from her face as the ruby lasers busily wrote coded information into her eyes. Once the lasers had stopped, the family left the bags and without a word, carried the device back to the village with them.

Thirty metres away, Jazz Gabnit was strolling confidently. She jovially tapped the face of her watch and up came the face of Ambassador Crunk.

"Hello guv?" she beamed. "The toy is active, repeat the toy is active."

9:53am
The Cabin, Cranston Woods

The projector, setup by Gim, wheezed and groaned like an elderly moose birthing a caravan.

"An invasion?" said Rosch

Gim pulled down a dusty projector screen.

"For the fifth time, yes," she said, "an invasion. The 'visitors' are not here for fun, nor is it their first time. But this you already know."

She returned her attention to the projector.

"Why me?" said Frank.

Rosch felt the familiar twinge of being treated like he was invisible but mostly felt disappointed he wasn't used to it by now.

"A long time ago," said Gim, "you were in Kyoto on a sake bender. You met my father, a scientist by the name of Mitsuo Genda."

Frank scratched his temple and thought long and hard.

"I can't remember…" he said, struggling to recall. "...Japan?"

"Whilst there, you did a tremendous service for my father. On his deathbed he made me vow..."

2014
Masamune Shirow Hospital, Kyoto, Japan

Mitsuo Genda, Gim's father, lay in a bed in the intensive care unit, tended to by a nurse and his devoted daughter. His withered frame was failing but he was still a man of great tenacity and conviction.

"Gimudzuke." he whispered. "I want you to-"

He was interrupted by the nurse solemnly placing the bed sheet over his face. With what little strength he had left, he wriggled in protest. The nurse bowed her head in apology and removed the bed sheet. Genda glared at the nurse before returning his attention to his daughter.

"You must help Detective Frank Ruggerman of the Western Tactical Unit," he said. "a shambolic but highly effective branch of the London Met. I owe him a great debt. He is a man of integrity who will be invaluable in humanity's fight for survival."

The nurse had reached once again for the bedsheet and without breaking eye contact with her father, Gim stopped her hand and put the sheet back down.

"How will I find him?" she asked.

The old man trembled as he leaned forward.

"He likes bars" he said, "bars and b-bus stops. You must promise me, you will protect him. The fate of the world depends on it."

Genda noticed the nurse standing dutifully by with a sheet at the ready.

"I don't like you." he said.

The old man shook and coughed and the life support machine sounded the beeping chorus of a life ending.

"Fatherrrrr!!" cried Gim, as Frank and Rosch listened, captivated by the candid account.

"That day I swore I would protect you," she said, "knowing that one day you would be called upon to expose a great sham. That sham is here. I moved to London and joined the police where I could keep you close."

"What did your father know?" said Frank, reaching down the side of the armchair for his lighter.

Gim clapped twice and the orange glow from the hearth and the many candles in the room lowered by half.

"My father worked in advanced communications for the Japanese space program."

The projector rotated one agonised notch and a black and white photograph appeared of four Japanese scientists, holding glasses of champagne and wearing lab coats outside the J.A.S.A. headquarters in Tokyo.

"He and his team intercepted a transmission." said Gim. "They traced its source back to a distant planet called Rivron 7. Upon deciphering, they discovered it was a warning... a prophecy. The message told of a race of creatures whose mission was to massively overstay their welcome on every livable planet in the known universe."

The next slide depicted a diagram of planets that had been systematically colonised by the Reticulants. The latest planet targeted, being Earth.

"Like a friend who needs your sofa for a couple of nights, and then stays for ten years." she said. "The Reticulants are colonising with the intent of bleeding the dominant species dry. My father believed that you Frank, are in a unique position with a unique understanding, to stop them."

"I'll agree" said Rosch, "that they're weird creatures with some shady dealings but I would hardly call appearing on *'Britain's Got Performers'* an invasion."

"Oh, come off it, Lando." scoffed Frank, "It's obviously a sham. You must have thought it strange when the British government was actively *encouraging* people to 'welcome foreigners'."

Rosch subtly nodded in concurrence.

"But I still don't get it, why me?" said Frank.

The next slide showed the facade of a bowling alley.

"In 1997," said Gim, "you led an investigation that exposed rigged, high stakes contests at a bowling alley in Slough."

The following slide showed a laboratory housing a dozen large tubes containing strange, genetic creations, suspended in liquid.

"The Reticulants had been ploughing the profits into genetically modified TV personalities. Thanks to you, they only got as far as... Justin Lee Collins."

"Who?" said Rosch.

"Precisely." said Gim.

The next slide shown by the bronchially wrecked projector, showed a picture of a handsome, middle-aged man on a university campus.

"Isle of Wight 2003," continued Gim, "you saved Bernard Hanklin, a university professor, from the electric chair, when you discovered his erratic behaviour was down to his use of condoms laced with LSD."

Both Frank and Rosch briefly contemplated the concept before recoiling.

"Little did you know" continued Gim, "he was a test subject for a wayward Reticulant General called Krablander. The experiment was yet another attempt...to spice up his marriage."

With the next rotation, the projector began making additional sounds of distress.

"Hackney 2012, you prevented a volcanic eruption underneath Bethnal Green by playing recordings of wildebeest mating at subsonic frequencies. That eruption would've exposed millions of dollars worth of tantamountium, a rare mineral Reticulants use in their Wi-Fi extenders. It is found in great abundance under the streets of Hackney. As well as your campaign to expose them, you have unknowingly thwarted them many times. Frank, you are more important than you can ever know. It is only you that can save this world from invasion. It is you Frank" said Gim, before looking to Rosch.

"...and him."

Cranston Village

Throughout that morning, Elizabeth had deployed the device on every villager they had come into contact with. Holding the shiny device between her little hands, Elizabeth walked at the head of a group now eighty strong composed of children and adults from the village. Silently, the mob shuffled its way along the lanes, searching through outhouses and barns, steadily making its way through Cranston.

A little while later, Elizabeth, followed closely by her extensive entourage, came to a stop. Just up ahead, Miss Elsa Copple, a teacher from Cranston, was busy changing the tyre of the school bus on the side of the road. The bus had been transporting the *'Lil' Cockers Gun Club'*, a local gun association for weapons enthusiasts aged 7 - 12. The sun was now beating down. As Miss Copple released the jack, she stood and wiped her brow leaving a smear of black grease across her forehead. She looked up into the windows of the bus and saw the faces of the gun club peering out at something behind her. She turned around and saw little Elizabeth, with most of the rest of the village in tow.
"Hello Elizabeth." said Miss Copple, squinting in the sun. Miss Copple surveyed the odd-looking collection of locals that had amassed behind Elizabeth before noticing the shiny device that Elizabeth held in her hands.
"Well, what have you got there?" she asked.

The Cabin, Cranston Woods

With it being sadly too late for the toilet, Gim gently lay Frank down in the bathtub and washed him. Frank draped his arm around Gim's neck and she carefully helped him onto the floor where she dried and powdered him. When cleaned and dressed, Gim steadily walked Frank back to the armchair by the fire.

A few hours later, Rosch, wrapped in a blanket, approached Gim in the kitchen while she was stirring 'old fashioneds'. Rosch felt the warmth from the timber beneath his bare feet and smelled the rich stew that was gently bubbling away. Gim was focussing on the drinks when Rosch spoke.

"Those waffles were quite something, thank you."

Without appearing to inhale, Gim responded.

"I think it only fair to tell you that I do not find you remotely sexually attractive in any way, on any level. You are like... Lord Fauntleroy love child of Bruno Mars and David Hyde-Pierce."

If Rosch had not been made speechless, he would have asked the Earth to swallow him.

"In addition." continued Gim, "Thank you. The recipe belonged to my grandmother. She grew up in Osaka and it involves a secret blend of rare herbs and spices you can only find in that region."

Rosch wrapped the blanket a little more tightly around him.

"Can I help?" he said, surveying the ingredients and bottles spread across the heavy timber work surface.

"You've seen me here for nearly three hours. Asking now just makes me want to say 'no' on general principle." replied Gim, without looking up from her stirring.

"I'm sorry." said Rosch. "I want to help."

Gim looked at Rosch, inquiringly.

"Okay. Help me bring him to the bar."

Gim and Rosch carefully approached Frank. Upon sensing Rosch, Frank lashed out.

"Toff crap Lando Judas piss!" he shouted, flailing his arms.

"You must save your strength." said Gim, gently subduing him. "You can berate him for his cowardly betrayal later."

Carefully and slowly, they lifted Frank to his feet, walked him over to the counter in the kitchen and sat him on a stool.

"He is able to process solid food again" said Gim, "but he will not survive unless he can make his own drinks."

"I thought it was the drinks that did this to him." said Rosch.

"No. That was your betrayal. He could never let on how it hurt him."
Rosch looked at the harried face of the old man.
"A man like Frank walks a very fine line." said Gim. "A magical, high functioning level of inebriation where his body and mind are in perfect harmony. In order for him to return to optimum capacity, he must retrain as a bartender."

Over the next few days, Gim encouraged Frank to practise the essential techniques of bartending. She held his hand while he wrestled against the shakes to stir ice in steady concentric circles. Frank would dribble onto the counter as all of his concentration was poured into fixing a good mint sprig onto a julep. The journey was hard and progress was slow. He would sob wretchedly after spilling the contents of a boston shaker, but Gim was a patient instructor. At the end of each session, Gim and Rosch would gently remove the chunks of pineapple from Frank's suit and put him to rest once again.

The next day, while Frank and Gim persisted, Rosch wandered the surrounding woods. He had gathered local fruits including limes, passion fruits and guavas in a basket he carried on his arm. As the sun descended, Rosch stopped to smell some luscious looking blackberries. The feeling of gratitude and harmony with the world around him was sadly shattered by the sight of a giant, rearing grizzly bear towering over him.

Later, back in the cabin. Gim managed the slightest smile as Frank successfully poured himself a quality daiquiri. Frank slowly raised the glass to his lips and savoured the sweet taste of victory. He laughed like a man who had never laughed before. Rosch, through the gaps in his bandages, saw the compassion between Gim and Frank, and as Rosch gently smiled, a few hundred yards away, Elizabeth led the rest of her village to the edge of a clearing.

After the sun had gone down, the mob had acquired torches, that is to say, they had set fire to the eight tallest villagers. They began to encircle the clearing, each villager looking to Elizabeth for the signal.

Back in the cabin, as the fire crackled, Gim adjusted Frank's blanket. Rosch cautiously removed one of the bandages from across his face and opened his medikit. Gim approached as Rosch winced at contact with the antiseptic swab.

"Let me see." she said.

She took the swab from him and adjusted his head into the light. As she cleaned his facial wounds, Rosch looked into her resolute face.

"Do you promise you didn't know about the bears?" asked Rosch.

"...No." she replied.

Rosch winced but was quickly calmed by Gim's impatience.

"Earlier" said Rosch, "you said I was important too."

"Yes." said Gim.

"...How?"

"All energy flows to the whims of opposing furies," said Gim. "Frank, is a mutated truth-junkie with an incisive imagination, an extraordinary eye for human weakness and an unwavering hatred of corruption."

"And me?" asked Rosch, hesitantly.

"You are his second. He needs you. In movie terms you are... Emilio Estevez. Misunderstood, hopelessly flawed but excellent in a buddy cop scenario."

A few minutes later, Gim and Rosch stepped out onto the porch. The night air was cold and humid. Moths collided with the glass on the smoky gas lamps that hung from the awning.

"Rosch." said Gim, sternly.

Rosch inhaled deeply.

"You know it's lovely how-"

"Rosch!" yelled Gim.

Gim dived towards Rosch and dragged him to the floor as a plague of bullets ripped through the timber of the porch, shattering glass and upturning chairs. Just then, Frank appeared at the door with a pistol in one hand and a rum and coke in the other.

"Get inside!" he yelled, firing into the treeline.

A bullet sent a large wooden splinter slicing through Gim's calf and she stumbled. Gritting her teeth, she dragged Rosch inside. Frank slammed the front door closed and began barricading it with anything and everything to hand. Rosch was scrambling for his pistol which hung from his armchair when he noticed the three villagers that were shuffling slowly in through the back door.

"The rear!" he shouted.

"Oh, shit the bed!" raged Frank, as he dropped a clip.

Gim grimaced as she tied a bandage tightly around her calf. Rosch fired round after round into the encroaching locals. They seemed almost oblivious to the impact of the bullets on their bodies, one, two, three shots, but still they shuffled onwards.

"Headshots Rosch." instructed Gim sternly, as she systematically put them down.

Rosch slid an armchair across the floor towards the back door, closed it and wedged it shut. Through the window, Rosch saw another trio of villagers step onto the back porch. He smashed his pistol through the window and fired.

Above Gim's head, a window broke inwards and four villagers reached slothily inside. Gim rolled forward and grabbed a bottle of vodka off the bar.

"No!" roared Frank.

She threw it hard against the window frame, showering the clambering locals in booze. She grabbed a nearby candle and threw it onto the floor underneath the window. The four immolated villagers ran back to the treeline and Gim put out the last of the fire in the cabin with the soda gun.

From the treeline, Elizabeth watched four of her minions race past her. The glow from the flames engulfing their bodies, illuminating the underbrush as they ran off into the distance.

Back in the cabin, Gim and Frank dropped several more locals that were approaching up the hill.

"Nice to see the English countryside is embracing tourism again." said Frank.

Rosch loaded another clip and fired through the window.

"Who in the effing arsenal are these people?" cried Rosch, hysterically. "What do they want?"

From her vantage point on the east side of the cabin, Gim peered out into the moonlit night.

"They're pulling back." she said.

"For now." said Frank, reloading. "They don't know how much ammo we've got."

Rosch checked his phone signal.

"Apparently I've got minus two bars." he said, confused. "We've got to get some back up out here."

"Not likely." said Gim. "This location was chosen as a remote hide away... I was not expecting the 'Wicker Man Ensemble' to show up."

"Why are they trying to kill us?" asked Rosch.

"It's not 'them'." said Frank. "It's the aliens. Mind control. For them it's as sophisticated technologically as you putting the kettle on."

"They must have spotted us en route." said Gim. "I have failed."

"Not even Gim." assured Frank. "Firstly, we're not dead yet. Second, you rescued us out of the fire but remaining hidden was never an option."

"Mind control?" puzzled Rosch.

"Yes." said Frank. "They expose a community to some kind of hypno-thingy, turn the villagers into 'night of the living dickhead' and we get disposed of without them getting their hands dirty."

"Target!" yelled Gim, firing twice. An incoming round exploded a window next to her and she fell to the floor.

"Gimudzuke!" cried Rosch.

"Lando! Help her." barked Frank, firing back.

Rosch scrambled over with the medikit and began wiping blood from Gim's face. Frank watched three locals walking

away from the car and flames begin to lick their way up the bodywork.
"Frank," said Gim, "can we clear a way to the car?"
Rosch reapplied the tourniquet on Gim's calf.
"Uhm." said Frank.
The explosion of the car illuminated Frank's face in a warm amber glow.
"Yes." he said. "But I'm afraid the eleven-hundred-degree temperature might prove too much for the aircon."
"Bastards." said Gim.
"What are we going to do?" said Rosch.
"Frank." said Gim, as Rosch helped her to her feet. "The sun is about to come up."
"Good." said Frank. "Lando, gather whatever you can find and barricade this place, we'll hold the perimeter."
Rosch assisted Gim into position overlooking the clearing and approached Frank at the front window.
"I hate to be the bearer of bad tidings," he said, quietly, "but I've got about three rounds left."
Frank opened his weapon to reveal four rounds."
"Yep." said Frank, quietly.

   The deep sapphire of the night was slowly fading into the grey violets of the dawn. Elizabeth stood in the tree line with the vast majority of her horde still at her side. She raised her hand and cried a most peculiar shriek. With that, the locals began to slowly advance in unison.
"They're moving!" yelled Gim.
Nearby, branches lashed against a windscreen, moving at high speed.
"Right." ordered Frank. "Once we're out, it's hand to hand. Everyone grab a weapon."
Gim took a large knife from the bar, Rosch took an iron from the fireplace and Frank grabbed a mannikin leg. From his window, Rosch saw a line of armed 'Lil Cockers' approaching, brandishing rifles.
"Here they come!" shouted Rosch.

Rosch fired his last three rounds, dropped his pistol and swung the heavy poker. Gim, gaffer-taped the knife to a broken broom handle that she had found under the counter.

Closer now, the unknown car thrashed its way through the dense woods. With a burst of acceleration, the car broke through into the clearing. Elizabeth turned and her face became lit up by high beam headlights. With a great burst of revs, she disappeared underneath the rampaging vehicle. Frank looked out towards the treeline.
"Wait a minute." he said, quietly.
In the distance, the unknown car careened across the open ground and up the hill towards the cabin.
"What is it Ruggerman? Talk to me!" called Rosch, dauntedly.
Frank peered outwards.
"It's... Oh shit."
As he drove the speeding car up the hill, Standards Officer Eugene Toltattler was listening to his favourite talk radio show.
"...And I for one just don't see what's unreasonable about that." said the voice of outspoken, right-wing irritant, Nigel Copraphage.
"Of course." replied the voice of seasoned host, Nick Khanute. *"If you don't like this government, if you don't like the visitors, then I'm sure Ha-Ha, then I'm sure, Venezuela Ha-Ha will happily welcome-"*
Toltattler pulled his car to a stop a few yards from the burning wreck of Gim's car, exited and jogged up the steps onto the porch. Inside, Frank, Rosch and Gim stared at him, speechless. Toltattler closed the door behind him and began.
"Gentlemen. Officer. After weeks of searching for you, I have-"
"For fucks sake Toltattler! Get down!" bellowed Frank, as a sustained volley of gunfire decimated the cabin. Once the firing subsided, Toltattler continued.
"Detective, assistant detective, officer-"

"I'm, full detective now." corrected Rosch, timidly, causing a flash of disgust on Frank's face.

"Kunnypacken," said Toltattler, "after not showing up for diplomatics duty for a week, you have been subsequently demoted back to assistant. I have your notice papers in my briefcase. I also require a statement of absence from you written-"

"What the fuck are you doing here!?" snapped Frank.

"Well, I-" began Toltattler.

"Heads up!" shouted Gim, as three locals mounted the porch.

Frank pushed through, out onto the porch, closely followed by Toltattler, Gim and Rosch. Frank caved in the head of a local with a swing of his mannikin leg, while Gim and Rosch beat back the other two with bone shattering blows. Toltattler dropped another three approaching locals with his revolver.

"As" BANG "the supervising assessment officer," BANG "I'm here to continue your" BANG "assessment."

Frank delivered a final blow to the last remaining 'Lil Cocker', before he clouted two other locals, knocking them over the edge of the porch.

"Jesus Christ Toltattler!" yelled Frank. "That was weeks ago!"

Toltattler clubbed a nearby local with his gun and fired at another.

"Until the assessment is completed," he said, "I must monitor you and your partner for as long as required until I am satisfied that all standards and practices are being adhered to."

With the porch cleared, they returned inside and reinforced the barricade.

"For example." said Toltattler. "It is clear you have both entered a hostile situation with a woefully insufficient complement of weapons and ammunition."

A volley of gunfire rocked the south wall.

"I see at least half a dozen children out there with weapons and the manual says any hostile engagement with suspects aged 8-12 requires at least one tactical 12-gauge be deployed for every three officers in the operation."

Gim and Rosch fought off the last remaining locals that had breached the east windows.

"One more charge like that and we are finished." said Gim.

"What are we going to do?" said Rosch. "All the ammo's gone."

"Case in point." said Toltattler. "As a properly equipped assessment officer of the Met. I have in my trunk the regulation arsenal for a hostile scenario engaged in during an assessment."

"Someone is going to have to go out to the car." said Rosch.

"I'll go." said Gim.

"You two stay here." said Frank. "Me and Toltattler will go. We've a better chance of bringing the weapons back if there's two of us."

"Nice try Ruggerman, but you are labelled under my assessment as a high flight risk so you will be staying here. I am the supervising officer and so I'll retrieve the weapons."

Toltattler braced himself to open the door and then looked at Frank.

"Lead your team." he said.

He took three deep breaths and opened the door, closing it again immediately as gunfire continued to destroy the front wall of the cabin. As the firing stopped, he spoke.

"...We may need a distraction."

"Wait! Look!" said Gim.

She directed their attention to the mountain of bric a brac that was housed under the stairs.

"Rosch, Frank, help me with this." she said.

Under her guidance, they assembled a complete mannikin, strapped it into a wheelchair and connected a set of bagpipes to an electric air pump, finally taping them to the mannikin. Frank kissed a bottle of brandy and poured it all over the chair. They pushed the wheelchair to the back door and out onto the path that led towards the road. Frank lit a cigarette and dropped it onto the chair before they pushed it down the hill.

"Wait!" said Gim, racing forward just in time to start the air pump cueing an intolerably loud drone from the bagpipes that sounded like a zeppelin dying of boredom.

The locals stopped advancing. For many of them, their slack jawed expressions developed notes of abject confusion. They watched as the flaming chair gathered speed, the mannikin's tethers tested to the brink as the chair bounced up and down, speeding towards the treeline.

"Go! Go! Go!" yelled Frank.

Toltattler raced out of the door and down the steps where he was confronted by a ten-year-old boy with a rifle. Toltattler dummy-stepped, bobbed and slapped the child across the face, sending him sprawling. As Toltattler reached the boot of the car, five locals converged on him. At that moment, Frank, Gim and Rosch attacked them with their assorted melee hardware. Toltattler removed two large sports bags from the boot.

"Let's move!" he shouted.

They raced back into the cabin and reset the barricade. Frantically, they removed shotguns and rifles from the sports bags and began loading shells into clips and chambers.

"Uhm!" shouted Rosch, drawing everyone's attention to the dozen locals that had just breached the back door.

Sweat pooled on brows as locals shuffled in through the back door and bullets slipped inside magazines. Gim was steadfast. She knew the AR-15 inside and out and she swiftly readied it for action.

"Officer." said Toltattler. "If you have not been properly trained on the AR-15 I am required-"

Without a word Gim slapped him hard across the face and with a tiny whimper, he refocused on loading. Gim slid the bolt into place.

"Firing!" she shouted.

The rest soon followed and the advancing locals steadily disintegrated as extremities and chunks of flesh were blasted onto the surrounding woodwork.

"Once we drop the first line," roared Frank, "we take positions. Gim, Lando take the veranda side, Toltattler, the porch."

As the body parts and viscera accumulated on the kitchen floor, still they came.

"There's too many Ruggerman." warned Toltattler.

"We need to carve a way to the car!" said Rosch. "It's our only way out!"

"All right. Fuck it." agreed Frank, turning back towards the front door.

Retreating towards the front entrance, Gim and Rosch held off the locals while Frank and Toltattler removed the front door barricade and began clearing the porch. Now through the door, they descended the steps, carving their way through the advancing locals. As they neared the car, a bullet hit Toltattler's shoulder and he fell, spinning to the ground.

"Bin him! He's done for!" shouted Frank.

"Frank! He's got the keys!" cried Rosch.

"Hold on buddy!" said Frank, assisting Toltattler to his feet. With the butts of their weapons, they cleared the last locals from the doors of the car. Toltattler pressed his keyfob, opening the central locking.

"Everybody inside!" shouted Frank, snatching the keys and throwing them to Gim as she entered the driver's side. With everyone inside, they secured the doors. Gim started the car and inadvertently the radio.

"...because the visitors aren't like normal immigrants, you know, they've got something to offer-"

Frank ferociously hammered the butt of his weapon into Toltattler's radio until the rhetoric was replaced by sparks and silence.

"...Sorry." he said, calmly.

Local faces pressed against the windows.

"Floor it!" yelled Rosch.

The car lurched forward and quickly became stuck in the quagmire of locals surrounding the car. With sluggish throbs of revs the car wrestled its way forward, churning up limbs and torsos. The wheels gained some traction and the car surged forward atop a mound of twisted corpses. As the car sped onto the dirt road, the alien toy, 'the Hypno-thingy' was crushed under the wheel, fizzing and sparking before its lights faded. As the car sped off into the woods, the remaining locals came to, confused as to their location and slowly realising the horror that surrounded them.

**Wednesday
1:12pm
John Fashanu Service Station, Windsor**

Underneath the overcast sky, Toltattler, Frank and Gim sat on a picnic table. Rosch approached carrying a large tray of sushi and elaborate looking cocktails. Frank removed two cocktails from the tray.
"It will be difficult to remain hidden from the aliens' watch." said Gim. "I suggest we head somewhere isolated and devoid of life, like Stoke or Leamington Spa."
"Officer" said Toltattler, "we were due back at HQ over an hour ago. Leathers is going to kill us."
"Oh, fuck Leathers." spat Frank, chewing an orange wedge.
"But what's Leathers going to say?" said Rosch. "And if the aliens *were* behind us getting attacked, then what's going to happen to us when we check in?"
"Being eaten out by Leathers is the least of your worries." said Gim.
Rosch shivered slightly at her choice of words.
"She's right." said Frank. "But we can't stay out here. If we remain AWOL it's just a matter of time before the Reticulants find a way to get rid of us. Nah, we have to return to the Met, stay visible."
"I don't think so, detective." said Toltattler. "You have just massacred the best part of a village and destroyed one of

Cranston's most popular hiking trails. You three will be subjected to disciplinaries and at least two years of sensitivity training."

Rosch stared despondently at a ladybird on the table.

"That's it." he said. "I'm finished. If I'm lucky maybe, maybe, they'll use me as a urinal cake."

"Give it a rest Ja Ja." said Frank, disdainfully. "No, Aunty Himmler will keep you nice and safe. Me on the other hand will be steam-rolled through a disciplinary hearing, tranquilised up to the eyeballs and banged away in a double quilted cell for the rest of my days. Nice and tidy."

"So why just walk back into it?" inquired Gim.

Frank slurped the last of his cocktail.

"It's like cottaging." he said. "Stay in a public space, wait for a loose opening, then look for the chance to catch 'em with their pants down."

"Lovely." said Rosch.

"Gim." said Frank. "Thank you."

"I swore to honour my father's blood oath to protect you." said Gim.

"Your old man must've been quite a guy." said Frank.

"He was, and he said he would never ever forget the great service you did for him."

After lunch, they got back into the car and headed back to the Met.

'A long time ago… in a bar far, far away…'

1978
Jimi Snuka's Sake Bonanza, Kyoto

Just off the main drag, Jimi Snuka's Sake Bonanza was open long after everyone else had closed. It was where the bartenders drank, along with some more salubrious types and the senior research team of the Japanese AeroSpace Association. On this night, Frank Ruggerman was 'in too deep to quit now' and decided to push through until dawn. Before ordering his next round, he stumbled his way to the toilet, stopping just shy of a bead curtain in order to let a man in a white lab coat pass through first. Once through, Frank continued on his trip to the lavatory but the man in the white lab coat stood a moment, feeling a tremendous respect quickly bloom for the drunkard who had just allowed him to pass. Internally, he swore he would honour this man.

EPISODE IX

Wednesday
4:10pm
London Zoo

As the rain hammered down, the accompanying white noise granted momentary absolution on the incarcerated of London Zoo. Rare, uncharacteristic outbursts of violent passion serving time alongside career offenders. The assembled species looked silently out through the bars, watching. The Orangutans peered out from underneath their makeshift, palm leaf umbrellas as Ambassador Crunk stood, looking at his favourite enclosure, 'Primates of the Banking Sector'. The rain danced on his black umbrella as he fed basil leaves in through the bars.
"Go on. Eat it all up." growled Crunk.
On the other side of the bars, a hefty man in a Saville Row suit blew a raspberry and rolled his well-fed torso forwards to grab the basil.
"Aren't they magnificent?" remarked Caroline Ahem, confidently as she approached Crunk in her motorised wheelchair. Crunk looked briefly in her direction before returning his attention to the caged creature in front of him.
"The souse is still alive." he said dryly.
"...And my nephew?" asked Ahem, with masterfully hidden menace.
"Inept." replied Crunk, "and yes still alive."
"Where are they now?" she said, mentally uncocking a pistol.
"They're coming home." said Crunk. "They'll be back in the city within the hour. When he's back, I need you to put

Ruggerman away for good. My attempts at removing him have proved... ineffective."

Crunk shook the last of the basil from the pack and threw the packet in through the bars.

"Nothing works on him." he exasperated. "He's like a splice job of the Queen Mother and Keith Richards."

"So, you want to use the 'rehab' option?" inquired Ahem, suggestively.

"Yes. Dose him up and tuck him away for the rest of his miserable life."

"That should be easy enough." said Ahem, lighting a cigarillo. "We have enough evidence on him to have him sectioned before the cheese and port arrives."

"There's one change." added Crunk. "I want your boy off the radar and the Western Tactical Unit shut down."

"Ambassador," said Ahem, reassuringly. "Rosch may be taking a while to find his feet but he's an asset-"

"Oh, get with it." snapped Crunk. "He's not even on the side you think he's on. He's more like the souse now than you can bear to admit. This burgeoning hostility towards us is going to ruin everything and until it's settled, I want him reassigned to the arse end of the ladder and Western Tactical gone."

Ahem nodded cordially and pulled away.

"I'm assuming he's worth more to you alive." added Crunk.

5:05pm
London Met Police HQ

The wet leaves on the trees outside the Met. sparkled as the sun poked through the clouds and began reclaiming all the freshly fallen rainwater. The forecourt was busy with civilians along with human and Reticulant officers preparing for the nightshift.

Toltattler pulled to a stop in a disabled space and displayed his 'Assessment Officer' parking sticker. Gim, Frank and

Rosch exited the car, scanning for signs of trouble. Through the passenger window, Toltattler called to Frank.

"Ruggerman. It is time for your performance review." he said, brusquely.

Frank halted the hunt for his lighter.

"You know what Toltattler?" he said.

Toltattler craned his neck and looked at Frank expectantly.

"Thanks."

"Save it." scoffed Toltattler. "You two are still under assessment. But now, I'm going to go to the hospital. My clavicle is shattered on the left side, I'm losing blood and I have now gone three days without a bowel movement...To be continued."

The engine started and Toltattler pulled away only to stop suddenly and blast his horn at a pair of children who had accidentally snagged their wheelchairs together on the crossing. After carefully surveying the scene, Gim turned to Frank.

"I still think this is a mistake." she said.

"I know you do Gim." said Frank, removing the unlit cigarette from his mouth. "But I need you to trust me now more than ever."

Rosch took a moment to check his phone, finding seventy-eight text messages that all read;

MY OFFICE

"It's Leathers." said Rosch, "I had better go."

Rosch turned to leave without goodbyes.

"Lando." said Frank.

Rosch stopped, turned and looked earnestly at Frank. After a moment, Frank groaned and resumed talking to Gim.

"Now this next part is crucial…" said Frank.

As Frank relayed his plan, Rosch slowly turned and headed for Leathers. His posture and walking pace resembled that of an overtired child at a wedding.

"What do you require me to do?" said Gim.

Frank showed Gim the front page of a newspaper displaying a headshot of Lorraine Kelly looking museful with a headline that read;

'VISITORS, BUDDIES OR BASTARDS?'

"Judging by this morning's paper," said Frank, "the aliens are still wrestling somewhat with their PR. They're assimilating rapidly but there's still a chance we can turn public opinion sour in time."
Gim listened closely to the old man, too focussed to notice his eyes burning brightly in the sea of ashen wrinkles surrounding them.
"I need you to watch the news." said Frank. "I want you to look for the cracks, look for a weakness, a way in, a quivering slip of a crevice, a trembling-".
"I get the picture." said Gim.
"Find us an angle to play. A phoney story, something that with a bit of pressure, we can crack open like a faulty Kinder Surprise. Everyone's got an entry point, and sometimes it just takes some fumbling before you find it."
"I have to say," said Gim, "I am reluctant to leave you to fend for yourself. Only four days ago I was washing and powdering your genitals."
"I know." said Frank. "You were very gentle on my tenderness. But this is where I need you now. This whole thing relies on you finding a way to expose the press's involvement in the invasion and incite the public. It's our only chance."

With that, Gim departed. Frank put his hands in his pockets, took a deep, calming breath and approached a bench, partially shaded by a willow. He sat down, smiling to himself and felt the warmth of the sun on his face. A little way down the street, three officers wrestled a violent Beefeater towards the road. They were halted by Paulo, the lollipop man. The suspect stopped struggling while Paulo dutifully looked both ways. Paulo, feeling confident and responsible, strode out into the road, flung his arms wide and smiled.

"Avanti, prego!" he beamed.

Neither the suspect nor the officers understood Italian, but the suspect roared and resumed his violent struggling and the officers escorted him towards the HQ entrance. Frank chuckled to himself as he had long forgotten the simple pleasure of people watching, without a surveillance team.

Across the forecourt, through the window of *'Diaper Dan's Ice Cream'* truck, an ice cream man accepted money for one of his frozen treats. Suddenly his demeanour changed as he spotted Frank, sitting only twenty metres away. The ice cream man threw a handful of change, roughly in the direction of his last customer and spoke into his cuff.

"Eagle boner, this is squat thrust. The boys are back in town, repeat the boys are back in town."

As Frank enjoyed his bench and the warm, fresh air, he removed a gin miniature from his jacket. He held up the miniature and for a moment enjoyed the shimmer of light on the tiny and beautiful glass bottle. He opened it, enjoyed the aroma and sank it. With arms outstretched across the rear of the bench and his legs crossed casually, Frank was feeling like the centre of creation when seven serious looking officers in suits and sunglasses approached and surrounded him. Frank remained content as the cuffs went on and they escorted him inside.

Chief Commissioner Leathers' Office

Something about the corridor in front of Leathers' office usually sapped all the air from Rosch's body, but not today, something had changed. From inside the office, Rosch heard a sustained buzzing sound and terrible shrieking. Unphased, Rosch knocked on the door and entered.

HAWKER STREET

The smoke in the air was even thicker than usual. As Rosch approached Leathers' desk, he noticed Reyka, standing in his usual spot by the window with his cigarette, fuming away relentlessly. Leathers sat at his desk, glaring at Rosch and brandishing a pair of tweezers attached to a thin wire. Rosch observed Leathers' tweezers hovering over a game of *'Operation'* and then followed the wires with his eyes and saw that they were attached via electrodes to strategic points around Renfield's body. Renfield looked in significant distress with copious brow sweat and his usual barbed demeanour now that of a frightened, broken lamb.

"sssssit." growled Leathers.

Rosch, obligingly did so.

"Kunnypacken." said Leathers, barely containing his 'Vesuvian' anger, "Needless to say that we...I...are very, very disappointed in you."

"Sir, if you consider-" began Rosch.

No sooner had Rosch opened his mouth when Leathers immediately stabbed the tweezers into the electric board game.

'GAZZZRRRRRRRT-TRRRT.'

Renfield's body contorted as the electricity surged through his bones. The sound of a furious tin hornet trapped in a chocolate wrapper filled the office, as did the sound of Renfield's anguish. The sound stopped and Renfield desperately tried to get his breath back. Rosch felt the usual twinges of anxiety as he watched today's instalment of *Tyrant's Gone Mental,* but he held his nerve and managed to mask his profound confusion.

"Assistant Detective," grimaced Leathers, "you've been given every chance along the way, every opportunity to demonstrate good judgement and yet you insist on smearing excrement all over the reputation of this station. The PM is under tremendous pressure to reopen the investigation into the death of Judge Pegg. It remains closed for now but if public opinion swings further afar then *'we'* will be investigated for the use of lethal force and *'you'*, were in charge of that fiasco.

"All due respect sir" replied Rosch, "but I didn't authorise the snipers or give the order-"
"All due respect nothing!"
'TRRRRRT-ZZRRRRRT-GATRRRRT'
Renfield's body writhed once again and he sobbed helplessly as the volts careened through him. As Leathers pressed the tweezers firmly against the copper contacts, Rosch looked on and managed to suppress a Cheshire cat smile into something much more '*Mona Lisa*'. The loud buzzing stopped.
"God damn you Kunnypacken." swore Leathers. "Your insubordination has cost this department dearly."
"But surely sir, in recent events there have been many occasions on which I believe my actions were exemplary. I-".
"Exemplary?!"
'GRRRRRRT-ZZZZZRRRRT-TA-TRRRRT'
Eventually, the sound ceased once again leaving Renfield weeping openly.
"Yes sir." continued Rosch. "We managed to acquire over a dozen complaints of misconduct from the National Theatre Board. We-"
"Kunnypacken I'm warning you!!!"
In a moment that hung silently, Rosch looked at Renfield, now a petrified husk of a bureaucrat. Rosch thought carefully. As he did so, he poked his tongue in his left cheek and slowly ran it along the inside of his bottom lip, before continuing;
"...We destroyed the saloon of the Horny Salmon Guesthouse whilst engaging a suspect."
'TZZZRRRRRRRRTT-GRRRRRRRRRT-TA-TRRRRRT'
Rosch stoically and arguably leisurely, continued his account as Leathers held the tweezers fast against the electrodes. Renfield's tears evolved into dry heaves and the little man's red bulb nose flashed Morse code messages of abject distress.
"We persuaded the Mayor of London to ban performances of Gary Barlow covers based on no evidence whatsoever.

We were trying to charge a murder on a feral beast man who turned out to be Tom Selleck, only for him to escape before we could arrest him."

The sustained electrocution was causing Renfield's mind to delete vital information including his national insurance number, his mother's face and his awareness of ABBA.

"...I went AWOL from a senior Visitor's close protection detail to save my partner from what can only be described as a demented alien clone of his ex-wife-"

"Rosch," said Reyka firmly, "knock it off."

The caustic buzzing stopped, Renfield was so traumatised he couldn't remember his own name and Rosch beamed a huge smile. As Leathers began to regain his composure, he frustratedly threw down the tweezers onto the game giving Renfield one last, short *'TZRRT'*. Rosch casually covered his mouth with his hand.

"Rosch," warned Reyka, "I don't think you'll find this all so amusing when you see your next assignment."

Rosch's manner slid subtly back into more diplomatic waters.

"I'm sure you realise that the Western Tactical Unit without any staff or senior officer has a precarious future so-"

"Fucking bastards!" roared Leathers, picking up the tweezers again and forcing them deep into the board game's innards.

'TZZZZRRRRRRRRRRRRRRT-GA-TRRRRRT'

Sadly, Renfield was once again terrorized by a sadistic but creative use of a well loved family board game. As the volts resumed their stampede through Renfield's nervous system, his body convulsed and he inadvertently spat the contents of the glass of water he was just drinking all over himself, sending the high voltage current wild.

"Leathers." attempted Reyka.

'TZRRRRRRRRRT-TRRRRT-TRRRRT-TRRRRRT-TRRT'

"Leathers enough." said Reyka.

Leathers removed the tweezers from the board, slowly placed them on the desk and Rosch covertly removed a tear from his cheek. Leathers began to return to a calmer but nonetheless menacing mood as smoke gently drifted from Renfield's unconscious and now incontinent torso.

"So...Kunnypacken," said Leathers, "...where would you *like* to go?"

The New Old Bailey

From underneath the London Met. building, there is an old, dank tunnel that runs all the way to the catacombs beneath the New Old Bailey courthouse. It was along this tunnel that Frank was being escorted by several members of Special Branch. Their echoing footsteps were muffled slightly by the extensive moss colonies that flourished around the dripping cracks in the ceiling. Eventually, they arrived at a large round chamber. Two agents grabbed Frank's arms and sat him firmly in a wheelchair.

"I'd like to see a menu please." said Frank.

Up ahead, from another dark tunnel that led into the round chamber, there came a steady rumbling sound, the sound of an overworked electric motor. From the darkness emerged Caroline Ahem in her motorised wheelchair. Ahem's hair was salon-fresh and her ruby dress cost more than most aircraft carriers. She came to a stop just in front of Frank.

"Ruggerman." she said, dryly.

"Aunty Goebles" said Frank.

"Hmpf, nice." said Ahem.

"I thought so." said Frank, smiling.

Ahem looked curiously at Frank.

"I have a question," she said, "all this...fuss, all this, cage rattling. What does it accomplish for you? What do you get out of it?"

"What do *you* get out of selling out your own kind?" replied Frank, "Apart from all the... money and influence."

"Yeah, that's pretty much it." she said, removing a hip flask from her pocket.

Ahem sipped her bourbon and gently replaced it.

"Well, Frank," she said, "you have reached the end of the line. After this performance review you will be suspended indefinitely for gross misconduct and the Western Tactical will be dismantled. Your days of free-spirited indignation are over."

"Oh yeah?" said Frank. "We'll see about that."

"No." said Ahem, tilting her head slightly. "We will."

Frank felt a sharp pinch as the hypodermic needle pierced the skin of his neck and sank deep into the tissue fibres. Ahem's assistant Grace, grinned with eyes wide as she pressed the plunger sending 10cc's of a custom concoction into his bloodstream. Frank's synapses were highly trained at working under the influence of intoxicants but even they were helpless against the tranquilliser he was just given. Ahem watched Frank's eyes fill with terror as he felt the iron bars of reality suddenly melt into spaghetti within his grasp. The precision engineered cocktail of sedatives shuffled its way through the synaptic corridors of Frank's mind like an old monk, closing up the monastery for the night, snuffing out candles as he makes his way to bed. Ahem leaned forward in her chair.

"So long, genius." she said.

As Ahem turned and pulled away, Frank's efforts to resist the drugs became limper, his eyes rolled and saliva descended from the side of his mouth.

The Special Branch officers pushed Frank's chair towards a large black double door and opened the large iron latch. The doors opened revealing the sound of hundreds of lively civilians, cheering and roaring. As they continued forward into the main courtroom of the New Old Bailey, Frank slurred and dribbled, his face assaulted by the flashes of dozens of cameras. Tier upon tier of dark stained oak balconies reached high up into the great dome that topped the building. Each balcony was packed with people in an ecstatic frenzy. In the hysteria, overexcited people tumbled from the higher platforms, a troupe of nuns from St.Otis' danced spiritedly and a non-plussed vendor hurled packets of peanuts at the unsuspecting.

Presiding was Judge Maudelin Marigold. Raised in Manhattan, emigrated to London and now in her sixties, she was amongst the most formidable judges of the British legal system. To try and quell the riotous cacophony in her courtroom, she banged her gavel, the action of which sadly knocked over her large pina colada.

"Oh, for fuck's sake." she said, mopping up the liquid with her robes.

She turned to the nearest bailiff.

"Get me another one will you? Right…"

She hammered her gavel, like someone destroying an infestation.

"Alright! This court is ordered to come to order."

The crowd fell quiet and the officers placed Frank in the dock. Just then, a petit man with a slicked side parting, and a chocolate brown suit bounced into the fray.

"Hi, my name's Mink Van Andrew, I'm going to be your lawyer today."

Frank's eyes drifted to and fro as he slurred, trying to focus on the voice that just spoke.

"What's with him?" asked Van Andrew, earnestly.

"Mr. Van Andrew," said Judge Marigold, "I have a long day ahead of me and I see Detective Ruggerman is in just the state I'd expect to see him in at 9:15 in the morning."

"Yes but-" said Van Andrew, spilling coffee on his documents.

"Frank Ruggerman" said Judge Marigold, "is a long serving member of the Metropolitan police force with a reputation for drinking…" She paused briefly to accept her replacement pina colada. "Thank you…that makes mine look safe enough to drive the kids home. Now, Detective Ruggerman has been called in for this performance review to assess his current professional capacity in light of a number of allegations of misconduct, and to determine the future, if any, of the Western Tactical Unit. Detective, do you know where you are?"

Frank gurned, gurgling.

"Well put." she said. "I have a barbecue with the mayor at three so if we can press on that would be 'lavvly'."

Bedsore Bob's TV & Electricals, Tottenham

Meanwhile, in a leading electronic goods shop, Gim had set up in front of a wall of flatscreen televisions, all showing different channels. She sat on a deckchair that she had commandeered and was making notes, her eyes scanning from screen to screen. She stopped a moment on the latest 'Pro-Visitor' celebrity infomercial.

Onscreen, Jude Law sat on a chair facing the camera, in a photography studio, lined with white linen. He wore a white t-shirt bearing a crayon drawing of a child and a Reticulant holding hands and a slogan that read; 'A Visitor Is A Friend You Just Met'.

"I want you to think of a different world," he pleaded, *"one...different, from the one we know and love. What if? What if the Romans never came to Britain?"*

There then began a sequence of top celebrities, speaking their thoughts on Homo-Reticulant relations.

Oprah : *"...Or the Anglo Saxons didn't welcome the Romans, but instead killed them on the beaches?... Think of Thanksgiving."*

Tom Cruise : *"The First People welcomed the pilgrims onto Fraggle Rock. What if, what if they had pelted them with rocks and faeces?"*

Seth Rogan: *"Or if the Aztecs said 'no get lost' to Christopher Columbus? I love burritos."*

Gim shifted her attention onto the next screen which displayed a new toy advert.

"How would you like to access all of your favourite cartoon shows like never before?" said a bubbly announcer.

Three children, aged 7 and up, bounced onto the screen and cheered as they picked up a metallic, spinning-top-like device, covered in shimmering red lights.

"The new model-F MedullaVision uses the very latest in Visitor technology!"

The children sat around the device calmly as it flickered red lasers across their retinas.

"Have all of your favourite cartoons accessible directly from your own brain!"

As the device finished its upload, the children stood up excitedly.

"All right!" they cheered in unison.

"Plus, the new neural net simulators allow you to bring your favourite characters to life and play with them in your own garden!"

The children raced joyfully around the fake garden set, miming shooting each other with guns.

"For the love of god Morty keep shooting!" said 8-year-old Jenny, *"You have no idea what prison is like here! Pshew! Pshew!"*

9-year-old Harry pretended to be shot, miming arterial spray as he slowly lowered himself to the ground.

On the next screen was C.U.N News. Gim watched as veteran reporter Walton Shalmanac delivered his report, standing with the crowd outside Frank's performance review.

"Today's performance review has caused exceptional controversy as Detective Frank Ruggerman is not only a deranged alcoholic, but also an outspoken critic of the Visitors. This reporter asks, if we must ask the question, is there room for xenophobia, in the modern police force?"

Despite the intense banality of what she was exposing herself to, Gim maintained her focus, her impeccable discipline holding as steadfast as her posture.

London Met. HQ. Leathers' Office

Reyka entered Leathers' office to find a flotation tank. From within, he could hear the muffled sound of loud and lively Irish folk music. Reyka pondered a moment before giving the subtlest of coughs. The lid of the flotation tank immediately sprang open, filling the office with music. Leathers, who was sporting a large, red wig and Lederhosen, leapt to his feet, stopped the tape recorder, popped an extra-large pipe in his mouth and approached Reyka until their noses were touching.

"Talk to me." he said.

Reyka took one step backwards and lit a cigarette.

"Councilwoman Ahem has put Ruggerman to trial with a performance review." he said. "She's also drugged him with an aim to permanently commit him to the dribble factory... and to dissolve Western Tactical."

"She can't do that!" exclaimed Leathers, his fervour dissipating away almost immediately because he knew she absolutely could. "Dissolve Western Tactical..." he said, mournfully. "And where will I be the next time a mutant cauliflower infests parliament? Or a sasquatch defecates through the skylight of a cocktail party? The W.T.U. was a landfill for anything that would otherwise tangle up resources meant for proper police work. Things like, orchestrating riots and housing the mentally ill. Ruggerman was a pain in the arse, but he got results... Is this what it comes to?"

Leathers peered thoughtfully at a signed portrait of comedian Frank Carson.

"In order to maintain," he continued, "one must suffer a permanent pain in the arse?"

Reyka stubbed out his cigarette on the wall mounted bear skin to his left.

"I think in the interests of maintaining," said Reyka, "when it comes to taking a pain in the ass...I'd take Frank Ruggerman."

The New Old Bailey, Main Courtroom

Prosecutor Shannon Crosswell was announcing the charges being levelled against Frank. An Oxford graduate, her black, curly hair had been subdued and wrapped into a tight bun.
"Your honour," she said. "I have here the details of over forty allegations of misconduct made against Detective Ruggerman and the Western Tactical Unit within the last two months. Detective Ruggerman, were you in the area of Little Toffle within the last eight weeks?"
Mink Van Andrew turned to Frank with hope in his face but saw only more gurning and dribbling.
"Your honour," said Crosswell, "the Detective is clearly too inebriated to continue and must be held in contempt."
"Miss Crosswell," said Judge Marigold, "I am very capable of deciding how my courtroom is run so when I…"

Suddenly she noticed a man in the front row standing up. Judge Marigold was momentarily lost in the vapours of a romance long forgotten. The man was former golden gloves and London Met. senior lab technician Jojo Binks.
"Uhm. Your majesty?" he said.
"Jojo?" she said, the look in her eyes flickering as opposing emotions jostled inside her. "I cannot have these proceedings interrupted."
"My sincerest condosoliations your honour," said Jojo, "but I feel I might be of some assistance. And, not for nothin', but I'd say he's been spiked."
"Mr. Binks, sit down." ordered the Judge.
"Trust me Maudie, I know when he's drunk and this? This is something else."
"Mr Binks," replied Judge Marigold, sternly, "you will refer to me in this court as Judge Marigold or your honour is that clear?"
"Apologies, your honour," said Jojo, pressing his palms together, "you know I uphold you in the highest respect. I was just thinking… I might be of use as a translator."
burp "Translator?" she said, quizzically.

"Sure." said Jojo, casually, "Frank and I go way back, we've been drinking partners pretty much since I moved here from Hackensack. Hey, do you remember a biology teacher at St. Spenglers? With the limp? Frank reminds me of him...I remember one time you-"
"Thank you! Mr. Binks you may sit with the defendant and hopefully you'll get some sense out of him."

Bedsore Bob's TV & Electricals, Tottenham

A solitary bead of sweat casually meandered its way down Gim's temple as exposure to this much daytime TV was eroding the foundations of her mind like a marauding termite colony. As an ad break began, another Pro-Visitor celebrity appeal had Alan Carr contributing;
"You might know what it's like to be an outsider. To be lonely. To feel about as welcome as a fart in a space suit."
Gim took a deep breath and crossed out a large portion of her notes.

The Ultimo, Just Outside Earth's Atmosphere

The Ultimo was the flagship of the Reticulant Beta 3 Invasion Services. With its design stolen from another species, it was by far the largest vessel created anywhere in the universe. Complete with regional dialects and timezones, the titanic ship hovered effortlessly above the helpless blue rock. The Ultimo was also home to the High Conqueror and it was outside his office, where Ambassador Crunk was currently sitting.
Bathed in a cool blue light, Crunk's large grey head looked down at the fibres of the luxurious carpet beneath his feet. He then flinched as a device on the wall next to him sounded a loud and peculiar, electronic fart. The door to the High Conqueror's office silently slid open and Crunk stepped inside. The High Conqueror looked as if he had been alive

for millenia. He sat at a large desk, underneath which was an aquarium in which everything had died. As he approached the desk, Crunk noticed a brutal, Jurassic looking warrior alien that was sitting on a sofa reading a magazine.
"May I sit?" asked Crunk, reluctantly.
"Love?" said the High Conqueror.
The brutal looking alien on the sofa looked up.
"Why don't you go home and get tea started?"
The long war-mongering creature nodded agreeably and departed, stopping only to give a kiss on the forehead of the High Conqueror.
"Yes yes, very nice, love you too." he said, dismissively.
As the warrior neared the exit, the door slid open. Upon stepping outside, the warrior collided with two small, servile creatures that were pushing a food cart instigating a very savage and one-sided brawl. The screams and roars of the fracas were hushed to silence as the door slid closed.
"Well?" said the High Conqueror. "Why don't you sit?"
"Because," said Crunk, "if I do, you're just going to say did I tell you to sit?"

The High Conqueror chuckled which sounded like emptying a handful of dry leaves from a wooden bucket.
"I knew I liked you for some reason, go on, sit down."
Crunk sat and immediately spoke;
"I've, never seen anything like this guy, he's-"
"Stop." said the High Conqueror, his voice growing weaker and more whispered with each passing eon. "What happened to you?"
Crunk sat, expectantly.
"Five planets ago, you brought an entire continent to heel and within a decade, they produced twelve seasons of some of the best televison any of us are ever going to see."
"That was a good planet." acknowledged Crunk, cautiously.
"Good? That two-parter with the Amish gangsters on the oil rig? Jesus H."
"That was a high point." admitted Crunk.

"And now?" rasped the High Conqueror, slowly standing, leaning on his bejewelled staff and approaching Crunk's side of the desk. "Crunk, you're a joke. We've got backwater countries on this planet torn apart by decades of civil war that are now subdued like cabbages watching reruns of '*Ducktales'*."

"Yes but-"

"And the UK is still a PR shit-house tornado fire because you cannot kill a man who's as likely to clap his hands as piss himself."

"If it was as simple as just killing him," grimaced Crunk, bitterly, "I would've done it, don't you think?"

"Don't even think about getting bolshy with me sunshine." growled the High Conqueror, moving closer. "Top and bottom of it is, we can only settle here and access all of their piss-warm TV shows if the humans are distracted enough to allow us to do so. Public opinion is everything and because of your inability to rein in Captain-continence, there's still a chance of this all blowing up in our faces like kissing a drunk fresher."

"I'm fixing it." said Crunk.

"Jimmy Saville, you are not Crunk, a pube hair away from running local radio on a shack planet in the outer fringes, you are."

"Don't Yoda me." scoffed Crunk, disdainfully.

"Crunk-"

"You know damn well if you post me out there I can't take my family."

The High Conqueror perched on the desk beside Crunk and loomed over him.

"Well I suggest you get cracking," he wheezed, "cos if I don't get my extra five seasons of *'Malcolm in the Middle'*, you'll be watching *your* kids grow up on dvd....Now get out."

Crunk stood calmly and strode towards the door. As it slid open, the cacophony of the brawl outside between the two servants and the warrior became audible again. Crunk did his best to avoid becoming entangled in the melee and was very nearly successful.

New Old Bailey, Main Courtroom

Mink Van Andrew had the floor.
"He exposed a corrupt televangelist for using naked pictures of dogs in, uhm, his infomercials. Which is really a bad thing to do...uhm, dogs have rights."
Judge Marigold replaced the stopper of a large brandy decanter and returned it to the compartment under the bench.
"Mr. Van Andrew," she said, "we are all very familiar with Detective Ruggerman's career high points but not one of those cases holds any bearing on *these* allegations. Miss Crosswell, please continue."
"Detective Ruggerman, whilst in Little Toffle did you also break into and hotwire a vehicle registered to a Mr. Sanderson?"
Jojo Binks leaned in to hear the secretory burblings of his long serving friend.
"He says the break in was a necessary ploy to engage the prime suspect, your honour."
Frank blew a long, slow raspberry into Jojo's ear.
"He says the investigation required him to lure the suspect into a location where he could be appropriately interviewed."
"And I suppose the same standard procedure required indecently assaulting a Tollaguska Beer mascot in Southend?" added Crosswell.
Frank twitched in his seat and dribbled again.
"Your honour" said Binks, defiantly, "at that time Frank was in a state of post traumatical distress after Judge Duane Pegg was murdered by a police sniper, under orders-"
The crowd erupted and Judge Marigold hammered her gavel.
"Enough!" she shouted. "God damn you Jojo."
Judge Marigold felt a twinge of pain in her heart.

"Maudie, you gotta listen to him!" cried Jojo.
"Bailiffs get him out of here!"
With that, seven bailiffs took to removing Jojo Binks from the room.
"Maudie, look in your heart!...The truth used to stand for something!"
The doors crashed open and closed as they led Jojo outside, Judge Marigold subdued the roaring crowd with her gavel and did her best to suppress the feelings within her.

Bedsore Bob's TV & Electricals, Tottenham

"I hate you! I hate you! I hate you!" said an onscreen TV chef, passionately tenderising a venison steak. Gim shifted her focus to the next screen as the C.U.N *'Teatime'* edition began. Derek Trough was delivering a piece to camera when he touched his earpiece and listened.
"Mrs Chandrasekhar, apologies" said Trough, *"but we now go live to an astounding breaking story involving a near miss on a train crossing just outside Drubble in Croydon. Shagney Kluft is on the scene."*
"Thanks, Derek." said Kluft. *"Just minutes ago here at this rail crossing, Mrs..."*
Kluft gently parried the enfeebled resistance of an elderly woman as she reached into her purse.
"...Helena Porter, a retired scuba diver, was out shopping when her electric wheelchair malfunctioned."
Mrs. Porter's efforts to speak were hampered greatly by her oxygen mask.
"She was shopping near her home in North London," continued Kluft, *"when she lost control of the chair and it carried her over 15 miles south through central London. Thanks to the city's comprehensive cctv coverage and videos contributed by the public, the entire journey is now available on 'Yourtube'."*
Gim watched as the C.G.I map traced Mrs.Porter's route through central London, the visuals complimented greatly

by the numerous videos and selfies that the people of London had dutifully recorded.
"After 4hrs, 3 chases and at least one attempt to stop the chair, it came to a stop here, on this rail crossing. Mrs. Porter was still unable to operate the chair even as the 14:27 to East Croydon bore down upon her. Mrs Porter, has the chair malfunctioned before and how did you feel?"

As she watched the news unfold, Gim observed that Mrs. Porter had been speaking continually beneath her mask and by analysing her body language, she quickly concluded that Porter believed that the chair had been sabotaged. Mrs. Porter angrily pointed offscreen. The camera adjusted to reveal two Reticulant officers, newly recruited to the London Met. leaning against their squad car. Kluft approached them for comment.
"Of course," she said, *"the heroes of the day, officers Gazbam and Deetlepush of the London Met. Recruited only hours before, they were on hand to rescue the stranded chair just seconds before the train careened through the crossing."*
The pair of Reticulant officers genuinely seemed more interested in the yoghurts they were eating than being interviewed.
"Officers, thanks to your bravery and quick thinking, you were able to save Mrs. Porter. How does it feel to be heroes?"
Reluctantly, Officer Gazbam gave a comment.
"We saw the old girl was in trouble. We did what anyone would do."
"Can I ask what you were doing in Croydon when you are based twenty-two miles away in Walthamstow?"
"...No." they said, in unison, re-entering their squad car.
"Well, there you have it. I know Mrs. Helena Porter is one old lady who thanks God for the visitors, and has never been so happy to miss the train."
Gim's eyes sharpened, subtly.
"Bingo." she said.

Gim licked the last of the tortilla chips from her fingers, grabbed her things and sprinted for her car.

The New Old Bailey, Main Courtroom

Whilst Crosswell had the floor, Mink Van Andrew had his head face down on the table.
"...for which you were forcibly detained by local police. Once released you were arrested again only forty-five minutes later for, it says here, urinating into a charity bin."
Frank slurred and continued dribbling on himself.
"All of which can be added to the fact that on September fourth you became embroiled in a dangerous hostage situation in which you subsequently lost control of the scene, resulting in the death of Judge Duane Pegg."
Frank contorted in his chair violently and Van Andrew sobbed openly.
"Please your majesty, make her stop! I can't…"
The crowd had become rambunctious again and Judge Marigold beat her gavel.
"Mr. Van Andrew!" she commanded. "This man is a liability. This kind of maverick tomfoolery no longer has any place in the modern police service. It is no longer acceptable to gun down an entire brass band, whilst investigating antique theft. Fist fighting and rectal violations are as archaic now as…casual racism or a collective TV viewing experience. No, Detective Ruggerman, if it was up to me and it is, I'd see you dismissed and prosecuted, I…"
Judge Marigold's eye was drawn to the notification of a picture on her phone. It was a photo of her and Jojo Binks, arm in arm at an anti-war protest. Accompanying the picture was a message that read;

"LOOK IN YOUR HEART MAUDIE!"

Her eyes, twinged subtly at the corners as the secretions came. She looked up at Ruggerman, lolling helplessly in his chair. She looked at Van Andrew who had his eyes closed firmly shut and his fingers crossed. Judge Marigold touched a fingertip on the phone screen and sighed.

"Detective Ruggerman," she said, "it is clear to me that your way of policing is done. We are in a new era. A man of your disposition, where once a champion of law and order, is now a hazard. I hereby rule that the Western Tactical Unit is to be dissolved immediately."

Hundreds of gasps depleted the air in the courtroom and high in a balcony, a despondent Hansen Olsen closed his eyes ruefully.

"Come on." said Chris, as he and Nathan wanted to beat the traffic.

"...its resources," continued Judge Marigold, "are to be distributed across neighbouring departments. By all rights, detective, you should now be dismissed and prosecuted for every single one of these charges. However, in light of your dedication to this job and several...external considerations, I find it inappropriate to deem you unable to reform from your current, flat out ego rampage that you call a life. I must promote the ideals of growth and rehabilitation. Therefore, I will judge in favour of sending you to a recuperative institute on medical grounds for treatment until you are deemed fit for service."

"Thank you, your majesty!" cried Van Andrew.

"Don't thank me." she said. "You can thank the good lord, the people, the fact it's happy hour and the maelstrom of social media pressure spearheaded by TV oracle and Elf-kin charisma wildfire Michaela Strachan."

Bang went the gavel.

The crowd roared once again as the performance review was closed and Frank was taken away.

EPISODE X

5 Hours ago
Drubble Train Crossing, Croydon

"...and this old lady has never been so happy to miss the train. This is Shagney Kluft, for C.U.N.Teatime."
With her sign-off, Shagney Kluft's smile disappeared. Her long serving friend and cameraman, Kareem Gill, stopped the recording. Kareem's mind had once been described as a complex maze where every turning led to something more stupid. His gentle and earnest face looked from behind his camera. As he tried to interpret the blend of disappointment and indignation on Kluft's face, behind him, Mrs. Porter's wheelchair came to life and she finally began her long journey home. Almost immediately, a spark fizzed on the left side of her chair and it came to a stop, sadly once again in the middle of the railway crossing.
"What's wrong?" said Kareem.
"It's all bullshit." snapped Kluft, painfully aware of the limitations of the forthcoming exchange.
"How do you mean?" said Kareem, his gentle, Yorkshire accent drifting on the breeze.
"I mean," replied Kluft, "that it's highly likely that we have just allowed aliens from another planet to swing a news narrative by placing an old lady on train tracks."
"What are you going on about!?" exclaimed Kareem. "It was aliens who rescued her!"
As Kareem spoke, both he and Kluft failed to notice the bell ringing and the barriers descending once again, either side of Mrs. Porter's chair.

"For Christ's sake, turn your brain on Kareem." yelled Kluft. "It was the aliens who put her there in the first place." Kareem shuffled uneasily as his brain provided him with its equivalent of 'File not Found'.

"Fucking scum bags." raged Kluft as she detached her microphone and stormed off.

As Mrs. Porter waved frantically to attract his attention, Kareem watched his friend depart. Upon noticing Mrs. Porter, Kareem quickly dashed to help her.

"Oh, bloody hell, sorry love!" he cried, assisting her off the tracks.

Hendrix Grove, Camden

Later that evening, Gim was following GPS directions to a flat, not far from the Stables end of Camden. The fact that the centuries old artform of tracking someone down using only police records and intuition had been replaced, by a maximum of 6 button presses on even the most basic smartphone held no sentimentality for Gim.

As Gim approached the address, she looked up and saw that all the lights were off. She climbed the stone stoop that led to the front door, scanned the names on the buzzers and pressed. After waiting exactly sixty seconds, she stood back and looked up at the window again. She returned to Shagney Kluft's profile on Twittlechat to discern a favourite hangout when she noticed Mulheyheyneys Pub a few doors down the street.

The facade of Mulheyheyney's bore blacked out windows and neon signs that told of house beers and spirits they hadn't stocked in decades. Sat under the windows were two lollipop ladies slumped, shoulder to shoulder with their legs outstretched.

"Bloody ninjas." slurred one of them as Gim passed by.

Gim opened the door and proceeded inside the dark and rowdy establishment. The venue was lined with television screens displaying all manner of sports coverage including

vodka tennis, horse curling and 'Aussie Rules' pig bingo. Carefully scanning, she slowly pushed her way through the inebriated patrons until she found her target. Sat at the bar and blowing bubbles into a glass of bourbon was Shagney Kluft.
"Miss Kluft. I am Gimudzuke Rerata. May I sit here."
"Help yourself." said Kluft, without making eye contact.
"Miss Kluft, I am here with the intention of recruiting you for a mission of tremendous importance."
"Look honey," said Kluft, "I think you're barking up the wrong trouser leg."
Gim's normally stoic face flashed the faintest hint of confusion.
"Are you suggesting I have the wrong… Shagney Kluft?"
"Point taken." said Kluft, swallowing the last of her drink.
"Today you helped an alien conspiracy win public favour by perpetuating a false narrative regarding the sabotage of an elderly woman's wheelchair and the placing of her in front of an oncoming train."
For the first time, Kluft looked into the face of her addresser.
"Today," said Gim, "I saw the same look in your eyes as I see now. You clearly understand that this world is being subjected to a great sham, yet you continue to perpetuate the establishment's, what you call, baloney."
"Easy there, little Miss Miyagi" warned Kluft, holding eye contact but also signalling the bartender for another whiskey.
Gim's face held steadfast save for the slightest raise of an eyebrow.
"Ah, what the hell can I do?" groaned Kluft, receiving her drink. "The news game has changed into something unrecognisable. It's all changed… and I've changed somehow. I don't even know what I do anymore."
"Your complicity and bottomless cowardice are easily apparent." said Gim.
"Ouch." said Kluft, burping.

   Just then, on the screen above the bar, Frank's performance review was turning out and the press were there in force. Frank was still deep in the throes of the tranquilliser he had been given and his appointed solicitor Mink Van Andrew disappeared, trampled underfoot by the swarming photographers.

"I'm afraid," said Gim, "today's example of your callous indifference to integrity is merely an amuse bouche."

She directed Kluft's attention to the TV.

"The aliens are of course," said Gim, "not new arrivals to our planet. They plan to openly assimilate and exist like parasites without contributing anything. Their greatest opponent...is this man."

"He looks brain damaged." said Kluft.

"In an attempt to derail his defence, I believe he has been drugged by the conspirators. Either that or he is drinking wine by the box again. What is important to note is that you have subverted the truth surrounding the death of an innocent man. A death for which Frank Ruggerman is being held responsible for."

As Kluft listened, she briefly pondered the term 'tough love'.

"Despite your betrayal marring your family name for generations to come, you can still make a difference." said Gim.

"...How?" said Kluft, leaning in.

"You are to turn the tide of public opinion against the aliens. Create a story that will rally the people of this country to resist. And, we need to see Frank Ruggerman released from the loony bin."

Kluft leaned back on her stool disdainfully and nearly fell off.

"It's impossible!" she yelped, grabbing the bar top firmly. "They've got celebrities, endorsements, Oprah!"

"We need to find something the public cares about more than celebrities." said Gim.

Kluft closed her eyes in despair. On the television, a video clip of nursery children visiting a petting zoo, inspired Kluft to momentarily fawn, the gesture being almost perfectly mirrored by Gim's indifference.

"Wait! That's it!" said Kluft, excitedly. "I don't know if you've noticed, but all the Reticulants I've met love two things, DVD boxsets and animals."
Never to miss a beat, Gim continued the thought.
"We must create a scandal involving the aliens and our animals." she said. "Somehow, depict the aliens as hoarding pet molesters."

On the television there appeared news coverage of a diplomatic meeting between senior Reticulant Deacon Smash and the Mayor of London, Harry Huffnagel. Huffnagel was showcasing his prize-winning racehorse Ginger to a galaxy of flashing cameras. Huffnagel's feigned smile gradually turned to explicit vexation as he continually batted Deacon Smash's hand away from his beloved horse. Kluft took a moment to inhale the rich layers of caramel and leather from her bourbon.
"We need a celebrity animal."

**Thursday
1:54pm
London Met. HQ, Gents Toilet, First Floor**

His eyes burning, Rosch raced over to the sink and began furiously rinsing them with water. Behind him in a cubicle, a flush of water only partially sent the contents of the bowl far away into the Thames River system. Rosch's vision began to clear and he saw a man approach him with his hands outstretched. Still wincing in agony, Rosch helped the man wash his hands and provided him with a handful of paper towels.
"Sorry." said the man.
As the man left, Rosch looked into the cubicle he had just vacated.
"Oh, Jesus Christ!" yelled Rosch, after the man, grabbing a fire axe and taking a mighty swing into the bowl.

St. Beadle's Memorial Hospital

Sat on a grey and foreboding heath, St. Beadle's looked about as welcoming as a cut-rate gulag managed by Norman Bates. Along one of the post mortem-blue corridors, two orderlies wheeled Frank on a trolley. Upon entering Frank's cell, they stripped him.
"Look at the state of this poor bugger." said Matt.
"Don't you know who this is?" said Jiff.
"...Bob Geldoff?" ventured Matt.
"Christ, you're ignorant." said Jiff. "He's a copper, had a breakdown and shot a judge or something."
"What?!" said Matt.
Frank could hear their voices but could still only dribble in protest.
"Yeah," said Jiff, "then he got done for being a racist. Xenophobic remarks or something."
Jiff recoiled as a stream of urine from Frank reached his face.
"Oh, bloody hell." he spluttered, repulsed.
Matt smothered the flow with spare hospital linen. Once they had fitted Frank with a fresh gown, they raised one end of the trolley and Frank's paralytic form slid down and onto the cold, tiled floor. As he lay in a heap, Frank tried to focus and steady his breathing.

10:31pm

Since his arrival in his cell, Frank's metabolism had been grappling with the sedatives in his system. The four walls of the cell, the colour of hypothermia, reached upwards, seemingly infinitely. Frank's vision was being obscured by a dense fog that shimmered and contorted.
Frank flinched as a moustachioed man pushing a trolley, appeared from nowhere and disappeared in a flash. The sound of Frank's own frantic breathing scorched his ears. For a moment, Frank was clear of mind and could see the

interior of his cell before it folded in on itself, the crumbling structure expelling the dense fog once again, leaving him blinded. Frank gritted his teeth as he clutched at the dissipating fibres of reality. He sat back, breathless against the wall. Then, slowly, a perfectly lucid vision of himself appeared from the fog, brushing particles off the sleeve of his jacket.

"Easy there, mate." said vision Frank. "How are you holding up?"

Frank managed only to hiss out a few scraped words.

"I'm so, so thirsty." he said.

"I know mate." said the vision. "If this place has a bar, I doubt it's up to much."

Frank's eyes continued to roll in his head as his words felt like sandpaper leaving his throat.

"I think I might be dying." said Frank.

"Nah, not at all," said the vision, "that's just the withdrawals talking. You hang in there, mate. Gim's going to find a way to blow this thing open and get you out of here."

"What about...dickhead Lando?" whispered Frank.

"Oh, he's well out the way." chuckled the vision. "I imagine Leathers has him working in the gents as an arse wipe."

Both Ruggermans laughed.

"He's a cretin." smiled Frank.

"Total cretin." said the vision. "Chances are, that's the last we'll ever see of the 'Star Wars kid'."

Frank smiled once again and gave a quiet sigh of relief. In that moment the vision disappeared and Rosch's face emerged, sobbing in Frank's mind.

"Ewok!" it cried, the sound so loud it nearly shattered Frank's eardrums.

"Oi! Stay with me!" said the vision sternly upon reappearing.

Frank's body was suddenly flooded with icy panic as he opened his eyes and saw that he was on the ceiling and about to fall onto the hard floor. Frank screamed and clawed at the air.

"Oi! Wake up!" said the vision, slapping Frank's face.

Frank fell backwards onto the floor and slapped his hands on the tiles, gripping them for stability. Breathless, Frank realised that he was alone in his cell. He closed his eyes and tried to focus.

Even though Frank was sitting, dribbling and unable to move, he became aware of a figure, standing facing the corner of his cell. As Frank spoke, the words seemed to conjure the vision of himself once again.

"Is there someone else in this room?" whispered Frank, his weight slumping forward, dropping a mouthful of saliva onto his gown.

"Yes." said the vision, warmly. "Just remember, she can only hurt you if you let her."

Suddenly, a pain tore through Frank's head like a chainsaw and he clutched his hands to his temples.

"Listen mate," said the vision. "from here...the withdrawals are going to get nasty."

Frank wrestled his eyes open to see he was face to face with a post mortem visage of his ex-wife.

"Real nasty indeed." she hissed, menacingly.

Frank's scream echoed around his cell but was inaudible outside it.

Shagney Kluft's Home, Camden

Kluft stood next to a flipchart in her charmingly cluttered front room. On separate sofas, Gim and Kareem looked on as Kluft summarised.

"So, Kareem," she said, "are we settled on the existence of Harry Potter?"

Kareem sat for a moment's ponder before enthusiastically nodding his head.

"Good." said Kluft, lifting a sheet of paper revealing a crude sketch of a horse.

"I must insist we press on." said Gim. "I estimate that Frank's alcohol withdrawals by now will be entering the Peter Jackson stage."

"Right." continued Kluft. "So, to recap, we are going to kidnap the Mayor's prize-winning horse, Ginger."
"Yes." said Gim. "Take it to a place that has frequent alien abductions."
"A specimen like that should be too much for the aliens to resist." said Kluft.
"But what happens once they take the horse?" said Gim.
"That's where we come in." said Kluft, "Kareem, get the camera. We are going to make a fake expose about the Visitors abducting exotic animals for greasy purposes. We'll feed the video directly into the Mayor's TV whilst he's having his breakfast. When he sees his horse is gone, he'll come banging down the walls looking for it back with a tirade of good old fashioned xenophobic speculation. The negative press for the Visitors will force people to choose sides. However... Ruggerman will *still* be in the laughing shack."
"I too see this problem." said Gim. "Frank Ruggerman is incarcerated and sober. If we don't see him released soon, the sobriety will tear his mind asunder. I estimate we have just under forty-eight hours before he goes full Kubrik."
"Well, let's just hope this works." said Kluft. "Kareem?"
Kareem sat on the sofa, scrutinising the room. Eventually, he looked to the right of his lap.
"Found it!" he cheered, picking up the camera.
"Great stuff, Kareem." said Kluft. "Now let's get packed, shoot the PTC, we're on the road in thirty."

9:22pm
The Home of Councilwoman Caroline Ahem, Wood Green

Ahem's study was a lavish feast for the eyes if you liked oak and despotry. At a desk, Ambassador Crunk sat at a computer whilst Ahem relaxed on her chaise longue.
"Argh! This isn't happening." wailed Crunk, his big grey head slumping into his little grey hands.

"Ah lighten up Crunky." said Ahem, throwing a Malteser into her mouth. "Look on the bright side. Your people will still be living here, it's just possible it will be immersed in distrust, resentment and prejudice. To be fair, that's all the rest of us get." she added quietly.

"Nah." grumbled Crunk. "If this goes south, the Boss will fling us to the arse end of the arse end of nowhere. Like, what do you call it? Benidorm?"

"Jesus." said Ahem, gravely, munching another Malteser.

"I've got to find higher calibre celebs for the TV segments." said Crunk.

Crunk began typing into a search bar.

"How is there no one more benevolent than Michaela bastard Strachan?" said Crunk. "There's got to be. Who haven't we had yet?"

"The Oprah segments have done magnificently." said Ahem, missing her mouth this time.

"Yes," said Crunk, "but you need new fodder every three days or it stagnates."

Ahem cocked another Malteser, ready for launch.

"What about Gerard Butler?" she said.

"Possible." said Crunk. "He might have too much integrity for this gig. We need popular celebs who'll say absolutely whatever we pay 'em to."

"He went on *Top Gear*." said Ahem.

"Did he now?" grinned Crunk.

1:13am
Mayor Of London Harry Huffnagel's Home, Bethnal Green

The only light came from the stout, wrought iron lamps that lined the long, brick driveway that led to the Huffnagel front door. In the darkness, next to a two feet high stone wall, Gim slid through the shadows dressed in all black fatigues. Following close behind and bearing the same striped black makeup, was Kluft. They paused at a large round terracotta pot plant, ten yards from the side door. Nearby on the main road, Kareem Gill was listening closely to his walkie talkie headset as he sat in a horse carrier truck that he had rented from his grandmother.

"Kareem?" whispered Kluft.

"Hello, Miss Kluft!" he said, cheerily.

"This doesn't seem right Kareem." said Kluft, surveying the entrance.

"She is correct." added Gim. "Who in their right mind would keep a racehorse in the house."

"Trust me!" said Kareem. "My cousin Errol says the Mayor treats that horse better than his own children. He lets it have breakfast with them all round the same table. Porridge for the kids and kippers and straw for the horse."

"No offence, Kareem" said Kluft, "but your cousin Errol gets lost in revolving doors."

"I'm telling you it's in the house! I can even see it on the thermograph."

"Ah, okay then." said Kluft. "Wait, What? Where the hell did you get a thermograph?"

"It's my dad's." said Kareem. "He bought one after he found a family of rabid badgers in the linen basket. Look, I can see a big yellow blob on the second floor."

"Do you mean upstairs?" puzzled Gim.

"Yeah." said Kareem. "And it looks like everyone else is in bed apart from one of the serving staff down the far end of the building."

"Now is the time." said Gim, as she began to creep further into the shadows toward the house.

"Okay. We're moving." said Kluft, "Radio silence."

Gim and Kluft crawled on their sides behind more large plant pots so as not to trigger the halogen lights. Once inside the black oak Tudor porch, they huddled close against the door. Gim carefully removed a small leather sheath containing fine tools. A lonely hoot from a howler monkey startled Kluft momentarily.

"Nice and easy there." soothed Gim, as she worked the intricate mechanisms of the door lock.
Click
Gim looked back over her shoulder at Kluft with a look that, although indistinguishable from her regular face, actually conveyed the most exquisite smugness. Gim carefully opened the door, stopping immediately as the creak of the door sounded like a giant tearing an oil tanker in half. Kluft grabbed hold of Gim's shoulders and froze. Gim looked deep inside herself and began to collate all of the collected wisdom of her training. With the winds of the masters in her sails, Gim carefully pressed on, slowly opening the old wooden door. The near deafening creak rattled the nearby, lattice glass windows, a slowly unfurling roar made of weathered timber, ground its way through all ear drums in the vicinity. On and on it went. As Gim pushed onwards and the sound filled the night, Kluft had her eyes shut tight as she bit down on her balaclava. After a period of what made a sneeze feel like the hundred years war, the sound stopped. In a twist of fate that was nothing short of miraculous, Gim looked into the darkened kitchen and saw no one. Gim looked back at Kluft who was simply beside herself.
"What is wrong?" asked Gim.
"Nothing, I'm fine." she sniffed, exhaling deeply and wiping the tears from her eyes.

After exactly sixty seconds, Gim was convinced that they could proceed and they both silently entered the house. Gim turned back to close the door when Kluft grabbed her and held her close.
"Don't...even think about it…" hissed Kluft, her eyes filled with mania. *gulp* "we'll only have to open it again when we come out with the horse."
Gim looked inquiringly into her comrade's face.
"Fair enough." she said. "Kareem, if I am correct, we should move north towards the rear of the house and the main stairs."

"That is correct, yes." said Kareem, confidently, as he traced his finger along a map of what was later revealed to be Cairo.

With only minimal moonlight creeping in between the cracks of the heavy rouge curtains lining the hallway, Gim and Kluft proceeded deeper into the house. After they crossed the front reception area, they passed through a corridor that was lined with photographs, each one depicting Mayor Huffnagel doing skydives. Kluft noticed that the last photograph in the line was different and displayed an elderly, grumpy looking man; *'Employee of the Month'* Ooga Chagga. Suddenly, Gim froze and in one fluid motion, she wrapped a gloved hand tightly across Kluft's mouth, spun them down to the ground and tucked them both neatly under a side table. A side door crashed open, spilling light from the pantry into the corridor. Through the door thundered a tea trolley pushed by an elderly, grumpy looking man.

"Ooga Chagga Ooga Ooga Ooga Chagga-" He mumbled to himself as he made his way down the hall.

The sound stopped as the man pushed the trolley into another side door and the corridor was dark once again. Gim and Kluft slowly emerged from underneath the table. After quietly spitting out fluff from Gim's glove, Kluft took the lead and they stealthily approached the bottom of the main stairs.

"We're at the stairs." whispered Kluft into her radio.

"Right oh, so," said Kareem, "it should be up them stairs and up on the right somewhere."

St. Beadle's Memorial Hospital

For the last few hours, Frank had been trying to control his thoughts against worsening hallucinations. Beginning with his name and address, Frank repeated the basic facts about himself, the mental process being similar to attempting to stack soap bubbles into a tower. He would get as far as his least favourite cup before the structure would invariably collapse into disarray. Frank sat against the wall of cold porcelain, dried tears staining his face, his eyes closed.

"Frank." said a calm, female voice.

Frank's spine flooded with dread.

"You're not here." whispered Frank, keeping his eyes clenched shut.

"What difference does that make?" said Beatrice. "Don't you take any comfort in my voice? In my face?..."

Frank tried to keep his eyes closed at all costs, he breathed deeply and tried to centre.

"...in my touch?" continued Beatrice.

Frank felt the sensation of a gentle hand against his shoulder and his resilience collapsed under the weight of long wanted affection. He slowly opened his eyes to look upon the face that once filled his days with sunshine, only the face he saw was not the face of his lost love, but that of a ghostly nun dressed in blue.

"Bottoms up Frank!" she roared, her mouth tearing at the edges as it expanded to the size of a bear trap,

"It's Happy Hour!!"

Frank screamed and hugged himself into a ball.

Mayor Of London Harry Huffnagel's Home, Bethnal Green

Carefully, Gim and Kluft crossed the last few steps leading onto the landing and froze whilst a smoke alarm went off in the far end of the house. It rang for approximately the amount of time it took Ooga Chagga to put down his cheesecake, move a chair over to the smoke alarm and press the button. Both equally overjoyed and baffled to have not yet been discovered, Gim and Kluft surveyed the first floor of the Huffnagel home. Kluft stepped forward and saw a series of carved oak doors, each with an ornate nameplate; 'Daphne', 'Carter', 'Phil' and 'Zulu'.

"Kareem," whispered Kluft, near inaudibly, "these look like bedrooms."

"Hold on you're dead quiet, I'll turn you up." said Kareem, adjusting the volume of his headphones.

"Carry on." he said.

"I said," whispered Kluft, "these look like bedrooms."

"Yeah!" said Kareem. "The heat signature is coming from what should be the room at the end of the landing."

Gim and Kluft observed a grand door at the end of the hall, exchanged glances and then approached.

"That's it!" said Kareem. "You should be right on top of it!"

Kluft steadied her breathing and slowly turned the door handle. The mercifully silent door opened to reveal a strange sight. Without sound, Kluft mouthed the words;

"You gotta be fucking kidding me."

Immediately in front of the door was a bed, upon which lay a naked and spread-eagled Mayor of London, standing next to the window was a large racehorse, named Ginger. After taking a moment to adjust to 'the new normal', Kluft whispered;

"Okay then."

With the immaculate poise of a glacier, Gim calmly approached the horse. On the wall, opposite the Mayor's bed, was a large, flatscreen TV. Kluft, removed a small electronic device from her vest and connected it to one of the inputs.

"What's going on? I can't hear nothing, hold on." said Kareem, turning his headphones to maximum.

Gim had untied the horse and was gently leading it out onto the landing. Huffnagel's slumbering body twitched and he emitted a loud crack of a snore, causing Kluft to freeze in terror and Kareem to recoil as his eardrums were shattered like china cups in a tumble dryer. Without breathing or a single heartbeat between them, Gim and Kluft waited as Huffnagel returned to the depths. As Gim and Ginger departed, Kluft carefully closed the bedroom door behind them.

Outside on the grass, Gim and Kluft led Ginger across the lawn and towards the road.

"Getting him down the stairs was much easier than I thought it was going to be." said Gim, quizzically, receiving enthusiastic nods of agreement from Kluft.

As they reached the main road, Kareem left the horse carrier to assist with the loading.

"She's a beauty isn't she!" bellowed Kareem, unaware of the level of damage done to his hearing.

"Jesus Christ Kareem!" hissed Kluft, covering his mouth. Gim squeezed a point on Kareem's shoulder and he immediately fell asleep and collapsed onto the floor. Kluft and Gim began to drag his unconscious body towards the cab of the horse carrier.

"Just for future reference," strained Kluft, "you can get the same effect by putting a bag on his head."

2:10am

The horse carrier drove along the dual carriageway. A fleet of paired red and white eyes bathed in the rhythmic pulses of yellow light from the street lamps. As Gim's face focussed on the road, Kluft attempted to gently rouse Kareem.

"Here we go." soothed Kluft. "Okay, that's right....You okay buddy?"

"What did you say?" shouted Kareem, smiling.

Gim cocked her pistol.

"It's okay, calm down." said Kluft, lowering Gim's pistol. "We just have to let your hearing come back."

Kareem decreased his speaking volume to a level where he couldn't hear himself, causing him to lose all control of his inflection.

"Did you manage to wire up the video feed to his TV?" he said.

"Yes." said Kluft, slowly and clearly mouthing her words. "And when the time is right, we hit the remote and the video will cut into whatever he's watching."

"Aye. That's right." beamed Kareem. "According to an expose in the *Daily Thompson*, the mayor is 97% likely to be watching TV at 09:15. Apparently, he never misses *Steve Backshall's Deadly 60*.

Kluft nodded and sat back in her seat.

"So," she said, "next stop, this week's abduction hotspot."

Into the glow of the headlights came a signpost for Hackney.

"It is not far now." said Gim.

Hackney Canal

The horse carrier slowly pulled through onto a layby and came to a stop next to the moonlit canal.

"This is the spot." said Kluft, reading from her phone.

Gim peered through the windscreen out into the night.

"There is nothing here." she said. "I see only an abandoned canal boat that smells like a urinal."

"Well, the app says it's here." said Kluft, opening her door. "Apparently this is the most frequent site, averaging two abductions a week for the last twelve years."

Once outside, Kluft and Kareem lowered the ramp at the rear of the horse carrier and Gim gently escorted the magnificent creature out and towards the canal. The fine hairs of the creature's broad back reflected the moonlight but otherwise, the beast's deep treacle colour looked black. Gim secured the bridle of the creature to a railing and with gentle caressing, she leaned her forehead against Ginger's neck.

"I am truly sorry." whispered Gim. "I hope we shall see you soon returned to your master. A good man needs your help."

Gim turned and left Ginger, joining Kluft and Kareem under a nearby hedge, a way back from the towpath of the canal.

"Are we gonna be here all night?" asked Kareem, his hearing slowly returning.

"For as long as it takes, Kareem." said Kluft.

"But it's freezing." pleaded Kareem.

"I know," hissed Kluft, rapidly losing patience, "if you can just bear with us."

"Let me just try somethin'." said Kareem, crawling out from under the hedge.

"Kareem!" whispered Kluft, at full volume.

"What the fuck does he think he is doing?" asked Gim, reaching again for her pistol.

"Kareem! Come back!" whisper-shouted Kluft.

Kareem smiled as he tenderly stroked the shoulder of the impressive animal. As Gim and Kluft looked on in disbelief, Kareem removed a can of spray cream from his jacket and curled a large cream spiral on the horse's back. Feeling satisfied, Kareem rejoined the gawking Kluft and Gim.

"Kareem…" said Kluft, "do you ever-"

Suddenly, a bright shaft of light descended on the horse from above and a low bass trembled the ground. Their eyes, all slowly ascended to view a silent, hovering spacecraft. Kluft's jaw was somewhere by her knees, Gim's face was a tempest of emotions, none of which reached her face and Kareem looked on with a most contented smile. A moment later, the craft whisked away with the horse inside and the canal boat was alone once again, gently bobbing on the dark water. The trio remained a minute by the canal. It was near silent, bar the gentlest lapping of the water against the brick banks and the murmurs of the Hackney nightlife in the distance. They returned to the horse carrier without a word, that was until Kluft asked;

"Do you always have whipped cream in your jacket?"

"No." said Kareem, earnestly. "I thought it were deodorant."

9:14am
Mayor Of London, Harry Huffnagel's Home, Bethnal Green

"Poxy!" exclaimed the Mayor, as he awoke in a start. He rubbed his face, put on his thick, black rimmed spectacles and turned on his television. In the horse carrier, out on the road in front of the house, Gim, Kluft and Kareem listened closely.

"He is awake, television is on." said Gim. "Be ready for the switch over in three...two…one, do it."

Kluft pressed a button on a remote and the Mayor's TV screen switched seamlessly from *Deadly 60* to a fake news segment prepared by Kluft and Kareem. As he sat on his bed, the Mayor pressed the now ineffectual buttons on his remote. After the initial disappointment of losing *Deadly 60* he became quickly engrossed in the current viewing.

"This is Shagney Kluft for C.U.N News bringing to you this warning for all animal lovers. This week has seen a rash of allegations against the Visitors. Citizens are claiming that rare and exotic animals are being abducted by the Visitors, for the purposes of forced, interspecies breeding, gambling and in some cases, tapas."

"Those poxy grey bastards!" barked the Mayor, his face brimming with indignation.

"We at C.U.N are advising anyone with a pet or possibly, race horse to keep your beloved animals close. Or your new Visitor friend might be dining tonight on horse-d'ouvres."

The Mayor clicked off his TV and called into his en-suite bathroom.

"Ginger!" he snapped. "Don't you worry girl, I won't let some little grey, haemorrhoid-headed alien get their grubby little hands on you...Ginger?"

"Ginger!?!" wailed the Mayor as he realised that there was no prize-winning racehorse in his bathroom.

"Poxy thieving grey bastard lying bastards!" he roared as he marched out of his room.

Outside on the road, Kluft was watching the Mayor's front door through binoculars. The door burst open and a barely dressed Mayor stormed outwards, followed closely by distressed aides and make-up specialists.
"Aaaaaand, we're off." said Kluft.
Gim pulled away from the kerbside and they began their journey back to Camden.

Back at Kluft's flat, all morning, Gim, Kluft and Kareem had been keeping a close eye on the news coverage.
"Wait! Here it is!" yelled Kluft, from the sofa.
A breaking feature on C.U.N News displayed a furious Huffnagel marching along the bank of the Thames, through a mob of press. C.U.N reporter, Walton Shalmanac, was on hand.
"Mr. Mayor! Do you believe Ginger has been kidnapped?"
"Yes, I bleedin' do, and by a poxy, thievin' alien no less!"
"What makes you suspect a Visitor of the abduction?"
The Mayor stopped a moment and spoke directly into the camera.
"Because that grey, balloon headed git Deacon Smash couldn't keep his filthy hands off her!"
"But Mr. Mayor-" began Shalmanac.
"Shut it Shalmanac! Look, I know it's him and if I have to give cavity searches to half his family tree I won't stop until I get my Ginger back!"

At that moment, in the London Met HQ, Reyka was entering one of the classier saloons in the Met building for a morning martini when he stopped and observed a TV screen featuring the Mayor's barnstorm.
"I'm going straight to the Met now to get this dealt with. Do you hear me Leathers!? I'm comin' down there!"
Reyka approached the bar where an officer in full uniform was polishing glassware and picked up the telephone handset from the art deco bartop. He waited for the acknowledgment of the operator before he spoke;
"...Ahem." he said, coolly.

Whilst he was waiting to be connected, Reyka turned his attention back to the TV screen where he saw the Mayor's fury overspill as he tumbled over two reporters, resulting in a mass brawl.

"Poxy!" yelled the Mayor, as he slipped over again, swinging his fists wildly in the fray.

Without taking his eyes off the screen, Reyka spoke;

"Councilwoman. I think you might want to get down here."

The Reticulant Secret Hidden Base, Droitwich

On the second floor and towards the rear of a hulking complex, were the animal enclosures. It was here where the senior Reticulants kept their prized specimens and where Ambassador Crunk was coming to see Deacon Smash. The space looked like an aircraft hangar filled with steel paddocks and energy-based force fields containing the more 'unpredictable' animals. Aliens of different species wore overalls and tended to the needs of the fauna. Crunk was preoccupied with his phone as he walked past cage after cage of bizarre and wonderful creatures.

"Alright Smash, let's make this quick," beckoned Crunk. "I need to wrap this up and get over to-"

Crunk froze as he looked up from his phone and saw Deacon Smash escorting his latest treasure with several labourer Reticulants.

"Isn't she a beauty?!" beamed Smash.

"Oh, Smash…" mourned Crunk, "what have you done?"

"Oh, come on," said Smash, "we've nicked weirder stuff than this! Look at her! She's amazing."

"You're supposed to keep it to rhinos, snow leopards, stuff no one's going to miss!" barked Crunk.

"Oh yeah, that leopard? Way too bitey for my liking."

"Smash." said Crunk, repressing his wrath admirably. "What you have here is a promethean V-bomb. You've nicked the most famous animal in the world, of organised gambling. They'll know it's us and when Huffnagel-"

"Oh, sod Huffnagel, he's a trouser sausage." said Smash, disdainfully.

"You don't get it Smash, he's a fucking lunatic. Right. You are going to go on TV backed by the biggest celebs with nothing on today and you are going to deny everything. You're going to explain how sad you are that such fake news serves only to stir up bigotry between species, are we clear?"

"...So I can keep her?" asked Smash, hopefully.

"Until I can find someone to frame, yes." said Crunk, as he turned and walked away. "Now go home and wait for a call."

"We're still going fishing on Saturday, right?" said Smash.

"Oh yes." whispered Crunk, to himself.

EPISODE XI

London Met HQ

Followed by his aides and a few more tenacious members of the press, Harry Huffnagel blasted his way through double doors as he marched towards Leathers' office.

"I want her found by tea time." he barked. "If that cretin Leathers knows what's good for him he'll give me everything I bleedin' ask for. Now, if you'll please excuse me, I need a slash."

The mayor pushed his way into the gents and while humming an old wartime showtune approached the nearest urinal. Just then, Rosch emerged from one of the cubicles wearing a WWII gas mask. He removed the mask revealing a breathless, sweaty and grimy face.

"Mr. Mayor?" gasped Rosch.

The Mayor slowly rotated his head towards Rosch before shaking and zipping his fly. Rosch looked at the Mayor keenly, he could hear the scrape of cognitive mechanisms recalling this familiar face. Rosch held his breath as the Mayor's mind crept ever closer to naming his addresser.

"Lyndon!" ventured the Mayor.

Rosch winced.

"...Lando." he sighed, mournfully.

"Sorry. Lando." corrected the Mayor. "Listen, I need you and Keith Floyd for a job. Some, low down, cheap, sleazy, poxy alien has nicked my Ginger, and you two clefts owe me big time for that Gary Barlow fiasco. I want her found and found fast. Now, where is that piss head Ruggerman?"

"He's been committed to St. Beadles." said Rosch.

"The daft cupboard?" scoffed the Mayor. "Bollocks. Right. Time to slap some sense into that donkey Leathers. I want you both on the road looking for that horse within the hour. And you get her found my son, or you'll think being an arse wipe is like courting Lulu."

London Met. HQ, Chief Commissioner Leathers' Office

Chief Leathers stood dutifully in the window next to Reyka whilst Caroline Ahem sat at his desk. Across from her, Mayor Harry Huffnagel looked intently through his thick rimmed spectacles.
"That extra-terrestrial dick bag nicked my Ginger." said the Mayor. "Now what are you gonna to do about it?"
"Mr. Mayor," said Ahem, smiling. "I hope you can understand the importance of maintaining smooth relations with the Visitors now more than ever-"
"Oh, leave it out!" snapped the Mayor. "You've not had half a million quid's worth of racehorse pinched while you were sleeping! Christ, to think he was in my house."
"I know you're upset." said Ahem. "It's just that for now our police resources are being prioritised for-"
"Don't give me that." scoffed the Mayor, disdainfully. "Western Tactical handles this kind of thing, doesn't it? What's that currently being prioritised for?"
"Ah-hum," coughed Leathers gently. "I'm afraid Western Tactical has been...dissolved due to allegations of...misconduct."
"Dissolved?!" roared the Mayor. "Listen. I need Frank Ruggerman *and* his monkey boy Fannypacker to get my horse back, so fill out the forms, turn the lights on and get the jump leads jumping because-"
"Mr. Mayor." said Ahem.
"Stop trying to canvas me princess! You need to-"
"Harry." said Ahem, stopping him dead.

All the perk and joviality in Ahem's face had dissipated and her demeanour had turned to granite. She held the Mayor in her iron gaze just a moment before she spoke.

"Listen close Harry, 'cos here's the thing. The deal with the Visitors means that in exchange for not destroying us, every TV production contract on the planet will be handed over to them. They and they alone will decide the fate of every TV show in existence. I would sincerely hate for… *'Salsa Time with Arsene Wenger'* to get axed, prematurely."

The fire disappeared from Huffnagel's face.

"...You can't." he said.

"You're a c***," snapped Ahem, "and what's more, you're a c*** who's going to realize just how far he is in over his stupid, bespectacled head. You are going to say no more to anyone about an abduction or Visitor involvement regarding that lame, polio-ridden horse. Frank Ruggerman is going to stay exactly where he is and Western Tactical stays kaput. One word out of you and Arsene Wenger will be slung back to managing premiership football teams. How would you like to do your salsa time with...James Corden?"

"Oh my god. You total, total can't." said the Mayor, nearly sobbing. "If anything unsavoury happens to that horse, I'll see to it you pair are manning the waltzers by Christmas."

The Mayor then leapt from his chair and stormed out through the door, accidentally concussing one of his aides in the process.

"Ciao, Harry." said Ahem, quietly, before adding;

"Leathers...a word please."

9:10am
Hendrix Grove, Camden, Shagney Kluft's Flat

The following morning, Gim stood in the middle of Kluft's living room, clicking the TV remote from channel to channel.

Click C.U.N *"-meaning that each boy scout had to eat his own bodyweight in fibreglass in order to escape-"*

Click JPAX News.*" -claims of sexual misconduct against him. In a bizarre twist of fate the president himself was later sexually assaulted by the entire starting eleven, of the Limehouse Rams-"*
Click BBBC News.*"-sixty three percent plastic and the remaining seventeen percent being a mix of Gaviscon and cocaine. In response, her majesty simply said-"*
Click...
Gim muted the TV as she and Kluft stood in silence. Kareem was sitting on the sofa, contentedly listening to his headphones.
"Not one fucking mention." lamented Kluft. "They've squashed it, the whole damn story."
"This is disastrous." said Gim. "I believe now Frank Ruggerman has less than four hours before alcohol withdrawals render his mind irreparable."
Gim began to tremble and Kluft held her gently by the shoulders.
"Gim, honey. I'm so sorry...We took our shot...They squashed it."
"Miss Kluft, I-" sniffed Gim.
Suddenly, on one of the sofas, Rosch awoke in a panic and agonisingly removed a tranquiliser dart from his neck.
"Argh! ...Uhm, Gim, can you just email me next time." winced Rosch, his eyes recoiling from the light.
"Apologies." said Gim. "Force of habit."
"Where the hell am I?!" inquired Rosch, desperately.
"Rosch, my name is Shagney Kluft. I'm a reporter for C.U.N News, you're in my home, you're safe here."
"Uhm..." pondered Rosch, attempting to massage the confusion from his brow. "...Shagney Kluft?"
"My mom was an L.A. hippy." said Kluft. "My dad's Korean, he loves *Pornhub* and-"
"Assistant Detective," interrupted Gim, "at this moment, we are at, how you say, Shitcon 1. Our plan to raise public distaste for the Reticulants has run aground. We must now break Frank free from St. Beadle's and the two of you must rescue the Mayor's horse Ginger from a-" Suddenly, a

hecklesome and cynical laugh emerged slowly from deep within Rosch's belly.
"Absolutely forget it." laughed Rosch.
"But Rosch-" began Kluft.
"Don't you dare 'but Rosch' me." he said. "I have tried with you people, I've tried and tried and so far, I've been vomited on, shot at, beaten-"
"Ravaged by a bear." added Gim, unapologetically.
"Ravaged by a bear and what has it got me? Demoted to a job that a recently widowed dung beetle would quit. I've been trying to-"
"What you've been trying to do, detective," stepped in Gim, "is to further your career by manipulating the investigations of the Western Tactical Unit. You have been informing on detective Ruggerman to win the favour of your superiors, all of whom you do not believe to be in any way trustworthy."
Rosch's eyes fell to the floor.
"You must not be surprised that your commitment to the white line in the middle of the road has brought you into conflict with Frank Ruggerman." said Gim. "He has integrity."
"But he's nuts!" yelled Rosch, "anyone can see that!"
"His talents being a product of psychosis is likely." said Gim. "But let us not forget that the facts surrounding the murder of Judge Duane Pegg have been whitewashed for the sake of the political elite to cover their collaboration with an invading alien force. You have a key part to play in this Rosch."
Rosch breathed deeply and sighed into his hands before looking around the carpet near his feet.
"...You said something about a horse?"

10 Minutes Later…

Rosch removed his smartphone as he raced down the front steps of Kluft's home. Gim, Kluft and an oblivious Kareem, still lost in his music, stood in the front doorway.

"Just give me half an hour." said Rosch, as he began texting.
"Rosch" said Gim, "we do not have time for this. Frank is-"
"Gim! Please!" pleaded Rosch.
Kluft turned to Gim whilst Gim's gaze held steadfast on Rosch.
"I can help." said Rosch. "Just half an hour....Trust me... Please."
Gim stared into Rosch's face. She exhaled deeply and gave him the slightest of nods. Validated, Rosch raced off and began making phone calls.
"What just happened?" asked Kluft.
"I don't know," said Gim, "but I sense a change in the force."
Gim and Kluft returned inside and Kareem emerged from his music just in time to see the door close and lock him out.

Thirty-Two Minutes Later...
The Olsen Twins Winnebago

As an extraordinary wind tormented the outside of the war-torn Winnebago, Rosch stood before Chris, Hansen and Nathan Olsen. The youngest member of the outfit, Hansen, leaned in his crisp suit against the window whilst he sipped from his mug. At a desk, sat Nathan.
"So what you're talking about is a two part rescue." said Nathan, to a rain-soaked Rosch.
As Rosch stood just inside the entrance of the hulking vehicle, Chris Olsen waved the bioscanner back and forth across Rosch's genitals.
"Yes. Knock it off. I believe so." said Rosch.
Chris quietly acquiesced.
"First," continued Rosch, "get Ruggerman out of St.Beadle's, then retrieve the Mayor's horse from an as of yet, unknown location."
"Most likely a heavily guarded, alien location." added Hansen.
"Yes." said Rosch.

"That may very well be in space." said Chris.

"...Possibly." said Rosch.

"No, I don't think so." said Nathan, flexing the back of his chair. "The moon is no go since the Russians turned it into a gulag for rogue social media bots. No...they're here somewhere."

"Well first things first." said Chris. "Freeing Ruggerman."

"That's not too tough." said Hansen. "I know St.Beadle's... I was sent there between the age of five and nine."

"You never told us this." said Chris, sympathetically.

"Things for the most part have moved on," said Hansen, "but back then, being addicted to KitKats was enough to see you locked away with the blueberries."

"Jesus." sighed Nathan.

"Meh. Time heals." said Hansen, placing his tea bag in the bin. "From what I remember there's a sewage pipe that…"

Rosch groaned and fingered his antibac spray in his pocket while Hansen described St.Beadle's.

"...runs in a straight line from the rec field, under the attack dogs' kennels and right behind each cell, separated only by a wooden panel at the back of the toilet."

Rosch gulped down the last of his sherry.

"Attack dogs?" he asked, reluctantly.

"Yes," replied Hansen, "you must ensure you close each junction gate correctly or else the dogs will be able to escape into the pipe."

"You'll also need a distraction." added Chris.

"A dinner lady of some kind usually does the trick." said Nathan. "Something real tasty to distract the guards."

"And what about the Mayor's horse?" asked Rosch.

"Well," said Hansen, "the horse is currently being held somewhere by Reticulants, we need to retrieve it."

The Olsen Twins then shared a moment of collective satisfaction.

"What?" asked Rosch, quizzically.

The Olsens all smiled.

"Send a horse to catch a horse, Rosch." said Nathan.

Sadly, that statement escalated Rosch's thinly veiled confusion into a sharp pain in his head.

"Well, there it is." said Hansen. "Rosch, here's the schematics of St. Beadle's. Make sure the dinner lady has something real tasty. We'll get to work locating this secret Reticulant base."

Hansen put the kettle on whilst Chris and Nathan eagerly took to their computers. In the awkward moment that followed, Rosch spoke; "I'll be off then." he said, opening the flimsy door and receiving a faceful of Baltic monsoon.

Shagney Kluft's Living Room

A little while later, Rosch stood before Gim and Kluft, who were silent and listening intently.
"Right…" he said. "...Oh, we need a bottle of bourbon."

St. Beadle's Memorial Hospital

Even though the hospital was located in central London, the barren, grey wastelands it sat on stretched to the horizon in every direction. A handful of naked, twisted trees dotted the landscape like skeletal cheerleaders that were there only to laugh at the new arrivals. The wind scoured the exterior of Rosch's black fatigues as he slowly raised the heavy iron grate that covered the entrance to the sewer system of St.Beadle's. As he heaved the huge metal slab into place, he was greeted by an olfact-aural combination of barking attack dog and effluence. Nearby, in the cab of the horse carrier they rented from Kareem's grandmother, Gim and Kluft watched as the disguised Kareem and his trundling lunch trolley were greeted by the St. Beadle's security.
"You're a bit late, aren't you?" said one burly guard.
"Hello!" said Kareem, cheerily. "It's crepes."

Kareem then pushed his trolley through the guards and into the building. The burly guard went to call after him until his colleague grabbed his arm.

"Don't," he warned gravely, "he's an idiot."

Inside the horse carrier, Kluft spoke into her walkie talkie.

"Okay, the milkybar kid is go." she said, "Chewbacca you are cleared for takeoff."

"Roger… and piss off." said Rosch, as he sat ready upon the edge of the iron grate.

With the joviality of derisive wordplay quickly leaving his mind, Rosch braced himself and cautiously lowered his body into the waist deep and ice-cold effluence that would lead him into the hospital. With a bottle of bourbon in a carrier bag, he held his breath and took his first steps into the water. The aroma caused the contents of Rosch's stomach to immediately attempt a bid for freedom but luckily for him, the crippling temperature had already frozen everything below his armpits. Rosch fought for his breath as the cold grasped his lungs and slowly stepped deeper into the tunnel.

Inside the hospital, Kareem's trolley trundled along an echoing corridor.

"Crepes." he gulped, his eyes drifting left to right as menacing murmurs began to seep from the cells. "Crepes? Does anyone fancy some crepes?"

Back in the sewer pipe, Rosch climbed from the main water channel, up onto a black concrete bank. He saw a narrow, brick lined pipe that was labelled, 'West Wing'. Rosch crawled over and peered inside. He saw that the pipe extended a long way ahead and was lined with what looked like empty fireplaces, all sealed by a wooden panel. Rosch was just slim enough to fit inside and he began the slow, arduous crawl towards the cells.

"Come out to California," he said drily, "we'll get together, have a few laughs." He chuckled once before his gag reflex buckled and the heaves wracked his body.

In the panic, he accidentally sprayed himself in the eye with his anti-bac spray. The sudden sound of terrifying and angry dogs nearby made him freeze solid in mid-heave. Once the barking dissipated, he slowly dragged his body along the pipe and up towards the first wooden panel. Carefully, he gripped the edges and worked it loose. He slowly removed it and looked inside. In the middle of the cell, stood a naked middle-aged man with a hula hoop swinging around his hips.

"Ignorant... bastards." he muttered to himself as he gyrated to and fro.

After noticing how the action of 'hula hooping' made male genitalia resemble a galloping horse, Rosch carefully replaced the panel and slipped back into the pipe. A few metres further along was the next cell. Rosch heaved his weight up the bank and began to dislodge the second panel. Inside the cell, lying on the floor, with dry tears staining his face, was Frank Ruggerman. The hole was just behind the toilet, Rosch slid the panel to one side and pushed his way through. With his legs still in the pipe, Rosch gritted his teeth as Frank grabbed him fiercely around the throat.

"You'll pay for what you've done you harriden!" screamed Frank, sobbing. "I loved you!"

"Frank! It's me!" gasped Rosch, pushing Frank away.

As the two lay gasping, Rosch spoke;

"I'm here with Gim, I've- urgh!" Rosch was choked once again by Frank.

"Fauntleroy Lando piss bastard!" he shouted, leaning his bodyweight on top of Rosch.

Rosch wrestled desperately and managed to remove the bottle of bourbon from the carrier bag. Frank's demeanour immediately shifted to that of a kitten.

"There it is," soothed Rosch, "nice and easy now."

Frank momentarily switched his attention to Rosch and then back to the bottle, then trembling, he reached forward.

In another wing, Kareem was busy serving crepes to some of the inmates.

"Crepes!" he called. "All the flavours... well, three."

An inmate called Hoyt, pressed his mean, grizzly and tattooed face through the bars.
"Well don't they smell real good?" he growled.
"You can have some if you like." said Kareem, pleasantly.
"They smell good like your mama's crevice!" roared Hoyt, as he reached through the bars and grabbed Kareem by the collar.
"Arrrrrgh!" he screamed. "Miss Kluft! Help me! I don't like it! I don't like it!"
Just then, the door at the end of the hall burst open and in rushed a squad of mean-looking guards.
"Oh, thank god!" cheered Kareem, as they rushed him to the ground and rained blow after blow upon him.
Inside Frank's cell. Rosch was attempting to wipe grime from his face and Frank was shivering as he lovingly nursed the bottle of whiskey. Outside the cell, Rosch heard the squad of guards storm past.
"Okay," said Rosch, "that's our cue. Right. Okay Frank, here we go."
With Frank weeping and swigging from the bottle, Rosch guided him through the hole behind the toilet and out into the pipe.

Eight minutes later and now outside in the fresh air, a perfectly lucid Frank threw the empty bottle of whiskey into a bush.
"And the Olsens think it's being kept here on earth?" he said.
"Yes." said Rosch, just about containing his admiration for the rejuvenative qualities of bourbon. "Or at least Nathan does, something about the Russians and social media."
"Makes sense." replied Frank.
As the two detectives stood in the howling wind, a horse carrier approached.
"Here's the cavalry." said Rosch.
As the horse carrier came to a stop nearby, Kareem stuck his bloodied and toothless face out of the window.
"In you pop!" he said cheerily.

11.36pm

The horse carrier pulled onto the piece of deserted wasteland that was home to the Olsen twins Winnebago. Leaving through the side door, Frank and Gim approached the driver's window.
"Kluft, you and Kareem stay here." said Frank. "To say they're a bit paranoid is like saying David Carradine was a bit fond of the rough stuff."
"Understood." said Kluft.
Frank and Gim were walking towards the Winnebago, when Rosch exited the horse carrier and began to follow. Upon noticing him, Frank turned and stopped.
"What?" he barked.
"Oh, come on, please," pleaded Rosch, "I-"
"Fucks sake, if you must." groaned Frank.

Inside the dilapidated but heavily modified recreational vehicle, Hansen Olsen handed Frank a large pina colada.
"Here you go, Frank." he said, smiling.
Nathan Olsen stroked his trimmed beard and flexed the back of his chair.
"So, the next step," he said, thoughtfully, "is to retrieve the horse from capture."
Rosch listened intently and Gim sat next to him, stirring her cocktail. Hansen Olsen plopped down in a chair with a mischievous grin and suddenly all eyes were on him.
"We think we have it." he said.
"Already?" said Rosch.
Nathan and Chris Olsen swung their chairs over to their respective computer workstations.
"Outstanding." said Frank.
"Now," said Chris, "the filtered emissions from their power generators made them very hard to spot. But we figured that a base that could house the transport ships would need to be huge, requiring lots of groundspace."
"With a large water source." added Hansen.

"So, we knew," continued Chris, "it would be out in the sticks, far from traffic."

"Once we figured that out" said Nathan, "we looked for sparsely populated areas with colossal amounts of broadband data usage."

"That gave us three options." said Hansen.

"And to narrow that down," furthered Chris, "I cross referenced which of the areas had the highest amount of *Nando's* deliveries."

"And that gave us here." said Nathan.

Rosch approached the workstation.

"Droitwich?" he said.

"The same." said Nathan, confidently. "We ran a whole bunch of other cross comparatives and this field in the foothills rang out loud and clear."

"How do we get inside?" asked Gim.

"It's actually exiting that's our primary concern." said Hansen. "Given what we've gathered from their technology, they'll most likely have the whole site cloaked, meaning we'll have no satellite pics that might show ways in or out."

"You'll be going in blind." said Nathan.

"Nice." said Frank.

"And if they catch you…" began Hansen.

"Then I guess we'll need to improvise." said Frank, lighting a cigarette. "What about getting in?"

The Olsen twins then relished in another moment of shared satisfaction.

"Classic Trojan." said Chris, making devil horns with his fingers.

Nathan Olsen reached into a cupboard and removed a pantomime horse costume.

"Et voila!" he said, triumphantly.

"Oh dear." said Rosch, under his breath.

"Relax, Rosch." soothed Hansen, warmly.

"Think about it." said Chris. "What's the one way you know of, guaranteed to get into the base? You've done it yourselves once already."

"Inspired." said Frank.

Frank appeared confident but Gim clearly had doubts.
"I am concerned that this will not pass for the real thing."
"Our studies," said Chris, "revealed that their security technology doesn't use light like ours. Theirs is molecular, more comparable to smell."
"Only like that of a bloodhound." added Nathan.
Hansen Olsen sipped from his mug of tea and placed it on the sink.
"So in order for the subterfuge to work," he said, "you'll only have to really, really, smell....like a horse."
"But that, I'm afraid," said Chris, regretfully, "we can't help you with."
"No," added Nathan, "there's one more person you're gonna need."

1:39am
Little Italy, London

With the horse carrier containing Gim, Kluft and Kareem, parked out on the quiet, suburban lane, Frank and Rosch approached the front door of one of the terracotta-coloured bungalows. Just as they came to the carved, wooden porch, the garage door heaved its way open, flooding the driveway with light and revealing the London Met, Snr. Lab technician, Jojo Binks. Jojo stood in his shaggy, pin striped dressing gown, his arms full of plastic containers and a large cigar protruding from his smile.
"Eyyyy!" he beamed, jovially. "I gotta say, you look like shit Frank, you okay?"
"Sorry it's so late." said Frank.
"Ah, forget about it. I was just watching TV." smiled Jojo.
Jojo, dumped the plastic containers on a workbench and approached Frank with his arms outstretched.
"Ey come 'ere, bring it in." he said.
Jojo wrapped his arms around Frank and Frank held onto his friend for dear life. After a moment, Frank sobbed.

"It's okay pal." said Jojo, placing a hand on Frank's neck. "It's alright. Work it out."
Frank eventually released his friend and sniffed.
"Ah." said Frank, relieved, smiling and chuckling. "Does the trick every time."
"Ey, what am I here for?" said Jojo. "You know Frank, this is a hell of a risk to rescue one horse."
"It's the only chance I've got to blow the Pegg coverup." said Frank.
"Ey, you don't gotta tell me twice." said Jojo. "So the Olsen's filled me in on what it was you guys needed. Thankfully, I got just the thing."
Frank and Rosch followed as Jojo entered his garage, closing the door behind them. Meanwhile in the horse carrier, Kluft and Kareem played a very one-sided game of 'slaps' and Gim wrestled with her own current inefficacy.

Inside the garage, Jojo pulled several chains across a steel rig that was built into the ceiling with dozens of high-pressure water spouts underneath. He then connected a thick hose pipe from a huge iron tank to the steel rig and beckoned Frank and Rosch over to him.
"You know," said Jojo, "I built this back in the eighties. I never thought I'd have to get the old broad out again."
"So, what's next?" Frank asked.
"You two, get in the horse costume." said Jojo. "Frank, you're in the front."
"Wait, why am I in the-" protested Rosch.
"Cos you're a horse's ass, alright?" snapped Jojo. "Plus, I need Frank to operate the field tracker."
Jojo relit his cigar.
"But-" said Rosch.
"Kid, would you get in the ass already?" commanded Jojo.
"Come on." said Frank, calmly.

Frank and Rosch proceeded to climb into their respective halves of the pantomime horse costume. Jojo assisted them both and then carefully attached them together in the middle. Then, he assisted Frank to put the head on.

"You alright?" asked Jojo, pausing before attaching the head.

"Yeah." said Frank, breathing deeply.

"You sure?"

"Yeah."

"Atta boy." said Jojo. "You're gonna be fine. Here's the touch pad for the subspace radio to keep in touch with the Olsens. If you're worried about detection, the touch pad also works as Morse code. It's configured to keep changing the encryption so it should remain hidden from their comms."

Frank took one last deep breath and nodded his head.

"Ah, you're all right." said Jojo. "Just remember to try and breathe normally."

Frank held his nerve against mild claustrophobia as the head was put in place.

"Now," said Jojo. "I put together a molecular based analyser using the data from the Olsens. For starters, we'll do an initial scan."

The pantomime horse, with its vacant face, stood despondently in the middle of Jojo's garage, beneath the sturdy metal rig. Jojo typed commands into a computer interface, the clacks of keyboard presses were closely followed by a rather stern, female, automated computer voice.

"Molecular scan initiated." it said. *"Acquiring subject. Subject acquired. Type human. Scanning. Detected: alcohol percentage at 135% lethal level. Detected: Jamesons, Jynx Voodoo, Flintoff Kingsize."*

From inside the horse;

"I slightly hesitate to ask Binks," said Frank, "but, how do you intend to disguise us?"

"That's the easy part." said Jojo. "Hey, I wanna tell you something, I might live another hundred years and still not find another life-or-death purpose for 800 gallons of matured horse urine."

Jojo typed another command into the keypad.

"Wait. What did he say?" said Rosch.

"Here we go." said Jojo.

"Camouflage protocol engaged." said the voice.

The dozens of high-pressure showerheads that loomed above the horse costume opened. 'CHOOOOOOOOM'. A dense, aromatic deluge of aged horse urine descended upon them.

"Oh... my... god." said Rosch.

"Calm down, Lando." said Frank, stoically.

"Oh, fuck off, Ruggerman." grimaced Rosch. "No one said anything about being drowned in 800 gallons of barrel aged horse piss ....Eurgh, Jesus."

"Just hold tight, it'll only take a few seconds." said Frank. "...Just be glad it's warm."

Frank and Rosch shivered and groaned as the urine seeped through the costume and into their clothes.

The showers ceased. Drips from the shower heads plopped and echoed. The panto horse remained still.

"You fellas okay in there?" asked Jojo.

"Just lovely, thank you mate." cheered Rosch with near terminal sarcasm.

"Right, so let's re-scan." said Jojo.

"Second scan initiating." said the voice. *"Scanning. Detected: Jamesons. 85 varieties of horse urine. Flintoff Kingsize. Subject. Human."*

"Eh." said Jojo, disappointedly. "Looks like we might need to give it a few more tries."

"Camouflage protocol engaged." said the voice.

'CHOOOOOOOM' came another thunderous roar as the shower heads pumped out gallons more of the eye-watering strength horse urine.

"Urgh, Jesus Christ." said Frank, as he tried to wipe his eyes.

"I've got to say Ruggerman" said Rosch, "this kind of makes me hope we get caught and tortured to death."

The showerheads eventually came to cease once again.

"Camouflage protocol complete."

"I hate to push Binks" said Frank, "but we are rather up against it for time here, mate."

"Scanning." said the voice.

"Believe me, Frank, I get it, but we gotta be patient. If we don't get this right. They'll spot you like a stripper at the last supper."

"Fair enough." said Frank.

"Detected: 85 varieties of horse urine."

Frank was waiting as patiently as he could, it was surely nearly over, but unbeknownst to him, Rosch was about to lose the battle with something very powerful inside himself. Then, in the silence;

'TSSS, TSSS.'

"What's that?" asked Ruggerman, scornfully.

'Uhm' said Rosch.

"Detected. Waitrose Anti-bacterial hand spray."

"Argh, fuck I'm sorry!" cried Rosch.

"Binks wait!" said Frank.

"Camouflage protocol engaged." 'CHOOOOOOOM'

Another monsoon of urine descended upon the saddest looking panto horse there ever was.

"You fucking dickhead, Lando!" bellowed Frank.

Jojo watched amused as the horse tried to kick itself in the testicles using its front leg.

"I am so sorry." said Rosch.

"Camouflage protocol complete."

"Oh please, dear god." said Frank, piously.

"Ruggerman," said Rosch, "do you think the coroner will mind if the 9ml shell she pulls out of my brain is soaked in horse piss?

"Binks, let's do this." ordered Frank, ignoring Rosch completely.

"Alright let's rescan again." said Jojo.

A while later, outside in the horse carrier, Kluft had joined Gim in the cab, Gim was staring intently at the closed garage door. A muffled 'CHOOOOOOOM' sound came from inside.

"What the hell's going on in there?" said Kluft, checking her watch, "it's been two hours."

"Something must be wrong." said Gim.

Just as Gim went to open the door of the cab, the garage door mechanism heaved into life and slowly began to rise.

"Wait." said Kluft, "Here they are."

Jojo Binks led the sad and wet panto horse, along his drive and towards the carrier. Gim and Kluft came out to assist, only to recoil at the breathtaking aroma.

"Wow." said Kluft.

"Here we go." said Jojo. "Remember, don't feed him after midnight. Heh heh. No seriously, you can't feed 'em at all, no more cigarettes neither. You guys, I gotta get back inside. Good luck to all of yous. Take it easy Frank!"

Gim lifted up the horse's head to speak to Frank.

"Yeah, thanks Binks." said Frank, warmly, before he noticed the look of indignation on Gim's face.

"Why are you taking Princess Liar?" she said. "I would be of infinitely more use than that gap year eunuch."

"Gim-" said Frank.

"And I overheard you on the phone before," she added, "you even tried to get Toltattler before me but he was unavailable, something about his bowels."

"You know I'm hearing all of this." said Rosch, from inside the horse.

"Good." snapped Gim. "Why not me, Frank? I can-"

"Because we might not make it." replied Frank briskly.

Gim paused.

"And if we don't." continued Frank, "someone needs to lead this fight. And that's you Gim."

"My father commanded me to-"

"Your father," said Frank, "is blessed to have you as a daughter. You're far too valuable to all this than to be the ninja bodyguard of a piss-artist like me. Your father believed in you, I believe in you...Plus, I'm taking Lando in case it gets all 'human shield-y'."

"Wow." said Rosch, muffled.

"Oh, be quiet Ja Ja." snapped Frank. "Right. Let's move."

With all in silence, and mostly with heads poking out of windows, the horse carrier made its way along the dark highway, towards Hackney Canal. After twenty-six minutes of lung-paralysing pungency, the vehicle finally came to a stop near an abandoned canal boat. Gim exited, surveyed the area, opened the back door to the carrier and assisted the panto horse down the ramp. Frank peered out through the eyes of the costume.
"This is Pegg's boat." he said.
"This is possible." said Gim, "It is also by far the most statistically likely spot for an abduction."
Gim led the squelching, urine-logged horse over to the canal side, her nose twitching and her eyes streaming. She took a long look into its sad, vacant face.
"Good luck to you both." she said, before taking cover in a nearby bush.

For ten minutes, they watched the motionless horse in silence, listening to the lapping of the water against the bank. Kareem then stood and approached the horse with his can of whipped cream. Sadly, his constitution collapsed as the smell returned to his nostrils. Kareem's eyes flooded, his knees wobbled violently and he squeezed the can releasing whipped cream into the air and all over himself.
"Kareem. It's fine." yelled Kluft, "Come back."
Coughing and spluttering apologetically, Kareem returned to the cover of the bushes. Kluft put her arm around him and took Gim's hand.

Sixteen Minutes Later…

"Should I get some more wee?" asked Kareem, thoughtfully. "I imagine it-"
A bright shaft of white light descended upon the panto horse.
"Shhh!" said Gim.
A low bass hum made the ground resonate.

"This is it." whispered Frank, "No sound."

The shaft of light pulsated and the panto horse was slowly lifted off the ground.

"Ruggerman." whispered Rosch, "I can't move."

"Quiet. It's just the tractor beam."

From the cover of the bushes, Gim, Kluft and Kareem watched as a panel beneath the craft opened, allowing the horse inside. It closed once again and the light beam disappeared, plunging the area back into darkness. With the gentlest hum, the craft departed and whooshed away.

"We must move quickly." said Gim.

"We have the coordinates for the location of the base from the Olsens." said Kluft. "Can't be too close but nearby enough to do a quick smash and grab. When they get out."

"...If they get out." said Kareem cheerily.

EPISODE XII

Holding Area, Reticulant Spacecraft, Somewhere En Route To Droitwich

Once the sounds of Reticulants nearby had passed, Frank attempted to assess their surroundings. Through the eyes and seams of the horse costume he could see only a moody orange glow coming from the strip lights that were embedded into the walls of the holding area. The only sound was the gentle hum of the craft's engine. The area was very warm and the air was heavy which greatly exacerbated the bouquet of being in the sodden horse. On a platform, with its bridle tethered to a railing, it stood motionless, save the wafts of smoke from Frank's *Flintoff Kingsize* that had begun to drift outwards through the horse's ears.
"Are you sure that's a good idea?" coughed Rosch.
"I am 800 gallons deep behind enemy lines Lando, yes I'm having a snout." spat Frank.
"Well, I'm just glad piss isn't flammable." said Rosch.
"Shhh! Quiet Lando." hissed Frank.
"What?" said Rosch, anxiously. "Is there someone there?"
"No." said Frank. "Just be quiet."
Rosch thought a moment in the silence.
"You know I am sorry about Pegg." he said.
"This is not the time, Lando." said Frank, forebodingly.
"Fine." said Rosch. "As you wish...but I've said it."
"Do you know what happens if we get caught?" said Frank, exhaling a lungful of smoke.

"You are talking to someone who spent over two hours being showered in horse urine." said Rosch. "At this point gastric surgery sounds like a Thai massage."
"Shhh, listen." ordered Frank.
The sound of the engine altered, suggestive of changing gears. Then, the hum of the engine grew louder and louder until it sounded like a long, drawn out boom, descending in pitch before a gentle tremor wobbled its way through the entire craft.
"Touchdown." said Frank.
Frank pressed the screen of the field tracker that the Olsens had built into the front of the costume. It came to life and bathed his aged face in a pale, yellow light.
"Droitwich. Spot on. Nice one, Chris." said Frank.
"What now?" said Rosch.
"Well-" began Frank.
Suddenly, both Frank and Rosch jumped as a loud creak indicated a heavy metal door being lowered to form an exit ramp nearby. As the ramp lowered, the dull orange glow of the holding area was gradually replaced with the bright lights of the Reticulant base.
"Here we go." whispered Frank. "Silence."

Two Reticulant zoo keepers ambled towards the panto horse, untied it and led it down the ramp. Through the eyes of the costume, Frank could see dozens of animal enclosures, some just paddocks, others cages or electrified. There were many exotic Earth animals including a group of giraffes and a myriad other bizarre and wonderful creatures from other corners of the cosmos. Finally, after securing them in a paddock, the Reticulant keepers left and went about other tasks.
"And now what?" said Rosch, dryly.
"Now?" replied Frank. "We wait."
The horse stood alone, in the conventional metal paddock alongside many others that filled the huge warehouse-looking space.
"...Where did you grow up?" asked Rosch.

Frank groaned explicitly.

"Don't bother Lando." growled Frank. "We don't have the time."

"We're just waiting!" said Rosch. "Why not get to know each other better?"

"Because, I know all I need to know about Darth Gap Year, thank you very much." said Frank.

"You don't know anything about me!" cried Rosch.

"Will you please get your head back in the game?" barked Frank. "I'm not going to tell you again."

"They died when I was seven." said Rosch.

"Agh, Christ." said Frank, removing another cigarette.

"What little I do remember feels cold and distant." said Rosch. "I remember my mother would wait patiently for my father to finish the Sunday supplements, before patrolling the village with the militia. Tuesday nights, after indulging in sherry, she would wake me at 3am to dance for her. She would laugh, clap her hands and occasionally spit. I didn't realise it back then, but they would be the only smiles she would ever show me."

"Jesus." said Frank, just before exhaling.

"Mostly, my childhood was spent going from boarding school to boarding school. All elite level, the best professors, the best resources. But all the privilege in the world, isn't a substitute for a family."

Frank, Rosch and the panto horse stood for a moment in silence.

"You done?" said Frank.

"Oh, for god's sake you total bastard!" barked Rosch. "Would it kill you to drop the animosity for just two seconds and talk to me? For fucks sake I'm here aren't I?"

Frank pondered a moment while he pulled on his cigarette.

"I'm from a small town near Seven Sisters. I grew up with my dad on a council estate, mum was in and out of the foreign legion. Anyway, I left school, got a job and wound up in a piss-soaked fancy-dress outfit with a total bell end!"

Suddenly, a loud 'clunk' echoed through the holding area as the last Reticulants left and the lights lowered to night mode.

"This is it." said Frank.

Frank slowly slipped his hands through the seam between the front legs of the costume and the head, giving it the look of a disappointing T-Rex. He and Rosch then shuffled forward towards the gate and Frank carefully undid the latch. Then, the now truly depressed looking horse stepped gingerly out of the paddock. Frank scanned left and right before selecting and then plodding down one of the many aisles of enclosures. In an office, two Reticulant zoo keepers were watching on a monitor.

"Stinky is out of his paddock." said one.

"Nah, it's alright," said the other, "the scanner detected *Flintoff Kingsize,* he's probably just off for a smoke."

"Ah, fair play."

Just then, another Reticulant zoo keeper popped her head into the office.

"Lads, the Jerk Store is about to fillet one of them 'blue whales', you've got to see this."

With that, they all left the office and went to behold the, to date, boldest endeavour of Kas Prabshit, the head chef at the *Jerk Store.*

Now freed from prying eyes, the oblivious panto horse continued on its way up and down the aisles, searching for the Mayor's horse. Frank peered left and right, each paddock revealing stranger creatures than the last. On his right, there came an enclosure containing a large, bright pink, primate like creature, only with a long slim body, lined with a hundred pairs of legs like a millipede. It shimmied up a large tree, wrapping itself around a branch before squawking like a chicken. Then came a family of fainting goats, all currently mid-episode. Frank came to a stop as they reached a cage that was triple reinforced and throbbed with the sound of a force field. Inside sat a solitary creature with its head bowed. A towering beast, it was approximately twelve foot in height and had its many long and barbed limbs folded around itself. Its closest equivalent here on Earth was the praying mantis, only this looked reptilian with bright blue scales and flashes of intense reds and oranges up and down its limbs. Frank looked in awe and briefly relished in the delivery of another wonder from this bountiful universe of ours. The creature slowly raised its head and peered curiously at the incredibly sad looking horse which seemed to find it so fascinating. From the front of its head, from underneath a bony top lip, protruded a set of saliva dripping jaws.

"Would you like a cup of tea Jeffrey?!" shrieked the creature, before headbutting the cage wall with a lightning strike of its long neck. The impact of its head shook the room and the forcefield flashed a screaming red in protest. Frank waited a moment to see if the terror induced heart attack would indeed finish him off. He remembered a mostly good life but was pleasantly surprised as his heart rate slowly normalised and his breathing continued.

"Would you like a cup of tea Jeffrey?!" it shrieked again, lashing out with the speed of a rattlesnake.

As Frank moved on along the aisle, he saw a sign that had been repeated in seventy-three languages, including English, that read;

'DO NOT ACCEPT OFFER OF TEA.'

At the end of the aisle, there sat a large enclosure, its walls were a shimmering hologram of a meadow in the morning. From small speakers in each corner of the enclosure, came the gentle sounds of birdsong and ambient music. Inside, stood the noble and impressive form of the Mayor's pride and joy, Ginger. Frank identified the entrance which was marked by a black, touch screen control panel. Inside the horse costume, Frank tapped the screen of the interface and tried to contact the Olsens. Inside the Olsen's Winnebago, screens fizzed and distorted sounds zapped between speakers.

"Chris, we need better than this." warned Hansen.

"Look," retorted Chris, "the energy field is designed to hide the base from detection. The cryptograph frequencies

change every thirty seconds. I'll only be able to lock in one in ten and then the window is, wait!...I've got it!"
"Frank, listen," said Hansen, "we're only going to have comms intermittently because of the cloaking field. Do you see the interface?"
Frank examined the interface on the paddock.
"Look for an icon like a scorpion." said Hansen.
A hiss of static scorched the ears.
"We're losing them." said Nathan.
"Chris?" said Hansen.
"Hold on!" Chris barked, typing frantically. "I just need to realign the Dimmock ratio."
"Got him." said Nathan.
"Frank! Hit the scorpion icon and swipe right on the touch bar!" shouted Hansen.
Frank performed said task and the screen fell to black.
"Hansen?" said Frank. "It's gone. The screen's gone black... Hansen?"
Back in the Winnebago, there was furious uproar and pointing of fingers.
"Guys! Come on now, get it together." yelled Hansen.
"Guys?" said Frank, anxiously.
"What's happening?" whispered Rosch.
Sweat had begun to drip from Frank's face onto the comm screen inside the costume. He looked out again, desperate for any sign of life from the interface.
"Fuck." he said.
An electronic 'twiddlydoodlydee' sounded from the interface and Frank heaved a sigh of relief.

On the screen there appeared a cartoon farmyard sunrise with a big beaming smile. The sun spoke with an abrasive digital voice that resembled a radicalised, electronic wasp. Frank hesitated, racking his brain for his next move. The sun repeated the same phrase only angrier. In desperation, Frank tapped an icon that looked like a barn. Then, a bright ping sounded in the affirmative followed by another garbled phrase that had the unmistakable, melodious inflection of 'Ah! Why didn't you say so!'. The sun emitted three electronic honks as three options appeared in a vertical row on the screen. The first icon depicted a cartoon of a farmer holding a clipboard, interviewing a sheep. The second had a picture of sheep stacked in geometric ascendancy. The third had a flame icon. Frank pondered his options carefully.

"Tick tock, dear." said Rosch.

"Piss off, Lando." snapped Frank, as he closed his eyes and tapped the second icon.

Frank's fervent prayer was interrupted by a cheery sounding ping. At the far end of the aisle, a commotion began in a high, steel fenced paddock containing a family of giraffes, whose heads and necks were peeking over the fence. The sound of engaging mechanical gears followed by despondent mews. Frank looked intently at the screen as he heard the sound of large cutting blades coming to life to his left. The mews from the giraffes became louder and Frank reluctantly peered to his left to see a hydraulic mechanism kick in and the heads and necks of the giraffes slowly lower out of sight below the top of the fence. The sound of the mewing and spinning razors became combined with the sound of crushing bone and splattering viscera. For a soul-crippling two minutes, the sad looking horse stood as the giraffes disintegrated. The last whirrs of the blades came to an end and the sound of automated high-pressure hoses filled the now empty paddock and made both Frank and Rosch wince terribly. Feeling genuinely bad about the giraffes, Frank persevered and assessed the other two icons.

"Frank?" yelled Hansen Olsen, inside the Winnebago.

"I told you that's the best we're going to get." said Chris.

"God damn it!" roared Hansen, throwing his handset across the room.

Frank took a gamble and pressed the first icon, that of the farmer interviewing a sheep. The screen fell to black again, the hologramatic meadow disappeared revealing a gate that clicked open. The panto horse carefully made its way into the enclosure and approached Ginger. Frank carefully

reached out and stroked Ginger's huge neck, before gently taking her bridle.
"Easy girl." whispered Frank. "That's it. On you come."
Slowly and tentatively, Ginger followed the panto horse out of the paddock.
"Wait a minute," said Rosch hesitantly, "do we expect to just trot our way to the exit?"
Frank led them over to a double set of doors with large glass windows and peered out.
"You know what? I think we're in luck." said Frank. "It's rodeo day."

Frank opened the double doors onto a high walkway that overlooked a large space of bristling activity like a vast, sprawling country fair. Aliens from across the systems were wearing cowboy hats and numbers. There were hundreds of stalls selling goods and concessions, several arenas surrounded by onlookers in which trainers would pit their foundling specimens or genetic creations in combat or dressage.

In one arena, a Reticulant cowboy encouraged a creature resembling a penguin, to manoeuvre around a paddock like a sheepdog, herding a flock of other creatures that looked like furry courgettes on legs. The Reticulant communicated with the small penguin by holding up different varieties of cheese and whistling. The penguin dutifully rounded up the creatures in a tight circle in the middle, at which point the penguin obediently sat next to them and awaited instructions. Then, from underneath the arena, the huge mouth of a carnivorous plant rose up and closed its jaws around the flock and the penguin. Whilst the plant was chewing, the Reticulant cowboy threw his arms in the air and thrust out his pelvis, receiving a standing ovation from the onlookers. Up on the walkway, Frank began to lead them down the ramp and into the fray.
"Nice and easy." he said.

The sounds of the rodeo festival grew louder as they descended the ramp and became submerged in the crowd.
"This sounds too busy." said Rosch. "Do we know how far it is to the exit?"
"Quiet Lando." hissed Frank. "You're going to get us captured."
With agonisingly slow progress, the panto horse proceeded on, leading Ginger through the mobbing patrons. An old Reticulant bumped into Rosch's end of the horse. Rosch froze. The old Reticulant made a grumpy gesture and went on his way.

Back on the first floor, Ambassador Crunk strode purposefully down the corridor that led to the holding area with the animals, followed closely by five members of his guard. As he walked, Crunk spoke into his communicator.
"Trust me, it's amazing." said Crunk. "The amount of meat on it...Yeah? Well this will feed your whole wedding... I'm just getting the official weight now. Okay bye."
Crunk entered the holding area and closed his communicator.
"Smash. Times up with the GG buddy. Time to get rid of it and turn it into 'horse d'ouvres'...Smash?"
Crunk turned the corner to find an empty paddock.
"For Fucks sake." snapped Crunk, "I want that horse found. Now."
Crunk's Reticulant guards nodded in the affirmative and spread out searching. A loud, caustic alarm that sounded like a retching fox, rang out dropping several of the Reticulant guards to their knees. Crunk, removed a keyfob and pressed the button, silencing it.
"Nice and low key, yeah?" he said.
The guards stared blankly at Crunk.
"Just get it found."

Down in the fray, Frank tried to see above the crowds. The entire area spanned a good square half mile with walls that ascended hundreds of feet. On the walls were giant screens displaying ads and trailers for the Reticula Autumn line up. On one screen, an alien in an apron waited patiently whilst three other aliens tried the culinary treat they had just prepared. The three aliens opened their mouths and long tongues stabbed into the bowl of food, knocking it over and spilling the contents everywhere. As the contestant alien began to cry, the three judge aliens smacked their lips and deliberated. The eldest looking judge cheered and the studio lit up and confetti fell from the ceiling. The audience clapped in jubilation and another judge took out a weapon and shot the contestant. Joyful music played and an alien logo that translated roughly into 'Good Enough To Die For' splashed onto the screen. Now becoming increasingly conscious of the effect the panto horse's aroma was having on nearby aliens, Rosch spoke:

"Do you have any idea where we're going?"

"Away from the paddock," said Frank, "and in a straight line so we eventually get to the edge. May I venture that if you've nothing of use to contribute that you keep your stupid, neurotic mouth shut."

"Sorry." replied Rosch.

Pushing their way between two stalls, Frank led them out into an open food court area with dining tables.

"I'm just going to head to those doors on the far wall." said Frank.

Frank came to a stop as he waited for a large bumbling creature resembling a sentient bean bag to pass by. Glancing to his right he saw something that floored him. Sat at a table, with her Reticulant partner having lunch, was his ex, Beatrice. For what seemed like an eternity, Beatrice was unknowingly being watched by the sad panto horse. The horse stood motionless as Frank saw the happiness and confidence in her face. Her partner said something and she burst out laughing. Frank felt the scrape of enjoying her happiness against his own loneliness. He did feel his judgement was impaired somewhat, but he could swear he had not seen that smile before.

"Ruggerman? What's happening?" whispered Rosch.

Frank sniffed but said nothing. Just then, two human-Reticulant-hybrid children bounced into view and sat at the table. Beatrice embraced them and wiped yellow mucus from their grey, oozing tentacles that protruded from their little faces. The children beamed smiles as they coughed, the glistening mucus dripping from their grey wrinkly skin.

"Ruggerman?" repeated Rosch.

Without a word Frank turned and continued onwards. Back upstairs in the holding area, Ambassador Crunk was approached by one of his guard.

"Guv. Two horses have just been spotted in the food court."

"Let's move." commanded Crunk. "Wait,...two?"

The panto horse and Ginger finally arrived at the perimeter of the rodeo. Alien patrons in cowboy hats passed through turnstiles and slurped from oversize cups. At that moment Crunk and his guard burst through a door and scanned for the horses.

"There!" barked Crunk. "Stop those horses!"

A Reticulant guard peered through a scope and fired a long-range energy-based weapon. Near to the horses, the beanbag alien was hit in the belly by an energy blast that began melting his insides. The alien clutched its stomach as it sank to the floor, dissolving.

"Shift it!" yelled Frank, pushing forward through the mass of patrons towards the exit.

Another energy blast seared over the heads of the rodeo patrons like a comet. It struck the rear of the panto horse, sending it careening into a stall of exotic vegetables. The energy rippled across the fabric of the costume.

"Argh! Fuck!" cried Rosch. "It's burning through the costume!"

"Wait, hold on" ordered Frank.

The fur of the costume was burning away furiously like phosphorus in water.

"Fuck! Get it off! Get it off!" cried Rosch.

Frank and Rosch fell to the floor and desperately scrambled to shake off the disintegrating costume. Crunk could not believe his eyes.

"It's the fucking souse!" he roared.

Crunk grabbed a weapon from one of his guard and fired another volley, killing several bystanders. Crunk and the guard charged down the platform and panic spread through the crowd as hundreds of species of aliens pocketed their winnings and helped themselves to unattended food stalls.

"Take the bridle!" Frank shouted, giving the reins to Rosch. "Out that way!"

Frank quickly salvaged the field tracker from the smouldering costume and began to frantically press the touch screen.

"*Featherlite* this is *Trojan*, come in." yelled Frank, as he and Rosch led Ginger through the gates and the swarming patrons.

They pushed their way onto a broad walkway, lined with barriers that led down a further 20-metre-wide ramp that was currently heaving under the weight of the panicked crowds.

"*Featherlite* this is *Trojan*, come in." repeated Frank.

Another weapon blast destroyed a stall behind them, much to the distress of the owner.

"Quick, in here." ordered Frank, pushing Rosch and Ginger through a side door. The heavy fire escape door closed shut behind them. They arrived at the top of a long gangway that descended in front of them for nearly half a kilometre. Steel grates lined the floor and walls, above their heads was a long string of grim, speckled lights that ran off into the distance.

"I think if we just keep heading downwards, we'll eventually get to ground level." said Frank, Rosch nodded in agreement. Hurriedly, Frank led Rosch and Ginger down the long metal gangway. A few minutes later, as they neared the end, they became aware of air coming in from outside the base.

"This looks good." said Rosch.

At the end of the walkway, they arrived in a huge air duct that ran perpendicular to the gangway. On the far wall of the duct, were huge extractor fans, each the size of a double decker bus. Beyond the giant, rotating blades, they could see the Droitwich countryside through the shimmering energy field that protected the base. Rosch looked left and right.

"Which way?" Rosch asked.

Suddenly, they became aware of commotion behind them up at the top of the gangway as Crunk and his guard burst in and were running down to them at full speed.

"Yes!" shouted Crunk, looking at his scanner. "Horse urine and *Flintoff Kingsize*, this way!"

"Move it! Move it!" shouted Frank, ushering Rosch and Ginger along the duct.

Just then, Frank, Rosch and Ginger experienced what many term, 'a glitch in the matrix'. The inescapable feeling of some kind of momentary kink in space time.

"What was that?" inquired Rosch, nervously.

"I don't know." said Frank. "But something has changed."

"How are you doing Frank? Lando?"

Frank and Rosch turned around to see the pleasant form of senior London Met forensic, Sodermine, lighting a cigarette. He inhaled, adjusted his brown trilby and returned his lighter to the pocket of his shabby rain mac.

"Sodermine?" said Frank, acutely aware of the Reticulant's knack for subterfuge. "What the hell are you doing here?"

"Well," said Sodermine, "it looks to me like a standard prison break scenario. Your captors are wielding greatly superior firepower as in you have no guns, but so far you guys seem to have the upper hand as in you're not dead."

"No," said Frank, with tangible existential scepticism. "I mean, why are you here?"

"Ah, you know me Frank, always first man on the scene. Someone's gotta be there when you arrive to give ya the skinny. First reports say your best chance of getting outta here is to head to the end of this duct and use a Z5 Particle disruptor, set to defrost. At that frequency when it's fired up in contact with a field junction box it'll temporarily kill the

camo-field. Meaning you guys can skedaddle out through one of the vents. You'll only have a few seconds though, and you don't wanna get trapped half way trust me. The energy field will fry ya like a pissed cannoli."
"Sounds good." said Frank.
"Wait." said Rosch. "But that means...someone will have to stay on this side to disrupt the field."
Even with the sound of Crunk and his guard getting closer, a solemn moment descended on all in attendance. Whatever happened, someone wasn't going to make it. Frank stroked his stubbled chin before turning to Sodermine.
"How are the kids?" he asked.
"Ah, they're doing great." replied Sodermine, cheerily.
Sodermine took out his wallet and began showing pictures.
"Millie just got signed up for the school play for the part of Oppenheimer....Here's Jeff doing his volunteer work down at the orphanage…"
Frank turned a beaming and callous smile on Rosch.
"...Oh, fuck off." said Rosch.
Sodermine and Frank stood, stunned at his outburst. Rosch's mind wrestled with its options momentarily before it eventually sat down in acceptance. Rosch looked at their faces, then again at the faces in the photographs and took a deep breath.
"Fair enough." he said calmly. "At least I'd have done one thing worthwhile. Can you just... I want to say-"
"Oh, pipe down, Ja Ja!" snapped Frank, "Crunk and his lot will be on us in about thirty seconds, and we-"
"Argh!" roared Rosch. "Will you not even let me die with some fucking dignity? You always-"
"Lando! Relax." said Sodermine, calmly, before turning to Frank. "...It's me."
"Sodermine, listen-" pleaded Frank
Rosch looked on as Frank protested. He couldn't hear Frank's words. Even as Frank became more animated and pointed vigorously at Rosch, he felt strangely more peaceful in himself than he could ever remember.

"It's okay." said Sodermine, placing a hand on Frank's shoulder.

"Sodermine no." implored Frank.

"Next time on the scene, I'll be there." said Sodermine, smiling. "The next time a lawyer is found head first in a chemical toilet with car magazines glued to his legs. I'll be there. I'll always be there Frank."

Frank looked curiously at his longtime colleague.

"What are you talking about?" he asked, incredulously.

A volley of weapons blasted the entrance to the air duct and Crunk and his guard tumbled over each other as they scrambled into the huge chamber.

"There they are!" shouted Crunk. His guards quickly gathered themselves and opened fire.

"It's been fun." said Rosch, ushering Ginger into motion and running for the end of the duct. The sounds of devastating weapons blasted and echoed around the duct.

"It's got me wondering though." said Sodermine, curiously. "If I'm here...where's the body?"

A shower of sparks covered all in attendance as a weapon blast impacted on the wall next to Sodermine.

"Sodermine!" roared Frank, as he grabbed him and pulled him inside a small maintenance area adjacent to the duct. Sodermine's face was bleeding badly.

"I'm alright, I'm alright." wheezed Sodermine, coughing blood spittle onto his face. Frank searched Sodermine's body and found the large piece of shrapnel lodged in his abdomen.

"Here..." croaked Sodermine, "...take my uzi." as he handed Frank the compact but effective automatic weapon. Frank leaned outside the area of cover and fired, causing Crunk and his guard to step back and hide behind a control console. Rosch paused as he heard the automatic fire and noticed that Frank was dangerously behind.

'Come on Ruggerman.' willed Rosch internally.

"Let's get you up." said Frank, heaving Sodermine to his feet.

Sodermine, grimaced as the wound in his abdomen tore further.

"I need you to help me into that junction." groaned Sodermine, pointing to a hub of mechanical controls situated ten yards further along the duct. Leaving Ginger, tethered to a railing, Rosch ran back to Frank, took the uzi and began providing covering fire as Frank shuffled Sodermine towards the junction box.

"That's right, just here." grunted Sodermine as Frank eased him into cover next to the junction box.

"Now look in that tool box," said Sodermine, clutching his middle. "You should find a Z5 particle disruptor, it looks kinda like an eggplant."

Frank removed the long black device.

"That's it." coughed Sodermine, "give it here."

Frank handed the device to Sodermine who clutched it close to his trembling chest.

"Now get outta here." rattled Sodermine, "You got ten seconds from when I stuff it into the junction box."

Frank hesitated, still unsure of where his friend, or at least what appeared to be his friend had come from.

"Trust me Frank, I'll explain another time. Go! Get outta here!"

Frank placed his hand on Sodermine's shoulder before racing off to join Rosch. With a further volley of fire, Rosch and Frank ran to rejoin Ginger.

"God this better work!" prayed Rosch as he, Frank and Ginger sped towards the vent at the end of the duct.

Two Reticulant guards emerged from around a corner with their weapons trained on Sodermine.

"See ya at the scene Frank." said Sodermine, as he jammed the black device into the junction box. Crunk shielded his face as his guards were knocked to the floor by the resulting explosion. Rosch couldn't help but notice the familiar shimmer of a still operational energy field, running across the vent as they got closer and closer, with only a few steps to go he closed his eyes. A surge of energy ripped along the full length of the duct, giant fans began to slow and the shimmering field disappeared, revealing the fresh air of the Droitwich countryside. Ecstatic, they leapt out through the vent and collapsed in a muddy heap in the soft, wet ground. A second later, the energy field kicked back in and the Reticulant base became invisible once again, leaving only the peaceful, misty countryside. As Frank and Rosch desperately tried to get their breath back, the horse carrier containing Gim, Shagney Kluft and Kareem skidded across wet mud and came to a stop nearby. With Gim at the wheel, Kluft and Kareem immediately ran out and began ushering Ginger into the back. Frank and Rosch leapt into the cab and with the all clear from Kluft they sped away.

With his guard mostly fatally injured, Ambassador Crunk watched through the energy field as the horse carrier smashed through a wooden fence and onto the road.
"Shit." cursed Crunk.
All those inside the horse carrier, except for Frank, who was sitting deep in thought, exchanged hugs of joy. Kareem wrapped his arms around Rosch.
"Well done mate." he said.
Kluft beamed a smile and rubbed Gim's shoulders as she drove.
"Okay," said Kluft, "time to arrange the unveiling."
Kluft sat back on a chair and removed her phone.
"Chief! Kluft." she said, excitedly, "No wait! Don't hang up! I know and I'm sorry, but listen...I've got something huge."

***

Back on the Reticulant base, Crunk stood considering his lack of options as the remaining two of his guards attempted to tend to their wounded comrades. After a moment, Crunk reached his inevitable conclusion.
"Sorry lads." he said, opening fire.
A more able guard leaned to protect his comrade and another tried to flee but all were consumed by the projectiles from the terrible weapon.

6:12pm

With a beep, the painfully slow door mechanism to Crunk's chambers began to slide open.
"For fucks sake!" roared Crunk, as he struggled to force the door. Eventually he slipped through the gap and fell inside. He immediately went into the bedroom and began removing documents from a drawer and a sports bag from a compartment at the bottom of the wardrobe. He dumped the sports bag on the bed.
"Commzapp." he barked.
A synthesized voice answered him.
"What dibnum please?"
"The Grublin." replied Crunk.
"One shagsplat."
Four ring cycles repeated on speakers as Crunk stuffed the last few essentials into the sports bag.
"Darling," said Arabella, Crunk's wife." I'm just off to the garden centre with Ramon, I've-"
"Listen." interrupted Crunk. "It's hit the fan, we need to run, now."
"Oh, darling," said Arabella, soothingly, "we had one of these, last planet. I'm sure you'll get some shmuck for brains to take the fall. What's dickhead said?"
"This is real!" snapped Crunk. "I need you to shut up and listen."
"Darling! How dare you speak-"
"Right, you have to shut the fuck up now 'cos in the next hour the Royal High Conqueror of the Reticulants will have his TV on. Within one minute of him finding out what's happened, the ZZ Top will be given their orders. Within another forty minutes they'll be marching up the drive and taking the front door off its fucking hinges. Next, they'll be stashing you and the kids away in black bags, do you understand?"
"Okay." replied Arabella, gingerly.
"Okay." continued Crunk. "I need you to get the kids out of school right now, there's bug out bags in the shed under the

floor. Take the next shuttle to Syberius 7 and book yourself into Slabnahm's Motel. Do NOT book yourself into the Sheridan, it must be low key and do NOT use your real IDs, use the ones in the bug out bag. If I'm not there by morning, take the kids to your cousins'.

"You'll be there though right?" asked Arabella, quietly.

"If not, it's because I'm dead."

"Okay." said Arabella. "I'm on my way. Be safe love, I love you."

"I love you too." said Crunk. "End Commzapp."

Crunk breathed a deep breath and completed his mental checklist.

"Commzapp ended." said the voice. "On a scale of 1 to 5, how did you enjoy your Commzapp?"

Crunk fired a round from his weapon at the intercom, causing a flurry of sparks and the lights to black out.

"Oh, shit the bed!" he spat.

7:35pm
The Grounds Of Buckingham Palace

Whilst in transit, Kluft had sold the expose of the millennium to her boss at C.U.N News. The Royal Family were currently holding a raffle, a huge gala event complete with a magnificent stage, press from around the world and a full orchestra providing an accompaniment to the proceedings. Kluft had convinced her boss to let them present Ginger on stage, 'newly rescued by the brave members of the London Met, from the evil and depraved hands of the Reticulants'. Thousands had gathered for the raffle but thanks to stalls selling organic cider, were well in the mood for something more interesting. A large portion of the crowd were wearing tee shirts bearing #justice4pegg and anti-visitor slogans, inspired by the tireless *Twittlechat* campaign of TV *She-Ra* and naturist Micheala Strachan. The horse carrier came to a stop behind the stage and Frank et al, exited and led Ginger up the steps and into the view of the gathered masses. Kluft made her way to the podium and began to speak.

"Ladies and gentlemen, I am Shagney Kluft of C.U.N News and I want to thank you all for coming. It is my distinct pleasure to introduce, newly rescued from a humiliating death, three-time winner of the Grand National and a Golden Globe for best breakthrough documentary, Ginger!"

The crowd erupted in joy. In the jubilation, a hang glider that was strapped to the Mayor of London, Harry Huffnagel, crash landed into the orchestra pit causing a flurry of slurred toots, snapping instruments and popping timpani. The Mayor laboriously unstrapped himself from the hang glider and wrestled his way out of the quagmire of musicians. Stepping on backs, he managed to climb his way up onto the stage. He raced forward and threw his arms around his Ginger. The crowd erupted in joy once again and an emotional Huffnagel approached the podium.

"I was lost without that horse." confessed the Mayor. "It truly humbles me that you have all embraced my Ginger, as a darling of the nation. She will from this moment on be remembered as a symbol of our pride and determination, no matter what shifty, greasy, thieving and above all poxy, alien bastards might try."

The crowd erupted in joy and the remainder of the orchestra played a stirring and patriotic number. At the rear of the stage, Rosch signalled to Frank to look to his left. Frank turned and saw the car of Chief Commissioner Leathers pull to a stop next to the stage. Leathers waved to the adoring crowd as he left his car and made his way on stage. In her country home, Councilwoman Caroline Ahem was watching the event on TV and sipping a Death Valley-dry martini.

"Get me Reyka." she said.

Reyka was once again watching the backroom live sport at the Lucky Orphan Restaurant in Chinatown. He removed his phone from his suit jacket pocket.

 "Councilwoman." he said, calmly. "Where do we stand?"

"Barefoot at the urinal." she snorted. "Ruggerman has Huffnagel's horse, it's all over the damn TV."
"And Crunk?" asked Reyka.
"Skedaddled. He's gone to ground somewhere to avoid being cast out to, I don't know, Benidorm I think he said."
"Jesus." said Reyka, imperviously.
"What do we do?" said Ahem.
Reyka took only a moment before his instincts kicked in admirably.
"The Reticulants have been exposed as hoarding pet molesters," he said, "hardly the kind of folk you want next door. Someone needs to swing. Charged with high treason for collaboration and endangering the public. The PM is the obvious choice."
"Naturally." grinned Ahem, sipping.
"Tomorrow night Westminster will need to pick their representative for the formation of an international committee of Reticulant affairs. This committee will oversee the responsible integration of the Visitors and reassure the public of the utmost and to be quite frank, brutal scrutiny that will be applied. It requires someone of extensive diplomatic experience. You want it?"
"Sounds good, Reyka," said Ahem. "...too good."
"Of course, it does." said Reyka. "We have a little work to do prior to your appointment. Needless to say we must ensure the other prospective applicants are... discouraged."
"Ha! I love it." chimed Ahem, biting an olive off a cocktail stick. "Call me in the morning with the names."
Ahem hung up and ordered another martini.

The Grounds Of Buckingham Palace

Chief Commissioner Leathers took his place at the podium, relishing in the attention.
"It is often at times like this," he said, "when words fail. But I can assure you of the tremendous depth, of satisfaction that I feel, at the reunion, of man, and horse."

The crowd erupted in joy, Ginger whinnied and the Mayor flicked a 'V' behind Leathers' back.

"Naturally," continued Leathers, "I am not so happy to see such a disgraceful abuse of power and coercion. Men and women in positions of great responsibility collaborating, against the interests of you, the good public. In this new era, I feel it essential that we utilise the very best resources at our disposal. Therefore, I hereby reinstate the Western Tactical Unit along with its relocation to a new facility, with double parking and a sensationally modest budgetary increase."

The crowd erupted in joy.

Rosch and Frank both waited for the inevitable catch.

"In addition to the existing members of the Western Tactical Unit, it gives me deep pleasure to announce the promotion of Officer Gimudzuke Rerata to Assistant Detective, accountable to Detective Frank Ruggerman."

The crowd erupted in joy.

Gim looked to Frank, who gave her a wink. She stood, centred herself and with her usual immaculate poise, approached the podium.

"It is-" she began, as Leathers draped a medal around her neck and directed her back to her seat.

"Yes yes," said Leathers, "and very proud we are of her. Next!"

At that moment, still suffering from frequent post-*Operation* twitches, Leathers' lackey Renfield rushed on stage and whispered in his ear.

"Agh!" barked Leathers, nearly deafening the audience close to the speakers, "Yes! The Western Tactical Unit will also soon benefit from the assistance of another rising star in the London Met. A man of fastidious time keeping..."

"Oh shit." mourned Frank.

"...Standards Officer Eugene Toltattler!"

The crowd erupted in joy and the orchestra played a late-night chat show motif as Toltattler jogged up onstage and approached the podium.

"Thank you, Chief Commissioner." said Toltattler, adjusting his spectacles. "May I just say that it is an honour to serve as a member of the London Metropolitan Police Service and I look forward wholeheartedly to working closely with the existing W.T.U. Our aim will be to create a new force for justice in this great city. I'm afraid however, that I must now leave you as I'm still very much on duty, it is approaching my lunch break and I think I may be due a bowel movement. Thank you."

The crowd erupted in joy.

Before leaving the stage, Toltattler approached Frank.

"Don't let all this go to your head, Ruggerman." he growled. "Leathers told me to have you boys on a very, very short leash."

"Yeah. Right." said Frank, nonchalantly. "As you were, Officer."

Toltattler smiled a sarcastic smile and departed.

Leathers retook his position at the podium.

"For the heroic rescue of Ginger, and the exposure of an insidious alien conspiracy, we recognize the linchpin of the Western Tactical Unit, detective Frank Ruggerman."

Frank stood and with formidable purpose, approached the podium. Once the ecstatic pandemonium of the crowd subsided, he began.

"Back in the 1980's, sixteen Dutch librarians were forced into exile after-"

Suddenly a mighty gust of wind tore down banners and toppled hotdog carts. Members of the crowd shielded their faces and held their children close. A loud, thundering bass hum vibrated the whole postcode and with a flurry of rippling electricity, a small Reticulant craft decloaked on the left-hand side of the stage. The crowd instantly became restless but hushed quickly as a large metal panel emerged from the craft and slowly lowered to form a ramp. From a wall of smoke, the Reticulant High Conqueror slowly walked his ancient bones down the ramp, leaning on his staff. As the High Conqueror approached the middle of the stage, the crowd grew angry, shouting xenophobic remarks.

A large man from the crowd, brandishing a bottle, stepped on stage, grinning menacingly as he approached the elderly Reticulant leader. Without looking at him, the High Conqueror pressed a button on his watch that released a long, thin, metallic arm from his belt. The metallic arm unfurled like a cobra before striking at incredible speed and attaching itself to the back of the neck of the angry man. The man's eyes began to bleed and rolled back in his head as he became immediately docile. As the crowd looked on in horror, the High Conqueror slowly walked his limp and pathetic man-puppet towards the podium. Slapping his hands clumsily on the podium and dribbling, the puppet man spoke with an unmistakably alien use of inflection.

"All right now listen." it said. "Oh firstly, my voice has totally gone, so I'm going to use this chimp. Now, let's not lose perspective shall we? We can destroy you all in a heartbeat by turning your bowels into molten lead. If you want to go all 'pitchforky' on us...well, you just have at it." The crowd stayed quiet.

"I thought so. Here's the thing, we are going to stay here because, you people have the greatest catalogue of science fiction tv shows this side of the Vandross system. We are bored and need passable content to while out our vast lifetimes. You may not like us, you may not trust us, I understand."

The puppet man turned and pointed to a man in the crowd.

"You." said the puppet man. "I met you at the salad bar in the hotel, you told me about your wife needing an operation."

"My dog." corrected the man, timidly.

"Whatever. Even with all I know about you, in my mind, you can live for a thousand years or you can die, right now and I don't give a flying fuck which happens. The point being that we do not have to like each other, but you are going to have to get used to us. So give us some laws or licences or whatever helps you sleep at night and get cracking making some more *Malcolm In The Middle*. Peace be with you."

The High Conqueror released the puppet man and he collapsed in a heap and vomited. The High Conqueror returned onto his ship and it departed with the same table-flipping turbulence with which it had arrived. A rumble of thunder cued a downpour onto the heads of the gathered.
"Well, there it is." smiled Leathers. "We all need to make sure…"
The last of Leathers' signoff was unheard as he walked out of range of the microphone. The Mayor, leading Ginger lovingly by the bridle, stopped off at Frank before departing.
"We all best be off then." said the Mayor.
"Nice one, Harry." Frank smirked.
"That's the last one of them, Princess." said the Mayor, sternly, with a pointed finger.
The mayor led Ginger carefully down the steps of the stage, followed by his advisors. Kluft was smiling to herself as Gim approached and tapped her shoulder. Kluft turned and smiled into the stoic face of Gim.
"Shagney." said Gim. "I find your facial symmetry pleasing. Would you like to join me for whisky? And perhaps intercourse?"
Kluft chuckled and took her hand.
"Let's start with a whisky." she said. "Come on Kareem."
Kareem spat out a mouthful of cavity insulation he had found under the stage and followed. Gim and Kluft approached the steps. Gim stopped for a moment with Frank.
"I shall see you Monday." she said.
"You will." said Frank.
Rosch sat looking at the floor. He rubbed his hands, breathed deeply and raised his head to speak before noticing that Frank had gone and he was now alone on the stage.

Monday
9:17am
The New Old Bailey Main Courtroom

Judge Marigold hammered her gavel as she tried to control the riotous mob that currently occupied her courtroom.

"I said enough, you assholes!" she roared.

The crowd quietened and she sipped from her supersize Cognac.

"Now," she said, "I see here that just prior to commencing this performance review the former PM has dissolved his original council in favour of a single representative?"

There came murmurs from the audience.

"That is correct, your honour." said Caroline Ahem.

"Councilwoman Ahem. Good to see you." said the judge. "*Wild Turkey*, rocks with a twist?"

"Why not?" said Ahem, warmly.

"Bailiffs!" screamed the judge. "Bring in the defendant."

The doors burst open and former PM Joffrey Wiff-Waff Donovan was wheeled in by two burly-looking bailiffs. The former PM was in a severe state of drug induced disarray. He dribbled onto the lapels of his suit as his weight continued to sink into the chair. The bailiffs wheeled him through the courtroom under the furious gaze of the audience before bringing him to a neat stop next to Caroline Ahem.

"Mr. Wiff-Waff Donovan," said the judge, "you stand accused of high treason, corruption and breach of the public trust, how do you plead?"

The former PM blew a raspberry and dribbled.

"Excellent." said the judge. "Councilwoman, you may begin."

Smiling grievously, Ahem accepted her drink and began her deposition.

8:32pm
The Dog And Hotpot Pub

Frank, Gim and Rosch sat around a table covered in empty pint glasses. On the TV, Walton Shalmanac was reporting for C.U.N News.
"The former PM's defence plead guilty to all charges. This just before the former PM was held in contempt, for defecating in the dock."
Frank sat deep in thought.
"You're thinking about Pegg." said Rosch.
Frank gave Rosch a disdainful look.
"Wiff-Waff Donovan has been held responsible for the invasion," said Gim, "and you have been exonerated for the death of Judge Pegg."
"Wiff-Waff Donovan was just the Emu." grumbled Frank, resentfully. "Someone had a hand up his arse and his strings were being pulled by a number of people. I don't know how many behind the scenes pigs are on the tit, but it all starts with Aunty Goebles."
After a moment's reflection, Gim stood.
"I believe it is my round."

After Frank and Rosch shared a silence that was comparable in both duration and awkwardness to the black death, Gim returned with a tray of drinks.
"Rosch," she said, "they didn't have *Bacardi Breezers* so I got you a *J2O*-2-D2." Gim erupted with hysterical laughter and dropped to her knees, clutching the table for support. Frank snorted and Rosch stifled a laugh of his own.
"Arseholes." he said, sipping from his bottle.

EPILOGUE

On the pavement outside *Slabnham's Motel*, Ambassador Crunk's wife Arabella and their two children, stood wearing hats, scarves and sunglasses. As Crunk appeared, the two children ran and embraced their father. After enjoying the reunion, Crunk stood and looked into the face of his wife. She stared at him, cautiously, before approaching and placing her large grey forehead against his. Twenty minutes later, they arrived by cab at the Offworld Scaggz Travelport, a long-distance travel service, situated on the edge of the Tempus nebula, a service preferred by those desiring a discrete exit. Crunk and his family showed the clerk their IDs. The clerk examined the documents closely, allowing one of his six eyes to drift over the faces of Crunk and his family. Once satisfied, they were given their tickets and made their way onto the crowded platform. Crunk ushered his family onto the craft and into a booth. Crunk opted to store their luggage under the chairs rather than in the overhead compartment. Once completed, Crunk stood a moment in thought.
"Have a seat darling." said Arabella, anxiously.
Crunk was clearly wrestling with something in his mind.
"Can you just give me a minute?" he said, before walking off down the gangway. As he reached the dining car, he removed his phone and began writing a text. A minute later, he sat down with his family and watched the dingy spaceport drift further and further away through the window.

Lake Taco

Reticulant senior Lieutenant Rabz, received and read a text as he walked along the jetty that reached out onto the surface of the vast, peaceful lake. The wind was cold and it was drying up the moisture on his large black eyes. On a small fishing boat, located at the end of the jetty, another senior Reticulant, Deacon Smash, was wearing full fishing gear and loading the last box of tackle into the boat. Smash looked up and saw his friend and colleague approaching. Also sitting in the boat, was a mean looking warrior alien, with huge scaly shoulders and fangs.

"Easy Rabz!" said Smash, cheerily. "Lovely out innit?...Where's Crunk?"

"Bad news, Smash." said Rabz, dryly. "Crunk has been held up."

Smash looked into the grey, wrinkly face of his longtime friend, before glancing at the warrior alien in the boat.

"Ah, come on, Rabz mate. You saw that horse." said Smash. "How about it, for old times sake?"

"Can't do it Smash. I'll see you around." said Rabz, before turning on his heel and leaving.

Deacon Smash watched hopefully after his friend as he walked away. Smash then sat down resignedly and got comfy in the boat.

"Let's go Hilda." he said.

The warrior alien started the boat motor, and they pulled away onto the deep. blue lake.

Back on the transport vessel, Crunk received a text, which he read, before placing his phone on the table and carefully placing his arm around his child, who was sleeping, snuggled next to him.

THE END

Thank you so much for reading my book. If you enjoyed it then please visit

WWW.HAWKERSTREET.ONLINE

To get more things Heskerton, kindly subscribe to my Youtube Channel – Rich Heskerton

I can also be found on Facebook, Instagram, TikTok

Please leave your reviews, likes and even share with the like minded.

THANK YOU

ABOUT THE AUTHOR

Born in Walsall, based in London, Rich Heskerton is an author inspired by the fringe and an unhealthy love of Robocop. He is preoccupied with the anguish of being human, the abuse of the natural world and troublesome streaming sites that won't let you re - bingewatch a series without restarting every episode. He is a Dj who served 7 years on Rude FM.COM and is a resident at the Blues Kitchen playing Soul, Funk and RnB.

Thank You

2000 AD / Armando Iannucci / All Crews Family
Rage Against The Machine / Charlie Brooker /
Dj Flight / Spaced / The League Of Gentlemen /
Futurama / The Day Today / Adam and Joe
Mike Judge / Rik Mayall / Mavis Staples
The Wu Tang Clan / James Brown / Doc Scott
The Thing / Adam Curtis / Portishead
Rude FM / Garth Ennis / The Blues Kitchen
On Cinema At The Cinema / Cypress Hill
The Fast Show / People Just Do Nothing / The X-Files
It's Always Sunny In Philadelphia / Paul Verhoeven
Sun And Bass / Red Letter Media / Big Train
Hunter S.Thompson / John Landis / Godless
Underworld / Mark System / Jenn Burke
Rupture / Public Enemy / Aliens
San Teodoro / Sir Arthur Conan Doyle
Blackadder / South Park
Sly And The Family Stone / Mash / Deftones
Steve Coogan / Dev Paradox
Beastie Boys / Vlog Brothers

Printed in Great Britain
by Amazon